The Cool Breeze of . ... - A new beginning

18 September 8.40 am

Is there such a thing as a gentle apocalypse?

Caila, notorious for her clumsy moments and indecisiveness, is asked by an alien species to help decide the faith of Earth, in less than a week. To make matters worse, she also needs to select seven companions to help rebuild a human population.

The surprisingly gentle apocalypse is the beginning of their fight for survival.

Titles available in the Cool Breeze of Spring series:

A new beginning
Rebecca's Diary (companion to *A new beginning*)
A flying start (available in June 2019)

Find out more at www.haszit.com

C. Attleya

THE COOL BREEZE OF SPRING

A new beginning

Haszit Ltd.

Published in the United Kingdom in 2019 by:
Haszit Limited

British Library Cataloguing-in-Publication Data
A catalogue record for this book is available from the
British Library

Second edition March 2019

Layout and design by Haszit Ltd.

ISBN 978-1-9164368-5-5

For Chris

Just a big thank you.

Prologue

Non erit sapiens

Of the 496 they'd seeded, only 13 remained among a population of more than seven and a half billion. How could he have got it so wrong?

Millions of years of research had been wasted!

Their evolution hadn't followed the pattern he'd expected. It wasn't a lack of intellectual capacity, some of them were terrifically intelligent. No, it was something else; they had allowed themselves to be guided by emotions and greed. Today, violence and cruelty ruled this species.

Mateos studied their faces. These 13 survivors were their last hope. The sedation worked well, they were relaxed and receptive. He invited the corvids in and observed how they joined their assigned Khered.

It was time.

"Greetings, Khered. This is the day, we hoped would never arrive. Recent events forced us to reactivate all Khered assemblies on Earth, to consult on a full reset of this planet. I can assure you that this decision was not taken lightly.

Human development saw admirable progress and horrific destruction go hand in hand. But this has now reached a tipping point, where the demise of your planet and all its inhabitants is unavoidable.

We are faced with the choice between the annihilation of Earth, and a hard reset.

Of the human population, only Khered, and their seven chosen ones, may remain. You are the last surviving human Khered, and the last Khered species to be consulted.

Other assemblies have reached a verdict, yours will be the final ruling, and will conclude this consultation.

In two days, you will meet again, but the process of restoring your memories and skills will commence instantly. During your meetings, you will discuss the options which are available to you. However, your final verdict will not be expected until the end of your last assembly.

Each of you has been assigned a Corvidaean Khered guide, to remain at your side throughout the consultation stage.

Before your next assembly, we will visit all of you individually to explain what is expected of you, and to answer any questions you may have.

Non erit sapiens."

The last day

Friday 13 September 2019

As Caila spotted the crow, flying from crossbeam to crossbeam, she reflected that she had never felt better than that morning when she arrived at the bustling and overcrowded station. She'd bagged herself a seat on the train, and her nap had done her a world of good. Between the swarms of stressed and grumpy commuters, she felt gloriously relaxed, exhilarated even. The air was filled with the aroma of damp clothes, bacon and coffee, but to Caila, today smelled like the first day of spring.

Then a niggle staged a brazen attack on her high spirits, '*non erit sapiens*'.

She tried to shake the kill-joy off, while she wondered where the spoilsport came from and what it meant.

"Cai… Cai… Hey Cai, wait for me!"

A familiar loud voice did the trick and instantly liberated Caila from her gremlin. Reluctantly she looked over her shoulder to spot Rob, hot on her heels, waving his copy of the Financial Times to flag his status as an economics professional. Escape was impossible, she would have to face him.

"This is the perfect way to end the perfect beginning of a perfect day," she muttered before plastering her best smile on her face to greet her colleague. "Good morning, Rob, don't you normally come in a bit later?"

"Well you know, my dear, the early bird and the worm and all that," Rob explained his unexpected presence at Victoria Station, at the peak of the London rush-hour. "But what are you doing here at this ungodly hour, Cai? I thought you had taken the day off."

"Yes, I did," dear Cai quickened her pace, "but I left my book in the office last night, so I'm just popping back in to pick it up, and then I'm off again."

"A book? You came back into the office at this ungodly hour to pick up a paper brick?" Rob frowned, as he accelerated to keep up with the small redhead. "You have heard of audio, haven't you? And streaming?" he shook his head. "Cai, Cai! This is the twenty-first century, my dear, and you really should sort out your priorities."

As she observed his condescending smirk, Caila suppressed the urge to tip the last of her coffee over his shiny black shoes. Instead, she upped her pace and hoped ignoring him would be enough to shut him up.

Neither Caila nor Rob noticed the majestic black corvid who landed on the lamppost above them. It let out a loud squeak, before it hopped onto the next post, effortlessly keeping up with the accelerating woman on the pavement below.

"Now tell me, Cai, what are your plans for today?" undisturbed by his colleague's silence, Rob enquired. "It must be terribly exciting, you were miles away. So, what is it? A hot date? I don't see that geeky husband of yours? Besides you look far too cute for a date with the hubby. Or is it a job interview? You are certainly dressed for the occasion! Come on, Cai, you can tell me. I am the soul of discretion."

Soul of discretion? Yehhh, right! Town crier more likely! Rob was really beginning to get on Caila's nerves, and why the hell did he insist on shortening everyone's name? She hated it!

"Well, you know how it is, Robbie, old boy. I realise that secrets are safe with you, but it's ever so complicated. And you know how sensitive these issues can be, office politics and all that. It's probably best to wait for the official announcement. Don't you think?" That should set some tongues wagging; add one good-sized gossip to a pool of receptive ears in a shiny glass and steel structure, stir well and enjoy the intoxicating tall tales. Caila swiped her badge to open the door.

"Morning, William," she greeted the receptionist as she sprinted through the lobby, and into the lift. On the fifth floor she was welcomed by the sight of empty desks and Rob's boss, who impatiently paced the floor next to her companion's workspace.

"Is that Jonathan, waiting for you?" Caila gave the grim looking manager a quick wave. "I'll see you on Monday."

She didn't wait for a response and dashed towards her own desk at the other side of the floor, almost taking down the watercooler as she stumbled over a loose bit of carpet on the way.

From behind her screen, a laughing Juliet observed the petite pricing analyst's clumsy and hastened escape, "Well, that's worth a picture for the album. You and Rob, amiably entering the office together." Juliet, the team's personal assistant, was in early as usual.

"Oh, hi, Juliet. I ran into Rob, just outside the station. He told me, he was being an early bird today because he wants to catch a worm. Or something like that," Caila's irritation waned at the sight of the cheerful P.A., and she laughed when she added, "But Juliet, you should never use the words amiable and Rob in one sentence."

"Point taken," Juliet stretched and reached for her bag. "Worm, is that what he said? Jonathan more likely! He told Rob to come in early today, to catch up on his work. Elise was sick and tired of covering for him, so she finally spilled the beans to Jonathan, yesterday afternoon. And he'd better not call him John again! Jonathan told me that if people insist on being hypocoristic, then it should be Jon not John. But, talking about worms, that reminds me, here are a couple of fresh eggs for your weekend breakfast. With complements, from Bertie and Matilda."

Bertie and Matilda were part of Juliet's ever-expanding chicken flock.

"And here's your book, you left it on your desk last night. Do you want to know who did it?" Juliet offered the paperback with a wicked grin on her face, "I finished it on my way in, this morning, I couldn't put it down."

Caila inhaled sharply as she accidently accepted the book with her left hand, and Juliet looked concerned but unsurprised when she spotted the bandages.

"It's nothing. Just a little disagreement with the oven. And, thank you and, no thanks," Caila laughingly refused Juliet's cheeky offer to reveal the plot of her whodunnit, "I'm going to finish it over a long and leisurely breakfast in Hyde Park. Don't forget to thank Bertie and Matilda, for the eggs. Enjoy your weekend, I'll see you on Monday."

***

Caila clumsily balanced a tray, as she manoeuvred towards a vacant table next to the shiny black grand piano in the centre of the restaurant of the Victoria and Albert museum. The marshmallows on her hot chocolate rocked like ships on a stormy ocean, and the white paper napkins soon resembled a wet sandy beach. With a sigh of relief, she lowered her tray onto the table and dumped the evidence of a morning well spend in Oxford Street, underneath. Her sunglasses which she'd clutched in her mouth, slid down and would have bumped off the table, if it hadn't been for an attentive stranger.

"Thank you," when Caila turned around to see who'd rescued her glasses, she spotted no one. "Thanks, ghost."

Caila grinned and slumped into her chair. She looked at the door, she could have been late; he was always late, about 15 minutes, usually. Then, as she stared at the ornate fireplace of the Gamble Room, whilst sipping her extra-large hot chocolate, she experienced a feeling of déjà vu.

'*Non erit sapiens. Khered*'.

"'*Khered*'? ..." mumbling irritatedly, she pulled her mobile out of her bag. "What's wrong with me today? This is ridiculous." But the tenable result of her search almost made Caila drop her phone, '*Non erit sapiens*' is Latin for, '*It is wise*'.

She glared at the fireplace, firmly appropriating blame for her irritating niggle to the gloomy marble that surrounded the firebox.

'*Annihilation of Earth, Khered. Your final verdict*'.

"Hey darling, it looks like you had a productive morning," Chris noticed the multitude of bags under the table. "Wow, did I frighten you, you were miles away."

Caila jumped at the sound of his voice, but quickly smiled again, Chris always made her smile. Was it possible for a honeymoon to last a lifetime?

"Chris!" she got up and stood on tiptoes to kiss her tall husband. "No, I was just thinking about this perfect day which, by the way, got even better now that you are here. I bought you a new sweater this morning, it's purple, I'm sure you'll love it. How did the software deployment go?"

"Almost perfect. If you give me a sip of your hot chocolate, I'll go and get us something to eat," Chris grabbed Caila's half-empty mug. "Mmmm, that's good. So, what would you like? A salad or a sandwich, or something else? Or would you like a bit more time to decide? They won't close until five o'clock, we have plenty of time?"

"Ha, ha. Very funny. But I checked the boards before I ordered my drink. They serve kale and cheddar onion tarts today. Could you get me one of those, please? With a mixed leaves salad?"

"That must be a personal record, my dear," Chris teased. "I still don't understand how someone who can never decide, can make a career out of decision making."

"It's simple, my dear Chris, I use algorithms and decision trees. Would you like to see the one I wrote to decide what to order at Pret a Manger? I have it on my mobile, so that I can use it every day, before I go out to lunch."

"Caila, you are hopeless," Chris laughed, "but yes, I would like to see it."

An hour later, after they'd finished their meal, Caila and Chris discussed how to spend the rest of their day. Not that it required much discussion, because their days out in London always followed the same pattern. Clothes shopping in the morning which, to Chris's relief, had already been done. Then lunch at the V&A, a quick tour through the Science museum, followed by shopping for books. Early in the evening, they would grab a snack before catching a quiet post-commuter train home.

So, it wasn't until they were on the 9.42 from Victoria, that Caila finally showed Chris his new sweater. And that Chris remarked, her hand did not appear to have given her too much trouble that day.

"My hand?" Caila looked puzzled. Oh, blimey, yes, she'd completely forgotten she'd hurt it. She examined the smudged bandages, "Right, my hand. No, it feels absolutely fine; actually, it feels like nothing ever happened to it. Do you think we should have a quick peek?" Caila reached for the edge of the plaster, which Chris had carefully applied to cover her angry blistering patch of skin.

"Are you mad? Don't touch that. Your skin was red and broken last night, and now you want to look at it on a dirty train, without washing your hands? That's asking for an infection. Wait until we're home, and then I'll refresh that bandage for you."

"Right, okay then," if Chris got into this kind of a mood, it was useless to argue. "Let me have a look at your Angular book, then you can have a browse through my TensorFlow."

Chris glanced only briefly in Caila's paperback before he demanded the return of his own purchase, "What are convolutional neural networks? Give me my Angular back, at least that makes some sense. Why don't you read your Corvus book, what's it called again? Oh, right, '*Gifts of the Crow*'? Why did you buy that, actually?"

"I don't know. Maybe it's because of that 'Game of Crows' thing, on 'Winterwatch'. Or maybe it's because London seemed full of crows, they were everywhere today. Unless it was one single bird following me around, which would clearly be ridiculous.

Anyway, I felt like learning a bit more about them, they are very intelligent, you know, and I like them. Chris! Don't laugh at me!"

***

"Right, careful now. You can have a quick look in a moment, before we cover it with clean gauze," Chris carefully peeled back the bandage which covered Caila's burn, "tell me if it hurts."

Not bothered by even the slightest bit of pain, Caila laughed as she watched how her husband concentrated on the task at hand. He could be such a fusspot, at times. But then she noticed how his expression changed, from concern to utter dumbfounded-ness.

"What? Chris, what is it? It's fine, I don't feel anything. My hand hasn't turned green or purple, has it?" Caila quipped, before she inspected the offending appendage.

And then she grasped why Chris looked a bit more than just a little surprised.

Her hand was perfect, no blisters, no redness, just perfectly healthy skin. Like… well… like the skin on her other hand. She compared them.

"I guess that means I no longer have an excuse for not doing the dishes?" staring at her smooth skin, she considered that no amount of moisturiser could improve on it. She could have sworn that her hand looked even better than it did last week.

"Come on, I know that you normally heal quickly, but this is ridiculous. Even for you. Your hand was blistered and painful last night. The skin was broken, and it was fire engine bloody red! This isn't right," Chris looked genuinely worried, even more so than twenty-four hours ago, when she'd actually hurt herself.

"Maybe yesterday wasn't as bad as it seemed. Besides, I'm not complaining. But, okay, if you are really worried about it, we can look it up on the Internet," Caila despaired at her husband's honest concern, she hated it when people fussed, even from Chris she accepted fussiness only in small doses. "I can hardly go and see our GP, to show him my hand, which healed perfectly fine after burning it a little bit!"

"A little bit much, you mean," Chris retorted. "But all right, let's have a glass of wine and then we'll have an early night."

As they switched the kitchen lights off, they were startled by the scream of a crow, who had taken up residence in their garden.
That night Chris slept like he'd never slept before, but for Caila the day was far from over.

Limited options

"Bonum mane, Caila.

Don't worry, Chris won't wake up. Would you like to talk here, or downstairs?"

Their bedroom was dimly lit, and Caila jumped as she spotted the intruder, "Who are you? What are you doing here?" she reached for her mobile to call 999. But before she could, her nightly visitor was at her side and, as he touched the back of her neck, she felt herself relax.

"It's you," she remembered her dream on the early morning train, "you talked about annihilation, and a reset of Earth. You said you would visit us, to explain the details. There were 13 of us, and you called us Khered. That is what's been bugging me all day!

This isn't a dream, is it? This feels real!"

Caila pinched herself hard and it hurt like hell, but she didn't wake up.

"No, this is not a dream, this is very real. Stop pinching yourself, Caila, you'll give yourself a bruise," her uninvited guest's touch was warm and soft, as he took her hand and rested it on the duvet. "My name is Mateos, I am a Neteru from the planet Etherun, and I'll answer all your questions in a moment. Just take a minute to settle down.

Are you all right? We are not in a hurry."

Oddly enough, Caila really felt fine. The stranger in her bedroom felt familiar, unintimidating and kind, even. But still, "Could you hand me my jumper, please? I feel kind of underdressed for the occasion. ... Thank you. Why don't you sit down? You are rather towering over me. Okay, I'm ready now."

Mateos sat on the edge of Caila's bed and studied her. He realised, that right now, only his human mask, which covered his Neteruian appearance, was visible to her, and he wondered how long it would take Caila to see through it. She appeared extremely relaxed given the circumstances, even for a first order Khered, "Let's start with a bit of background. You may start to remember things, as I speak, but don't worry if you don't.

A long time ago, the Neteru initiated an experiment, building an ecology from scratch, on a distant planet."

"On Earth," Caila interrupted him.

Mateos smiled, "Yes, indeed, on Earth, that is what you call your planet. There are strict rules for these kinds of experiments, there need to be, because the equilibrium of the Universe is easily disturbed and, if something goes wrong, the consequences can be catastrophic.

We populated your planet with a variety of species, and the aim of the experiment was to observe how different species would evolve, interact and balance themselves out.

Earth species started out with a mix of mental and physical qualities, and for a long time the initial balance remained. However, recently, humans developed into the dominant species, and, as I mentioned during our earlier meeting, this was characterised by both great progress but also by enormous destruction. Initially we hoped that your progress would overtake, and ultimately, eliminate destruction, but we were wrong.

And now we arrived at a point, where we need to decide how to address this problem, to avert a Universe-wide catastrophe. We have a number of options available to us, which I will lay out to you in a minute."

Caila looked over her shoulder, to check on her sleeping husband, she wondered why he didn't wake up, and found herself surprised that she was not worried by that fact.

"Caila?!" Mateos sounded irritated when he noticed her distraction. "First, I will explain how you fit into this process. You are a Khered, a direct descendant of one of those seedlings. The genetic blueprints of most of our seedlings were based on species which could be found on Etherun. Humans were of special interest to us because they were based on Neteru, and we hoped to simulate our own evolution by studying yours.

While species evolved and changed, a small part of the Khered's basic genetic structure remained unaltered, in what you call your DNA. To avoid overlapping generations as much as possible, this particular string of DNA is inherited from grandparent to only one grandchild."

"And when you seeded Mesu, the Khered were intended as a backup. Within our DNA you preserved skills and memories that you can reactivate when you need to return to the initial state. It's like a kind of hard reset, isn't it?" Caila interjected triumphantly.

"That's right. And it obviously works, because you are already starting to remember; I never told you that our word for Earth, is Mesu. But I am not entirely surprised, your lineage presented us with some problems in the past. Your ancestors recognised visitors and remembered bits of Neteruian science and technology.

You are a first order Khered, that is a descendant who retained more than the expected amount of memories and skills, as well as their backup DNA. We had a hard time keeping you safe. Originally, there were 29 lines of first order Khered, and you are the only one left. 23 were lost during witch hunts. Humans really did evolve in a most undesirable direction. Burning witches!? How ignorant can you …?

But that's not the issue now. I apologise.

A number of you did not procreate - does that sound familiar? - and then you, Caila, were almost weeded out by security services."

"So, those shapes I saw, they were real?" Caila felt relieved, she was not going mad. "There have been a lot more of you over the last few years, not only Neteru, other species visited Earth as well. And you visited me before, quite a few times actually. Years ago, you showed me

Etherun. It was beautiful," Caila smiled at the memory of their trip to the magnificent planet, but then, with alarm, she remembered Mateos's last remark. "But hold on! You said that I was almost weeded out, that sounds rather alarming. And it is not something I take lightly."

Mateos eyed her stoically, "Do you really want to hear about that now? You are quite safe, as long as you keep your head down. This problem was dealt with a long time ago."

"That sounds ominous," Caila did her best to copy her interstellar guest's poker face. "But really, yes, I would like to know."
Then her attempt at a poker face turned into a victorious grin, "And you don't need to try and keep your disguise up all the time, you never used it before, and I can see right through it. It doesn't bother me that you are a bit opaque, or grey. I like the kind of hazy look, it suits you, and I don't need to see your emotions, I can feel them."

"Right then, thank you," Mateos dropped his mask and a tall, ghostly grey-coloured shape remained, "that is going to make life a lot easier for me. I'll tell you a bit about your birth, if you promise not to tell anyone, about me showing you Etherun. It isn't exactly standard procedure.
A little over a century ago, Earth authorities became aware of Khered. We had called an assembly and one member of the group contacted their country's security services. Fortunately, she did this before she was able to identify any of the others, but governments have been on alert ever since,

and, based on her description, they believed they could identify Khered by certain physical characteristics.

Now, some of your ancestors, were not as inconspicuous as they should have been, and your grandmother was identified as a Khered, and subsequently eliminated. At that moment your mother was in the last stages of pregnancy. Fortunately for us, however, she very unwisely decided to go abroad, on holiday. She went into labour and gave birth to twins in a hospital in the Netherlands. One boy and one girl.

In that same hospital, at the same time, another woman gave birth to a child, a stillborn girl. We switched you, before the security services could get to you, and that's why you are still here, and safe."

Caila paled, she was stunned, "You are telling me that, ..., that my parents were not my real parents? And that I have, or had a brother? What happened to him, and what happened to my birth parents?"

"I'm sorry, Caila, I'll tell you all about them, later. For now, just know that your brother is safe. And that you live in the country of your genetic parents, that is why you feel so at home here.

I know I told you that we are not in a hurry, but maybe we should concentrate on the current issue. Sunday morning you are required to attend an assembly, and you need time to think about your options. I will tell you all about your birth family, later. I promise."

Caila deliberated how the story about her birth explained a lot. She decided to let it rest for now, but Mateos definitely owed her more detail. Lots of it.

So, still annoyed about the yet to be revealed other half of her life story, she agreed, "All right then, Mateos, maybe we should move on, from me almost being weeded out, to the total annihilation of human life on Earth. Give it your worst, you can skip the sales pitch. Just the facts, please."

With a feeling of relief, Mateos dived right in, he had already given her more background than he was allowed to convey, "No doubt, you heard about the Doomsday Clock, and how it was recently moved to two minutes to midnight."

Caila nodded.

"Well, that is a typical example of human optimism. It is closer to a millisecond, than it is to two minutes to midnight. In addition to randomly killing each other, you are poisoning your atmosphere and the oceans, and every living being in it; you are driving other species, you depend on, to extinction. At this rate it would have taken you approximately one Earth century to wipe yourselves out.

However, right now, you have some serious madmen in charge, who are playing with chemical, biological and nuclear weapons like children in a toyshop. And to top it all off, they are preparing to use them.

Imminently, this will result in a disaster which will not only affect Mesu, but also the rest of the Universe. It will put the Universe's carefully maintained balance and peace at risk.

We decided that there are, a couple, …" Mateos wavered, Caila needed to really grasp this, "… sorry, did I say couple? I am supposed to say, we are giving you the choice out of four options. I will give them to you in the order of preference, as decided by the assembly on Etherun.

Our preferred option is to reset Earth. All species will remain as they are, except for humans, all humans will be removed.

The second option is similar to the first one, but now human Khered will remain on Earth to restart and supervise new human populations.

Third, we wipe Earth clean and leave it as we found it, bare; and fourth, we do nothing.

I left out some details, but you don't need to concern yourself with those, at this stage.

Do you have any questions?"

Caila looked back at Chris, blissfully unaware and peacefully asleep. There was no way, that would be impossible. Mateos could not be asking that of her, "About the second option, the one about Khered restarting a new human population. You don't really expect the 13 of us, to do that on our own, do you?"

She must have looked petrified, because Caila felt how Mateos used his touch to relax her. But, while he brushed against her shoulder, she also felt something else, something that surprised her: he was amused. He laughed at her! Well okay, maybe it was ridiculous to consider that they'd planned something so foolish. But it wasn't that funny!

"Don't worry, it will not just be the 13 of you. Statistically, the chances of a successful restart, using only 13 humans, would be incredibly slim. Or, more accurately, you wouldn't stand a chance," Mateos noticed Caila's relief as she watched Chris again, "and, yes, you can keep your husband, even if I would strongly advise against selecting your companion on such an emotional basis. That would have been your next question, wouldn't it?"

"Yes, it would have been. Thank you, … I think," Caila was visibly relieved, but also confused about his strange remark regarding Chris. "You mentioned that other Khered assemblies already agreed. Are you allowed to tell us what they decided? And what happens if we can't come to a consensus?"

"At this moment I cannot tell you about their decisions, or what will happen if you come to a different conclusion. You need to feel free to make up your own mind. We don't expect all 13 of you to necessarily agree, although that would, for obvious reasons, be the best outcome. You can also present realistic alternatives, but ..." Caila felt a change in the Neteru, as if he'd pulled up an invisible wall to hide his feelings, "... but keep in mind, the Etherun assembly and other Earth assemblies have already voted."

It felt like the temperature had dropped several degrees, and Caila was reminded of the way, Mateos had brushed over the last two of their four options, "I think I understand.

You are basically asking us to decide between a total and a near total human extinction? There are no other realistic options, are there? I'm not sure I like that, it scares the hell out of me. How much time do we have?"

"Trust me, Caila, the alternative would be a hell of a lot scarier. You have seven days to decide. From tomorrow, you will meet up regularly, with the other Khered, and after the last meeting on Friday morning, we will ask you to present your verdict. We are not asking you to leave your hearts, as they say here on Earth, out of it. But remember that your head can lead you to what is right for your heart. If you settle on the second option, you will need to choose your 'chosen ones'. Each Khered may select up to seven companions to join them, after the Event," then, sensing Caila's panic at the overwhelming amount of decision making she faced, he added, "don't worry too much about it, I know you can handle this. And I'll be here for you if you need me. What more could you possibly ask for?"

Caila couldn't help but smile, "If that's your attempt at humour, then it's not brilliant. But thanks anyway. Can I ask just a few more questions, please?
Will there be time for us to prepare, between our decision and the Event, as you call it? And, will the Event be, how am I going to say this, … disturbing, or painful for the others? For the people who will be removed?"

"There will be some time for you to prepare. I cannot tell you how long you have exactly, but I'm afraid it will be limited," Mateos said. "The Event itself will be very quick, you will hardly notice it, but afterwards it will take some time for you and your chosen ones to adjust to the new situation.

The humans we remove from this planet, will not be aware of the Event, before, or even while it happens. They won't experience any kind of distress, or pain."

It wasn't much of a comfort, as far as Caila was concerned, the result would still be the same. But at least it was something, "Thank you."

Then she remembered something he'd said during their earlier meeting, "That crow! There was only one crow in London today, wasn't there? Is it really going to follow me around?"

"Don't worry. The crow is only there to help you, just in case you need assistance while I'm out of touch," Mateos wondered if she would swallow this official line, he would be disappointed if she did.

And Caila had no intention of disappointing him, she felt offended by the Neteru's brush-off, "Oh, come on, you've been straight with me from the start. You can't seriously ask me to believe, that these crows are not going to indulge in a bit of '007' activity for you?" If he really thought she was going to believe that, then he had another thing coming, "And does, 'while I'm out of touch', mean that you will be constantly hovering over me as well? That you are assigned to keep an eye on me, permanently from now on?"

"Relax, Caila, there is no need to get angry. Yes, I will be here, most of the time. As will be the crow Khered, who has been assigned to you. But I'm sure that in your case, it will be only for your security, and not for surveillance purposes.

Now, do you have any other questions for me, before I let you go back to sleep?"

Caila looked at the dark window, there was no sign of dawn yet.

And yet, sleeping was the last thing on her mind, "Just two. First, what's my best corvid friend's name? It would hardly be polite of me to keep referring to him or her, as 'crow'.

And secondly, what do you believe would be smart questions to ask right now?"

"Crows do indeed have names, but they would be very difficult to pronounce for you. Why don't you ask him yourself, tomorrow morning? And a smart question for you to ask right now, would be, 'How much sleep do I need to be well rested and prepared for the Event?'

And then I would tell you, that you definitely need a few more hours tonight."

Mateos got up and looked down on his Khered, "Goodnight, Caila. Call me if you need me, I'll stay close by."

"But I'm wide awake now, and besides, I don't feel like sleeping. Don't go yet, Mateos," she loved the sound of his name, it felt as if she'd said it a thousand times before today, "I might think of more questions." But even while she said it, Caila started to feel drowsy as Mateos touched her head. "He's a tricky one", was her last thought, before she drifted off, into a deep dreamless sleep.

Reluctant to leave her, Mateos lingered, her spheream was developing in the exact same shade as her auburn hair. He reached out and touched it.

When he was this close to Caila, it was hard not to think of her. They were so alike.

Maybe at the end of all this, he would finally have her back.

OOVII

Saturday 14 September

Caila spent the next day juggling, what felt like two lives. The feeling that Mateos and Armageddon were nothing more than a scene from a vivid nightmare quickly disappeared, to be replaced by the sense of a phantasmagorical reality.

Her crow Khered proved real enough, and not without a sense of humour, as he landed in their garden to introduce himself while she and Chris were having their breakfast.

- I apologise for interrupting your morning meal, Caila, but I do believe I ought to introduce myself, sooner rather than later, since we are going to spend more time together, over the next few weeks, than we will with our own partners. –

Caila's mouth fell open as she watched the magnificent corvid, who was perched on the Cotoneaster next to the bird table and looked her straight in the eyes.

- My name is Khrhhsh, but for you to attempt to pronounce that, Mateos assured me, would do serious damage to your *plica vocalis*. I therefore followed up on his counsel and came up with an appropriate alias, more considerate to your human vocal cords. You may call me

Oviy, that spells double-O-V-I-I, – Khrhhsh took a bite from the bird food, Chris had put out before breakfast. - Mmmm, these grease sprinkles are excellent quality, but I do prefer peanuts; regrettably, we may experience a serious shortage of this nutritious legume in these parts of the world, in the very near future. Fortunately, however, that will be compensated, by the loss of a significant number of nuts of another kind.

Oh, Caila, really, you should keep up some sort of decorum whilst you enjoy your breakfast. –

- Can you hear what I think, Oviy? – whilst recovering from her coughing fit and furiously mopping up the tea she'd spilled, Caila tried to send the unblinking crow her thoughts.

"It's okay, Chris," she sounded horse as she reassured her husband, "you can stop banging my back now. I'm fine. I just had a bit of a clumsy moment. Is that the mail I hear, it sounds like he chucked a brick through the letterbox?"

That was perfect timing, mail was the only thing that managed to distract Chris from almost anything, at any time. And true to form, Chris was out of his chair and on his way to the hall, before Caila had a chance to finish her sentence.

Grateful for the diversion, Caila focussed on her tête-à-tête with her avian chaperone, who informed her that this method of conversing, was known as lectanimo. An utterly efficient form of communication used between activated

Khered and Neteru, OOVII assured her, as he munched on monkey nuts.

- I'll ask Chris to leave out some extra peanuts, – Caila combined offering Chris's services, with practising her newly acquired communication skills. - Do you prefer au naturel, or would you like them chopped up and sprinkled with some crushed mealworms? –

- That is most kind of you. But there is no need for Chris to chop them up, although a sprinkling of mealworm powder would not go amiss, – Khrhhsh a.k.a. OOVII politely accepted Caila's offer. - Would you mind if I asked my partner to join me, occasionally? Shrssthy is also partial to peanuts. –

Caila wondered if all corvids were as articulate as OOVII. This was completely unexpected, and she loved it, - By all means, Oviy, … – then she caught on to the bird's Fleming-ian reference. - Oh right, OOVII! … Did Mateos spill the beans about our conversation last night? –

Stoically, OOVII informed Caila that, of course he had been comprehensively briefed by Mateos, and this included disclosure of the initial reservations, Caila had voiced regarding Khrhhsh's intelligence role in the unfolding events, - I am not one for snooping, but I am convinced that total disclosure will simplify and expedite the process at hand. –

- OOVII, it is then, – Caila loved the corvid's wit, - and I could not agree with you more, with regards to total disclosure. Could you give me a quick recap of the decisions taken so far, and an update on the timeline leading towards the upcoming Event, please? –

- Nice try! Mateos mentioned that you are a tricky one. Those were his words, not mine. I believe that our Neteruian liaison already informed you that this information cannot be disclosed to any human Khered at this point. But again, it was a nice try.

Now, for the practical aspects of our arrangement. I am required to stay close to you, at all times, wherever you go. But there are some issues to consider. Your commute into London is something I cannot or indeed would not like to join into. The ideal solution, and Mateos agrees with me here, would be if you stayed at home from now onwards. – Caila opened her mouth to object.

- Pray, allow me to finish, Caila. I realise that, at this juncture, you cannot break free from your commitments. Furthermore, such an abrupt change to your daily routine might draw undesirable attention towards you. What I would propose, is that you go to your place of work as normal, on Monday morning. You will be accompanied by Mateos, and a friend of mine, in London, is ready to step in, if need be. Then, when the occasion presents itself you will stumble and hurt your ankle. This will surprise no one, Mateos assured me that your reputation for having *clumsy moments*, as he put it, is well established. –

Her jumper still soaked with spilled tea, Caila's attempt to look suitably indignant was not convincing.

- You will then make you way home where, as I observed earlier, you can honour your professional commitments under my supervision. –

- My team leader will be chuffed to hear that he is being replaced by a corvid. No, don't worry, OOVII, I know, I won't tell anyone. And thanks a lot, clumsiness is not my favourite image to present to the world, – Caila wondered how long and how intense Mateos had been observing her to know about her tendency for clumsy moments. - However, there is one flaw in that little plan you and Mateos cooked up last night. I am the worst actress in the world, and even if I manage to stumble convincingly, I still won't be able to pretend to be in enough pain, to warrant working from home for a week, or so.

I don't think this is a very good idea, OOVII. Besides I'll be safe at work, especially with your friend in London keeping an eye on me. –

And more importantly, the last thing Caila wanted was for her colleagues to make a big fuss over her, while she was on the floor in the office, attracting a lot of attention to herself and her ankle, feeling completely and utterly embarrassed.

- I am terribly sorry about this, but Mateos was insistent you should remain at home as soon as possible, where we can most effectively supervise you. And I tend to agree with him on this issue, – Mateos had informed Khrhhsh about the security issues surrounding his Khered. - If the acting is what bothers you, then I can put your mind at ease. Mateos suggested helping you out with a gentle push, and it is fairly straightforward, for him to give you a realistic injury, it is the opposite of how he helped heal your hand. Don't fret, Caila, we have it all in hand. –

Before Caila had a chance to inform OOVII, she fancied that idea even less than the first one, the elegant bird announced, - Ha, I see that Mateos has returned, and I believe your husband is also attempting to attract your attention. I'll see you later, Caila. –

Chris was indeed trying to attract her attention, and Caila had felt Mateos's presence even before OOVII mentioned him. Concluding she had to make a choice, she decided to ignore the alien who was planning to trip her up and hurt her ankle, and to instead concentrate all her attention on her loving husband, "I'm sorry, darling, I was just looking at that crow in the garden, they hardly ever come out to the back. What did you say?"

"I only said, that we agreed to look for new curtains in Tunbridge Wells. But it is so lovely outside that it would be a shame to drive out to town and then spend most of today trudging from shop to shop. Would you mind terribly if we stayed at home instead, and maybe did some reading in the garden? We can even pick up some food, for one last barbeque, this year." Chris sounded sincere while he clutched his C# and Angular books.

Caila smiled, against those new books, replacing their worn curtains had never stood a chance. Besides, Chris was right, it was a lovely day, and maybe the last chance to laze about in the garden this year.

Their last chance ever, possibly, if the Neteruians decided to wipe the earth clean of all humans, so why would they even bother to look for new curtains.

"I think that's a brilliant idea. How about mackerel, corn and bananas for on the barbeque? And some of that really good vanilla ice cream to go with the bananas? Let's go. Why don't you get the car keys, while I put the butter and cheese back in the fridge?"

An hour later, after they'd settled in their sunloungers, Caila glanced at Chris and considered there was no way in hell she could ever choose to stay here on Earth without her husband. She didn't care if Mateos was unhappy about emotional decisions.

Then she regarded the Neteru, who'd made himself at home, in the wooden arbour, in the far corner of their garden, - I don't know what you have against emotional attachments, Mateos. But for me it is with Chris, or not at all. – And when he ignored her, she challenged him, - and just so you know, I will go into work next week. –

Two minutes or a millisecond?

Was he right? Was it really this close to midnight?

Caila considered that everything Mateos had told her last night, sounded perfectly reasonable. Stockpiles of chemical, biological and nuclear weapons were scattered all over the planet. But would anyone be actually mad enough to use them?

True, not everyone in charge could be described as the brightest star on the political firmament, some were actually complete idiots. But you would have to be a complete dimwit to start chucking nukes around.

And what about killing each other, poisoning the atmosphere and the oceans, and driving other species to extinction? Was it really as bad as Mateos believed it to be? Of course, they'd made a big mess, she conceded. But was it bad enough to justify removing all humans from Earth?

Caila browsed through the news on her mobile, there had been another school shooting in the US; bombings, killings and chemical attacks in the Middle East; knife, gun and acid attacks in London. And that was only a small part of one day's worth of bad news. How could she defend that? How could anyone possibly defend that?

Then there was that little problem of the growing hole in the ozone layer.

And plastic, polluting the oceans, poisoning all species who depended on Poseidon's realm.

Global warming, and almost extinct northern white rhinos, tigers and orangutans. The last Bolivian water frog was desperately looking for a mate, online. The latter would actually be funny, if it wasn't so sad.

'There is no way, we can still fix all of those things,' Caila watched a bee, it's little hindlegs laden with pollen, fly from the Buddleia bush to the Sedum plant next to her chair, 'even if everyone agreed to chip in'.

But then she remembered that sweet little girl in the supermarket, offering her haggard mum the last of her sweets.

And that lovely old couple she met on the train last week. They were so happy together, and so proud to tell Caila about their first grandchild, who was about to graduate from university. She'd studied climatology and would be the first in their family to graduate.

With so many good people, why was humanity dominated by a handful of ignorant fools?

'Mateos, you charming and fiendish Neteru,' Caila pondered her nightly meeting as she eyed her extra-terrestrial liaison, who seemed relaxed in the corner of her garden, 'do you realise what you ask of us? Do you truly expect us to support you in killing all, or most of humanity? Because of a handful of idiots?

Why couldn't you have just got on with it? Whatever, 'it' is.'

Tension building

Sunday 15 September

Sunday morning arrived too soon.

Yesterday had been perfect. Chris, not keen on ants disturbing his meal at the best of times, had surprised her by agreeing to a picnic style tea, on a blanket, in the garden.

Days like that should never end. But, even forever, would not have been enough to prepare Caila for her early morning meeting.

Caila had a restless night and woke up early to find Mateos sitting next to her, "Bonum mane, Mateos. I hope you're here to tell me that the meeting has been cancelled, and that the end of the world has been postponed, indefinitely."

Still, before he answered, she realised her liaison was in too serious a mood to deliver such a happy message.

"Bonum mane, Caila. How are you? No, it's nothing like that. I just thought we should have a quick chat before the assembly, to see if you have any questions, and to reiterate the aim of this meeting. Are you ready to meet your fellow Khered?"

While she gave him a vague nod, Caila thought he was trying to sound more chipper than his demeanour betrayed.

She could easily read his feelings now, and felt he was trying to hide something from her.

"Right then," Mateos continued, "from our point of view, the main focus of this meeting should be on the choices I laid out to you earlier; we would like you to discuss this in as much depth as possible. You may become better acquainted with your fellow Khered, but please keep this brief, and do not reveal any personal, identifiable details. I will be …"

"What's going on?" Caila interrupted him. "Has something happened?"

Mateos took a couple of seconds to consider how much he should tell her, "At this moment there is nothing for you to worry about. But I must insist you don't disclose any information that could identify you or reveal your location. Will you please keep that in mind?"

Caila got that same inexplicable feeling from him, that she'd experienced earlier. It was a mixture between concern and something deeper, something not immediately related to the reset of Mesu.

"Blast," she thought, "it's Earth, not Mesu, I'm not a Neteru!"

"All right, I will," she reassured him, "I'll be careful. I survived until now, and I am planning to stick around a little bit longer. That is, if you don't blast all of us of the face of the Earth, during that blasted Event of yours. And don't say 'don't worry', again! I'll decide when I need to worry or not."

"No worries, I won't."

When Caila gave him, what she hoped was her most withering look, he added, "Don't bite; I was just trying to lighten the mood, my dear Caila. And I have just one last question for you before I let you go to your meeting. … 'Do you really find me, charming and fiendish?'"

With that parting shot he vanished, leaving Caila open-mouthed and speechless. He couldn't know that, could he? Oh, blasted lectanimo!

- Mateos, if you are listening now, then I will let you know that I am less than impressed with you. You, sneaky snoop!

–

But Caila didn't have time to dwell on her burgeoning relationship with her Neteruian liaison. Because, after a quick glance at her blissfully sleeping husband, she was whisked away, to her first Khered assembly.

Your funeral

When she looked around, she found herself, not in a cold meeting room, but in her dream cottage. Snuggled up on a comfortable chair, under a soft lilac coloured throw, cradling a mug of hot strong tea. It was her favourite, Empress Grey.

Caila noticed it was impossible to make out the features of her fellow Khered. Everyone was an identical impression of a human shape, obscured by a uniquely coloured haze. She couldn't remember if it had been like that the first time they met.

Not looking forward to the discussion ahead, but uncomfortable with the awkward silence, she plucked up her courage and decided to kick things off.

"Hi, you all. How are you?" Caila hoped she sounded more confident than she felt. "We all know why we are here. Maybe we should start this meeting?"

The soft green shape next to Caila agreed, "We probably should. Does anyone have a suggestion, on how to handle this?"

"Yeh, leave it to me, I am used to leading meetings. Let's start with the basics, who's who: name, age, where we live; that kind of stuff," the brown form pointed at the pink silhouette, on his right, "you go first."

"Maybe we should leave those details, for now. There will be more than enough time to get better acquainted later. Unless, of course, we get exterminated before that 'later' arrives; in which case our names, ranks and serial numbers will be irrelevant anyway," Caila was rewarded with a muffled laughter, and considered that Mateos would have been satisfied with the way she'd sidestepped the brown shape's suggestion.

"How about this? We say where we stand, on the options that were given to us by the Neteru. And instead of trying to remember everyone's names I suggest we ..." she hesitated for a moment whilst studying the differently coloured shapes around the room. "I assume everyone can see that we are all different colours? Yes? Do you all see me as ...," she quickly re-checked the colour that had enveloped her since Saturday morning, "Red? ... Right then. Hi, I'm Red, and of the four options given to us, one, a reset without a human population, two, a reset including human Khered, three, wiping the planet clean completely, and, four, doing nothing.

Of these four options, I favour numbers one and two. Over to you, Green."

"Hi, I'm Green. Thanks, Red, I do agree with you, but I believe that we should also put forward an alternative option. There are so many good people around, maybe the

Neteru can do a selective reset, getting rid of the nasties only. I guess you're next, Blue?"

"Yes, I believe I am," Blue said in a soft voice, "I'm not sure about this yet. I don't want people dying because of us. May I choose option four, please?"

"Of course, you may, Blue," Caila, a.k.a. Red, reassured her, "that's why we are here. How about you, Pink?"

"First of all, I would like to say that I loathe pink, the colour pink, that is. But I agree that this is a practical solution, given the absence of an annotated seating plan, so you can call me Pink, for now. Well, I'm happy with any of the first three options. Life is a great big humbug anyway. Your next, Snow White."

"Hi all, I'm White," White chuckled, "and I agree with Red, it should be one or two, we made the mess and we should take responsibility for it. Your turn, Brown." White chuckled again.

"Green! I think you are on the right track. We need more choice. These guys are not giving us a fair chance," Brown sounded as confident, as Blue had appeared shy. "We need to show them who they are dealing with. I say bring it on! … Now, I don't want to brag. But I am a very, very, successful businessman. And I have an extremely high IQ. I am well-known and very well-connected. Yo… We need a leader, folks. And I am the best man to lead our team. What do you think, Green, do you support m…"

"I'm sorry, Brown, if I may interrupt you for a moment," what a twat! Caila tried to remember who he reminded her of, "that is a very kind offer, and we will discuss the possibility of selecting a chair later. But at this moment this is a shared responsibility with equal input from all, and some of us haven't had a chance to speak up yet, let's continue with Purple. Purple, which options do you favour?"

"Hi," Purple gave a little wave and looked at Pink, "I'm Purple, which by the way is my favourite colour. I believe …"

A consensus emerged, that humans had messed up badly, and they should accept responsibility. This wiped options three and four of the table, which, Caila believed, were dummy options anyway, even if Mateos had not outright confirmed it, the other night.

"I think that was pretty clear. Most of us prefer the first two alternatives, so I believe we should compare and discuss these choices further. We should also discuss a possible fifth option," Caila sipped her tea. "Personally, I believe it will take a seriously good sales pitch to convince the Neteru to even consider a new option, we need to come up with some good arguments there.

Then of course, there is the point raised by Brown. Do we need a leader, or a chair?

Just now, you showed that we are all pretty disciplined. So, I don't believe we need a leader. But we might want to select a chair, to make sure we all get to say our bit. How about that?"

"Brown, I agree with Red," Yellow seconded Caila, "I don't believe that we need a leader, but a chair wouldn't be a bad idea. And since Red appears to have already successfully taken up this role, I propose we ask Red to continue. Would you mind chairing these meetings, Red?"

"I'm happy to do it, that is, … if no one objects."

Yellow scanned the room and after an approving murmur, concluded, "That's agreed then. Red, you have the floor."

"Thank you. Let's quickly agree on an agenda, before we proceed," Caila improvised. "How about this? From our introductions it's clear that we can drop the last two options. So, let's first discuss one versus two.

After that, anyone who has a suggestion for a fifth alternative, will get the opportunity to present it. And then, if there is still time left, we can briefly discuss those options, so that we can think about them between this assembly and the next. We'll finish off with any other suggestions or remarks. Is that okay with everyone? …

Right. Who would like to give us their reasons for strongly supporting or rejecting a reset with or without human Khered? … Grey? You go first."

Grey kicked off a lively discussion which centred around two arguments.

Was it fair for a tiny, select group to remain on this planet while the rest of the human population was removed? Orange and Lilac had strong feelings about the injustice of this, especially about the selective bit. While Grey felt that, if push came to shove, they owed it to all the good and decent people, still out there, to restart and build on the best qualities and achievements of humanity. This provoked an acid reply from Lilac, that they knew people worthier than themselves, to build on this inheritance.

The second discussion centred around the practicalities of being left behind. Blue, who seemed shyer than the rest of them, was worried about organising her group, and keeping them healthy and happy. Violet made a valid point that option two would put them at a distinct disadvantage over all the other species on Earth. "Without our tech and toys," they said, "we will be like kids, lost in the woods". That remark got a giggle out of Blue. But Yellow noted that, even if they lost all their toys, they would still have something that was more valuable to their survival than gadgets: their brains.

Slowly but surely, consensus shifted towards the second option. But, before deciding, Lilac wanted more details on what the Neteru called, their '*chosen ones*'. And Blue wanted to know if they could still meet after the Event.

The discussion moved on to a possible fifth option, and Green kicked off by repeating their selective, '*get rid of the nasties only*', suggestion.

Which prompted Pink to enquire, how you recognised a nasty. Brown's solution, to eliminate the prison populations, was met with an angry retort from Lilac, who informed them that some of the biggest crooks lived highly respected highlifes, on the outside.

"Let's stick to the outlines, for now," Caila could see the discussion on nasties, taking a truly nasty turn. "We can think about the details, before and during our next meeting. Does anyone else have a suggestion for a fifth option?"

Blue hesitantly raised their hand.

"Yes, Blue, do you have an idea?"

"I'm not sure, this is probably a silly idea. But could the Neteru maybe just get rid of the bad stuff we made? Like the guns and bombs, and those kinds of things, maybe," Blue sounded terrified, fully expecting to be put down, for coming up with something foolish.

And true to form, Brown obliged, "Don't be naïve, how could we ever keep the bad guys in their place without guns? I never heard anything so stu…"

"Stop it right there, Brown. No. Shush," Caila furiously silenced him. "Number one, Brown, we treat each other with respect here; if you can't do that, then you shut up." She softened her tone as she addressed Blue, "And number two, Blue, I think that is a brilliant idea, with a bit more detail, it might make a convincing case. Thank you. Yes, Yellow?"

"I realise we shouldn't go into detail right now, but Green's idea could be combined with Blue's clean-up. Thanks, Blue, I think you're onto something here."

Blue appeared to glow a bit brighter, "Thank you."

Caila gave Yellow a grateful smile, before she realised that he or she probably wouldn't notice, "Those are two good ideas to consider. Thank you, Blue and Green.
Anyone else? No? Going once, going twice, gone."

"Next subject," Caila continued. "Any other questions, suggestions, concerns or whatever else is relevant to this situation? Yes, Pink?"

Pink's haze radiated grumpiness, "Well, yes, I would like to know if there is a reason why we are the colour we are. And, I would like to know if I can change mine?"

Their unexpected moan brought about a roaring laughter.

"I am serious," Pink complained, "I detest pink."

"I'm sorry. I know it's not funny and you don't give the impression of being the pinkish type. But I think we all just needed some release, after the previous discussions. I'll add it to my list, to ask my Neteruian liaison. In the meantime, is there another word that we can use to address you?
Oh, hold on, your colour reminds me of the Pink Tiger. Or was that a panther?
Well, anyway, would you mind if we called you Tiger, until we can sort this out? You sound more like a Tiger than like a Pink."

It took Pink no more than a couple of seconds to decide that there were worse things than to be compared to a tiger, "I like Tiger, but I would also still like to have my colour changed, if possible".

"Right, Tiger it is then, and I'll ask about the colour change. Anyone else?

Yes, Violet?"

"If you are making a list of things to ask the Neteru, then could you also ask them what kind of a timeline they have in mind? And, if any fifth option is going to be considered seriously. If they don't, then we might as well remove it from our agenda, during our next meeting."

"Good points, I'll add them to my list," Caila hoped she could remember the growing list of questions. "Have you always been this practical?"

"Not really, you lot seem to bring out the best in me."

"Does anyone else have a question for my list?" Caila wasn't sure, but she thought Black tried to attract her attention, he hadn't said much until now. "Yes, Black?"

"Can you please ask the Neteru, if there is a possibility of accidental survivors?"

Black's question took Caila by surprise, "That is an interesting question. Would you expect accidental survivors? And would that be good or bad?"

Black explained, that in the case of a disaster, it was likely that Government officials and their protection detail took shelter. And that it would be hard to predict if they would be friendly or hostile.

This reminded Caila of Mateos's insistence not to share any personal information, and she imagined that Black might not be far off the mark, "Thanks, that is a good question. Anyone else?"

Oh no, not Brown again, "Yes, Brown? Please go ahead, do you have anything for our list?"

"No, mister or mizzz chair. Merely a very sensible suggestion." Brown emphasised every one of these last three words, "I don't like the idea that we all have an equal vote. Some of us are better placed than others to oversee the gravity of this situation. We should have voting rights based on our age, education, gender and country of residence. Let's share these details, right now.
Blue, you go first."

Even before Caila could put a stop to it, Tiger, formerly known as Pink, exploded, "Hold on, Blue, not a word. I think we need to discuss this first. Red, please?"

"I agree with you, Tiger. Would you like to be the first, to comment on Brown's proposal?" Caila snuggled deeper under her throw, almost feeling guilty, she suspected she was going to enjoy this bust-up.

"Pleasure," Tiger obliged and sat up straight. "Putting the weighted system aside for now, I believe you said age, education, gender, country of residence?
One, where does gender fit into this? I believe that the myth of gender-linked brainpower was debunked ages ago. But maybe you are too young to remember?
Two, I believe we heard enough from everyone to conclude that age and education, whatever those are, are irrelevant here. Every single one of us made intelligent contributions to the earlier discussions.

Three, where the hell would geographical location come into the equation?"

An uneasy silence followed Tiger's outburst.

'Why did I ever agree to chair these meetings,' Caila despaired, 'please, get me out of here.' But instead of running, she summarised, "I don't believe anyone could disagree with Tiger's stance on gender equality. However, if anyone would like to challenge Tiger, then please go ahead. ... No one? Good.

No, just one moment please, Brown, you'll have the opportunity to respond in a minute.

Ok, age and what was it again? ... Education, right. Thanks, White.

I tend to agree with Tiger. Every person in this room has had their say in the earlier discussions, and I believe we can all agree that the subject matter was challenging. Judging from your input I would say that, every one of us is in possession of more than sufficient intellectual capacities, combined with a good measure of common sense.

Would anyone like to comment? ... No one? We're on a roll.

That leaves geographical location, which has me flabbergasted as well.

Brown, would you care to elaborate, please?"

"Fine, if no one agrees. But the differences between male and female brains are well documented. And if you don't care about a half educated 12-year-old getting equal voting rights? It's your funeral!" ungracefully, Brown conceded on

the first part of his request. "But even if you are not as intelligent as I am, you must see how important geographical location is. Let me spell it out to you.
Some of us represent only very small countries. While others represent very, very big nations. That brings more responsibility. And it deserves a bigger slice of the vote. Surely, no one can argue with that."

'Why is everyone looking at me?' Caila panicked and decided to go for the well-worn meeting technique of '*stall and waffle*', while her hands nervously braided the tassels of her throw, "Thank you, Brown, that clarifies your stance immensely, I can see now, where you are coming from. Most governments and international organisations do indeed work on this principle. And I agree that, on first sight, it might also appear appropriate, in this situation. ..."
Yes! Caila felt like punching the air, she had an idea, "However, in the current situation, none of us are actually representatives of our countries. We represent the entire population of Earth. The way I interpret that, is that each and every one of us represents an equal share of this planet's human residents.
Please, anyone, let me know if you disagree?" Caila swallowed and wondered if anyone would mind if she hid under her throw.

"Seriously, Red, if you are not already a politician, then you should be. That is a perfectly solid argument, let anyone have a stab at sinking that," Yellow exclaimed. "We should put this to the vote. Who rejects Browns proposal for weighted voting rights?"

Twelve arms shot up.

"That's decided then. No weights. Oops, I'm sorry, I kind of took over from you, but I feel very strongly about this."

"No worries. I'm glad we got this cleared up. I'm sorry, Brown, but I guess your proposal was rejected. No hard feelings? I'm sure that as a successful businessman you are used to '*win some lose some*'. Please, let us know if you have any other ideas."

"Right, anyone else? …

No other suggestions?" with a sigh of relief, Caila rounded off their first round of discussions. "Well then, you all know what we need to consider before our next meeting. And I've got my list of questions to challenge my Neteruian contact. Remains for me to say, that no doubt our liaisons will let us know when we will meet again, and it has been a pleasure getting to know all of you, even if it is under less than happy circumstances.

Enjoy the rest of your day. Or, sleep tight, and don't let the bedbugs bite."

Big brother

It was still only half past six, when Caila checked her alarm clock, no time had passed during her meeting. Chris was still asleep, looking peaceful and happy, blissfully unaware of the impending end of the world. She stroked his back, maybe she should wake him. She was wide awake and craved distraction.

As if on cue, Caila's wish was fulfilled, though not in the way she'd planned. From outside her window, a familiar voice interrupted her reflections.

- A very good morning to you, Caila. I trust the assembly went ahead as planned. Mateos requested of me, to pass on this message, immediately upon your return. –

- Good morning, OOVII, I hope you had a restful night, despite Mateos's predawn request. And how's your lovely wife, this morning? –

- Why, thank you. I had a very restful night indeed, and my wife is still in the Land of Dreams. Mateos asked me to inform you he has an urgent matter to attend to; he will return as soon as possible.

Furthermore, Mateos requested that all your curtains should remain undrawn, to facilitate an unobstructed view of the interior of your present position, – OOVII hoped that by rephrasing Mateos's request, he would increase the likelihood of Caila's cooperation. A hope, that was immediately crushed by her response.

- Open my curtains, to … what? – Caila was stunned. - So, I can be watched 24/7?

No thank you, I would like some privacy, thank you very much! I know that Big Brother, Mateos is watching me most of the time, but when he is away, I would like to have at least a tiny bit of privacy. Especially at night, when I am with my husband; I can assure you that I am quite safe when I'm with Chris.

Please tell Mateos there are limits, and that this is one of them. No wait! Don't bother, I will tell him myself, when he returns. –

Caila punched her pillow, all she wanted, was some time alone with Chris, before the inevitable madness ensued. Then, she snuggled back under the duvet.

But she'd misjudged OOVII's determination.

Mateos's instructions had been clear and left him in no doubt that there was no room for negotiations, - Caila, be reasonable. I understand your position, I treasure my own privacy. However, Mateos would not have made such an invasive request if he had not considered it to be of the utmost importance.

May I suggest a compromise, please? Would you agree to open your curtains, if I promise to avert my gaze, when you require a moment of privacy? – Khrhhsh reasoned that, Caila's partial cooperation would be better than no cooperation at all. Although he doubted, Mateos would agree.

\- You are really worried about Mateos's reaction if those curtains are not open when he returns, aren't you? – Caila understood the corvid's predicament. - All right then, but I'm only doing it to keep you out of trouble. I still believe Mateos is flipping out over nothing, and I will let that overprotective control freak know, as soon as he returns. – Carefully, Caila slipped out of bed, not wanting to disturb Chris, before she'd had a chance to come up with a reasonable excuse for her unusual behaviour. She quietly opened the curtains, and was rewarded with a view of OOVII, perched in front of her window, against the background of an enormous bright full moon.

And then, the inevitable happened.

"What time is it? Oh, Caila, what are you doing? It's only half past six, it's Sunday. Close those curtains and come back to bed, please."

\- Thanks, OOVII, how would you explain that to your wife? –

"Good morning, darling. Look out of the window! Isn't it beautiful? I just remembered that there was going to be a super moon tonight. Don't you think it's gorgeous? Let's keep the curtains open. The other day, I read, that if you wake up to the light of the last super moon of a year, you will have good luck until the 31st December." Caila climbed back into bed and snuggled up to Chris.

\- OOVII, you promised to look away. –

"Who knows," she kissed her husband's neck, "we might even win the lottery."

"You are crazy, darling," Chris turned around and pulled her close as he kissed her, "but I love you."

True to his word, OOVII did not turn around until Caila told him it was okay to do so, - You can turn around now. I'm starting to believe that we can make this partnership work. You are the most reasonable corvid, I've ever had the good fortune to meet. –

"However, do you think that crow got that egg into our garden? Surely, it's much too large for him to carry in his beak. It looks like a chicken egg," Chris was fascinated by the enormous shiny black bird, enjoying a late eggy breakfast. "At first, you hardly ever see crows at the back, and then, they make themselves perfectly at home, having their breakfast right under your nose. It is a beautiful bird. I wonder if it has a partner, I believe they usually come in pairs. What does your new book say about that?"

That book doesn't tell me how to deal with a polite crow, when he informs you that those eggs on your kitchen counter look extremely tempting. Caila looked guiltily at the empty egg box in the kitchen, not sure how she was going to explain their rapidly diminishing supply to Chris, "Yes, I believe they pair of for life. I'm sure his wife is around somewhere. He is gorgeous, isn't he?"

"That is, assuming it is a *him*. Although, such a handsome bird can only be a male, of course. … Ouch, don't hit me, darling. That reminds me. Did you colour your hair this morning? It looks great, but you left a red handprint on my stomach."

A red handprint, what the …? I could kill Mateos, Caila fumed as she lifted Chris's sweater, "Yes, and no, it's a new touch-up temporary, colour-spray thingy, I must have got some of it on my hands, sorry about that. Does it really look good?

My hair I mean, not your handprint," Caila stood to inspect her shiny auburn locks in the mirror, her husband was right, it looked picture perfect, not one brown strand dared rear its ugly head. "Yes, it does look very natural, doesn't it?" Then she quickly steered the conversation to a safer subject, "How's that new marmalade? It was on offer this week."

"It's good, but I still prefer strawberry jam," preferring food to fashion, Chris took the bait. "What would you like to do today? Home or away? I really should have a look at some legacy code, before tomorrow morning's meeting. But if you would like to go out, I could do it tonight, and maybe leave a bit earlier in the morning."

Chris's request gave Caila an excuse to keep Mateos happy without appearing to give in to his demands. Besides, Chris would not relax until he'd done his prep. So, that would be killing two birds with one stone. Or, feeding two crows from one box of eggs, which would, no doubt, sound kinder to OOVII's ears.

She also had a feeling that Mateos would be back soon, and with Chris working, she wouldn't have to divide her attention between the two men.

***

One thing she was clear about. If, as she suspected, it came down to a choice between no humans at all, or just a few, then she would go for the few. While Chris occupied the sofa, frowning sceptically at his laptop, Caila was curled up in a comfortable chair, pretending to read.

She was convinced humans could play a valuable role in Earth's ecology, but they would have to up their game considerably. It wouldn't be a walk in the park either. Growing carrots was slightly more complicated than chucking them in your basket in the supermarket. And how did you get rid of a headache, without aspirin? Books, that's what they needed, lots of them. A library. And people. Useful people. A farmer, a doctor, ... what more?

Overwhelmed, Caila despaired that seven companions, felt a bit thin on the ground. Maybe they could convince the Neteru to allow them some more.

And, who should she pick, to stay with her after the Event? She hated those words, '*chosen ones*', they sounded so pretentious. As if it would be a privilege, to be asked to hang around after the apocalypse! Asked? They would not have a choice in the matter either, would they?

Number one was a no brainer, that could only be Chris.

Then there was Steve, she'd briefly worked with him, a couple of years ago, but he had become their best friend. He was intelligent and a passionate gardener, which would come in useful when they were growing those carrots. Steve was a package deal with Richard, they'd married only recently, but had been a couple for over ten years. Richard was good-natured and patient, and as an engineer he might know something about building useful things. Off the top of her head, Caila hadn't the foggiest what kind of useful things needed building, but it seemed to make sense. Besides she liked having Steve and Richard around. Bluebell and Banjo should, of course, also join them; those two guys were dotty about their cats.

That took her up to four, only four more to go. But who? She hit a blank, and suddenly, asking the Neteru for more companions became a less appealing option.

- Caila, I need you to call in sick tomorrow morning. You are not leaving this house. –

Completely lost in her thoughts, Caila hadn't noticed Mateos's return; and from the looks and sounds of it, he was in a foul mood. Fine, let him be. Caila didn't care. She wanted to retain some control over her rapidly out of control spinning life.

- And a good morning to you too, Mateos. How are you today? I am fine, thank you for asking, – Caila sensed that her sarcastic comment did nothing to improve his mood. - And I would like to point out to you that I am not ill or otherwise incapacitated, so I'm not going to pull a sickie tomorrow. I never did that before, and I'm not going to start now. Even if the world is about to end. –

That had the effect she aimed for.

Mateos's mood changed from foul to furious, as he growled, - I just told you that you are not leaving this house! That was an order, not a request! –

His Khered's mouth fell open in surprise.

- No, shut up, I'm not in the mood for an argument. If necessary, I will give you a valid excuse to call in sick. I'd rather not, I prefer you mobile and alert. But believe me, one way or another, you will not leave this house. Got that? – Mateos radiated frustration and fury.

But Caila, who normally hated confrontations, was less than impressed. Mateos looked kind of funny when he was this angry, not intimidating at all. She didn't know why, but there was something very familiar about this situation. Suppressing a giggle, she informed her enraged liaison, - Has anyone ever told you that you look terribly handsome when you are angry? All you have to do is ask nicely, and then, maybe, I'll say yes.

Come on, you should know by now that shouting at me is counterproductive. –

The Neteru studied his Khered and wondered how much she remembered. How much of her DNA was preserved in Caila? They were so alike, he couldn't risk losing her again. He composed himself, there was too much at stake, - My dear Caila, would you please stay at home, tomorrow morning? I would not burden you with such an impertinent request, if it was not essential to your safety. At this moment I cannot fully explain my reasons, but I promise you that I will do so later. … Truce? –

'You'd better say yes, my little Tia,' he thought, 'because I will not let you leave this house'.

- Truce! – Caila exclaimed victoriously. - And, I wouldn't actually mind extending my weekend for a little bit. But I don't like lying to Juliet, she can see right through me. Would working from home be an acceptable alternative? –

- As long as you don't leave the house, – he quickly accepted her offer, before she had a chance to change her mind. - Promise? –

- Promised. Is Chris safe, or should he stay at home as well? – worried that, if this was so important to Mateos, there had to be a serious threat. - Does this have something to do with Brown? He was really pushy this morning, trying to find out who we all were. No one gave anything away, by the way. –

- I am aware of that. Sorry, we had no choice; we had to monitor your meeting.
Keep Chris at home, they might try to get to you through him, – Mateos cast an irritated glance in Chris's direction. Why did she have to complicate things by being in such an intense relationship? - I believe you were given a list of questions for me, during your meeting? –

- Yes, I was. And thank you for your concern regarding my husband, – Caila noticed the way he'd looked at Chris, and his attitude towards her partner began to annoy her.

- You completely ignored my second question about Brown, so I'll take that as a 'yes'. And since you were eavesdropping, you know the list as well as I do.
So, shoot. –

Ignoring her snipe about his behaviour towards Chris, and the remark about Brown, Mateos obliged, - I already instructed all liaisons to elaborate on your chosen ones.

And no, we cannot distinguish between Green's 'nasties' and others.

Yes, you may tell Blue that you can still meet up after the Event. Thank you for telling Brown off, when he attacked her, she is very young but with some support she will be fine.

Pink Tiger then, that was unexpected and highly entertaining. I'm terribly sorry but spheream colours stick for life, it is hard coded. Would you like to tell Tiger, or would you prefer their contact to do that? –

- It's okay, I kind of like Tiger. I'll tell him. Or her. –

- Black's accidental survivors? There is not much I can add there. He is right, there is now a significant chance of accidental survivors; and if there are any, then there is a real risk that they are Government officials with armed escorts. Only a small number of the highest security bunkers can possibly shelter their occupants from the beam that triggers the Event. We will do what we can, to limit the risk this poses to you all, but I cannot guarantee anything. This is one of the reasons for bringing the Event forward. –

- So, the Event is a given? Does that mean, that option four is of the table? – Caila asked him to confirm what she'd already suspected.

- Officially, no. Unofficially, yes, – Mateos admitted, - but that's between us, Caila, don't let it get any further. –

- All right, – Caila gave her word, - don't worry, I won't tell anyone. –

Mateos continued with Violet's timeline, - That, I'm afraid, may just have got condensed. But you will all be ready in time.
And the fifth option? As I mentioned before, we will listen to you, but our hands are tied. That was everything on your list I believe. –

- Yes, that was everything on my meeting list, – with option five, following option four, into the bin, Caila concluded, -but I also have some personal questions. –
She quickly glanced at Chris, who was still engrossed in his code; not very good code judging from the deep frown, which hadn't left his forehead since he'd opened his laptop. Then she turned her attention back to Mateos, who appeared relaxed now that she'd agreed to stay at home, - Are all crows as posh as OOVII? –

- Ov-i-y … who? – Mateos was thrown of balance, until it dawned upon him that she meant Khrhhsh. - Oh, you mean Khrhhsh! I didn't see that one coming. Most corvids are well spoken, but Khrhhsh is from a high-ranking family, so maybe he is a bit more eloquent than most of his species. Do you have any more of those pressing questions, Caila? –

- This was important. Well, to me it was, – the worst actress in the world, made a lamentable attempt at sounding aggrieved. - Mateos! Are you laughing at me? Well, never mind.

But there is one other thing, it is not really a question, it is more of a request. I need you to slow down on the fixing trick, Chris is starting to notice. And what's the deal with me leaving a handprint on his skin? You can't seriously expect me not to touch my husband for a couple of weeks, or for however long we have until the Event. –

As Mateos rushed over to examine his Khered's oblivious husband, Caila gasped when she noticed the change in Chris, - How...? What ...? What is going on, Sets? –

But the Neteru didn't answer her question, he looked grim, his good mood had disappeared, - Upstairs, Caila. Now. Alone. –

Messy families

Upstairs, in the study, Caila felt oddly calm, "What's going on here, Mateos?

Please, tell me that I don't have to worry about my husband glowing fire engine red.

And tell me, that in your Neteruian world, it is perfectly normal to leave a handprint on your partner's skin. And then I want you to tell me that everything will be fine, because if something happens to Chris, I ....

No, don't try to adjust my mood. I know what you are trying to do. That trick worked yesterday, but not anymore."

'And that is exactly the problem,' Mateos thought, 'you are developing too fast, and too far, for a Khered'.

"Caila, Chris's glowing, in itself, is nothing to worry about. It is similar to your own spheream. And it would have happened anyway, after he'd consented to become an activated Khered, as one of your chosen ones.

What is unusual, is that you initiated the process, normally this can only be done by a Neteru. Let me see your hand, please. ... No, the other one, the one you burned last week."

"That is the one, the wound was gone by Friday night," Caila lowered her hand onto her desk. "It's like my hair, I guess; I had an overnight root touch-up. And my knee, the one that's been giving me problems since I had that skating accident, it feels fine now.

That's what I meant, when I asked you to hold back on the fixing tricks. Chris is starting to notice."

"The purpose of this fixing trick, as you call it, is to get you in an acceptable condition for the restart. I fixed your hand, but I only got rid of the blisters, to prevent infection. The wound should still be visible and sensitive. I healed your knee, but I didn't do anything about your hair," Mateos stared at the wooden cat figurine in the window while he considered how much he should tell her. Breaking any more rules presented a risk, however, if he waited too long, she might start putting two and two together. He should probably stick to the wider picture; hell, he couldn't explain most of it himself.

Caila shifted in her chair, impatient for him to continue.

"Not all Khered received the same DNA insert. We created different trial groups, and we expected them to evolve and reactivate in different ways. …

But your insert is unique, it contains an additional sequence. And I believe, that it is this extra sequence that is causing your reactivation to speed up, it also appears to give you some Neteruian abilities.

Now, about Chris. … Neteru commit to a partner for life, but when they find a partner who is from a different species, that partner can choose to become Neteru. It is purely practical, it aligns the couple's abilities and lifespans.

Can you tell me where you touched Chris, and what you were thinking when you touched him?"

Caila blushed, as she remembered the moment, she'd rested her hand on Chris's stomach, "I put my hand on his stomach and I thought, well, just normal things, I guess. I was happy and relaxed, and I thought about how much I loved him, and that I never wanted to lose him. How we belonged together."

Her liaison gave her a look of despair, "That sounds like you performed your own conversion ceremony. Usually it is conducted in a more formal setting, with witnesses. Chris must have been unusually receptive, or you would not have been able to do this without his consent. Was Khrhhsh watching you?"

Caila shrugged, "You asked him to keep an eye on us, and I believe his wife was with him."

"Then they must have unwittingly taken on the roles of witnesses, allowing you to convert Chris into an activated Khered," then, impassively, Mateos concluded, "Congratulations, Caila, you are now officially paired off on two planets."

His Khered considered the implications and decided she rather liked it, "That isn't too bad then, is it? Although I never imagined I'd get married without noticing. I'm sure Chris won't mind either. He loves me."

"Mateos, that bit of DNA, the extra insert you gave me, what was that?" she studied her nebulous alien liaison. "It's not turning me into a full-blown Neteru, is it? … I'm not sure I'm ready to be turned into a hazy red cloud, not just yet."

"I don't think so; those fixes you affected, only restored your human body. However, I believe that, given time, you will be able to return to Etherun," realising he'd slipped up, he digressed. "But, later today, you will have some explaining to do, preferably before your husband starts asking questions."

"Yes, that is going to be an interesting conversation," his Khered admitted, "for which you will be present to help me, of course?"

Then it registered what Mateos had said before he changed the subject, "But hold on, rather like that skating injury of mine, you did some serious skating around the issue, to distract me from something you said earlier. What did you mean when you said that I would be, 'returning', to Etherun?

Who did you nick that extra bit of DNA from, that you gave my ancestor? And who is Sets? That is what I called you downstairs, and it is your name, isn't it?"

"My name is Mateos, Mateos Heruset. Heruset is my middle name.

The only one to ever call me Sets, was my sister, usually when she needed a favour or when I had to get her out of trouble. She left a copy of her DNA, before she left Etherun. She never returned.

You, Caila, or your ancestors, never lived on Etherun, but Tia's DNA insert seems to be creating memories for you. It also appears to have evolved, to give you traits which she possessed. That was never my intention, and I did not foresee you would be so like her."

Caila was not sure how to react to this revelation. The Neteru's apprehension confused her. Mateos had been lots of things since she'd first met him, but he had always been confident. Holding on to her anger, she tried to ignore the sympathy she felt for him. This explained why they were so at ease with each other, "I guess no one on Etherun was partial to your little experiment? Am I a clone of your sister? And is that why you visited me, when I was younger?"

"No, you are not a clone," Mateos sounded indignant, "give me some credit. I wouldn't do that, Tia would kill me. No, you inherited some of her personality, and the colour of her spheream. She was the same shade of red, it's the hair colour you were born with. I changed it to brown, shortly after your birth, to disguise your ancestry. Your Khered lineage all had the same auburn hair."

"And I liked that colour so much that I used a bottle to undo your prudent recolouring exercise," Caila thought it was rather funny.

"Yes, and now it restored itself," Mateos confirmed dryly, "you'll no longer need those bottles."

Caila laughed, "Do you know how difficult it is to stay angry with you?

Would you mind if I accepted you as an honorary brother? I always wanted one.

What happened to Tia?"

"I'd be honoured to have you as an honorary sister. But I'll tell you about Tia later," Mateos relaxed, Caila seemed to take it all rather well. "And to answer your earlier question: no, no one on Etherun is aware that I used Tia's DNA, and I would be in serious trouble if it came out."

"And I would probably be poked and pricked, as a novelty Khered, and be assigned a new liaison," Caila concluded horrified. "Yuk, I'm not partial to poking and pricking, and you are kind of growing on me, Mateos. So, you can tell them whatever they need to hear when I do something weird and I'll do my best to keep my Neteruian tricks under control."

Caila glanced at the clock, "Did you do your time trick again, or should I worry about Chris becoming impatient? Can you teach me how to stop time, it could be very useful?"

"I don't think that would be wise. You still have a lot to learn, so I'm going to keep a close eye on you. Accidently marrying your husband is one thing, but messing with time is in a completely different league. Don't even think about trying it.

It is not a trick by the way, it is applying Etherun time to Earth. And I haven't used it, so Chris is probably expecting the surprise you promised him, very soon.

Let's get back to business, before he walks in on us. I need to leave you for a while, but I'll be back tonight. Khrhhsh will be there for you, while I'm gone.

One last thing before I go. How are you getting on with your *chosen ones*?"

"I don't know," Caila pulled a face, "I have friends and then again, I don't have friends. If you know what I mean? … Probably not, that's gobbledygook," even to Caila's own ears, it sounded like gibberish. "Chris is number one, of course. And after this morning I believe I haven't left him a choice, have I?

Then there are these two guys that I really trust, and I think they can handle it. Life after the Event, I mean. They have been together for ages, they are smart, and they have some useful skills, …" remembering Steve and Richard's pets, Caila interrupted herself, "oh, but Sets, can they bring their cats, please? Bluebell and Banjo, they absolutely dote on them."

Mateos eyed Caila suspiciously. Was she seriously asking him to look after a couple of cats? Yes, apparently, she was, "Caila, cats won't be harmed during the Event. They may be a bit disorientated, but they will be fine."

He looked at Caila, who just stared back at him, "But if you insist, I'll isolate your two felines and deliver them safely to their new home."

"That's brilliant, I knew I could count on you!

As for the other four, of course I know people, but they should be able to adjust to living in a decimated world. And,

I would like them to fit into our group, as well as be useful. There are two more who might be up to the challenge, but I need to give numbers six and seven a bit more thought. I was thinking of someone with medical skills."

"I believe I can help you there. Do you trust me?" Mateos tried to conceal his enthusiasm. "I know someone with medical skills who would fit in perfectly, his name is Peter Overwood."

Caila shrugged, "Of course, I trust you. And that's one less thing for me to decide."

"I'll be on my way then. And," Mateos reminded her, "hold off on explaining what happened to Chris until I'm back, it will be easier for you if I'm here to support you. Also, your next and final assembly has been moved forward to Tuesday morning. We expect you to come to a consensus then. When I told you earlier the timeline had been condensed, I meant it. We encountered substantial problems and need to speed this process up. I don't believe the breach will affect you, but I can't be certain, so whatever you do, Caila, do not leave this house."

London – 10 Downing Street

The Prime Minister scrutinised Marcus, her head of MI5, while she tried to make sense of what she'd just been told. How was she going to respond? How could anyone possibly respond to, … this?

"Marcus, let me recap, please. You want me to call a COBR meeting to discuss the threat of an imminent alien invasion. Additionally, you would like me to authorise the elimination of the woman who is the alien's human contact here in the United Kingdom. Or did you say Earth?"

"That is correct, Madam Prime Minister," Marcus confirmed curtly.

"And this is based on evidence which originates from the United States, gathered during the Salem witch trials. And more recently from a man who claims to have attended a nightly meeting with these aliens and their human contacts here on Earth," Samantha held up a pale freckled hand. "No, hold on Marcus, I want to make certain I understand this correctly. This man did not recognise any of his fellow human attendees because, like the alien chairperson, they were all disguised as colourful clouds.

However, this suspect is implicated because she is a first-born red-haired woman. And, approximately fifty years ago the CIA eliminated her grandmother for the exact same reasons; because she was the eldest female child and had red hair. This operation, executed on UK territory, was not approved by us, nor was it made known to us, until you were briefed by the head of the CIA earlier today.

Marcus, there is one point that I am not quite clear on yet. Are you asking me to authorise the elimination of only this particular first-born, red-haired woman? Or are you seeking authorisation for the elimination of all first-born red-haired women in the UK?" Samantha twisted a strand of her ginger locks around her finger.

"I can assure you that red hair is not the issue here, ma'am, it merely forms part of the evidence against this woman," realising he was fighting a losing battle, Marcus decided to give it one last shot. "Madam Prime Minister, I realise that this is unchartered territory. But the threat is unprecedented, and the evidence is solid, it comes straight from a specialist branch within the CIA and it has been confirmed by specialists within our own service.

There is no evidence any other person or persons in our country are colluding with these aliens. The target in question, is a confirmed security risk and plans for the invasion are in an advanced stage. However, we have strong evidence an invasion cannot take place, without the support of this woman, or her associates."

"Marcus, so far, we enjoyed an excellent working relationship. Any evidence originating from your team always proved timely and reliable, and I never hesitated to accept your recommendations," the Prime Minister sat down behind her desk and folded her hands. "However, in this instance I cannot oblige. I refuse to act upon evidence gathered by witch hunters against red-haired women. That is one step too far."

Samantha pressed a button to call her P.A., "John? Marcus is ready to leave now.

And, could you please inform my husband that I will join him for lunch. In about 15 minutes?"

She stood and extended her hand, looking her security chief straight in the eyes, "Goodbye, Marcus."

"Alastair, how are you? I do apologise for disturbing you whilst you enjoy your well-deserved Sunday roast, but this can't wait. It concerns Marcus," the Prime Minister listened to her Secretary of State as she watched Marcus stride out of Downing Street. "Yes, that's right, I'm talking about our head of MI5. I suspect he suffered a mental breakdown and I want him send on sick leave without delay, pending medical evaluation."

Samantha turned away from the window and frowned irritated, "I appreciate that, Alastair, and I am very well aware that Marcus is a key figure in ongoing operations. However, he completely lost the plot and we need to let him go before he inflicts irreparable damage. This could cost us the next elections."

She nodded while she considered the practical implications of an instant suspension.

"All right, tomorrow morning at the latest then. And, thank you, Alastair. Enjoy your pudding."

Marcus took one last look at the official residence and office of the Prime Minister. Fools, the lot of them! His phone buzzed.

"Yes." …, "Right." …, "Thank you, John."

The bitch! But he had more strings on his bow.

He pulled a different mobile out of his pocket, "Mr Thurogood? Marcus here. I need to speak to you on a matter of national security," he scanned Parliament Street for a taxi while he listened to Baldwin's token objections.

"This has the potential to bring your party back into Government," spotting a black cab, Marcus raised a hand, "Tonight, eight pm, leave the backdoor open."

Chris shines

"Do you want one?" Chris offered his wife a chocolate from the box of Belgian Seashells she'd given him earlier, and Caila smiled when she realised that Chris's favourite chocolates had been sort of an impromptu wedding gift.

After Mateos had left her, Caila spent the rest of the afternoon thinking about her remaining three '*chosen ones*'. She was happy to leave the mysterious number seven, to her honorary brother.

What worried Caila, was how her companions would react to their new Khered status in a deserted world. It was impossible to predict how anyone would respond to being asked to stick around, while all their nearest and dearest were gone. Not that she would leave them a choice; they wouldn't find out until after the Event.

She'd briefly toyed with the idea of random selection, but quickly discarded it as unworkable, she needed people who could live and work together. People who she knew could adjust to this new life.

She desperately wanted Steve and Richard to join them, but they were their best friends and hurting them was the last thing she wanted. Still, Caila realised, that if she selected them pain was unavoidable. Steve and Richard loved their extended families and friends, and they stood to lose them all because she was too selfish to let them go. At the same time Caila realised that there was no way she could not choose them, they were her best friends and she trusted them completely.

If she was going to vote for a reset including Khered, she really didn't have a choice. Blasted Neteru! Caila grimaced. Or should that be blasted humans, for creating this horrible mess in the first place?

Juliet would be a perfect fourth choice. She had disappointed her parents by shying away from a career in the theatre, and you'd be hard fetched to find anyone less like her Capulet namesake. As a personal assistant she kept teams running smoothly and managers on a short leash. But more importantly, she grew her own, kept chickens, goats and ducks, and made her own cheese and bread. And she had no close family or friends to speak of.

Then there was Luke, 29 years old and not a fan of social occasions. His honesty sometimes bordered on the embarrassing, he was an extremely logical thinker and absolutely bloody brilliant. His parents, massive Star Wars fans, had christened him Luke Jedi. A fact they'd lived to regret, when Luke's critical dissection of the series significantly affected their enjoyment of this epic drama. Caila had met him a couple of times, he was a software developer like Chris, they worked together, and got along perfectly well.

Luke might not be too charmed by Jenny, however.

Jenny would be the youngest of their group, she was only twenty years old, and Caila realised she would be taking a risk with her. Jenny had a mother and a brother whom she loved dearly, and she adored her little nieces. She was a slave to her make-up and hid her insecurity behind a wall of constant chatter. And she loved partying. But she was also incredibly creative when it came to problem solving, and more intelligent than she gave herself credit for. Jenny adapted quickly to new circumstances and was fun to have around. She was a risk worth taking.

One engineer, two mathematicians, two IT guys, an econometrician and a smallholder personal assistant. Caila pondered that there were worse starting points for a new civilisation than Geek junction. Mateos's medical professional would fit in just fine.

***

With her homework done and dusted, Caila felt smug when she turned her attention to her brightly glowing husband, "No, my dearest darling, that's all right, they're all yours. What's left of them anyway."
Chris had managed to munge through most of the box of chocolates, it would be gone before the sandman called tonight.
"Is something wrong with your eyes? You keep squinting."

Chris peered at Caila, "It's probably the light, the sun is going down behind you. You are surrounded by this red haze." Chris closed his eyes and shook his head, "How about starting dinner? It's getting late and I'm hungry."

Maybe that's not the best of ideas right now, Caila worried. She knew for certain that her spheream wouldn't fade in the kitchen. And when Chris walked past the mirror in the dining room, he might notice that hers was not the only red cloud in the house, "Let's wait a couple of minutes, you can't possibly be hungry after eating all those chocolates. Why don't you come and look at the sun set, the sky looks gorgeous?"

That much was true, it was a beautiful evening. Would sunsets still be this beautiful after the Event. She remembered reading that dawns and dusks could be especially bright because of pollutants in the air, reflecting the sun light.

- Caila, my dearest Caila, what have you done? I believe congratulations are in order, – OOVII watched them from across the street. - But you won't be able to hide this from Chris much longer. He is a beautiful shade of red, much brighter than yours. –

- Why, thank you, OOVII. But we were married, long before we got married this morning. And I'm sure Chris won't mind, once I explain how it happened.
Do you have any idea what's keeping Mateos? I could use his support. Chris is starting to ask questions. –

- I was informed that there has been an escalation of earlier problems, up north.

But maybe I can be of assistance? My wife frequently succeeded in explaining the inexplicable to me. –

- Thank you for offering, I might take you up on it, if I can't convince Chris this is nothing more than an innocent reset of Mesu. And that I'm an activated Khered, and accidently turned him into one as well? Did I forget anything? ... Oh, OOVII, what a mess! –

- Mesu? ... Really, you should mind your Ps and Qs. Earth will sound more familiar to Chris. –

"Caila? Hey, Caila," Chris put an arm around his distracted wife's shoulders, "you were miles away, again. I can still see your cloud. Maybe it's the alien side of your family shining through? .... Wow, darling, don't choke. I know that I'm funny, but it was not that hilarious! Shall I get you some water?"

'You don't know half how very - not - funny you were,' Caila thought, as she wiped the tears from her eyes and tried to get her coughing spell under control, "No, it's fine, I was choking on a bit of nothing. Just hold me for a moment." With Chris's arms safely wrapped around her, she heard OOVII mumbling in the background.

- This is going to be interesting. It will make up for my lack of sleep. –

"I believe your haze is rubbing off on me," Chris looked over her shoulder and inspected his arm, before he followed his wife's gaze out of the window and froze. With the sun disappearing fast, their cloudy reflections gazed back at them, in a perfect mix of two clashing shades of red.

Caila considered she should have taken a chance on shepherding Chris to the kitchen, Mateos would not be happy about this. She faced her husband and took his hand, "Chris? Yes, I can see it too. It's nothing to worry about. Let's sit down for a moment, then I'll explain."

Still holding Chris's hand, Caila sank back onto the sofa, "That joke you just made, about my alien side of the family shining through? … You were actually spot on. I know that this is going to sound a bit strange, but please hear me out."

While his eyes remained firmly fixed on their sphereams, Chris showed no signs of relaxing.

"You always said that I had to be from another planet. Well, I'm not, not really. But a tiny bit of me is, just a teeny-weeny bit of DNA. And that little bit has always been dormant, until last Friday, when it was reactivated.

I know you noticed some strange things happening to me, my burned hand which healed too quickly. My hair when it coloured itself red, overnight. That handprint, I left on your stomach. And me being a bit distracted, over the last couple of days.

Darling, last Friday, my alien DNA was activated. It is related to a species called the Neteru, they live on Etherun. Earth is a Neteruian experiment. Well, life on Earth is anyway. …

Apparently, we are on the brink of completely messing up our planet, and that in turn, would have a knock-on effect on the rest of the universe.

The long and short of it is, that they want to do a reset. There are a number of options, but the one that is relevant, is that Khered, that's me and a few others who were born with Neteruian DNA, act as reset elements for the human population. It's kind of like reverting in GIT. When you seriously messed up you chuck out loads of versions and restart almost from scratch," throwing in a bit of software jargon didn't help relax her husband, "but I'll tell you about that later.

Now, for some reason, my reactivation is going a bit faster than expected, and that's why you are becoming like me. I accidently performed some kind of Neteruian wedding ceremony, when I touched you this morning.

Don't worry, Chris, it's not a problem and it's not dangerous, I wanted to keep you anyway, I just speeded up the process.

I'm sorry, I know that this sounds rather far-fetched. And I should have prepared better before telling you all this, but I'd hoped that Mateos, my Neteruian contact, would be back to help me explain things to you.

Chris? … Please, Chris, say something."

Chris looked at his wife and blinked. She'd always had a vivid imagination but this was over the top, even for her. Something had happened last Friday, he was certain of that, Caila had not been herself these last couple of days. But aliens?

It almost sounded like she believed what she was telling him, "Caila, darling, I don't know what's going on, but …"

Chris looked around their living room and then back at Caila. Nothing else in the room was surrounded by a halo, and Caila's hand was completely healed; the same hand which now softly stroked the back of his neck.

Despite the bizarre situation, he felt himself relax, "but, …. well, something did happen. Maybe you had a bad dream? There must be a rational explanation. It's probably screen-eyes. Let's take a couple of days off, we've both been busy, we could do with a break."

Caila watched in wonder how Chris loosened up after she'd touched him. And screen eyes? That was brilliant! She realised she could have avoided this entire drama by blaming their sphereams on screen eyes.

'Thank you, Chris,' she thought, let's just run with that version, "I'd love to take a break to give our overworked screen eyes some well-deserved rest. Maybe we can both work from home tomorrow, and then we take the rest of the week off. Can you do that?"

"I'll try," Chris agreed. "Tomorrow morning, I'll call in on that meeting, and then I'll handover to Luke. He can also take care of that conference call on Wednesday, he won't like it, but he's the only one who knows what he's talking about and he won't accept any nonsense. That's a deal then. What are we going to do next week, apart from visiting that planet of yours?"

"Ha, ha, that is very funny. Let's get some food on the table, before we catch the next shuttle to my alien home."

***

How Chris could eat a plate full of Italian meatballs, after munching through an enormous box of chocolates was beyond Caila.

Italian meatballs? Remove sleeve and film, then cook for 30 minutes in a preheated oven. Caila considered that maybe she should look for a real recipe. Growing tomatoes and herbs shouldn't prove too difficult. But then she remembered the main ingredient.

- OOVII, you are not vegetarian, are you? –

- A balanced diet is essential, Caila, – the obliging corvid advised, - I can recommend insects as an alternative source of protein, but I understand there is a general aversion amongst humans to the consumption of insectum. –

"What was that?"

"What was what?" surely Chris could not have overheard OOVII's remark, it was too soon for him to pick up on lectanimo. Or not?

"I'm sure I heard someone talking about eating insects. Someone with a posh accent."

Obviously, it was not too soon, - Thanks, OOVII. Care to come in, and explain this one for me? – Caila chided the smart crow, making sure she excluded Chris from their conversation. - And where the hell is Mateos, when you need him? –

- You called, milady? Did you miss my stimulating company? –

"And what …, who is that?" Chris stared at Mateos who, in his unmasked form bore hardly any resemblance to a human.

Caila, who was used to disasters by now, was the first to recover and made the introductions, "Chris, this is Mateos. Mateos, you remember Chris, my husband.

And OOVII, I don't believe Chris is ready to take up your alternative protein source suggestion. Mateos, could you get dressed, please?"

It took the Neteru a moment to realise that Caila referred to his human mask but then he obliged instantly.

"Thank you. Could you please explain about, … well explain about everything, please?" Caila requested incoherently. "I tried earlier, but I think Chris believes that I've gone potty."

"I clearly remember asking you to wait until I got back, and I told you not to use your skills. How hard is it for you to follow orders?" Mateos ignored Caila's shocked husband, as he rebuked his wayward Khered. This afternoon had been difficult, but he had some good news that he'd looked forward to sharing.

"Yes, I clearly remember that you asked me to wait until you got back," Caila replied sweetly, "but I believe I can still use my own judgment occasionally. Please don't expect me to blindly follow all your orders all the time. And I prefer requests, not orders.

This afternoon, Chris's spheream became rather pronounced, and he noticed mine as well. That's a little detail you could have picked up on before you had a go at me, thank you very much. And you used that hand trick on me too. Remember? How did you know I used it on Chris?"

"You left an imprint, on your husband's neck," Mateos turned his attention to Caila's husband. "How do you feel, Chris?"

Chris had followed the exchange, between Caila and their unexpected guest, with increasing bewilderment, - *If Caila is going mad, then so am I. How do you think I feel?* – He opened his mouth to declare that he felt fine, but before he could say anything, their visitor, who had settled in their most comfortable chair in the corner of his living room, answered his unintended lectanimo.

"Caila has not gone mad, Chris, and neither have you. You feel confused right now, but that will pass."

- Fuck. Can you read my mind? You'd better say no, or, even better, nothing at all. –

"Only when you address me directly, Caila can hear you too. It is not strictly mind reading, the correct term for it is lectanimo. It is a form of mind communication," Mateos explained patiently. "If you have any thoughts that you don't want to relay to either of us, then don't address them to Caila or to me. Your wife has become quite proficient at it since we met. You overheard me and Khrhhsh, or OOVII, as Caila calls him, because we addressed Caila's direct environment, instead of Caila directly."

"Are you telling me that everything Caila told me earlier is real? About her alien DNA, and about resetting Earth?" Chris realised that 'alien' was maybe not the best word to use, it did not sound like a very polite way to address this, uhm …, alien? "I apologise for the word alien, but I forgot what Caila called you."

"That's fine, no offence taken. I am a Neteru. I don't know exactly what Caila told you earlier, but that sounds about right. She was very concerned about not being allowed to be candid with you from the start."

- Don't worry, I didn't go into details about the Event, – Caila addressed Mateos directly, - and thanks for being nice to Chris. –

- No problem, you could have chosen a worse partner. By the way, I need to speak to you later. Privately. –

"Are you two talking behind my back?" Chris had sensed the interaction between his wife and the Neteruian. "And, can I ask you something?"

"Caila thanked me for being nice to you, she knows that I am concerned that her emotional attachment to you might put her at risk," Mateos decided that befriending Caila's partner would be better in the long run, than alienating him. "What would you like to know?"

"You mentioned a hand trick that Caila should not have used," Chris felt the back of his neck. "What was that all about?"

"Caila's reactivation is taking place at an unexpected pace. So, when you were upset earlier, she applied a

Neteruian relaxation technique. I used it on her when we first met.

As a Khered, she should not have been able to do that, but somehow, she managed. I'll remind her later not to experiment.

I'll give the two of you some privacy now, I'm sure that there are things you would like to discuss."

- I'll be back later, Caila, – Mateos reminded her before he disappeared. - Something happened, we need to talk. –

An unexpected offer

Chris took the news that the world was about to end surprisingly well. He didn't press Caila for details when she asked him not to. And when she told him that Mateos had asked them not to leave the house, because it might put them in danger, he fussed even more than the Neteru had, suggesting they should use webcams to monitor the area around their home, and the first three cameras peered into the dark night before they turned in. No doubt, Mateos, who had discretely retreated to the study, would approve, Caila despaired.

"Night, darling. And no more tricks while I'm asleep, please," within minutes Chris was fast asleep and it didn't take his wife too long to follow.

"Caila, we need to talk."

Caila stirred grumpily and pushed the bedside lamp over in an attempt to shoo her liaison, - Go away, Sets. –

"I can help you wake up properly, if that's what you prefer?" effortlessly, Mateos caught the lamp and replaced it; reluctant to wake her he'd watched her sleep for a couple of minutes, softly snoring and totally relaxed, but he needed to speak to her, "Please, Caila, it won't take long. Or I'll tell everyone that you snore."

Caila opened her eyes and sat up carefully, not wanting to disturb Chris.

"I don't snore," she muttered, still half asleep. "You probably heard your own brains squeaking and creaking, while you tried to figure out how to wake me up without using your Neteruian tricks."

"That would be physically impossible. But I could ask Khrhhsh to check if someone is sawing down trees?" Mateos teased her. "He deserves fair warning if his home is under attack."

"Oh, Sets, you are impossible," Caila gave up. "All right then, what is it?"

"I have good news and bad news. Which would you like to hear first?"

"Give me the bad news first, please, it will probably sound better while I'm still half asleep. Then you can give me the good news when I'm fully awake," Caila rubbed her eyes. "And Sets, could you please hand me my jumper? Thanks."

Mateos appeared serious, but not overly worried, "We have a problem up north. One of the Khered betrayed us, and this almost resulted in the assassination of another Khered.

Caila, I don't think the Earth's authorities will be able to trace you, but from now on, we will keep you under constant observation. I asked Khrhhsh to draft in the help of some of his fellow corvids, and I'll help Chris connect the rest of those webcams first thing tomorrow morning. We should cover as large an area as possible."

'That figures,' Caila thought, 'now I have two men fussing over me, plus a bunch of overly conscientious crows. Happy days!'

Then she remembered Brown's behaviour at their meeting, and how he'd persistently fished for personal details, "Would that rogue Khered happen to be Brown?" she sensed how Mateos raised a mental barrier, "You can tell me now, I guess that from now on only twelve of us will attend the assemblies?"

"All right. Yes, it was Brown," Mateos admitted, "he has been removed."

Caila swallowed, that sounded rather final for Brown, "I won't ask, what you mean by 'removed'. If I trust you on resetting Mesu, then I should trust you on this as well.

Is the other Khered okay? Brown didn't go after Blue, did he? He was rather bullish with her, or him, during the meeting."

"No, it wasn't Blue. And yes, the other Khered is safe for now. And despite all his misadventures, he doesn't give his liaison half the trouble you give me.

Now, are you ready for the good news?"

"If you're not going to tell me what exactly happened, over there up north, then you might as well," Caila plumped her pillow and pushed it behind her back, she was eager to know what, despite the problems with the other Khered, got Mateos in such a good mood.

"During the Assembly on Etherun, we discussed the possibility of moving suitable activated Khered to our planet after the burn-in period. How would you feel about that? You told me you found Etherun beautiful."

Caila was stunned. Mateos had mentioned the possibility of her return to Etherun earlier, but she hadn't given it any serious consideration, or taken it seriously for that matter. True, she remembered more about her earlier encounters with Mateos now, and about her visit to Etherun. But moving to another planet would be, well, what would it be…? It would be exciting. Caila's face lighted up, "That would be brilliant! But I'm not going without Chris, of course."

"Absolutely. I'm starting to warm to your partner, he truly cares for you and takes your safety very seriously. All activated Khered would be considered. Your chosen ones will become activated after the Event, if they consent, and then you can all remain on Mesu during the burn-in period," Mateos was pleased with Caila's reaction, there was so much he wanted to show her and as a Neteru on Etherun she would be safe. And Chris? Well, he'd proved to be pleasant company, and an acceptable partner for Caila.

"How long is this burn-in period actually?" this was the first time he'd mentioned it.

"Not very long at all, only 107 years, it'll fl…" Mateos didn't get very far.

"107 years?! You've got to be joking. Do you know how old I'll be by then? My skin will be sagging around my feet,

I'll have had five hip replacements and my bones will be crumbly as chalk!" Caila looked horrified as she faced her amused honorary brother, and she understood. "But that's not going to happen, is it? As well as that healing trick, the reactivation triggered some kind of age fixation. We are going to be aging in Etherunian time. Sets, how old are you actually?"

"If you believe 107 years is old, then we won't even go there. But I led this project when we seeded Mesu; you are the mathematician, so you do the calculations. Remember, Neteru don't have the disadvantage of a physical body."

"Delightful! I look forward to my one thousandth birthday already," Caila imagined the candles on her cake and laughed. "But seriously, earlier you said that Chris would have become an activated Khered anyway, after agreeing to it. Will all my companions be offered that choice?"

"All your chosen ones will be adjusted to become Khered, but they will only be activated if they agree to it. Activation will provide them with mental and physical advantages to make your task, of restarting and supervising a new human population simpler. Did you make your final choice yet? Who your chosen ones should be?"

"Yes, I did. Would you like me to tell you their names?"

To Caila's surprise, Mateos laughed, "Not unless those names are wholly unique, I need a bit more detail. No wait," Mateos hesitated, "let's try something else. Let me touch your hand, and then you concentrate on your choices."

When their sphereams touched, Caila felt a strangely familiar sensation as a connection built up between them, then she stared at Mateos and concentrated.

After only a couple of seconds, Mateos let go, "That is Steve, Richard, Juliet, Luke and Jenny? Right? If you are sure about these people, I'll visit them and prepare them to remain untouched by the Event.

Chris will be safe, you took care of that yourself. I checked, and you did a good job. I'll have another chat with him tomorrow morning, we need to discuss how to keep you out of trouble until the Event. Maybe we should attach a bodycam or a tracker to you?"

"Ha, ha, that's not funny," when Mateos showed no signs of amusement, Caila warned him, "Don't you dare, Sets!

Oh, and by the way, how can I be sure that you're going to visit the correct Steve, Richard, Juliet, Luke and Jenny? Those are only first names."

Mateos made contact again and showed her the images of her five lucky, or unlucky companions to be, "Are those your chosen ones? ... I thought so.

Now it's time for you to go back to sleep. Or was there anything else?"

"Thanks, Sets. Just one little thing, please?" Caila bit her lip, trying to keep a straight face.

Mateos noticed it, and smiled, "I'm not sure I like the sound of that, Tia. What do you need from me?"

"It's nothing big, really. But do you remember that you promised to take care of Bluebell and Banjo? Steve and Richard's cats? Well, Juliet has a few chickens, goats and ducks; she talks about them all the time. You will get them safely to us, won't you, Sets?" Caila did not wait for an answer. "I knew I could rely on you, Sets, you're the best."

On that note, Mateos quickly left the room, fearing he'd be moving an entire zoo after the Event, if he didn't learn how to say no to Caila.

London – Backdoor politics

"Sir, Mr Thurogood, the Prime Minister is not qualified to decide on the right course of action in this matter. Her emotions and lack of experience led her to ignore the facts, and the consequences of her inability to act will be devastating.

The intelligence on this issue comes from reliable sources and it cannot be ignored. The security of this country, even the bare existence of the world is at stake. We need to investigate this threat thoroughly, and act without delay.

That is why we need you to step in, Mr Thurogood. We need someone who is strong and experienced, to lead this operation."

"You do realise that it is my neck on the block, if this turns out to be a snipe hunt. And if it transpires that I advised you how to proceed in this matter?" Baldwin eyed Marcus shrewdly. "I don't want any of this leaked, before the next election campaign. How reliable is this source of yours?"

"Sir, it is not a question of how reliable; I consider a source to be either reliable or unreliable. And I can assure you sir, that this particular source is reliable," Marcus didn't like Baldwin, but he was predictable and useful at a time like this. "The information comes straight from a specialist branch within the CIA, and our target has been confirmed by specialists within our own service. Their family have been known to have close ties to this group, for generations. We need someone, who is not held back by prejudices, to take responsibility and approve this operation, so that we can act and eliminate this alien threat, once and for all. For our country and for the world."

"Just make sure you keep it low key and keep my name out of it. And whatever happens, from now on you communicate directly with me; the Prime Minister can indeed, not be trusted on this issue. She is to be kept out of all matters of national security.
Feed her some red herrings on Middle Eastern terrorists, to keep her occupied. Understood?"

"Perfectly, sir! I will not disappoint you."

Pleased with the result, Marcus turned on his heels and left Baldwin's house the same way he'd arrived 15 minutes earlier. Through the backdoor.

Cat out of the bag
Monday 16 September

Monday's uneventful start did not hint at the dramatic turn it would take before noon.

Shortly after eight o'clock, Caila sent emails to Juliet and her manager, explaining she had to deal with a family emergency - that wasn't too far from the truth, she reasoned - and she would have to work from home today, possibly a bit longer.

Juliet replied instantly and reminded her that Daniel was out of the office that week, she told Caila she'd let the rest of the team know. Then, Juliet being Juliet, followed up on her professional email with a personal text, urging Caila to let her know if she needed any help or a chat.

Caila thanked her and added that she would treat her to a large latte and all the gory details later this week. Which, she guessed, would probably not be too far from the truth either.

Downstairs, Chris and Mateos had been in deep conversation but they looked up and stopped talking when Caila entered the living room. The two remaining webcams had been installed and a monitor showed a jigsaw projection of their entire neighbourhood. This would raise some eyebrows, if anyone noticed.

"Right guys, I'm sorry to interrupt your man-chat, but how about getting started? We need to get to work. Mateos, will you stay with us today?"

Both men appeared in high spirits, "I told you she'd be annoyed about being excluded," Mateos grinned at Chris "she is dying to know what we were talking about."

In a fruitless attempt to disprove that point, Caila send a cushion flying in their direction.

"I guess she is," Chris agreed with his new best friend, "don't worry about her hitting you when she throws things, her aim has always been miserable."

Chris's revelation was followed by another cushion, which knocked an empty wine bottle of the table.

"You see? … You should only worry when she aims at something else. But you are right, darling wife of mine, we should get to work. Up to the office, chop-chop!"

"I will be here most of the day," Mateos followed them into the study, "I only need to leave you alone briefly, to help with some preparation for the Event. Khrhhsh knows how to get hold of me, if something happens while I'm away."

When Caila looked out of the window she noticed that the curtains of the Higgs's spare room were still closed, but a raft of crows scattered on the surrounding roofs and gardens distracted her.

Mateos didn't leave until eleven; which was just after Caila noticed their back neighbours' curtains were still closed, and just before she realised this wasn't normal.

"Chris?"

"Yes?"

"Do you have a camera on the Higgs's upstairs windows?"

"What?" pre-occupied with his work, Chris looked up from his screen. "Yes, I think so. Why do you ask?"

"The curtains of their spare room are still closed, and it's term time; they normally only have the grandchildren during the holidays. Can you see if there has been any movement, or unusual activity? It doesn't feel right," Caila sensed something was wrong and called in reinforcements, - OOVII? Are you there? –

- Good morning, Caila and Chris. Yes, I'm on the roof. Is there a problem? –

"I could be wrong," Chris sounded alarmed, "but it looks like there is something sticking out between those curtains. I can't make out what it is exactly, but it reflects the sunlight, it could be a lens, or something similar."

- OOVII, could you check out the house behind ours, please? There might be something funny going on behind that upstairs window on the right, – Caila heard rather than saw the flutter of birds before OOVII returned with a disturbing message.

- Someone, who no-one has seen before today, arrived at that house early this morning. We cannot spot him in any of the other rooms at this moment; and a lens and a microphone are directed at your home. I'll ask Mateos to return immediately, stay away from the windows, please. Bugger, … –

Caila and Chris looked up simultaneously, startled by OOVII's uncharacteristic outburst.

- … more unidentified individuals entered the surveillance area. Stay put. –

- Did you catch that? – at the same time, Caila scribbled an illegible note to inform her husband of what OOVII had said. - Don't talk out loud. –

- I heard. OOVII is right, it is getting crowded out there, there is no way we can get out without being seen. We need Mateos to help us. –

- We are here, – Mateos materialised accompanied by a second Neteru. - Devyn, we can get them out if we cloak them. You take Chris, his spheream has developed far enough to be manipulated. I'll take care of Caila. … Dev?! –

- What's going on here? – completely absorbed, Devyn stared at Mateos's Khered.

- Never mind that, – Mateos barked, - use the side door, it's a blind spot, then take a left through the neighbouring gardens. If we lose touch, we'll meet at the domus. Do it, Dev, now! –

Devyn peeled his gaze away from Caila and concentrated on Chris, - Right, Chris, here we go, – he touched his shoulder and Chris disappeared, - lead the way, I can see you. Mateos and your wife will be right behind us. –

- Come on, Tia, Chris is safe, it's your turn now, – Mateos touched Caila's shoulder and concentrated, but nothing happened. - Damned, Caila, don't resist! –

- I'm not, really, I'm not," Caila replied desperately, "I may be stubborn sometimes, but I'm not stupid. –

Mateos tried again before he gave up, - Damn, there is too much Neteru in you. I can't manipulate you anymore. You'll have to do it yourself. –

- What? How? – Caila panicked. - I don't know how to do that. –

She could do a few tricks by now but making herself invisible was completely different.

- Relax and concentrate. Imagine yourself as Chris was when he left. You can do it, - while Mateos attempted to coax Caila into relaxing, they were interrupted by loud banging noises downstairs.

"Armed police; open the door. Armed police!"

- Relax, Caila, filter them out. –

"Armed police! Open the door. Now, or we will break it down," a loud crash immediately followed that warning.

'Apparently, they don't believe in giving fair warning,' Caila felt the floor of the study vibrate, - Mateos, it's useless, I can't do it. But I might just be able to get out and into the neighbour's garden. –

Caila had their annoying runaway bamboo patch in mind; if she could reach that, it might buy them enough time. She didn't wait for a reply and hurtled down the stairs with a cursing Mateos in hot pursuit.

However, before Caila could reach the utility room, the front door gave way and she heard the horde of raiders stampede into the hall.

Instinctively Caila hid behind the door, and through the crack between the door and the frame she spied the first raider in black as he stormed into her kitchen.

'I can do this, I only need to relax and concentrate. You, lowlife toe rag, you're not going to get me. I'll show you!' Caila focussed on the guy with the balaclava, and while he kicked the door, she felt herself morph into a copy of her uninvited destructive guest. 'That's not how your mummy taught you to open a door, bambino,' Caila pulled her shoulders back and strode into the kitchen.

"All clear, move on!" she hollered, before stomping out of the backdoor to open the garden gate. Faced with a small army of extra troops she ordered them, "Move inside, they're upstairs. …

Move!"

She stepped aside before confidently plodding in the direction of a control vehicle, "The remains of an unidentified male and female have been found on the first floor. Inform HQ. Now! … Are you bleeding deaf?

Stop picking your noses and get a move on!"

Just then, a murder of crows landed in the tree next to her house, making enough racket to distract the officers in the van.

- Thanks, OOVII, – Caila turned away and purposefully marched into the direction of the officers guarding the entry to the estate.

- Mateos, are you there? – Caila hissed, she could use a bit of help here. - Is anyone looking? –

Caila veered into a carport between two houses, and while she ducked behind the car, she dropped her disguise, - Sh… Ships, this is bloody hard to keep up. Now what? –

- I am glad that you trust me to help you, other than running after you. What kind of a performance was that? I asked you to cloak. –

- Sets?! – Caila looked aggrieved at the fuming Neteru. What was his problem? She was the one doing all the hard work here.

- We'll talk later, – Mateos decided to let it go for now, his Khered was not out of danger yet. - You need to cloak to get out of here. Take a minute to rest but we should hurry, I believe they're catching on. –

Caila took a deep breath and fruitlessly attempted to cloak, - Flip, why can't I do this one? – When she closed her eyes for the third time, Caila was startled by a cat brushing up against her legs.

'Hi, Carrot, long time no see,' and an outrageous idea took shape as she stared at the gentle ginger feline. 'No, I couldn't, could I?' she wondered, if maybe she could.

Caila concentrated and experienced the same weird sensation as before, when she had morphed into the police officer.

Carrot hissed, and Caila, not keen on a catfight, shot out through the front gardens and out of the estate.

Caila didn't stop running until she reached the fields at the far side of town, where she dropped the cat mask and slumped down under a tree.

"How's that, for masking?" Caila was dog-tired, but rather chuffed with herself. "I'm exhausted. Let me catch my breath for a moment. Where do we go next?"

- That was utterly brilliant, – OOVII landed on a branch above them. - But Caila, why did it have to be a cat? There are truly fairer creatures around. –

- Thank you, OOVII, for the distraction just there. I would have tried for a crow, but I don't think I can fly, – Caila laughed, relieved to have put some distance between herself and her aggressive visitors.

But Mateos eyed his Khered severely, as he reproached them both, - No, you can definitely not fly. Don't put ideas into her head, Khrhhsh, she is in enough trouble as it is.

Devyn and Chris are waiting for us a bit further down, it's not far, so let's get going. I want to get you out of here, and under the cover of trees.

Khrhhsh, can you follow us please? –

Still on a high after her feline inspired escape, Caila wondered what got into him. They were safe now, and even if she had not done exactly what he'd told her to do, she still felt she had done brilliantly well. She shrugged and got up, "Lead the way, milord!"

Wordlessly, Mateos pulled Caila in front of him, where it would be easier to keep an eye on her.

***

It took them fifteen, icily silent minutes to catch up with Chris and Devyn, who were waiting for them near the Last Chance Animal Rescue centre, just outside of town.
Chris, not normally prone to public displays of affection, threw his arms around his errant wife and pulled her close, "I was scared to death when you weren't behind us. What happened?"

Caila released herself reluctantly from his comforting bearhug, "I'm sure Mateos can explain it better than I can. But I …" unsure how much she could say in front of the other Neteru, she stole a glance at Mateos, "… but he had some problems cloaking me."

"Good morning, Caila," Devyn stepped forward to introduce himself, "in the confusion of the moment, Mateos omitted the introductions. My name is Devyn.
Why don't you take five minutes to rest, before we continue to your domus?
Mats, I believe we should take a moment to catch up?" The tension between the two Neteruians was tangible.

Caila looked at Mateos, and after his curt nod, she hung back with Chris while they watched Devyn and Mateos argue.

"She looks like Calia, and her name is Caila; I heard you call her Tia, and she called you Sets. And you can't control her. What's going on here?" Devyn tried to restrain his anger. "There is a lot more to this, than an activated Khered developing faster and further than expected. I believe you owe me an explanation."

Mateos looked at his best friend; they had been inseparable when they were younger, Devyn, Calia, and him. And, for a long time, Devyn had had a hopeless crush on his sister, "Are you sure you want to know, Dev? This could put you in an awkward position.

I will protect Caila, no matter what happens, but there is no need for you to become involved."

"I don't believe you've ever had any reason to doubt my loyalty to you, or to Calia," Devyn replied coldly. "And you already got me involved, the moment you called me over to help you. Just tell me what this is all about, we don't have much time."

"I won't get into details then," Mateos shot a quick glance at his Khered, who eyed him worriedly, "but in addition to Khered DNA, I inserted some of Calia's DNA into Caila's ancestor.

They are first order Khered, and their lineage always stood out because they not only retained the complete DNA sequences, but also expanded on them. Caila displays Neteruian skills and memories which cannot be explained in any other way.

Because she has partly reversed to Neteru, I was unable to cloak her, she needed to do it herself. However, for some reason, she couldn't cloak, but she did manage to morph into another human, and a bit later into a cat."

"So, that's why you were so eager to support me, when I suggested we should allow suitable activated Khered to move to Etherun, after the burn-in period? You were probably planning to suggest something similar yourself.

Mats, do you realise how horribly wrong this could have gone? It still can. You have broken so many rules, I won't even begin to list them ..." Devyn looked at his friend in despair. "And, of course, that is why you insisted I should help you with this problem, and no one else. You know how I felt about your sister, I would have done anything for her. All right, I won't give you away. But remember, she's Caila, not Calia!

How did she end up with a name that close to your sister's anyway?"

Mateos realised how much he asked of Devyn, but in his heart, he'd known that his friend would never let him down, "Believe it or not, she changed her name to Caila, shortly after moving back to England. Her Dutch name was difficult to pronounce in English, so she came up with Caila."

"Boy! Are you in trouble! She came up with that name, even without being activated?!

You'd better keep a very close eye on her, Mats," Devyn didn't envy his friend. "Come on, we should get a move on and deliver those two safely to their domus."

My home is my castle

It took them almost an hour to reach their new home, or domus, as Devyn called it.

While Mateos and Chris led the way, engaged in an animated discussion on the beauty of the Garden of England, Caila followed lackadaisically, accompanied by a stand-offish Devyn.

As he escorted her to her domus, Devyn kept his eyes firmly fixed on Mateos's back whilst attempting to keep his engagement with his friend's Khered to a minimum. Mats had manipulated it, so that he and Caila would walk together, but he had no intention of being drawn into Mats's problems any further than he already was.

"Are you a liaison for one of the Khered, like Mateos is?" Caila realised it was not a very imaginative question, but she was desperate to break the uncomfortable silence and, as far as small talk went, it was one step up from discussing the weather.

She rolled her eyes when she was rewarded with nothing more than a short, "Yes, I am," from the aloof green Neteruian.

- Mateos, you can't do this to me, – Caila decided to address Mateos directly, to plead her case. - That arrogant friend of yours obviously has a problem with me. Can you and Chris, please come over and join us? Please? –

- That is not very polite, Caila, – Mateos didn't budge, - besides, I have matters to discuss with Chris. Devyn is my best friend, and he was a good friend of my sister's. You can trust him. He is just a bit rattled, after I told him about your background. Be nice, I'm sure that's not too much to ask for, after a morning of nothing but ignoring my advice. –

'That's the last time I ask you for a favour,' Caila muttered. - No worries, I can be nice as pie. –
She turned her attention back to her reluctant companion, making sure Mateos could hear her when she asked, - Devyn, what are your thoughts on pie? –

Confused by the curious question, Devyn stopped abruptly, wondering if he'd heard correctly, "I'm sorry, I believe I misunderstood. Did you say pie? And why are you using lectanimo?"

- Yes, pie, – Caila glanced innocently at Mateos's back, - I was just thinking, should I make sweet strawberry pie, or sour cherry pie? –

"I don't believe …" Devyn started, but then he caught Caila's wide eyes focussed on his friend's back. - Right, Caila. I'm not sure how Mateos fits into this conversation, but he is out from now on. Mats, stay out of this, I need to talk to your Khered privately. –

"Now, as for you, Caila, Mateos informed me of your lineage, and I'm not happy about it.

You …, this unfortunate situation could land Mateos in big trouble if it came to light, so I would appreciate it if you took it a bit more seriously."

As she realised she'd misjudged him, Caila felt bad about her silly joke. She bit her lip as she regarded the loyal Neteru and apologised, "I'm sorry Devyn, I was out of order. And, believe me, I do take this seriously. I admit I was a bit miffed when Mateos told me about this DNA lark, but I like Mateos." Caila smiled as she watched the grey Neteru, walking beside her husband. "No, that is actually the understatement of the century. I always wanted a brother, and Mateos feels like the big brother I never had. I would never intentionally hurt him or do anything that could land him in trouble. I don't know if it is his sister's DNA that causes the connection between us, or something else, but I felt it from the first moment we met.

And I apologise about the pie joke. Mateos told me to be nice, so I thought 'nice as pie', and then, sweet pie, … sour pie. I'm really sorry, it wasn't a very good joke. It was pretty bad actually; I have never been any good at jokes."

Caila stared at the ground, and when Devyn stayed silent, she looked back up at the Neteru, who appeared to study her intently. She gave him an apologetic smile.

"Calia's jokes were pretty awful, most of the time."

"Calia? Is that Mateos's sister's name?"

"Calia Antia. That's where Mateos's nickname for her, Tia, comes from. Mats is right, you are very much like her. Mateos and Cals were thick as thieves."

"Mateos told me that you are best friends, and that you were a good friend of Tia's as well. What happened to Tia?"

"I'll leave it to Mats, to tell you about Tia. But we grew up together, the three of us," Devyn smiled and changed the subject. "Mateos told me that you morphed into a cat, but that you could not cloak yourself. What happened?"

"I don't know, I relaxed and concentrated like mad, exactly like Mateos told me to do, but nothing happened. But then, when I saw that police raider guy, and later on, the cat, I just looked at them, and concentrated and changed shape.
It's harder to imagine myself as nothing, I suppose, maybe that's just one step too far for me."

"I think I know where you went wrong, Caila," the soft green Neteru laughed. "Cloaking is not like morphing, you don't transform yourself into something else. You imagine an opaque spheream around you. Maybe the best comparison would be, putting on a soft warm coat. Does that make sense?"

'I guess it does,' he thought, as Caila vanished instantly. Devyn could still see the air vibrating around her, but he knew that she was invisible to humans.

"Why didn't Mateos explain it like this?" Caila glowed in her success, as she dropped her cloak. "It's easy! Exhausting, but easy."

The rest of the track was spent in amiable conversation. Devyn began to trust Caila, and Caila found him to be kind and patient. It soon became obvious to her, why Mateos and Devyn were best friends. As they passed St. Peter's church, Caila regaled Devyn with the condensed version of the story of Henry VIII and Anne Boleyn, whose father was buried there. Devyn had just observed that English history was remarkably interesting, when Caila, as usual, looking any which way but in front of her, inelegantly bumped into her husband's back.

Chris had stopped to inspect their new home, which Mateos had pointed out to him.

"How do you like our new abode? It's a little bit bigger than what we're used to, but I'm sure you can manage the dusting and the hoovering."

Caila followed his gaze, and her jaw dropped.

"I believe she is actually speechless, Chris," Mateos chipped in, "that's one nil for us."

"You are joking. You are, aren't you? Come on! Chris? Sets? ... Devyn?"

No one answered.

"That's Hever Castle! No, come on, you are having me on. I'm not going to fall for that. Besides it's open to the public, it's too busy. Very funny, but I'm definitely not going to fall for it. Nice try. ... Now tell me, where are we really going, I'm getting tired."

"It really is Hever, Caila," Devyn was the first to take pity on her, "it makes perfect sense to have this as your domus. It has all the space you need for you and your chosen ones, it can easily be secured, and it won't be too difficult for you to establish a reliable food production on these grounds.

And, yes, it was open to the public, until this morning. But due to 'subsidence', the castle and its grounds were evacuated earlier today. Until the Event, you will run into some security staff and surveyors, they are your Neteruian guards. Their masks are visible to all humans. And, Caila, it's probably best if the Neteruians, who are guarding the castle, remain unaware of your unexpected skills."

"I understand, Devyn. You are a true gent, which is more than I can say for those two over there," Caila nodded in the direction of Chris and Mateos. "Shall we go home then?" Caila smiled at Chris, this was a special place for them. They had spent numerous afternoons picnicking on the lawns and exploring the castle. The entrance hall leading to the Inner Hall on the right, and the Drawing Room with its secret door and baby grand piano. And on the left to the cosy Library, and the Morning Room with its priest hole. The beautiful Dining Hall lay in the middle, one of its doors still secured by one of Henry VIII original gild locks. The upstairs Long Gallery and the bedrooms were magnificent. Some years ago, they'd spent two expensive, but brilliant nights in the Edward VII suite in the Bed & Breakfast extension. It had been their best holiday ever.

"I wonder if our room is still available, Chris?"

They decided that, until the Event, Chris and Caila would be safer in the castle than in the Edwardian Wing.

The thicker walls provided better protection against heat seeking equipment, and there was no shortage of hiding places.

After Mateos and Devyn had introduced them to their guards, who provided the couple with safety helmets and hi vis jackets, the castle's new occupants did a quick round of the restaurant and the tourist shop to stock up on necessities. Laden with bags, filled with sweets, books and stationary, candles, food and drinks, towels and slippers, they re-joined Mateos and Devyn in the Library. The Neteruians interrupted their discussion and watched on in amusement as Caila dressed the sofa with an assortment of throws and cushions, before she flopped down and replaced her shoes with a pair of comfortable slippers.

"Wow, that feels good. Don't mind us, please continue your conversation while Chris and I settle in," Caila offered Chris a second pair of slippers, "it's lunchtime."

Chris and Caila munched their way through a plate full of sandwiches and sausage rolls, while Mateos and Devyn stood next to one of the many bookcases, discussing their next steps.

When they were ready to finish their meal off with an assortment of fudge, Devyn came over to say goodbye, "Chris, Caila, I need to go now, but Mateos will tell you what's going to happen next. I'll visit you again soon. Stay safe." With that advice, the moss green Neteru vanished.

Mateos joined his Khered on the sofa, throwing a disapproving look at the table full of sweets.

"I saw that look, but we need something sweet to recover from the shock of this morning," Caila challenged him.

"Sugar is not an appropriate remedy and you are not suffering from shock," Mateos responded automatically, before he realised that his honorary sister was provoking him. "Chris, your wife's sense of humour is absolutely horrendous, you should spend the next few days helping her improve on that."

Chris shrugged, "I tried, but it's hopeless, I suffered for years."

"Thanks for that, Chris. And you too, Mateos," Caila's attempt to look offended failed miserably. "When did you two become best mates?"

"Your husband is a very sensible man, young lady," Mateos smiled, before he continued in a soberer tone. "Now, before I go, there are a few things you should be aware of. Devyn and I requested an emergency assembly on Etherun, so, I will be gone for a while. Khrhhsh and his family moved into the castle grounds, and he will be there for you whenever you need him.

Caila, we may bring the final assembly forward even further. So, be ready.

And because you are in a unique position, you and Chris both being activated before the Event, you are permitted to bring Chris up to date on the details of this process.

That reminds me," Mateos turned to Chris, "I would like to check that you are ready for the Event, one last time. Do you mind?"

Chris shrugged, he trusted the Neteruian completely, "No, go ahead, please."

Mateos positioned himself behind Caila's husband and touched his shoulders, and Chris wondered how the touch of a species with no physicality could still feel so solid.
It only took a couple of seconds before Mateos let go again and reported, "Good job", while he looked at Caila. "Right, if there is nothing else, then I'll be off now."

Caila jumped up and opened her mouth to speak.

"Anything but chickens, goats or cats," Mateos warned her.

"I wouldn't do that to you, Sets," the Khered gave her liaison an innocent smile, "but, could you get us some underwear, please? We didn't have time to pack before we left home. For me, any colour will do, as long as it's not yellow, brown, beige or champagne pink, I'm not fussy. But I do like silk."

A shocking little detail

Chris and Caila spent their first afternoon at the castle exploring.

They selected Henry VIII's bedchamber as their bedroom and finished the private tour of their new home in the study, where Chris discovered a secret door. While her husband worked his way through stacks of rubbish, Caila studied a series of crystal balls, neatly lined up on the mantelshelf.

"I agree with you, I don't think they will accept a fifth option; the process is in a much too advanced stage. For that same reason, I believe you can safely disregard option four," Chris breathed heavily as he lurched another bulky box into the study.

"But this is for you to decide, Caila. Like it or not, it's your heritage, and I don't envy you for it. The other day, I heard someone say that a, 'clinical analysis of evidence', is needed by members of a jury in a trial. And I believe that is what they are asking you to do here.

It won't be easy, but no matter what you decide, I'm behind you."

"You were well ahead of me this morning!" Caila changed the subject, she'd made up her mind and wanted to forget about it for now. She wasn't looking forward to their final meeting, some time tomorrow.

"Mateos assured me, the fault was entirely yours," Chris teased. Mateos hadn't told him what exactly happened that morning, but he could tell that something had gone seriously wrong, and that the Neteru had been terribly concerned about his wife's safety.

"Yes, I believe he was not entirely happy with me," Caila peered into the dark space behind the door.

"No, he wasn't, and I don't think you've heard the last of it. And rightfully so. Mateos does his utmost to keep you safe, you really should listen to him, darling. He worries about you, and so do I."

"I know, there were just some technical hiccups, but everything worked out fine in the end," Caila reflected it could have ended pretty badly if they'd caught her, and she took a deep breath before she continued. "Chris, there is something else I need to tell you about the reset."

She was relieved that Mateos had finally allowed her to share the details of the process with her husband, "All of us were asked to select seven '*chosen ones*', as the Neteru call them. Humans who won't be harmed by the Event. Those chosen ones will join us, to help restart a human population."

"Do you mean you need to ask seven people, to leave all their friends and families behind, to team up with us in an empty world?" Chris frowned, he'd believed that choosing between those four options was tough, but this was even worse. "That could be a hard-sell."

"I can't ask them before the Event, obviously, so they won't really have a choice in the matter," Caila realised how harsh this sounded, even if it was undeniably true. "But you are right, I'll need some good arguments to explain why they are still here, while the rest of the world has been removed.

I already made my choices, and last night I gave them to Mateos, so that he can prepare them for the Event. He'll insert dormant Khered DNA, which they can have activated later. Would you like to know who they are?"

"If we are going to share a home with them, and I guess that's why Mateos opted for something as big as Hever, then I should probably know who our housemates will be. I'm glad I wasn't involved in this part of the process, my darling, but I'll support you when they arrive," he smiled encouragingly, more confident than he actually felt at that moment. His wife would need his support; a clinical analysis of evidence, and emotions didn't usually go hand in hand.

"Right," Caila took her husband's hand, "you are the first one, of course, and you are already activated. Are you happy with that?"

"Delighted, my darling," Chris kissed her nose, "I didn't really have a choice in the matter, but it's still good to know I don't come last."

"Then there are Steve and Richard."

When a monstrous spider came crawling out of one of the boxes, Caila let go of her husband's hand and quickly put some distance between herself and the hairy arachnid, "Ouch!" she rubbed her hip after it painfully collided with the sharp corner of the writing desk. "What do you think about them?"

"And excellent choice, I can live with those guys," Chris liked the two men and understood why Caila had chosen them, but he expected the couple would give her a hard time, they were extremely attached to their families and wide circle of friends.

"Good," his wife proceeded, not giving him too much time to think about it, "and then there are Juliet and Luke."

"Is that Juliet, as in Juliet, the P.A. with the eggs and the chickens? Of course! That's what Mateos meant when he told you, no more chickens and goats! I never met her, but she sounds interesting. And Luke? Do you mean Luke Jedi, from work?"

Caila nodded.

"That is a sensible choice. I like him, Luke is a genius at rationally approaching problems and he will love the piano in the Drawing Room. He'll fit in really well."
Whereas Steve and Richard were very emotional, Luke was the polar opposite.

"And then, …", Caila hesitated, "then there's Jenny."

"THE, Jenny?!" Chris was stunned. "Come on, Caila, she is going to drive Luke mad. She is a non-stop chatter machine. Although, it would be interesting to see who is hiding behind all that make-up. Whatever made you choose her?"

Until now, Caila's choices had made perfect sense, they had been predictable even. But, Jenny?

"Jenny is not that bad," Caila defended the young woman. "Yes, she talks a bit more than the rest of us, and her make-up is a bit intense. But she is also incredibly intelligent, and she will approach problems from a completely different angle than the rest of us.

Besides, if we need to restart a population, we need younger people. And Jenny will be the only person in the group who has some experience taking care of children."

Chris looked dumbstruck.

"Come on, Jenny is a bit different from the rest of us, but she is not that bad," Caila had expected some questions about this choice, but this was over the top. "Chris?!"

"Children? … Caila, surely … How is that going to work out? There will be the two of us as a couple. And honestly, we are way, way beyond that age.

And Steve and Richard, well, that's not going to happen is it? And Luke and Jenny are as incompatible as they come."

"Don't worry about it for now, I'm sure it will all work out, we'll ask Mateos about it, next time we see him. And I am not beyond that age. Well not, 'way-way', beyond that age, as you so kindly put it. Thank you very much." Then, when she noticed her husband was still worried, she reassured him. "The Neteru are singularly rational. I'm sure they don't expect us to produce loads of babies. That would not be efficient."

'They'd better not', she thought.

"Drop it, for now?"

"All right then, let's ask Mateos about it," Chris agreed reluctantly. "But you said you were allowed seven companions, I believe we arrived at six, with Jenny."

"Oh yes, that's right," Caila remembered her mystery guest. "I mentioned to Mateos that I would like to add someone with medical skills to our group. And apparently, he knows of someone who will fit in, so I'm going to trust him on that one. I'm hoping for an experienced doctor, who combines brilliant general practitioner skills with surgical expertise. His name is Peter Overwood."

"It's a shame we can't look him up on LinkedIn, I feel kind of lost without my laptop and phone. But I trust Mateos, he seems to genuinely care about you," Chris's stomach rumbled. "How about dinner? It'll soon be too dark to go out and fetch it."

Chris and Caila collected their dinner from the Moat restaurant, dressed in their best surveyor's outfits, under the scrutinising eyes of OOVII and a small army of Neteruian guards. Since they were not allowed to cook hot food, dinner consisted of a Ploughman's and fresh bread, followed by carrot cake and coffee. As Caila sipped a glass of port later that night, she considered that Mateos could have dropped them in a worse place.

"You've always been the odd one out, Caila," Chris's response to his wife's switch at birth, was laconic, "and this is a more credible explanation then the milkman. But I'm glad they switched you, I might not have met you if they hadn't."

Mateos returned only briefly, shortly after they'd settled in their new bedroom. He informed Caila that her final assembly would be in half an hour. And after a hurried, "don't worry about it, you'll be fine", he disappeared again. Caila then had a short restless slumber, before she was whisked away to this much dreaded final meeting.

The beginning of the end

Cradling her mug of hot strong Empress Grey, Caila scanned the room and wondered who of the Khered had been attacked; Brown had disappeared together with his chair, but the others were still there.

"It's good to see you all again," Caila started their final meeting. "I don't know how much you have been told by your contacts, but Brown has left our group and won't return."

When no one expressed surprise or regret at that announcement, she continued, "Circumstances forced the Neteru to speed up the consultation process, so this will be our final meeting before the Event. We need to inform the Neteru of our decision at the end of this assembly.

I suggest, I start with the replies to our list of questions before we do a quick around-the-table, just saying which option we would vote for. Depending on how close, or how far apart we are, we'll then have a discussion to try and reach a consensus. Does that sound reasonable?"

After some of the cloud-cladded attendees nodded in agreement, Caila kicked off with the first item on their agenda, "I was assured that everyone received additional

information about our chosen ones. Has that happened? …
Yes? Okay.

Number two, Green, this was your question I believe? It
won't be possible to distinguish between the good, the bad
and the ugly. I'm sorry about that."

Green shrugged, as if they'd already expected that.

"Blue, we will still be able to meet up after the Event,
that's good news, we'll all need all the support we can get.

Tiger, I'm sorry, I wish I could be the bearer of better
tidings, but you are stuck with your colour, forever.
Apparently, it's hard coded."

"That's a big flaw in their system," Tiger snorted. "Let's
give it some time, we are all smart, maybe we can fix it for
them."

Everyone laughed; trust Tiger to lighten the mood.

"Next, Black, I believe? My Neteru contact confirmed
that there is a real chance of accidental survivors, and you
were right about them probably being Government officials
with armed escorts. The Neteru will try to limit the risk, but
we should all be aware of it. Any survivor who is not one of
your chosen ones may pose a threat. There is of course, also
the chance that they are friendly, so, there's no need to panic
and attack every stranger who comes along but keep your
guards up.

Thanks, Black, that was a good question."

Black gave a barely visible nod, and Caila pushed on.

"Violet, with this meeting being moved forward, you
probably already guessed there is no fixed timeline. But I

have been assured that we will be given sufficient time to prepare.

And our fifth option? They will listen but their …, and now I quote, 'hands are tied'."

"That was our list. Let's move on to the round-the-table. Choose only one option this time. One, a reset without a human population; two, a reset including human Khered; three, wiping the planet clean completely; four, do nothing; and five, a fifth option.

White, would you like to start please?"

"Option two for me, please."

"Purple?"

"Two, please. Grey?"

"Two. Black?"

"Two."

"Lilac?" …

Only Green and Lilac preferred a fifth option, while everyone else agreed on option two.

"That was quick, and we are pretty close," Caila was glad they seemed to move in the same direction so quickly. "Green and Lilac, you chose a fifth option. Would you care to elaborate, please?"

Green began, "My idea is not so much different from option two; I would just like our group of chosen ones to be a bit bigger than eight. 50 maybe? It would improve our chances of survival. What is your idea, Lilac?"

"I was thinking along the same lines, but instead of chosen ones, I would rather be assigned random companions."

Caila noticed Black shifting in his chair, as if he wanted to reply to Lilac's suggestion, but was not keen on attracting attention to himself, "Black? Would you like to respond to Lilac or Green?"

Their short reply, "Yes, I would, please," reminded Caila of Luke, "Okay then, Black, tell us what you think of the fifth options, that Lilac and Green proposed, please."

"If Lilac prefers randomly chosen companions, they wouldn't need to ask the Neteru to assign them. Lilac could randomly select them herself."

While Lilac considered Black's suggestion, Caila agreed, "I think Black has a point. If you feel strongly about selection being unfair, then maybe you could pull random names from a phone book in your region. Or, maybe use pins and a map. Or …, well I don't know, something like that? Is there anyone else who would like their chosen ones to be random, rather than selected?" Caila looked around. "No one?"

Yellow raised their hand.

"Yes, Yellow?"

"I believe that by selecting our chosen ones, we can make sure we have the combined skill-set that will put us in the best possible position, for the challenges that will no doubt face us. I have no problem with anyone randomly drawing their companions, but I would not like to see it imposed on all of us."

"Thank you. Would anyone else like to say something about random selection?" Caila scanned the room again. "No one? ... Well then, Lilac, would you be happy with that solution? Every one of us is free to select their chosen ones in whatever way they believe is best, random or personal selection?"

Lilac shrugged, "I can live with that."

"Thanks, Lilac."

"Now, for Green's proposal of larger groups," Caila pressed on. "I should admit that I thought the same thing, a couple of days ago, but I found it hard enough to select just seven companions. Adding another forty would drive me bonkers.

Would anyone else like to comment on Green's proposal? ... Yes, Grey?"

"I wouldn't mind having a few extra. Not 50, but double what we've got now?"

"Like Red," Tiger jumped in, "I would find it hard to think of anyone else I would like to add to my group." Several of the Khered nodded, before Tiger added, "And maybe, this will resolve itself after the Event."

"What do you mean by that?" Caila wanted to know.

"Thanks to Black's question, we know that there is a realistic chance of accidental survivors, friend or foe. That would be the solution to both Green's and Lilac's proposals.

It would increase the numbers, and it would be kind of random," Tiger looked at Lilac. "How about that?"

"I was already happy with the first solution," Lilac responded, "but you made me even happier. Thanks, Tiger."

"Grey, can you live with that?" Caila asked. "Stick to our seven, then pick up survivors, if there are any, along the way?"

"Definitely."

"Green, how about you? There is no hard and fast guarantee there will be any additional survivors, but from what my contact said, I believe there is a very real possibility there will be."

"It's a risk. But I'm willing to accept it. It might be too hard to convince the Neteru anyway. It would take more time to select and prepare fifty companions, and with the way they are speeding things up, I don't believe they would go for it."

"I think you are right," Caila took a sip of her tea, "about speeding things up, I mean. Thank you. Is there anyone who would like to change their original choice, at this moment? … Yes, Green?"

"It's option two for me now," Green joined the majority.

"Option two for me as well, please," Lilac followed suit.

"That makes it unanimous," Caila concluded, "unless anyone else would like to change their vote?" she waited a couple of seconds before continuing. "Okay, just to make it official then. All in favour of option two, raise your hand, please."

Twelve hands shot up.

"That's all twelve of us in favour of option two," this was final, Caila felt cold and shivered. Their consent would set the ultimate component of the process, to reset their planet and the removal of billions of people in motion. She was convinced any other option than the first two would have been rejected by the Neteru, and that this was the only way to maintain a human population on Earth. But right now, she felt like running away, running away from this choice, and from this responsibility.

However, instead of running she stayed put and requested with a steady voice, "Is there anything, anyone would like to say or add, before we call the Neteru in?"

After a moment of silence, Tiger spoke up, "None of us asked to be involved in this decision. We were not invited, we were drafted.

And I am convinced, that all of us would have gladly stayed oblivious of these events. However, we were placed in this situation and had to make a choice. In our minds, we all know that realistically we only had the choice between the first two options; between giving up, and having a future for humanity.

We chose to have a future. How about starting it all together? As one?" Tiger reached out to Blue and to White, "Red?"

Caila linked hands with Green and Orange, "Thank you, Tiger."

As she watched how their group formed a chain, Caila took a deep breath, "Is everyone ready to call the Neteru in? Just relax and concentrate, while you think of your contact."

Caila sensed Mateos's presence as he arrived behind her, and looking around the room, she saw a Neteru appear behind each Khered.

Devyn stood behind Black, and he was the one who spoke, "Khered, have you come to a consensus?"

"Yes, we have," Caila answered.

"What have you decided?"

"We selected option two. A reset of Earth, of the human population, only Khered and their chosen ones remain."

"Is your decision unanimous?"

"Yes, it is," Caila felt Orange squeeze her hand reassuringly.

"Thank you, Khered," Devyn continued, "this makes the verdict of all Khered assemblies on Earth unanimous, the Etherun Assembly will abide by your decision.
We will inform the other assemblies of your verdict and initiate the reset Event. Your contacts will provide you with further details."

"Unforeseen occurrences forced us to bring the Event forward," the dark blue Neteru behind White took over from Devyn, "you may request meetings, but I urge you to retain your anonymity until after the reset."

Then Caila heard Mateos speak up behind her.

"Prior to the Event, your Neteruian contacts will arrange your meetings. However, after the reset, you are free to initiate assemblies yourself. I would like to ask you to select a suitable liaison. …"

Before Mateos had a chance to continue, Yellow interrupted him, "That's easy. Red is our chair, so I nominate Red as our liaison. Is everyone okay with that? Yes? …

Right, you're it, Red.

Oops, I'm sorry, there I go again, I should have asked first."

"That's fine," Caila considered that any subsequent meeting would be child's play compared to these first ones, "I'm happy to act as your liaison, if no one objects."

Unfazed by the interruption Mateos continued, "We will let you know how to contact your liaison. And, Red, I will teach you how to initiate meetings."

Devyn concluded, "Thank you for your cooperation, Khered. We will leave you now, to allow you to wrap up your meeting. *Non erit sapiens*."

After the Neteru had disappeared, a heavy silence hung over the room.

"Let's hope we have been and will be wise. Assuming that, '*non erit sapiens*', translates the same from Neteruian, as from Latin."

"That's impressive," Tiger quipped, breaking the solemn atmosphere. "Are you a scholar?"

"Not really," Caila confessed, "I'm more a Googler than a scholar."

Her admission prompted Orange to suggest, "Maybe we should ask the Neteru for dictionaries. Let's throw in a request for a Neteruian encyclopaedia, on life in the modern Universe."

"I wouldn't mind learning a bit more about our nearest and furthest neighbours," now that the decision had been made, Purple came also out of their shell.

"Speaking of which, I'm looking forward to learning a bit more about all of you guys," Yellow announced. "After the Event, of course."

"Same here," Caila agreed, "and let's hope we have lots of time to get better acquainted."

"Is there anything else, anyone would like to discuss?" Caila felt empty, all she wanted right now, was to get back to Chris and into her warm bed, "Then I think we should call it quits. We'll all be busy over the next few days but if anyone would like to meet, for whatever reason, even for just a chat, ask your contact to call a meeting."

As an afterthought, with her own misadventures in mind, she advised, "Stay safe, everyone."

London - Priorities

"You messed up!" Baldwin was fuming. "Badly.
You used 47 highly trained men, to botch-up the arrest of a humdrum suburban couple.
And what did you accomplish? They slipped through your incompetent fingers, you have no idea where to find them, and you attracted more attention than the ruddy world cup finals."

"Mr Thurogood, I accept full responsibility for these failings. Our targets were forewarned and assisted in their escape by the invading force. This merely proves our point, how urgent and complicated this situation has become. We need to regain control and smoke these collaborators out, asap, and eliminate them. My men are tracking any known associates of our target, as we speak.
I was informed by the head of the CIA that an attack is imminent, but we were also assured that without these Earth contacts, the attack will not, and cannot proceed.
However, as a precautionary measure, I moved the most senior members of our Royal Family into an Ac3-level bunker. The Queen refused to leave her country, but the Prince of Wales and his eldest son with his wife and children have been secured."

"I'm not sure the Royal Family should be our priority at this point. If the worst happens, this country needs strong leadership and I can provide that.

Eleonor and I should, without delay, be moved into one of these top tier shelters."

"Sir, I am not sure that can be arranged at this moment," the head of MI5 began to regret his decision to involve the sneaky opportunist, "without attracting the wrong kind of attention."

"Marcus, I have perfect faith that you can arrange this little thing for us.

After all, ..." Baldwin's smile did not reach his eyes, "... who else is going to reserve a place for you in their shelter. I have it on good authority that your suspension will be announced tomorrow morning; how long your life, or your period of disgrace will last, lies entirely in your own hands."

"Sir, I will have an armoured vehicle collect you and the shadow chancellor, from this address, in one hour exactly."

Lists and feather quills

Tuesday 17 September

After she'd returned from the final assembly, it had taken Caila hours of twisting and turning to fall into a deep dreamless sleep. But the next morning sunlight streamed into her new and unfamiliar bedroom, challenging her to accept last night's decision, and move on.

"Wake up, darling, here's your breakfast, it's almost nine o'clock," Chris walked in, balancing a large tray, heaped with salmon and cream cheese sandwiches, orange juice and tea. "Mateos asked me to let you sleep, he'll be back to talk to you later. Move over, please, it's been ages since we had breakfast in bed."

"Mmm, that smells delicious. Did he say anything else?" when Chris frowned, his wife clarified. "Mateos, of course. Who else? You seem a bit distracted, is something wrong?"

"Apart from a world that's about to end, you mean? Mateos told me what you decided," Chris stared at the large hourglass. "You know that I've never been the most sociable of creatures, but now that society is about to be cancelled, it feels odd. I never enjoyed work socials, or any socials at all, actually. But if feels strange that I will never have to endure them again. And ..." he smiled at his wife,

"I never dreamed, I'd be in for such a drastic career change."

"No, I don't think any of us did," Caila thought back of last night. "Do you think we made the right decision? I don't believe 'doing nothing' was ever a realistic option. And removing all life from this planet, just because we messed up, well …, that wouldn't be right, would it? So, it basically came down to two options, restarting with, or without humans.

Or, as Tiger put it yesterday, to a choice between a future for humanity, and giving up.

Do you think it was selfish to choose a future? Last night, after I returned from that meeting, I kept seeing faces of people who will, quite soon, not be around anymore. Not anyone special, but people who I always took for granted, like the mailman, the girl at the station, our neighbours, …"
With an apologetic smile, Caila looked back up at her husband, "I'm sorry Chris, I shouldn't lay this on you, the decision has been made, it's done now. And I didn't give you much choice on your Khered, or activated Khered, status either."

"No, you didn't, but I would have agreed anyway," he was reminded of his shock at discovering their red sphereams and seeing Mateos for the first time, "and if it came down to a choice between a future and giving up, then I would probably have made the same choice."

"Thanks, you're the best husband ever," Caila rubbed her temples, she could do with some fresh air. "I have a blazing headache. Let's go out for a walk in the gardens, before we start organising humanity's new future. The roses are still beautiful.

And don't worry about missing those socials, there are going to be at least eight of us, so we can always organise one for you to suffer your way through."

"At least?" Chris regarded his wife with surprise, while she chucked cold water on her face. "I thought you said it would be just us, and six others?"

"That's right, but there may be some more," Caila went on to explain the possibility of accidental survivors. "So, we may expect, some unexpected company from time to time."

"Let's hope Black and Mateos are wrong about them being aggressive or armed, we have quite enough on our plate, as it is," Chris contemplated the consequences. "But, if they are, we should start thinking about how to deal with them, it's best to be prepared."

"Yes, I guess you're right," Caila thought about it for a moment, before suggesting, "Darling, would you mind being our head of security? I realise it's not very democratic, but I believe you would be the best person for the job."

"Well, the number of vacancies for software developers might be a bit limited in the near future, so, head of security is a good alternative. If we can get the power back on, then maybe Luke and I can set up some kind of CCTV system. How about that?"

"That sounds geeky, but also terribly useful. Right, my darling, we should get serious about those preparations. Where did I leave that blasted jumper?"

Chris grinned from ear to ear as he held up a pretty gold-coloured box, decorated with red ribbons.

"Chris, what is that?"

"Just a little something Mateos dropped off earlier. I believe it is your size."

Caila jumped to grab her present before she excitedly pulled at the ribbon and lifted the lid. Then a blush crept up her cheeks as she stared at a pile of beautiful underwear. All of it silk, and all of it red.

***

Caila and Chris were busy making lists when Mateos returned later that morning. Chris made good progress but Caila struggled with a feather pen and ink, which she insisted on using because it suited the ambiance of the stately Library. Annoyingly, the quill had behaved significantly better when Chris took her up on her challenge, to show that he could do better. And now, there was no way she was going to admit defeat.

OOVII had also joined them, and perched on the back of a chair, he generously furnished his human companions with advice. On his insistence, raw peanuts were added to the list of nutritional necessities.

Mateos observed the trio for a while. They were getting on so well together; it reminded him of his comfortable friendship with Devyn and Tia, when he was younger.

Caila was the first one to notice him when he moved further into the room, "Hi Mateos, we are making lists of things we need to collect after the Event. Would you like to help us? You have good taste, thank you for your present."

"Always happy to be of service, milady. Good morning, Chris. Good morning, Khrhhsh," the Neteru noticed Caila's ink-soaked hands while he greeted the others. "Has she been giving you much trouble?"

"Nothing we can't handle, but we are happy to see you, some help is always appreciated," Chris looked up at OOVII, with whom he had struck up a firm friendship. "Right, OOVII?"

- Most certainly, Chris, – the corvid remained dignified, as ever, - I could not have expressed it better, myself. –

"Much as I would like to join in the fun," Mateos got back to business, "there are some matters I need to discuss with Caila. Urgently."

"Spoilsport!" Caila retorted laughingly, before she assured him more seriously, "No, it's all right. Do you need to speak to me alone, or can Chris and OOVII stay?"

- Count me out, – OOVII flew onto the windowsill, - it is time for me to inspect the grounds. – He elegantly sailed out of the window, taking a beakful of peanuts for his wife, who was feasting on windfall outside in the orchard.

Chris put his notebook down and started to get up, but Mateos stopped him, "No, please stay, it'll save Caila time, later on, in bringing you up to date. And with that pen, she will need all the time she can get, to finish those lists."

Caila threw him a quasi-pained look.

Then in a sober tone, Mateos announced, "Following human Khered consensus, we acquired final approval to deploy the telumparticula. This produces a beam, which will allow us to remove specified objects and species from Mesu. Sorry, Chris, that's Earth.

We will deploy the beam as soon as we have the telumparticula in place. I expect it to be no later than tomorrow afternoon," he looked from Chris to Caila. "All humans will be removed, except Khered and their chosen ones. Caila, your chosen ones have been prepared, they will be untouched by the beam and will know where to find you, after the Event. We will also remove weapons and contaminants that pose a threat to the future of this planet and the wider Universe."

"So, we don't need to worry about nuclear waste, or explosions as storage containers wear thin?" that would have been the last thing they needed. "That's a relief, and Blue will be chuffed that you are getting rid of the '*bad stuff*'."

"That, she will be," Mateos had met the slight young girl earlier, "it was one of her main concerns. She is young, and she hasn't had an easy life so far, but with a little bit of help she'll manage."

That reminded Caila of her husband's earlier concerns, "Mateos, Chris asked me about children. As much fun as it would be to make them, I would not like to be a production line for the next generation. That is a definite no-no for me," Caila hugged a large cushion, for support.

"Production line? That's an interesting way to describe it. And it would keep you busy and out of trouble," to his satisfaction, he noticed that Caila was about to take the bait.

She opened her mouth, ready to take him on.

"But, my dear Caila, please listen to me before you have a go at me. Khered are few and far between, and childbirth in humans is not without risk. That is why we decided that Khered children should be created in a similar way to young Neteru. It is comparable to the process of in vitro fertilisation here on Earth, but at no point does a parent carry the child in vivo. I trust, you find this solution acceptable?"

"I guess I do," Caila studied the figurine of a woman and child, above the fireplace. "And if you could deliver them potty trained, and make them skip puberty, it would be simply perfect."

"Caila, don't forget that I have seen you grow up," Mateos reminded his Khered. "You are the perfect person to deal with a stroppy teenager, experience is still the best teacher. Am I right, Chris?"

Chris decided that claiming ignorance was the best strategy, "I didn't know Caila when she was in her teens, so I can't possibly comment."

"That was smooth, Chris. But I hope I put your minds at ease. The Neteruian method also provides a solution for human males, whose anatomy prevents them from carrying a child. Each Khered will receive an infant which is based on their own individual DNA. They will form the starting point of a new human population."

"But before we get stuck in the details of the restart, there is something else I need to discuss with you," in a sterner mood, Mateos proceeded. "Your ancestors, Caila, and those of one other Khered have since a previous leak been known to the intelligence agencies. We had hoped that, because of your messy past, your switch at birth, your frequent moves and your name changes, you'd stay undetected until the Event. But your past only delayed detection and yesterday they caught up with you. You are safe now, as long as you stick to our rules.

However, security services are investigating everyone close to you. Fortunately, you don't have a wide circle of close relations, you have lived extremely private lives so far. The only contacts to attract attention were …"

"Steve and Richard!" Caila cried out. "Are they safe?"

Mateos looked worried, "There is a problem, Caila, that we need to discuss urgently."

Steve and Richard

Richard had left for work two hours ago, and Steve reflected that working from home as a contractor, definitely had its advantages. No cattle class trains, no aggressive drivers and no office politics.

His home office looked out over the normally quiet cul-de-sac. But today, it was unusually busy for a Tuesday morning, or for any morning or time of day.

'I hope Bluebell and Banjo watch their steps,' he worried about their cheeky felines, 'I should keep them in, when they return from their morning walk'.

Steve made sure he had a signal and checked his phone again, there was still no message from Richard. He could not shake the uneasy feeling that something had happened, this was not like Rich. And where were those cats, they'd normally be dancing on his keyboard by now, demanding their midmorning treat.

Restless, Steve went downstairs to make himself a cup of coffee and, as he filled the machine with water, he heard a car pull up.

He looked out of the kitchen window and felt the blood drain from his face.

Out front, a police car had pulled up, and two officers with solemn faces made their way to his front door. A couple of seconds later, there was the inevitable knock.

While he opened the door to them, Steve squeezed out, "Richard?"

"Mr Owen, Steve Owen?"

Unable to say anything, Steve just nodded.

"Can we come in, please? We have some urgent news for you."

Completely numbed, Steve let himself be led to the sitting room.

"Sir, I'm afraid I have bad news for you," the female officer addressed him compassionately, "this morning, your husband, Richard Gardener, was involved in an accident. He is in a serious condition in hospital."

In hospital. Relieve flowed through Steve, that meant Richard was alive.

"How is he, is he badly hurt?" tears blurred his vision. "I need to go and see him. Where are my car keys?"

"You are in no condition to drive, Steve. Your husband has been airlifted to a specialist unit in Pembury. We will take you there immediately."

The officers stood, and Steve followed them to the door, mechanically picking up his keys from the hall table before dropping them outside after an unsuccessful attempt to lock his front door. The male officer picked them up and handed them to his colleague, who locked the door before she settled next to Steve in the back of the patrol car.

During a tense ride, the female officer unsuccessfully attempted to distract their distraught passenger, informing him that her name was Sophie, and enquiring how long they'd been married.

Steve answered her questions unthinkingly and hardly noticed the road as they left Ashford; but after sipping from a kindly offered water bottle, he finally felt himself relax. Becoming drowsy, almost.

"Don't worry, Steve, that's normal," Sophie comfortingly laid a hand on his shoulder and offered him another sip of water, "it is the shock settling in."

Steve came back around when the car stopped in a wooded area, it was a different car, he noticed, not the police vehicle he'd got into earlier.

"You gave him too much, he's not used to it."

Steve heard how the male officer scolded his female colleague. What was her name again? He felt disorientated, and had trouble remembering.

"Get him active. I'm not going to carry him for three miles."

'Sophie,' now Steve remembered, that was her name. He felt how she nudged him patiently, whilst still keeping him in an iron grip.

"Come on Steve, wake up, we need to walk from here."

***

Richard checked his phone again, it was not like Steve not to reply.

Whilst, with a growing feeling of unease, he tried to decide between giving Steve a call or sending him another text, his manager appeared next to his desk.

"Richard, could you come with me, please? To Janet's office. It's urgent."

Richard glanced at his phone and followed Helen reluctantly; he noticed that Janet was not in her office, but two police officers were studying his every move as he approached.

"Mr Gardener, Richard Gardener?" the female officer enquired.

Richard nodded.

"Please, sit down, Richard, we have bad news for you. Your husband, Steve Owen, had an accident this morning. He is in a serious condition, in hospital."

One of the officers offered him a glass of water and he took a sip.

"What happened, where is he now?" Richard was confused. Steve was at home, nothing bad could happen at home.

"Your husband had a bad fall, he was airlifted to a specialist unit in Pembury. We will take you there immediately, Mr Gardener," the officer nodded towards Helen, who was now waiting outside the glass cubicle with his coat and bag.

Helen came in, and gently put an arm around his shoulder, "Go with the officers Richard and take as much time as you need." She gave him a quick hug before she handed him his belongings.

A patrol car was waiting outside the office and, after they got in, the female officer offered him another sip of water whilst assuring him, "We'll be there soon, Richard; my name is Sophie."

Richard felt himself getting drowsy.

"It's the shock, Richard, try to relax. We'll have you with Steve, in no time at all."

Recriminations

"What happened?" Caila snapped, as she was close to tears, she would never forgive herself if something happened to Steve or Richard.

"Mateos, are they safe?" Chris worried. "They are our best friends, they were Caila's first choice, they would have been mine as well."

"We are keeping a close eye on all your chosen ones, and all others appear safe and undetected. They aren't close enough to you to come onto the radar of the intelligence agencies. Yet.

However, Steve and Richard were both picked up this morning, by …"

Caila felt the blood drain from her face, while they were interrupted by an angry interaction in the Outer Hall.

Mateos got up and moved into the direction of the disturbance, "One moment, please."

"Excellent," his voice sounded muffled, dulled by the castle's thick walls. "Follow me, please."

Donning his human mask, Mateos was followed into the Library by an agitated Steve, and two unfamiliar looking Neteru, perfectly disguised as police officers.

"As I was about to tell you, Caila," Mateos calmly continued his earlier explanation, "earlier this morning, Steve and Richard were both picked up by us, just before the intelligence services moved in."

Caila flew of the sofa and threw her arms around Steve, "Steve, you're safe. I thought something terrible had happened to you and Richard."

Then she furiously turned around to face Mateos, "Are you out of your mind, you scared the hell out of me? Is Richard safe as well?"

With an inscrutable expression, Mateos replied, "What comes around goes around. Now you know how Chris and I felt, yesterday.

And yes, Richard is also safely on his way to the castle."

Chris looked from Caila to Mateos and shrugged, before he steered the utterly confused Steve onto the sofa, "It's good to know that you're safe. And that Richard is also safely on his way. Let's sit down, Caila will explain everything in a minute."

Then, deciding to be the voice of reason, he urged, "Caila, we were very worried about you yesterday, and this is not the appropriate moment for you to test if your looks can kill our Neteruian contact. Mateos, I believe Caila got the message. Can we all be friends again, please?"

Chris felt like a parent soothing a couple of petulant siblings, "That's better. How long until Richard arrives?"

Mateos looked questioningly at the two uniformed Neteru at the door.

"No more than five minutes, they were right behind us," the female officer answered, "do you still need us, or can we go back now?"

"Thank you, we'll be fine. You may go back to Canada. Could you please tell Devyn, I'll see him later?"

Not a minute after they'd left the room, an angry Richard was led in by two other, almost identical looking officers, who blocked the door when an emotional Steve ran up to his husband and pulled him close, "Rich, I thought I'd never see you again!"

Chris noticed that Mateos was getting restless and realised they probably didn't have a lot of time to get this sorted. He nudged Caila who, still miffed with their liaison, shrugged. "Come on Caila," he whispered, "Mateos means well, he cares about you."

Caila raised her eyebrows and sighed, "Steve, Richard, could you come over here please, and sit down for a minute? We need to talk," she got up and gently pushed the tearful, reunited couple in the direction of the sofa.

With a quick glance in his direction, she addressed Mateos directly, - Do you have time to stay a bit longer? Convincing them of an alien plan to reset Earth may take a bit of Neteruian back up. – She smiled apologetically when she added, - And I apologise, Sets, I know that you worry about me, sometimes. –

- More than just sometimes, – Mateos watched his troublesome Khered, and returned her smile. - Yes, I do have some time to spare. And, I'm sorry too. I shouldn't have scared you like that. Now, you'd better get started, those guys are badly disorientated, and your husband is probably wondering what we are talking about. –

"Don't worry," Caila grinned at Chris, "that was just a kiss and make up with the second man in my life."
In a rare display of coordination, she caught Chris's cushion before it had a chance to hit her. Then she quickly returned her attention to the confused couple who were silently watching them from the sofa.

"Hi, you two. I'm really sorry about the scare, but there was no other way to keep you safe," Caila gave them a reassuring smile. "How are you now?"

Steve, with his arm firmly wrapped around Richard's waist, replied, "Somewhere between utterly confused and massively relieved, Caila dear. Those two over there," he pointed in the direction of the two Neteru at the door, "are they real police officers? They told me that Richard was badly hurt and in hospital."

Richard looked at his husband, "They told me the same thing, about you. I'm so happy you're okay."

"I don't like this, Caila, what is going on here?" Steve glared at his friend, making it obvious he was not happy with her, "You know that I have always considered you and Chris best friends, but if this is a joke, then it is not a very funny one, I'll let you know." His voice faltered as his irritation gave way to outright anger, "And what did those two give me, … us, to knock us out?"

Caila glanced at Mateos, who answered for her, "The effects of mito alone, sorry, of relaxation by touch, would not have been powerful enough to assure timely and discrete transportation to Caila's domus. We also administered a light sedative, it should be completely out of your systems by now."

"Thanks. Steve and Richard, this is Mateos," Caila made the introductions before she started her explanation. "Do you remember when we talked about everything that was wrong in the world? The aggression, the pollution? It was a couple of weeks ago? You said that, if you were in charge, you would handle things differently, and the world would be a better place?"

Steve didn't reply and continued to view Caila furiously.

"Well. It appears that no one is in charge, not anymore," Caila grew increasingly nervous under Steve's persistent glare, "no humans, I mean. There is no easy way to explain this, and you are not going to believe me, but just hear me out. Please.

Out there," Caila waved towards the ceiling, "there is a planet called Etherun, and that's where a species called the Neteru live.

A long time ago they decided to do an experiment, seeding life on a remote planet, called Earth. They seeded lots of different species, and recently one of these species, humans, became dominant and made a terrible mess of things. And now, it is so bad, that we are about to completely destroy our own little planet. And that in turn, would have serious implications for the stability of the rest of the universe.

So, they, the Neteru, decided that they needed to reset Earth. This involves a big clean-up of the mess we made, and …, and they will remove most of the human population.

Only a few of us will remain. Chris and I are two of them. And you and Richard will stay as well. That's it, basically."

Steve and Richard looked bewildered, either this was some kind of elaborate stunt, or their friends had completely lost their marbles.

Richard was first to find his voice again, "Caila, I don't know how you organised all this. Or why. But you will have to come up with something better than an alien invasion."

"I see," Caila wasn't sure how to respond, she was well aware how incredible her story sounded. "Steve?"

Steve pointedly ignored Caila and glanced at Chris, "This is a bit too far-fetched for me. Where are the cameras?"

Chris looked at Caila, who nodded, urging him to confirm what she had told their two friends, "I realise it appears far-fetched, I found it hard to believe as well. Caila left out a few details, but that really is basically the long and the short of it."

Mateos stepped in and took over from Chris, "One of the details Caila left out, is that she is a Khered, a direct descendant of the first seedlings on Earth. She, and seven humans of her choice, will remain on this planet, after the reset Event.

Her first choice was her partner, Chris. You are her second and third choices. Your DNA has already been adjusted to allow you to remain untouched by the telumparticula, the Event, but you will also be given the choice to become activated Khered, like Chris and Caila."

"Mateos is from Etherun, he is here to organise the reset," Caila looked at the Neteru by the door and threw Mateos a pleading glance.

He understood and told them that they were free to re-join Devyn.

After they had left, Caila continued, "Mateos does not really look like he appears to you at this moment. He uses a kind of mask, an overlay. It's not that he looks scary, just a bit different from us."

She got up and walked over to her friends, "Mateos, would you mind?"

While Mateos dropped his mask, Caila slipped behind the two men.

"What the …?" Steve jumped up from the sofa, half taking his shocked husband with him.

"It's fine guys," Caila was quick to touch the backs of her friends' necks, "he is just a different species. And he is quite friendly most of the time, when he's not being terribly bossy, that is."

When Richard and Steve sank back onto the sofa, Caila let go of them.

She glanced at Mateos and considered that he didn't look bad, actually. Grey was not her favourite colour, but he was quite handsome. And while she admired her new honorary brother, before walking back to re-join her husband, Caila had a brief vision of three young Neteru, one red, one green and one grey, against a beautiful Etherunian background.

Mateos gave her a questioning glance but didn't ask anything. He had just had a recollection of Tia, Dev and himself, hanging out when they were younger. From Caila's reaction, he could have sworn she had seen the same thing. He touched Steve and Richard shoulders briefly, "Caila is right, I am just another species." Then he reactivated his mask.

Steve and Richard recovered quickly from the unexpected sight of the opaque grey shape floating towards them. His touch, even after he had morphed back into a human, felt light. It felt like there was nothing at all, but at the same time it felt solid and comforting.

"So, this is real?" Richard asked Chris, who to him, seemed the sanest and most reliable person at this moment.

"It is very real."

A tense silence hung over the Library, while the two men let reality sink in, "If this is true …? I have a sister, we have parents, and nieces and nephews."

Caila sank down onto the sofa, next to Steve, "I know, and I am so sorry. But the Event is inevitable, it will take place, no matter what. It will be quick, and no one will be aware of it as it happens. That is right, isn't it, Mateos?"

Mateos nodded, "It will take less than a second. Your families won't be aware of anything, before or during the Event. If we would not intervene, the consequences would be devastating, and you and your families would suffer greatly, even if they survived."

He glanced at Caila, as if to ask her permission to continue, but her face was drained of all colour as she looked like she was about to burst into tears.

His Khered swallowed before she gave him a short nod.

'Shit', he thought, 'she must have seen it. But that's impossible'.

Distracted, he turned his attention back to Steve, "You and your husband have been prepared, you will be untouched by the beam. Afterwards you will live your lives either as dormant or activated Khered. Caila will explain the consequences of both options later."

"Caila?" Mateos realised he should talk to his distressed Khered, but he should have been out of here ten minutes ago, "I'm so sorry but I really need to go now. I'll be back as soon as I can, probably later tonight. I believe we need to have a chat. Khrhhsh will be here to keep an eye on things."

"Yes, we do need to talk. Thanks for everything, Sets," Caila fought back her tears and bit her lip, "I'll see you later."

"How? Where's he gone to?" Steve had just witnessed Mateos disappear into thin air.

Caila kept her eyes fixed on an old magazine on the footstool in front of her, "I don't know, preparation, a meeting, or helping one of the other Khered. I'm not sure," she looked up, "but Mateos is right. If they didn't intervene, things would go wrong. So terribly wrong that you would not want to be around to tell. This is the only solution."

"Are you all right, darling?" Chris could see that something had upset his wife badly.

"I'm fine, it's nothing to worry about," and with a faint smile at Chris and her guests, she continued. "There is nothing I can do to help your families, and I'm really sorry about that. But I care deeply about you, and I believe you can handle life after the Event. That is why I asked for you. There will be four others, joining us later."

"I know you meant well, but why in heaven's name would you assume that we would want to hang around here, when all our family and friends, and the rest of the world are gone?"

"I considered that, believe me. You and Richard are our best friends, and I wouldn't want to hurt you for anything in this world. But I had no choice, I trust you, both of you. And I know of no one who is better suited to help rebuild a fairer human population.

Yes, I admit, it was probably selfish of me as well. I chose you because you are our best friends, because I trust you, because you are intelligent, because of your skills, and because I think you will fit into the group. You can blame me for that if you want, but it won't alter the facts. You will be here after the Event, as Khered.

Why don't you two have some time alone, to discuss it and let it sink in?" Caila's throat hurt, and her eyes were burning, she couldn't breakdown in front of her friends, "You can use the Drawing Room. There will be a Neteru with you, but you can talk freely. It's at the end of the hall to your right."

Steve and Richard took her up on her offer. And the moment the door closed behind their two friends, Caila curled up on the sofa, and started sobbing uncontrollably.

Too much information

"Caila, what is it?" Chris ran over to his wife. "Darling, what's wrong?"

Clinging on to Chris, Caila continued to sob uncontrollably, "Five … minutes …."

It didn't take her all of five minutes to recover, but this was still the most upset Chris had ever seen his wife, "Is it about those stroppy guys over there, in the sitting room? They weren't happy with what you told them, but that's hardly surprising given the circumstances.

First you give them the biggest fright of their life, then you tell them that aliens are about to change their lives forever, that none of their friends and family will be around to see it, and to top it all off, you tell them that you are the person responsible for keeping them around. That's enough to upset the most stoic of men, and to be fair, my darling, being stoic is the last thing anyone could ever accuse Steve and Richard of."

That last remark earned Chris a watery smile from his wife, "No, they're definitely not stoic. But that wasn't it. Of course, it is part of it, because I don't like seeing them upset or angry with me. But what else could I have expected? It would probably have been easier after the Event. A fait accompli is easier to accept than the inevitable, even if the inevitable is unavoidable."

Caila continued her conversation using lectanimo, - Can you concentrate on me, please? And lock everything else out. I will tell you what it was that upset me, but we need complete privacy, even from the guards. –

Chris regarded her with surprise but did as he was asked, - Like this? –

- Yes, like that, – Caila paused for a moment to try and make sense of what had just happened. - When Mateos said that the consequences would be devastating if they didn't intervene, he somehow, inadvertently I believe, projected an image to me of what would happen, or rather, of what would have happened. And it was pretty disturbing to say the least. I am not going to try and show it to you, or even describe it, because it was so horrifically bad, and I believe that I was not supposed to see it. –

- Mateos told me that you are, … what was it again? – Chris remembered the conversation he'd had with their liaison, on their way to their new home, - A first order Khered, and that you developed a bit faster than the others. Maybe you are even surprising him, and that's why you saw this. Is that why he said that you needed to have a chat, later on? –

- Developing a bit faster? That's one way of putting it, – Caila wished she could tell her husband the whole truth. - Yes, I believe he noticed I picked up on those images, so I guess that's what he will want to talk about. But I didn't want to leave you in the dark, after I released the waterworks on you, you seemed a bit worried. –

- That is the understatement of the century, I have never seen you this upset before. You really had me worried there for a moment. It must have been terribly disturbing, to get you in such a state. –

- It was. The Neteru are making the right choice, the alternative would have been horrendous, – Caila tried to shake the image of burned bodies and scarred and emaciated survivors. – Thanks, darling, I feel a lot better. I'll talk to Mateos later, but now I want to think about something else to try and get those images out of my head. How about getting back to human chat mode?
And, would you like some sandwiches before we get back to those blasted lists? –

When they returned from the restaurant, Caila quickly glanced into the Drawing Room, where Steve and Richard appeared to be engaged in a heated discussion. She decided it was best to leave them to it, but half an hour later she asked one of the Neteru guards to bring them something to eat and drink.

Two hours later, while they were discussing shoes, what kind, how many and where to find them, Caila glanced at the clock.

"Go on, just go and ask if they need anything," Chris sensed her restlessness, "and if they're not ready, then you leave them a bit longer."

"Steve? Richard?" Caila knocked softly. "Can I come in, please?" she looked around the door, "Oops, I'm sorry. I'll come back later."

Steve and Richard were locked in a passionate embrace on the antique sofa, and Caila had already turned around when she heard Richard call after her, "Come in, Caila. It's safe, we discussed your little bombshell and we would like to talk to you. Don't worry, we won't bite."

As she nestled herself in the comfortable armchair by the fireplace, Caila studied their faces, "Are we still friends?"

"Of course, we are," Steve reassured her, "I guess I had a bad case of shooting the messenger. Can we ask you some questions now?"

"Shoot!" Caila shot back.

"Caila, Caila. That was almost funny, young lady," Steve shook his head in mock exasperation, before he continued in a more serious tone. "How certain are you that this reset is necessary? I know what that bloke said, but we want to hear it from you."

Caila shivered and wrapped her arms around herself, while the images she'd inadvertently seen, shot through her mind again, "One hundred percent necessary," her voice was soft but steady, "I have no doubt. You'll have to trust me on this."

Gazing at the two Neteru, at the far end of the room, she thought it was lucky she'd learned to separate her thinking from lectanimo, "And I want you to know that you can trust Mateos too. He won't lie to you, he may not give you all of the details, but I know he won't lie."

Steve and Richard exchanged a glance.

"I can live with that. I trust Caila and Chris," Richard told Steve, "let's leave it at that. … Is there nothing at all you can do for our families?"

"No, …" Caila shook her head slowly, she'd expected this question. "No, I'm so sorry, but there is nothing I can do for them." She looked at the two men on the frilly sofa, "I hope you don't blame me for choosing you to survive. It was the hardest thing I ever had to do in my life, deciding who I wanted to stay with me. Not only because of the choice of who our companions were going to be, but also because I knew how much I would be asking of them, and how much they would have to leave behind."

"We kind of expected you to say that, and we understand," Richard studied the continuous pattern of the freeze above the fireplace. "I'm sorry we came down so hard on you earlier, it can't have been easy for you and Chris either."

"No, it wasn't, but we've had a bit more time to adjust to this new situation than the two of you have. And we didn't have a couple of fake police officers scare the living daylights out of us."

"Yes, that was definitely the worst moment of my life," Steve squeezed Richard's hand, "when I got that knock on my door. One more question though. That Neteru, what's his name again, … Mateos, mentioned that you would explain the difference between a dormant and an activated Khered?"

Caila grimaced, "Let's go back to the Library then. Chris isn't completely up to date on that subject either, so I might as well have you all together while I explain."

When the trio arrived back in the Library, Chris announced that he was happy to see everyone on friendlier terms again, and Richard wanted to know if Caila's blue hands were in any way related to the badly stained feather pen on the writing desk. Chris asked him how he'd guessed, and then put Richard in charge of preventing Caila from getting her hands on the sealing wax in the souvenir shop.

"I would be extremely grateful if you would all be so kind and stop using me as your main source of amusement. Thank you very much," Caila snuggled up on the sofa, next to Chris, leaving only two separate armchairs for Steve and Richard.

The two men promptly dragged them close together in front of the fireplace, "Right, to be activated or not, that is the question?" Steve hooked his foot under a footstool to pull it closer.

"Chris. Steve and Richard asked me to explain about the Khered versus activated Khered option. And since your conversion was a bit hasty, I …"

"Hasty doesn't even begin to describe it, darling," Chris teased, "but don't mind me, please, continue."

"As I was saying, …" Caila obliged whilst rolling her eyes at her husband, "… was a bit hasty, you should hear this as well.

If you decide to remain a plain Khered, you will stay as you are; you already received the extra string of Khered DNA to keep you safe during the Event. This part of your DNA will then remain dormant for the rest of your lives. But it will be transferred to one of your grandchildren, and then one of their grandchildren, and so on. You get the drift. If you choose …"

Chris coughed at that last word, an action which earned him another disapproving look from his wife.

"… to become an activated Khered, you will also stay mostly as you are right now, but that extra string of DNA will be activated. Mateos can do that for you and you won't feel a thing.

This has some advantages. You will, for example, be able to use lectanimo to communicate with Neteru, and with activated Khered from all the different Khered species here on Earth. And the Neteru will be able to fix you. …

Oops, I'm sorry, that didn't exactly come out right, did it?" embarrassed and desperately searching for the right word, Caila continued, "What I mean is that, … for example, I burned my hand rather badly last Thursday, and then Mateos fixed it for me. Like he fixed Chris's eyes." Caila's fingers came perilously close to the aforementioned organs of the visual system as she pointed at her husband, who swiftly moved his head out of harm's way and took a bow, "See, no glasses, no contacts. Healing! …That's the word I was looking for, they will be able to heal you!

Then, like with dormant Khered, some of your offspring will also be Khered, it jumps from grandparent to one grandchild, but they will be dormant, so they won't have this healing advantage.

And, as a dormant Khered you would live out your normal human lifespan, but as an activated Khered you will remain on Mesu, …, I mean on Earth, for the entire burn-in period after the Event. Any questions?"

"Caila, young lady, I hate to break it to you," Steve grinned triumphantly, "but you can't have failed to notice that Rich and I are not likely to produce offspring."

Caila nodded earnestly, giving Steve her best fake sympathetic look, "And I am aware that this has always caused you enormous pain and sorrow. However, …" she knew very well they had most definitely never regretted not having children, "I am happy to announce that the Neteru found a way around this problem, and they will assist all Khered, male and female, in producing at least one child of their own."

"Caila!" Chris watched the horrified couple and shook his head as he admonished his wife, "Really, Caila! Don't worry, guys, I have been assured that the issue in question will be produced in vitro, and the final product will be delivered when it is ready to be fed and diapered. And Caila has kindly included someone with baby expertise, in our team."

"Thank you, missy, for scaring us half to dead, that was very wicked of you, I will let you know," Steve sank back into his chair. "Chris, Rich and I are grateful for the additional information, so very kindly supplied by you."

"Yes, thank you," Richard was keen to steer the conversation away from turbulent baby waters. "So far, choosing the activated option sounds like a no-brainer. But that lecta-something, you mentioned earlier. What is it exactly? And the other Khered species, what are they?"

"Lectanimo. That is communicating without talking out loud. Activated Khered can use it with other activated Khered and with Neteru. It can be really useful when you want some privacy in a crowded room," Caila conveniently ignored Mateos's advice on lectanimo etiquette. "And the other Khered species are crows, dolphins, whales, … bees, …," she frowned while trying to recall which others Mateos had mentioned, "there are more, I believe, but those are the ones that I remember. So far, I've only met OOVII, my Crow contact, and he is very smart and very posh, everything you would expect from a corvid."

"It almost sounds too good to be true," Steve took another chocolate from the box on the table, "a tiny painless adjustment and you live happily and healthily ever after. Bob's your uncle!"

He noticed Caila's hesitation, "Or is there a catch?"

"I wouldn't call it a catch, not exactly, it just depends on how long you want to live.

Do you remember I mentioned that you will be expected to hang around for the burn-in period? For the, *entire*, burn-in period?"

While Steve and Richard nodded, Caila looked away, OOVII and his friends were scouring the lawn for corvid delicacies, "Well, that burn-in period lasts 107 years, that's kind of why they give you the health benefits."

Then Caila remembered this would also be news to Chris, and when she looked back into the room she was greeted by a wall of stunned silence, until Steve finished some mental arithmetic and reminded her.

"Do you realise that I will be 144 years old, by then?"

Caila gave him a wide smile, "Yes, but such a handsome 144-year-old, Steve," she assured him, "Thanks to the health benefits."

When the laughter died down, Caila concluded, "Yeh, but all joking aside, I don't want to influence your decision. It's up to you. But obviously I would be chuffed if you chose to become activated, so that we can stay together."

"I understand. We'll talk about it tonight, and then, tomorrow morning, we'll let you know what we decided," Steve promised. "Is that all right with you?" he asked his husband.

The rest of the afternoon was spent amiably chatting away and working on their shopping lists, before they had their dinner in the grand Dining Hall where a stern Black Prince and an even sterner Henry V looked down on them. With the no-cooking-allowed-until-the-Event rule still in place, the food was not nearly as impressive as the beautiful room and the five-meter-long oak dining table, but nevertheless, the salads and the incredibly messy Eton mess tasted delicious.

Mateos still hadn't returned when they decided it was time to turn in that night.

But, when Caila and Chris showed their friends their new bedroom, the cosy Waldegrave room next to theirs, Caila found that her Neteruian brother had kept his word.

On the red bedspread of Steve and Richard's new four-poster bed, two contented cats lay blissfully sleeping, their food bowls empty and a litter tray strategically placed in the adjoining oratory.

The couple yelped, "Bluebell, Banjo!" as they raced over to hug their unruffled cats.

A Neteru guard followed them into the room, and Chris quietly closed the door behind them.

While they walked over to their own room, and settled for the night, Caila wondered what was keeping Sets.

The alternative

"Caila, wake up."

Caila tried to shake off Chris's hand as he nudged her gently, "I'm tired, le'me sleep." She turned around and tried to ignore the now more urgent prodding. It had taken her ages to fall asleep, and her sleep had been interlaced with a string of nightmares, each spectre more horrifying than the previous one. She was tired, dog-tired.

"Wake up, sleepyhead, it's me, we need to talk. Come on, I need you to wake up."

As Caila half opened her eyes, it dawned on her that it wasn't Chris but Mateos, "Sets, you're back. What time is it?"

"Very late. Or very early. That depends on how you look at it, we need to talk, Caila. Come on down to the Morning Room. Here's your jumper."

Caila stretched and reached out to accept the woollen garment before she, still clutching her pillow, stumbled out of the unusually high bed.

"What's going on?" Chris woke up, as Caila accidently pulled the duvet away from him.

"I need to talk to Caila. We're going downstairs. Is that okay?"

"Yeh, that's fine," not fully awake, Chris grumbled and pulled the duvet back up to his chin, "night."

Drowsy with sleep, Caila followed Mateos downstairs, but when they entered the Morning Room, she shivered as a blast of cold air woke her up properly, "Oi, it's cold in here. Can't we go to the Library?"

- No, I need you to concentrate, – Mateos closed the doors, - and we need complete privacy. Come on, focus. –

Holding on to her pillow, Caila sank down on the worn and itchy carpet, avoiding the flimsy looking three-legged chairs, which would no doubt topple over if she tried to utilise them for their intended purpose. Then she looked Mateos in the eyes, and focussed until there was nothing left in the room except the two of them, - Like this? –

- Yes, that's it. We need to talk about what happened, earlier today. I believe you picked up on something you weren't meant to see. –

- Do you mean the three Neteru; was that you with Devyn and Calia, on Etherun? Or do you mean the horror movie? –

- Both, – Mateos realised he had been right, even if it should have been impossible, - Caila, those were private thoughts, how did you access them? –

He sounded kind and patient, but Caila could tell he was not happy about what happened that afternoon. Understandably so, she would not like it either if her honorary brother dug around in the deepest and darkest corners of her mind, - I don't know how it happened, but it wasn't on purpose. They just kind of flashed into my mind. The first one was okay, but I was not exactly excited about being made partial to that second one.

Is it normal for Neteru to pick up on random thoughts, or memories, from each other? –

- No, it is not, it is incredibly rare, actually. And they were memories.

How do you feel now? I noticed that seeing the Mesu disaster images upset you badly. I'm sorry, I would have talked to you sooner, but I had no choice. We are accelerating the process and I need to be part of the preparations. –

- I understand. But those images, that I picked up on? Is that what would happen if you wouldn't intervene? –

Mateos simply nodded, and Caila swallowed hard, - Surely, no one can be that sick. What was that? Nuclear, chemical, biological? Who did that? –

Mateos noticed the tears streaming down her face, he sat down next to her and pulled her in his arms, - It's all right, Tia, it's not going to happen. We caught it in time.

It is a weapon combining all three; there are some sick minds around. And more than one side would have used it if we hadn't intervened. It is a gruesome weapon, and traces of it would have seeped out through the Earth's atmosphere. The effect would have been devastating. Most life forms on this planet would have been annihilated, dying a slow and painful dead. Some unfortunate survivors would have been left behind, growing increasingly sicker and weaker, on a planet where everything they touched, was poison to them. I don't believe it is relevant who would have started it, because multiple parties would have joined in, and used this weapon. There is no good or bad here; just evil, all over. –

Mateos paused as he looked at Caila's tear-stained face, - But you should not have witnessed any of this. It was unnecessary for you to see it, because none of this is going to happen.

The telumparticula will remove humans quickly, and also what Blue called, the bad stuff; the weapons and the contamination. You will make a new start, on a clean planet. –

Caila rested her head against Mateos, - Thanks for explaining.

In a way, I'm glad to know how bad the alternative would have been, it was just a bit unexpected, – she felt how he was about to retreat from her. - Sets, may I ask something else, please? –

Sensing that her next question was related to her access to his first memory, Mateos agreed reluctantly.

- Has this happened to you before? I mean picking up random memories. You said it was very rare, – when he hesitated, she guessed. - Was it you and Tia? –

- Yes, it was, – he studied the image of Catherine of Braganza, on the stumpwork mirror - You are not going to let this rest, are you? –

Caila shook her head.

- Tia and I were twins, and twins are very uncommon on Etherun. A Neteru can request to have a child, like I explained earlier, but to prevent overpopulation, this is ordinarily only granted when a Neteru dies or leaves the planet. When my parents time came, multiple Neteru had left, and they combined their requests, asking for twins. Twins with part shared DNA.

I can only guess, but I believe that is what caused a strong connection between me and my sister. Tia sometimes caught some of my memories, when I wasn't careful, and I caught some of hers. I think your DNA, the part you inherited from Tia, is causing the same issue. From now on I'll have to be more careful when I'm around you. –

As he studied his honorary sister, Mateos hoped Caila hadn't inherited Calia's ability to scan memories at will.

Sensing how painful this topic was for him, Caila didn't push him for more information, - If you had known, what you were getting yourself into when you inserted that extra bit of DNA into my great-great-something-great-grandmother or father, you would probably have thought about it twice. But you're stuck with me now. Should I be more careful when I'm around you? I wouldn't want you to pick up on all those dark secrets that lie scattered around in my brain. –

- I haven't picked up on anything from you yet, but I probably could if I tried, – he noticed Caila's mischievous grin. - Caila, this is serious. Listen, young lady … –

- Oh, Sets, would it really help if I worried about it? It is what it is.

I promise I will take it seriously, and I'll try to stay out of your mind if you promise to stay out of mine. Don't look so worried, you'll give yourself wrinkles. –

Mateos tried hard, but it was impossible to remain serious when his honorary sister was in such a mood. The resemblance to Calia was uncanny, - It's lucky then, that wrinkles don't show on me, like they show on you. –

He was rewarded with a smack from Caila's pillow, the one she'd clutched close since he'd woken her up.

- Sets, there is one more thing, – Caila was serious again. - It was you, with Devyn and Tia in that first memory, wasn't it? –

When Mateos didn't respond, she continued, - I don't ask because I'm being nosy, or anything. But can you tell me if, after what happened in that memory that I picked up, the three of you were told off for being late? By an older, yellow, no, … a gold coloured Neteru?

I didn't pick that up from you, it just followed when I thought about it, later today. –

- Caila, – Mateos wasn't sure how to react to this revelation, - first of all, how did you know that the gold coloured Neteru was older? –

His seemingly unrelated question surprised Caila, - Well, that's obvious isn't it!

Your colours become richer as you get older. You and Devyn and Tia in that memory were relatively young, I would say the equivalent of a human in their teens.

And most Neteru walking around on the grounds here at Hever, are probably the equivalent of humans in their early to late twenties. And you are, I believe, the equivalent of around fifty. Am I right? But that golden Neteru was a lot older, he was very old. Well over a hundred. –

- That is frighteningly accurate, for most Khered it would be impossible to guess the age of a Neteru. The golden Neteru that you saw, is my great-grandfather. He did indeed tell us off for being late; and the only way for you to have known that, is if you have access to Tia's memories, – he looked at Caila, who was clearly exhausted. - Maybe we should let this rest for now, I promise we'll talk about it later. –

Too tired to object, Caila agreed, - That's fine. And I promise that if I remember anything embarrassing about you, I won't tell anyone. –

Mateos grabbed a throw from the Library and threw it around Caila's shoulders before he walked her back upstairs. Back to her warm bed, and Chris's welcoming arms.

But before he settled down for the night, he looked down on Caila while she drifted off to sleep. He smiled as he was reminded of Devyn's words: '*Boy, are you in trouble*'.

A new beginning

Wednesday 18 September

"Caila, wake up, please."

Not again, Caila buried her head in her pillow, it was way too early.

"Come on, we have guests, remember? Wake up, darling."

Caila sat up reluctantly, and with her eyes still half closed, she challenged her lively husband, "Do you have any idea what time it is?"

"At the third stroke, the time will be seven eleven precisely," Chris announced cheerfully before he tapped the enormous brass warming-pan next to the fireplace, three times. "Time to get up, my sweetheart, we have a busy day ahead of us. Steve, Richard and I were planning to go and explore the castle after breakfast, to see if we can find any more secret passages. Do you want to go with us?"

Caila groaned, "I should have known, put three guys together in a castle and all they can think about are secret passages."

She heard Steve and Richard's door open, and Steve calling out to them.

"Rise and shine, darlings. Time for breakfast."

"All right, I give up," Caila admitted defeat, "I'll be downstairs in five minutes."

Pickings from the restaurant were still rich, so while the group discussed the day ahead, Bluebell and Banjo enjoyed the same luxury salmon breakfast as their human companions.

"You know, I read about a secret passageway leading out of the castle, and there is a secret cave and tunnel structure somewhere on the grounds," the table next to Richard was covered with old maps and floorplans, "maybe they are connected?

This is exciting.

And, Caila? Steve and I decided that we would like to be activated. Chris needs all the help he can get to keep you on the straight and narrow, over the next 107 years."

"That's great news. Although I'm sure I am perfectly capable of keeping myself on the straight and narrow, thank you very much." To prove that point, Caila chased after her hairclip which had escaped while she tried to adjust it; in a perfect curve she'd launched it backwards towards the fire place, where it finally came to rest between the fresh logs.

But, before she had a chance to dig it out, Mateos handed it back to her, "You were saying, Caila?"

"Just a clumsy moment. Good morning, Mateos, I didn't see you come in," Caila accepted her clip and continued her struggle to fix it into her hair.

"Maybe that's because you were too busy chasing that hair thing of yours? Good morning, Chris, Steve, Richard," Mateos moved over to Caila's companions on the other side of the table. "Steve and Richard, have you decided if you want to be activated? You don't need to decide right away, but I can activate your DNA now if you want to, before Caila and I leave you for a while."

Caila threw her liaison a quizzical look, - Are we going somewhere? –

"I will tell you in a minute," Mateos replied out loud, not very subtly reminding her of proper lectanimo etiquette.

"Was that Caila doing lectanimo?" Steve asked.

Mateos nodded, "Yes, and it was not a very polite thing to do in company," he looked accusingly at Caila, who promptly stuck her tongue out at him, and followed it up by her sweetest smile. The Neteru shook his head and returned his attention to Caila's friends.

"Richard and I decided we would like to be activated," Steve glanced at the armour in the corner of the Dining Hall, "Caila said it wouldn't hurt."

"She was right, it is not painful," Mateos assured him, "you won't feel anything, other than me touching your back."

"That's good then," Steve looked slightly less worried, "because Richard has a very low pain threshold."

"Says the man who," Caila cut in, "very nearly fainted when he suffered a papercut."

"Those are official office secrets, I'll let you know," her friend regarded her with an indignant expression, "and it was a very deep cut, it took more than a week to heal."

"Don't remind me," his husband enlightened their friends, as he revealed with an exaggerated sigh, "I was on cleaning duty for more than two weeks."

Mateos rested his hands on Richard's back and concentrated for a few seconds, before repeating the process with Steve, "That's both of you activated, you will start to notice the effects later today."

"Caila, can we talk now?" Mateos turned to his Khered. "Privately, please."

But his Khered, who had been concentrating on lifting a fork loaded with too much scrambled egg to her mouth, had another clumsy moment as she startled and promptly dropped the utensil, sending her egg flying onto her husband's plate and clothes.

After a quick, "Sorry, Chris," she ran after her honorary brother, into the Inner Hall.

Caila sat down in the far corner of the open space, between father and son Tudor and as she regarded the antique Spanish warming table in the middle of the room, she mused that it could be modern again, soon.

"So, today is the day?" she asked, keeping her eyes fixed on the two red-copper bowls.

"Yes, we are almost in place now," Mateos studied the portrait of the rotund king above Caila's head, "we expect to launch within the next fifteen minutes."

"That is earlier than I expected," Caila looked up and sensed Mateos's unease as he was reluctant to meet her eyes. "There is something else, isn't there?"

"Caila, there is something I need to ask," Mateos sounded hesitant, "All Khered, all of the original twelve, are required to witness the Event. However, because you are in a special position I requested, and I have been granted, an exemption for you. It is too dangerous for you to leave these grounds before the Event, and I would prefer it if you accepted."

"But you didn't really want to ask, because you expected me to refuse?"

Mateos didn't respond, fearing she might take it as a challenge.

"Are any of the others exempt?" Caila pressed, she needed to know, but her liaison stalled. "Come on, Mateos, we crossed that 'I'm not at liberty to divulge'-line a long time ago."

"There is one other and he accepted, Devyn will witness the Event for him. Caila, be sensible, the moment you leave this place, you put yourself in danger." Mateos forced himself to remain composed, if he pushed too hard, he knew she would insist on going.

"Where would I have to go, to witness the Event?"

"It would have to be somewhere crowded."

'Caila, please,' he thought, 'don't do it'.

"Why would they like us to witness it?" Caila felt Mateos was attempting to manipulate her into accepting the exemption, but it didn't feel quite right. "Don't look at me like that, I can't decide if I don't have all the facts."

"They would like you to be able to give an accurate account of the Event," his voice was strained, "but I can do that for you."

"When I voted for this option, I became co-responsible for the consequences, … for this reset," Caila attempted to articulate why she needed to do this. "I need to witness it, I have no choice."

"Caila, you do have a choice," Mateos felt his patience slip. "Just say no!"

Raising her chin, Caila determinately looked at her liaison, "I will go."
Then feeling how he was about to lose his temper, she pleaded, "Please understand why I need to witness this, I really can't accept the exemption."

Mateos fumed, "I forbid it."

"You what?" Caila was momentarily stunned. "You forbid it? In your bloody dreams, Mateos. I told you the reasons why I need to go, and I will go." Caila stood, ready to walk out, "You can come with me, or I will go out alone."

Mateos realised he could not stop his Khered from walking out, but he was sure as hell not going to let her leave this place on her own, and he snapped at her back, "We'll go together." Taking a moment to compose himself, he decided to give Caila a proper dressing down later. Right now, he had to concentrate on keeping her safe and there was only one sure way to do that, "Do you remember when I took you to see Etherun? How we travelled there?"

Not convinced that this wasn't a ploy to distract her, Caila eyed him suspiciously, but she nodded anyway.

"I use a similar method to travel between places here on Mesu, and I can take you with me."

Caila nodded again.

"I need you to touch my hands and accept the image I project to you; and the moment we arrive there, I want you to cloak yourself. Do you think you can do that?"

Remembering the raid on her home and her earlier cloaking fiasco, Caila hesitated, maybe this wasn't such a good idea after all, "I think so."

"Just remember how Devyn explained it," Mateos reminded her. "We'll do a test run inside the castle, before we do it for real. Are you ready?"

As Caila held out her hands and closed her eyes, she caught a brief glimpse of one of the little girl's bedrooms in the '*dog kennels*', and when she opened her eyes again, they were in the pretty green room. She quickly imagined her soft warm coat and looked up at Mateos, "Is this acceptable?"

"Almost, just cloak a bit earlier and we're there. We need to go for real now," he decided to give his Khered one last chance to change her mind, "Are you sure you want to do this?"

Caila nodded, she had no choice, "Yes, I'm sure."
She held out her hands, but then remembered she hadn't told anyone she'd be going out. She needed to let Chris know, - Chris … –

***

London Victoria? Caila was surprised, only five days ago, she'd walked over there on the other side of the concourse before Rob caught up with her on their way to the office. She breathed in deeply when she, once again, smelled the familiar aroma of damp clothes, bacon and coffee.

Then, out of a seemingly unbreakable habit, Caila looked up at the announcement boards, heralders of many delays and cancellations, it was 8:38 and 59 seconds.

She startled when Mateos roughly pushed her out of the crowds, closer to the wall, and hissed, - I told you to cloak. –

And then, when she looked at her image in the shop window, Caila noticed that something had gone terribly wrong. Whilst attempting to contact her husband at the last moment, she'd morphed into a perfect copy of Chris.

- I'm sorry, it was a mistake, – Caila scrambled to rectify her error but made it worse by losing her disguise altogether when she was distracted by Rob, who rushed across the concourse towards the exit.

Noticing his former colleague, Rob came to a sudden halt and called out, "Hey Cai! Caila! Where have you been? The police were in the office on Monday, asking about you."

Caila panicked. She heard Mateos cursing behind her as Rob's insistent shouting attracted the attention of armed police officers.

One of them mouthed something into his radio while they started moving towards her. Desperately, Caila attempted to back away as the officers closed in on her, but when she looked over her shoulder, she noticed two more policemen approaching her from the other side.

- Caila, cloak! – Mateos frantically tried to get through to his Khered. - Now! –

But Caila, paralysed with fear as the officers raised their guns, managed nothing more than a softly whispered, "I'm sorry, Sets."

Then, Caila felt a cool breeze, and the station smelled like her garden in spring.

She was not the only one who noticed, commuters smiled, and looked up to see where it came from.

And then, there was nothing. Only the cool breeze of spring, lingering in the air.

The cool breeze of spring

Juliet had already been in the office for almost an hour, and it was stuffy as ever, with the heating on too high and too early in the year. She watched Jonathan impatiently pacing behind Rob's desk, he had asked his analyst to be in at eight-thirty and it was now eight-thirty-eight.

The office started to fill up slowly. Juliet looked at Caila's empty chair and wondered what had happened to her. On Monday the police had been around asking questions. They wanted to know when she'd last been in the office, and where she would be if she was not at home. As far as Juliet knew, they'd left empty handed. Which was fine by her, they had been extremely disagreeable, and Ginny had left the office in tears after they'd questioned her. Poor girl.

That's better, Juliet felt a cool breeze touching the back of her neck and smiled, it smelled like spring. She looked up from the document she was editing.

Her colleagues, they all smiled: Jonathan, Ginny, Alice and Mark. And then they vanished.

***

Jenny arrived at London Bridge. Why had she ever given up her job in Tunbridge Wells? This commute was killing her. She had planned to rent a flat in the city but had been beaten by the astronomical London property prices. As an econometrician, she should have known better, that was the kind of thing she should have foreseen.

Jenny sniffed as she walked past the pastry stall. Should she? No, she shouldn't. She definitely shouldn't.

"One bacon butty please, with butter and mayo. How's business today, Toby?"

While she frantically searched for her purse and kept up a mostly one-sided conversation with Toby, she dropped her bag, scattering her precious possessions over the grubby station floor. "Awww, ..." Clumsily she dived down to grab her stuff, all the while muttering to herself.

When she finally looked back up at the counter, Toby was gone.

Jenny straightened herself and looked around. The station was empty, everyone had disappeared. There was just a cool breeze and the fresh scent of spring. And her bacon butty on the counter.

***

"Good morning, Luke!" From behind the reception desk, Sasha brightly welcomed her colleague into the office. "How are you today?"

Why she insisted on saying the same thing every morning, even when it was clearly not a good day, was beyond Luke, "Good morning, Sasha." Luke had learned that this was the correct response to avoid further questions. He quickly walked to his desk and hiding behind his monitor he checked the little clock in the bottom right hand corner of his screen, it was eight-thirty-five and twenty-nine seconds. They were the first ones in the office.

Chris had not been at work since Monday, when he'd worked from home. Yesterday, police officers had visited the office, asking all kinds of stupid questions.

"Do you know where Chris is?"

Luke had told them, he did not.

"Do you and Chris discuss friends, outside of work?"

"No."

"Have you and Chris, ever discussed places where he likes to go to?"

"No."

Then the detective asked him if he and Chris talked about anything at all at work.

To which Luke had answered, "Yes."

At that point, the detective had let out a deep sigh and asked him, "What do you mostly talk about then, with Chris?"

"Design patterns, in C#."

In despair, the detective had walked out, and Luke had observed him talking to Sasha whilst pointing back at him. Sasha had shaken her head and tapped her nose, and when the detective came back into Mark's office, he'd instructed Luke to go back to work.

Luke wondered how anyone like that could ever be expected to solve a crime.

He hoped Chris would be back soon, he'd read an interesting article and wanted to discuss it with him. Luke checked the time again, eight-thirty-nine and fifty-three seconds; he glanced over his screen.

Sasha carried a glass of water as she walked back to her desk, followed by Mark.

A cool breeze followed them into the office, and the air smelled of spring.

Then his colleagues vanished, only an empty glass and a puddle of water remained.

Luke stood, and walked over to the window. He witnessed how the houses across the street disappeared, together with the street lights and traffic signs. They all vanished until only nature remained; where buildings had been, only bare soil was left behind. And the only sounds he heard, were the soft hush of gently waving branches and the melodious chirping of birds.

Luke picked up his bag, his little Puccini bust, and his and Chris's 'I Wear Glasses So I Can C#' mugs, then he walked out of the office for the very last time.

Once outside, he looked back and witnessed how the office disappeared, like all other buildings it appeared to sink into the soil. He paused and thought, he should go to Hever, that is where Caila was, Chris's wife. It would not be much further than twenty kilometres, he would walk four one-hour stretches and take three 15-minute breaks, he could be there before two o'clock.

***

"No, no, no! It's not fair. You never allow me to do anything. Everyone is going," Rebecca was outraged. Tightly holding onto Flock's reins, she yelled at her father, "if you loved me, you would let me go."

"Becky, we told you before, you are too young. All the others are at least sixteen," Rebecca's father despaired. "Besides, Mrs White won't allow it, not without our consent."

"Good morning, Mr Riverton, how are you?" Joan White had noticed the escalating argument and decided to investigate. "Hello, Rebecca, are you ready for your camping trip?"

Determined that she would not have her own way this time, Rebecca's father replied for his daughter, "Rebecca will not join you on your outing, Mrs White. I was under the impression that a signed consent form was required, or am I mistaken?"

An astonished Joan looked from father to daughter, "But I received your consent form earlier this week. Please, let me check for you, Mr Riverton. Yes, here it is, signed by both you and your wife."

The adults turned to face the teenager to demand an explanation.

But the furious 12-year-old had other plans, she mounted her horse and rode off, quickly disappearing behind the dense treeline behind the stables.

When Rebecca returned, one hour later, her father and riding instructor had vanished. The stables and fencing were also gone.

Rebecca dismounted and plopped onto a tree trunk, with a heartfelt, "Isn't that just typical for adults, Flock!" before sinking her teeth into her marmite sandwich.

***

"No, sir, this is exactly to your brother's specifications. Once the room is sealed it cannot be opened from the inside, for one full week. Unless a separate release code is entered on the outside panel, to confirm that it is safe to exit."

George peered inside the sparsely-stocked bunker, which was meant to guarantee his brother's family's survival in case of an uninvited visitor, or a nuclear attack. He didn't understand too much of the contractor's over the top explanation of the latest reinforcement technology: multiple layered concrete, alloy combinations, or something like that. All he understood was that, in the absence of his brother, he had to sign off on the blasted thing. Where was his brother anyway?

"And you are in possession of this release code?"

The contractor nodded.

"And you insist that before I sign off on this project, I lock myself into this vault? I then need to unsuccessfully attempt to exit these quarters, using my internal code. And then, following a successful failure, I will contact you and you will release me from my confinement by entering your code on the exterior keypad?"

"Yes, sir, that is exactly right," the contractor was close to despair, first he'd fruitlessly tried to convince George's brother to drop this particular safety feature, and now he had to convince George of the benefits of the opposite. "Your brother believed it would prevent his children from being released into a potentially hazardous situation."

"Let's get on with it then," George checked his watch, "I need to leave in twenty minutes." Then he held his hand out to his fiancée, "Oh no, my darling, you're going in with me. If I get stuck in there, then at least we will be stuck together."

With a playful pull, he ensured himself of her company inside his brother's new metal mini-mansion, but before he closed the heavy door, George checked one last time with the contractor, "You are sure that you have the correct exit code, Mr … uhm", what was his name again? "…, Smickolth?"

John Smickolth nodded, relieved that he was making progress; this project had been a pain, but it would provide a boost to his business.

Locking the door, George considered he would have felt better about it, if that bloke hadn't looked so damn nervous. He gave his fiancée a cheeky grin and a kiss, "Cosy, and still all the mod-cons one could wish for."

"Just get us out of here, darling. I wasn't planning on spending my hen party in an overpriced Wendy house. Let me see that code please."

Gemma entered the release code and her fiancé attempted to open the door.

"I would call that a successful failure, wouldn't you?" but when George pushed the speaker button on the intercom, he was met by only silence from the other side.

"Come on, Smickolth," he mumbled, "answer me, please. We haven't got all day."

He checked the basic communication device, there was nothing obviously wrong with it. Nothing could be wrong with it, stripped from all modern technology it was designed to remain in working order even if the rest of the country was completely wiped out. He tried again, with the same unsatisfactory result, "Darling, I believe we just got the day off. Would you like to …" he scanned the room for useful items, "… would you like to read a book or play a game?"

"George, that isn't funny, let me try," Gemma hit the speaker button a couple of times. "It's dead!"

"Don't worry, darling, they'll have us out of here in no time at all. Worst case," George teased his fiancée, "we are stuck here for a week."

Neither of them realised at that moment, how dead-on he was.

***

Jenny left the deserted station, munching her bacon sandwich.

London was gone, and to her big surprise, she wasn't at all surprised. While London Bridge station disappeared behind her, she turned to where she expected Tooley street to be. It was easier than expected, only one single building was left standing in this big city.

Two minutes later she walked into a cycle shop, where she selected a sturdy white bike and a pretty wicker basket to hold her bag, before exchanging her smart-casual for more comfortable sporting gear.

As Jenny stuffed her work clothes into her basket, a high-pitched scream made her jump. Quietly as she could, she sneaked to the window and peered out.

"Ahwww," she laughed nervously, when she saw two cats hissing at each other, as a mouse made a lucky escape, "you scared me, you naughty kitties."

Walking back to her bicycle, she noticed the jackets next to the till. They were to die for! Tentatively, she checked the price tags and sighed; the amazing coats were way above her budget.

Or, not? A grin spread across her face as she remembered the current state of the economy. She found two in her size and bagged them both, a red one to wear straight away, and a purple one for later. As an afterthought, she also grabbed a helmet and some energy bars.

Pedalling south, she looked over her shoulder and witnessed how the cycle shop followed the rest of London, into the ground.

Ten minutes later Jenny arrived at Kia Oval, where she found a woman in sensible blue biking gear waiting for her. She had managed to attach several bags and baskets to her bicycle, and greeted Jenny pleasantly.

"Hi, I'm Juliet. I believe we're riding to Hever together. Would you like something to drink, before we set off?"

"Oh yes, please. Thank you. My name is Jenny. I completely forgot to take drinks, but I have some energy bars. Would you like one? There is berry-mix, chocolate, apple-cinnamon, and honey."

Juliet chewed her mixed berry bar in silence while Jenny told her about her experience with her dropped bag, her bacon butty and the quarrelling cats.

Before they mounted their bikes to head south, Juliet knew all about Jenny's lucky charm, a little wooden cat she always carried with her, and about her disastrous crush on the muscular personal trainer at her local gym.

Older or wiser

Chris, Steve and Richard had only just finished their breakfast when Devyn arrived at Hever.

"Good morning Chris, I'm glad to see that your guests arrived safely," Mateos's friend looked around the Dining Hall. "Where is Caila?"

"Oh, hi, Devyn. How are you? This is Steve, and this is Richard. Caila, as far as I know, has gone out with Mateos," Chris wasn't worried, as long as his wife was with their Neteruian liaison, she would be safe. "About twenty minutes ago they went into the Inner Hall and by the sounds of it, they had an almighty argument before they left."

"Would you mind if I hung around for a bit? I need to talk to Mateos," he knew his friend had been dead set on keeping Caila safely inside the castle, something that obviously hadn't worked out. "So, ..." he turned to the two new guys, "how are you two getting on here? I notice that Mateos activated your Khered DNA."

Five minutes later, as they walked from the Dining Hall to the Drawing Room, to show Devyn the baby grand piano, Caila and Mateos returned to the Inner Hall.

Devyn looked to his left at the exact moment they reappeared, which was only seconds before Mateos decided to give Caila a long overdue piece of his mind.

Mateos's voice was loud and clear, "Do you have any idea how close you came to being killed out there? I explicitly told you that this was too dangerous; and I clearly remember instructing you to cloak. I took you with me because we had very little time and you left me no choice. Next time, Tia, I would appreciate it if you listened to my advice. And accepted it! I am the oldest!"

An outraged and shaken Caila didn't hold back either, "I told you it was an accident and I apologised. What more do you want, do you think I enjoyed that?
And, for your information, Sets, we are exactly the same age, we are twins. Remember?!"

"Twins?!" Mateos furiously spit back. "Yes, technically we are, but my production was started before yours. That makes me the elder."

"That may be so, but we were delivered at the same time, in the same pod. Which basically means that, …" Caila stuck out her chin, attempting to look taller, "if my production was started after yours, then I developed faster than you did. That makes me smarter than you."

Devyn smiled, all this sounded remarkably familiar to him, but when he noticed the stunned look on Chris's face, to whom this was obviously news, he decided to put a stop to it. Attempting to hide his smile, he rushed into the Inner Hall and cut Mats off before he could tell Caila that she'd slowed down since delivery was taken, "Mats, Cals. Maybe you should turn it down a notch, you have an audience."

When Caila and Mateos turned towards him, the startled looks on their faces proved too much, and Devyn laughed out loud, "Come on you two, you've had this argument before, more than once. I'll take those three over there into the Drawing Room, while you sort this out."

Then he addressed the two squabblers privately, - I don't know how many rules you have broken and frankly I don't want to know. I saw you arrive, just now. Don't worry I won't tell anyone, and I was the only one who noticed. All I care about is that you arrived back safely, both of you. You two sort things out between the two of you before you come and see us in the other room. You will have some explaining to do. –

With that, he ushered the others into the Drawing Room and closed the door firmly on the bickering siblings.

"I'm sorry, I panicked," Caila flopped down on the bench in the alcove, off the Inner Hall, "please, understand why I had to go, it's not something I enjoyed, but I needed to witness the Event."

"All I want, is to keep you safe. I would never forgive myself if something happened to you, especially if it was because of something I could have prevented," Mateos sat next to his Khered, "but I shouldn't have shouted. I'm sorry."

"Devyn said we had this argument before. Is that true? I assume he meant you and Tia."

"A number of times," a peacock landed on the armrest next to Mateos, and the Neteru smiled at the beautiful butterfly as it showed of its bright colours, "and almost word for word. My next move would have been to tell you that you obviously slowed down since delivery was taken."

"Sets, ... Mateos, we both know that I am not Tia. But there is a bond between us, a very strong bond, and it is getting stronger every day. When you started that argument, I just reacted," Caila hesitated, she didn't want to ask this, but she had no choice. "I would understand if you wanted to assign me a different contact. This, ... these memories and everything else, it must be difficult for you."

"Is that what you want?" the butterfly glided onto Mateos's outstretched arm. "A new liaison?"

"No, of course not," entranced, Caila watched the peacock as Mateos allowed it to move onto her open hand, "I wouldn't know what to do without you, I'd miss you like mad. You are like a big brother to me. But I don't want you to get hurt."

"Then let's keep it like this," Mateos eyes followed the butterfly as it went in search for a safe place on the gallery high above the Hall, "No doubt, there will be more surprises in store for us, and it will take adjustments on both our parts, but I'd miss you too. And Caila, I know that you are not Calia, but a lot of the time you feel very familiar to me, like a sister." Then he teased her, "A *big* brother, eh?"

Caila looked for something to throw, but when she didn't find anything, she settled for simply saying, "Only as a matter of speech, of course."

"Mateos, can I ask you something else, before we go in there?" Caila nodded towards the Drawing Room, and the Neteru eyed her questioningly.

"London was gone," she'd seen what was left of the city, "how much of the world has been removed?"

"We used the domus of activated Khered as midpoints, and only what lies within a 17- kilometre radius of those points has been preserved. With the exception, of course, of the nasty things, they are all gone. You have 28 days to forage for whatever you need. Then these areas will also be purged and, for you, only Hever and its surrounding village will remain."

"Tiny, but perfectly formed," Caila studied a crack in the wall, less infrastructure meant less worries, "I can live with that."

"You won't have a choice, but I will be here to help you," her big brother reassured her. "Now, we should probably go in there to explain what's going on."

Five pairs of eyes looked up at them, when they entered the Drawing Room. Bluebell and Banjo's promptly closed again, and the felines resumed their favourite pastime. Devyn didn't look up from the piano, he continued to play a gentle melody, as he enquired, "All sorted?"

But the other three men stared at them as if they saw
Mateos and Caila for the first time. Then Chris asked,
"Twins?"

"You can tell them everything," Mateos nodded at Caila
while he went against his own lectanimo etiquette, and
added, - As much as you believe you can tell them. The
entire castle is safe, there is no risk of anyone listening in
now that the guards have left. –

"This is going to sound incredible," while she shifted
some cushions and sat next to her husband, Caila started her
explanation, "I know I said it before, but it is true. … Again.
Steve, Richard, you don't know this yet, but I have been
developing a bit faster and further than other activated
Khered.

Chris, I know that Mateos told you that this is because I am
a first order Khered, and I never denied it because it is true,
but there is more to it. I couldn't tell you earlier, because it
could hurt Mateos if anyone overheard, … if it got out. And
I don't want that to happen."

"I can trust you, can't I?" Caila looked at Steve and Richard.
"I know you never blabbered, Steve."

"Don't worry, I'm not much of a '*blabber*' either."
Richard reassured her.

"Right then, there is not that much to tell, actually,"
Caila decided to go for the bare-bones version. "Apart from
Khered DNA, Mateos inserted some extra DNA in my
ancestor, it was a string that belonged to his sister. We

believe it is that extra piece of DNA, that causes me to develop at the pace I do.

I also sometimes get some memories that belonged to Calia," Caila carefully avoided using Sets nickname for his sister. "And, apparently, I look a bit like her, we are the same beautiful shade of red.

But, because inserting that extra bit of DNA was not part of the official experiment, it could land Mateos in a lot of trouble. And possibly, me as well.

The only other person who knows about this is Devyn, he found out last Monday. He already gave Mateos a serious telling-off, but Mateos's secret is safe with him, and they are still best friends.

All of you, in this room, are my best friends. And you know that I don't use that word lightly, certainly not in the Facebook sense of the word. I hope we can stay friends and keep this piece of information safely between the six of us." She scanned the room before adding one last little word, "Please?"

"Calia was my friend, a very good friend. And although I don't approve of what Mats did, the result is not too bad," Devyn was the first to speak. "Caila, it's not only the way you look like Calia. The only ones who ever managed to get Mats to lose his temper like that, are you and Cals, you know exactly how to push all the right buttons. I'd be happy to be friends with you," he turned to Mateos. "Mats, can I see you for a minute. I need to get back to Lucas, before we review the effect of the telumparticula, later today."

"And I thought we were done with the big revelations. You could have knocked me down with a feather, Caila, when you said you were twins. But your secret is safe with me, with both of us. Right, Steve?"

"We were best friends before and we still are, I won't tell on your ..., what is he of yours? ... Your genetic brother? Half-twin? Well anyway, I won't tell on either of you," Steve agreed with his better half, "Mateos has been very kind to us yesterday and this morning, it won't be too hard to be friends with him."

Caila looked at her husband.

"I told you before, that I suspected you were from another planet; Etherun is just a couple of extra lightyears away," Chris had no problems with his new brother in law. "But seriously, darling, could you please try to take Mateos's advise a bit more often? He only wants to keep you safe. And, so do I."

"Hear, hear. So do we all," Steve concurred. "And, now tell us, what did you get up to this morning, to get Mateos in such a state? Or shouldn't we ask?"

"Yes, you may, and I probably should tell you about it now," Caila nestled closer to Chris. "You know that the Event was scheduled for today, for this afternoon at the latest?

Well, it just happened. Earlier, Mateos explained to me that the twelve original Khered were required to witness it, but that he'd got me an exemption because it was too risky for me to leave the castle grounds. We had a bit of a discussion and, in the end, we agreed we should go together. Would you like me to tell you about it?"

When they regarded her in solemn silence, Caila continued gently, "It was very quick. We witnessed the Event at London Victoria, and one moment everyone was stressed out and rushing about. And then there was this cool breeze, and it smelled lovely and fresh. Almost like spring. I could see how people relaxed and smiled, and next, less than a second later, they had all vanished."

"So, they didn't notice anything?" Steve wanted to know. "No pain, no fear?"

"No, it was exactly as Mateos promised. That last moment was peaceful and relaxed, I'm sure it was the same for your families," Caila assured him, before pausing to let the news sink in.

"But there is more. Afterwards we went outside, and London had disappeared. Mateos told me that it is not just London, the Neteru left only a 17-kilometre radius around Hever intact. We have four weeks to stock up, until the telumparticula will be reactivated, and then most of that will be gone as well. We'll have to make do with only Hever and the village."

"That could attract survivors to this area," Chris noted worriedly.

"There may be accidental survivors," he explained to Richard and Steve, "and since there is a good chance, they are officials who bunked it out in a shelter, they could be hostile."

"We don't expect there to be very many, if any, of those bunkers, and we don't know where they are," Caila said. "But Chris is right, there is a very real chance that, if anyone survived in such a shelter, they harbour less than friendly feelings towards us."

"Then that drawbridge could be useful after all, we should see if it still works," the idea of reinstating the fortifications appealed to Richard. "And also, that portcullis."

"Yes, we should," his husband agreed, "but if the prime minister drops in, accompanied by some royalty, I look forward to seeing them help us dig for, uhm, … for survival." Steve pictured it in his mind and laughed, he liked what he saw.

"We should stock up on wellies then, and on spades," Chris showed his practical side. "But maybe, we should do some food shopping first, before the others arrive. Waitrose lies easily within our 17-kilometer range, I believe even most of Tunbridge Wells might still be there.
Do you know how much time we have before they arrive?"

"No. But we can ask Mateos, when he comes back."

"What would you like to know?" Mateos appeared at the Drawing Room door. "I'm sorry, I don't have long, today is going to be packed with evaluations and meetings, so you won't see very much of me until sometime tomorrow."

"That's okay, I can be quick," Caila gathered her thoughts. "First, Steve and Richard have decided that they are happy to be your friends; second, Chris is happy to stay friends with you; third, can we go out today; fourth, when can we expect the others, my chosen ones; fifth, do we still have water, electricity and gas; and sixth, did you remember to move Juliet's menagerie?"

Nonplussed, Mateos replied without hesitation, "First, thank you Steve and Richard, I'd be happy to be friends with you as well. Second, Chris I am glad we can stay friends. Besides you and I need to pool our resources, to keep Caila out of trouble. Third, yes, you can go out, the next seven days you should be safe. Fourth, I think Juliet and Jenny will arrive around one o'clock, Luke won't be far behind and Peter will arrive later this afternoon. Fifth, your taps and most of your appliances will still work, it is not gas or electricity as you know it, but it is safe to use, safer even and cleaner. I'll let you know if this remains available after the first 28 days. And sixth, Juliet's menagerie? I remembered   Bluebell   and   Banjo,   didn't   I? Now, I really need to go. I promised to visit Devyn's group before the assembly."

Before he left them, he quickly added, "Have fun today", before he disappeared.

"That gives us a couple of hours before our new housemates arrive," Caila said. "Any suggestions?"

"We can forget about our house, that will be gone," with a hint of regret, Steve cut his last ties with his old life, "but we could have a look at yours, to see if you want to salvage anything before it disappears."

"Let's do that," Chris agreed, "and then we'll drop in at Waitrose on our way back to Hever. We should prepare something nice for dinner tonight, now that we are allowed to cook hot food again.

I wonder if those cars still work? On Mateos's cleaner energy source, of course. But first, let's find ourselves rooms in the Edwardian Wing, and have a quick shower. The castle is nice, but the facilities are a bit basic."

Chris and Caila moved into the same room, where they'd spent one glorious Valentine's weekend, so many years ago. And, after a tour of the bed and breakfast, Steve and Richard decided on the suite next door; furnished with a spectacular four-poster bed and a chaise longue.

When they eventually regrouped in the breakfast room, Richard asked Chris to settle a dispute on the correct pronunciation of that particular piece of furniture. But their friend diplomatically avoided taking sides by suggesting they should settle for, 'a long chair', until they'd had a chance to look it up in a dictionary.

Munching on apples, which they'd picked up in the orchard, the foursome made their way to the car park, where Steve nudged Caila and remarked that he looked forward to checking out at the supermarket without that infernal machine telling him he had an unexpected item in the bagging area.

Little did they suspect, that today, the unexpected item would appear well before they'd even reached the checkout.

.

Unexpected item in bagging area

"It should be safe to cross now."

"I wasn't checking for vehicles," out of habit, Chris had indeed stopped to check for cars before turning into the road, "but the Highway Code states clearly that after an apocalypse non-mechanic horsepower poses a significant risk to health and safety."

He pulled out and drove slowly past the Henry VIII pub. The roads were deserted, and his concern that they would have to slalom around scores of abandoned vehicles proved unfounded; the telumparticula appeared to have removed all cars which had been occupied, together with their drivers.

"Remind me to ask Mateos about zoo animals," Caila spotted a team of galloping horses, "horses are one thing but coming up close and personal with a pride of lions is quite another."

Edenbridge felt alien, yet familiar. The abandoned High Street was in stark contrast to the unconcerned one-handed clock which, oblivious of the current state of affairs, informed them that it was sometime between ten and eleven.

Boyce's bakery was deserted, with their freshly baked sausage rolls at risk of going stale; until Steve alarmed Chris by requesting an emergency stop, before rushing out to bravely rescue his favourite pastry.

The doors to their old home were barricaded. And when they peered through the window, they were confronted with a scene which likened the before-picture of a reality tv show, where an army of declutter-ers and cleaners were called in to tackle years of neglect.

Chris picked up a large branch and shattered a window.

"Bastards, that was completely unnecessary," expecting chaos, Caila had not been prepared to encounter this degree of destruction. "What did they expect to find inside a television?"

Upstairs wasn't much better; the contents of their closets were strewn across the floor and the mattress had been cut open. Close to tears, she stared at their torn wedding picture. From the corner of her eyes, Caila caught a reflection of Steve and Richard in the mirror, they'd lost everything. At least she and Chris had some mementoes of their old life left.

She took a deep breath and turned around, "How terribly rude of them, if any of them were still around, I would tell their mothers to put them on the naughty step."

The three men watched in stunned silence as she picked up a Welsh love spoon, wiped it clean and dropped it in her bag. Then they roared with laughter.

"We were so worried about your feelings and you threaten them with the naughty step," Richard picked up a chair and, failing to notice its half-broken leg, made to sit down on it. Then, with an elegance that could not be

matched by the most accomplished of dancers, he slid down
onto the beige carpet.

"If you are quite finished, darling?" Steve hiccupped,
while he attempted to pull his unfortunate husband up from
the litter-strewn floor. "This is starting to resemble a
comedy of errors."

Chris lent him a hand, and together they pulled Richard free
from the splintered remnants of the chair.

"Let's just find what we want to keep and get out of here,
it will all be gone in 28 days anyway," Chris smiled when
he picked up his new purple sweater. "It was only last
Friday you gave me this, but it feels like a lifetime ago."

They ended up taking lots, cramming the van and their
old car with tools, books, clothes, pictures and Christmas
decorations. Caila also insisted on taking their drinks
cabinet, because it had funny rotating shelves. And at the
last minute she ran back into the garage to collect a battery-
operated motion detector, in disguise of a blue tit. Caila
explained that the constant twittering of this very lightly
triggered device had irritated Chris immensely. So, when
they'd moved into this house, he had banned it to the garage.
But one day, when he walked back home from the station,
he was once again greeted by the same insistent twittering.
He'd scoured the street to locate the source of the irritating
sound, only to discover a real life exuberant little bird,
greeting him from a tree across his new home.

Steve and Richard followed Chris's sixteen-year old people carrier to the supermarket in the centre of town where they parked close to the entrance, and while Caila lingered at the plant display, they were startled by a soft gurgling sound.

- I believe that sound originates from the perambulator, by the window, – until he spoke, none of them had noticed OOVII had accompanied them on their outing, - it is next to the shopping trolleys. I presume it is a young human, attempting to attract your attention. This is an unexpected development!

Are those your new companions, Caila? –

Caila and Chris looked up at the corvid who'd landed in the tree next to the terrace while they turned to walk towards the pram.

- Good morning, OOVII. I hadn't noticed that you accompanied us. Yes, that's Steve and Richard. Mateos only activated them this morning, so I'll have to translate, – "Oops," Caila stumbled as she looked over her shoulder to introduce her friends. "That handsome corvid up there, is OOVII, he is our crow Khered contact. OOVII just told us he spotted a baby in that pram over there."

An infant crinkled its tiny nose, as it noticed the four unfamiliar faces peering into its cream-coloured pram.

"Yes, that is definitely a baby. I don't believe it is a hostile armed official, so we'd better take it home with us," Caila looked up to find the three men watching her in anticipation.

Then Chris crouched down and picked up a handbag, which had been dropped next to the pram, "Do you think this is the mother's? Maybe we can find out its name."

After some rummaging, he pulled out a mobile, "That phone isn't much help, it is stone dead. Oh, hold on. I think the baby's mother's name is Mrs A. Whiteshift." Chris held up a credit card, before replacing the phone and card wallet to resume his search, "That's better, it's a family photo."

He showed it to the others and turned it around, "but there's nothing written on the back, and there is nothing with the baby's name on it in here, and no address. There aren't any car keys either, so they must have lived close to the supermarket. Definitely, somewhere in town.

I think we should take this bag and keep it, it's the only thing the baby has left of their family."

"Thanks, it's not much, but it's better than nothing. I'll push the pram if you get the trolleys," Caila caressed the baby's cheek and smiled when she was rewarded with a little yawn. "I think we need to do some extra shopping."

They got their grown-up food shopping out of the way before they visited the unfamiliar baby isle, where once again Caila was treated to three enquiring stares.

"What? Oh, no...! How should I know? I don't know anything about babies. You choose," Caila singled Richard out, "you are an engineer. That's got to be better than an analyst or a coder."

But Richard raised his arms in mock despair, "Sorry, baby changing was not on the curriculum when I was at uni."

They studied the tiny baby and then stared at the well-stocked racks, stuffed with an otherworldly assortment of diapers and formula, until Chris pulled out a random box.

"This picture looks a bit like him, or her; it says nine to fourteen kilos. How heavy do you think he is?"

Four pairs of eyes observed the now blissfully sleeping baby, trying to guess its weight, but then Richard's face lighted up.

"There are scales in the veg section."

"I've always known that I married you for more than your good looks," Steve padded his husband on the shoulders, "Come on, Caila, lead the way."

Richard had been right, but once again, when they arrived at the scales, the men watched Caila expectantly.

"You want me to put it on there?" Caila panicked. "I don't know how to hold it. What if I drop it? Or hurt it? And those scales are cold and dirty."

"Darling," Chris laughed, "since this whole thing began, you have been as cool as those cucumbers over there. And now you panic over a tiny little baby? Come on, let me do it. Put some tissues on the scales, please."

Chris carefully picked up the baby and pulled a face, "It definitely needs those diapers. Right little boy or girl, you weigh about six kilos." He returned the baby who was still miraculously quiet, to the pram.

Since they hadn't the foggiest how many diapers a baby went through in a day, or how fast the baby would grow, they decided to commandeer all packs in that size and above. They also took most of the formula, and, just to be on the safe side, a bit of everything else from the baby isle.

With the unexpected guest, expecting a comfortable ride home, they appropriated an extra vehicle. Another people carrier, for which they found the keys in one of the abandoned handbags in the supermarket, it had a baby seat neatly strapped to one of its backseats.

"Caila, darling, I never approved of your choice of car. It is not very trendy," Steve confided in Caila as she took possession of her new set of wheels, "but now it starts to make sense. And it still looks better than a white van."

When they arrived back home, just after one o'clock, they found Jenny and Juliet patiently waiting for them on the terrace outside the moat restaurant, their new bicycles parked in the shade under the barbecue area.

At the sight of the two familiar women, Caila bolted towards the younger one, "Jenny, I'm so glad to see you!" she gave the astonished girl a quick hug before pointing towards Steve, who was reluctantly pushing the pram. "You know about babies, don't you? You told me that you did loads of babysitting."

Overwhelmed by the enthusiastic welcome, Jenny merely nodded.

"Oh, bless you! Jenny, that's Chris, my husband, and that is Richard. And the guy over there, the one with the pram, that's Steve, he's married to Richard. In the pram, we have a little baby, we found her at the supermarket this morning. Can you please help us? We're at a bit of a loss. We don't know if it's a boy or a girl, or their name, or how old it is. I think it needs changing and feeding, but we have no idea about the how, or what, or how much."
Jenny performed a mock curtsey.

"Hi you'all, nice to meet you," she greeted the others hurriedly and rushed over to inspect the pram's contents. "Ohw, you are so pretty! I'm Jenny, what is your name, little one? We'll take very good care of you. Awww, you need a clean nappy and a nice warm bottle, don't you? Are you a boy or a girl?"
She looked back up at the others, "We'll have to think of a pretty name."

Steve shrugged.

"Don't you mind all these strange people, little one, I'll take care of you," Jenny took control of the pram and demanded, "Caila, where do we go?" Then she instructed a bewildered Steve, "I am going to need baby wipes, powder, diapers, a bottle warmer, a bottle and formula. Then I'll teach you how to change him. Or her."
Jenny resolutely marched off with the pram, accompanying Caila to the cottages, leaving Steve no choice but to follow them with the requested baby items, which Richard had hurriedly and cowardly handed over to him.

Chris and Richard walked over to greet Juliet, who had followed the baby scene with an amused expression on her face, "She is a bit of a whirlwind, isn't she? I enjoyed every minute of our ride to Hever, but I haven't managed to get a word in edgeways since we left London."

"Caila believes it's how Jenny hides her insecurity," Chris said. "I wasn't too sure at first, about her inviting Jenny, but I think she'll be all right, and after the way she took charge of our little bundle of joy, I am downright grateful to have her onboard.

Let's show you your new home first, there is still an ample choice of rooms.

Later on, we'll help you find a suitable place for your animals. Caila asked her contact to move them to Hever, and when I last saw them, they were having a ball in the rose garden, but we should probably find them a more suitable place to graze. There is plenty of grass for the goats to trim around here."

"Chris!"

Chris turned around when he heard a familiar voice. He smiled, he'd never seen Luke hurry or stroll. His former colleague walked towards them at his usual casual pace, his back slightly hunched. After he'd caught up, Chris made the introductions.

"Luke, this is Juliet, and this is Richard. Juliet works, … used to work with Caila, and Richard is a friend of ours. Luke worked with me as a software developer."

"Nice to meet you, Luke," Juliet extended a welcoming hand, "Chris was just about to show us our new home. Maybe we should all have lunch afterwards."

They found Caila and Jenny in one of the rooms of the Edwardian wing, where Jenny had already changed the baby. Steve was just ahead of them, carrying what looked like the bare bones of a cot.

"Thank you, Steve, just put it over there, please," Jenny left it to Steve to struggle with the cot while she carefully returned the baby to its pram before turning around to inspect the newcomer.

"Oh, hi. You're new," her cheeks turned crimson. "I'm Jenny."

Jenny's reaction surprised Caila; Luke was a handsome man, but not Jenny's usual muscular he-man type, "Jenny, this is Luke. He worked with Chris. Oh, and Luke, this is Steve. We worked together for a while, and he's a good friend of ours."

While he gave two incompatible pieces of flatpack furniture the dead stare, Steve asked their final companion hopefully, "Hey Luke, do you know how to assemble a baby bed?"

"You have that the wrong way around," his eyes fixed on Steve's project, Luke walked over to help him out, ignoring Jenny and the baby, "you need to release that catch, then push there, and secure that latch over here."

"That is brilliant," Steve looked on in astonishment. "Thanks ever so much."

"Chris, could you help Luke choose a room, please? And then we'll all meet up in the Dining Hall of the castle for a spot of lunch," Caila's stomach reminded her that she hadn't had anything to eat, after her interrupted breakfast. "Oh, and Luke? You play the piano, don't you? Then we have a surprise for you.

Not sure how to respond to that half remark, half question, Luke nodded. But then, as he looked at Chris, he was reminded of something and opened his bag.

"I brought you your mug, Chris."

During lunch, the Dining Hall livened up as they occupied almost half of the chairs around the massive table. Clutching their new green dinosaur soft toy, the baby slept peacefully in its cot next to Jenny's chair. Two plastic ducks, dressed up as Anne Boleyn and Henry VIII, were keeping watch from the bottom of its bed.

Steve hadn't been able to locate a baby monitor yet, so the girl had insisted he'd find her another baby bed to take into the castle. Before she ate, Jenny fed the infant and announced she was a girl of around three months old. This initiated a fierce debate about suitable names, a discussion which continued in the Drawing Room.

While the others moved extra chairs to the centre of the room, Caila took Luke aside and showed him the piano, in the corner near the window. She explained her plan before excusing herself, announcing she'd be back in a minute.

Careful not to spoil her surprise, Caila glanced into the room to make sure everyone had found a seat, and that Luke was in position behind his new instrument. When she gave him a wave, he played the first notes and Caila walked in, singing, "Happy birthday to you, happy birthday to you, happy birthday dear Jenny, …"

The others quickly joined in while Jenny blushed from ear to ear, hiding her face in her hands. After Luke finished the birthday song, he continued playing a gentle classical melody, which sounded vaguely familiar to Caila.

"Jenny, a very happy birthday to you, from all of us. This is your 21st birthday, and it is the first birthday in this new world," Caila placed an enormous cake on the table, "that makes it a special occasion. I was going to tease you about being the youngest in our group, but since you no longer are, I probably shouldn't. And you have already proven that there is at least one subject you are a lot better at than any one of us." Caila handed Jenny two small boxes, "We got you some presents. And don't forget to make a wish when you blow out your candles."

"Awww, I don't know what to say," lost for words, Jenny blew out the candles and concentrated on unwrapping her presents. "Thank you, that's lovely, thanks ever so much." She admired a pretty travel size manicure set, which

Caila had found in the souvenir shop, and with unsteady hands she put on the golden necklace.

Jenny was spared further embarrassment when Luke stopped playing and walked over to the window, announcing that a car had pulled up outside the drawbridge.

Alarmed, Chris got to his feet, "Steve, Rich, come to the door with me. Luke, keep an eye on that car. If, whoever comes out of it has a gun, or any other weapon, you come and tell us."

"Juliet and Jenny," Caila also rose to join the men as they walked to the door, "can you keep an eye on the baby, please? I'm going with Chris and the boys."

"Maybe you should stay inside?" Chris was worried. "Mateos would kill me if something happened to you."

Just then, Luke stuck his head around the door, and reported, "It is a man of about your age, Chris, and he is alone. I can't see any weapons."

"Thanks Luke, can you stay with Juliet and Jenny, please?" Caila requested. "I think we can handle this. Chris, I'm coming with you, I think I know who this is. And if it isn't? … Well then there's strength in numbers."

She looked out of the window and saw a man of about her own age cross the courtyard, but when he reached the door, he seemed uncertain how to proceed. So, before the men could stop her, Caila reached for the handle, and opened the door.

"Good afternoon, my name is Peter Overwood," Peter was tall and his accent distinctly RP, "I believe I am expected."

"Hi Peter, I'm Caila. Would you mind if I asked you a question, before we allow you in?" Caila felt like a gameshow host as she quizzed their unfamiliar caller.

"Not at all, Caila, by all means, ask away."

'He kind of sounds like OOVII,' Caila liked his accent and, somehow, he looked familiar to her. She wondered if she'd seen him on the telly, "What do you do for a living, Peter?"

"I am a veterinarian, I have, or more accurately, I had my practice near my home in North Wales. Not far from Betws-y-Coed."

Caila swallowed, "Yes, then we were told to expect you."
With a sheepish grin she turned to her husband, who had also caught on and was desperately trying not to laugh.

- A medical professional, my dear? I would say that Mateos interpreted your request rather loosely. –

Somehow, Caila managed to keep a straight face as she welcomed Peter into his new home, "Peter, this is my husband, Chris. And this here is Steve, and his husband Richard. Please, come in and meet the rest of our group."

In the Drawing Room, while she introduced Peter to the others, she noticed how Chris studied the vet intently, but when he caught his wife's questioning look, he shrugged and said, - It's nothing, he just appears familiar. –

The cake on the table and the wrapping paper next to Jenny's chair were obviously a dead giveaway, and when he spotted the celebratory items, Peter congratulated the birthday girl and apologised for arriving empty-handed. To make amends, he offered her first choice of the eggs from his chickens who had accompanied him on his journey eastwards. This prompted Juliet to match his offer with fresh milk from her goats.

As she watched her group, Caila considered Mateos had been right, Peter seemed to fit in perfectly. And what are humans anyway, but just another Earth species.

"Jenny, how about cutting that cake? Peter, there is tea and coffee in the thermoses, on the side table. Please, help yourself."

Then Caila looked at Steve and blinked as she spotted his spheream for the first time. Wow, that was bright. But she smiled when she followed Steve's concerned gaze. That was brilliant!

"Juliet, would you mind helping Peter find a room, after we had our tea? And, then you will probably want to get your animals settled, before it gets too dark. Let us know if you need any help with that."

"What breed are your goats, Juliet?" taking his tea and a piece of cake, Peter joined Juliet for an animated discussion about their livestock.

Caila walked over to Jenny and the baby, she crouched down and stroked its tiny clenched fist, "How are you getting on with her? She is a contented little thing, isn't she?"

"I need to bathe her tonight," Jenny looked into the cot and smiled proudly, "I can use the bath in my en-suite, but a real baby bath would be better."

"We will get her a new one tomorrow, when we go shopping in Tunbridge Wells, just make a list of all the stuff you need. But first we'll go to your place to pick up some of your belongings." Caila looked at Luke, "Could you help Jenny find a baby bath, please? If there is one in the hotel. No, not right now, Luke. There's no rush."

"Are you matchmaking?" Chris enquired doubtfully, after the two couples had left the room. "That's not like you. Peter and Juliet might work, but you can forget about Jenny and Luke."

"There's an idea! But no, I'm not," Caila nodded towards Steve and Richard, "I think we need to talk to those guys, from the looks of it, they might have some questions."

"Yes, there wasn't really time this morning, was there?" Chris eyed the two glowing men. "But judging from their sphereams, a chat is long overdue.
Hey guys, it's not your eyes, it's real. They are a bit bright, brighter than ours, but I like your matching colours."

"A bit bright?" Steve squinted, as he examined the yellow haze enveloping his partner. "Rich looks like he's been sprayed with luminescent paint!"

"You're a good one to talk! May I borrow your sunglasses, Caila? Steve shines brighter than the sun at noon. Is this permanent?"

"Yes, I'm afraid it is, you are stuck with it for the rest of your lives. It's called a spheream and it's only visible to activated Khered. Have you noticed anything else yet?" Caila tried communicating using lectanimo, - How many cupcakes, in a baker's dozen? – but she didn't get an answer. "I guess it's too early. Sometime later today, or tomorrow, you should be able to use lectanimo. It's not difficult; but remember to concentrate only on the person or persons you want to communicate with, or you could end up with rather embarrassing situations. And don't be surprised if OOVII introduces himself, he will want to get to know you better.

Oh, and, Steve, your eyesight will be restored as well. I wish I'd known this a couple of years ago, I could have saved a small fortune if I hadn't had my eyes lasered."

"Who's next?"

That evening they played a game of, '*what I'm going to miss most*'. Juliet had come up with the idea, to identify gaps in their shopping lists.

"Peter?"

"*What I am going to miss most*, …. I believe, I will miss my practice most of all," Peter's profession had been his lifelong passion, "being a vet, and working with animals."

"That's easily solved. How about adding medical equipment to our shopping lists? There will always be sick or injured animals," with Caila's request for a medical professional in mind, Chris suggested, "and, what would you say about re-training as a doctor? For humans?
The Neteru can heal us when our Khered DNA is activated. But, in time, we'll have children, who won't have that benefit. They will need a doctor, and possibly someone who can train a new generation of medical professionals."

"I like that idea," adding another species to his list of patients appealed to Peter. "It would be challenging, but I'm up for it. Would you mind if I appropriated the holiday cottage to convert into a clinic? I could start collecting supplies and find textbooks from the nearest town tomorrow. It would also be good to have an assistant to help me with procedures, or someone who can occasionally stand in for me."

"I'd like to give that a try, if you will have me," Juliet was no stranger to first aid kits. "I have been an assistant most of my life, and I have all the first aid certificates you could possibly imagine."

"The job is yours," that afternoon, the vet had enjoyed chasing chickens and goats with his prospective assistant. "I believe, we will make a great team."

As the evening drew to a close and the bottles of wine contained no more than alcohol vapours, they ran out of ideas and the discussion meandered into a light-hearted chat.

'Dr Who', was Caila's final contribution, she'd waited almost a year for the new series. If the Beeb hadn't delayed the second series with Jodie Whittaker, it could have aired before the Event.

Luke added sheet music and musical instruments to their lists and offered to teach Jenny to play the piano when she said she'd miss music. Jenny looked doubtful, because her taste in music was more Little Mix than Giacomo Puccini, but she gracefully accepted Luke's offer.

And, when Steve said he'd miss strong creamy hot chocolate, they were launched into a fierce discussion between milk and dark chocolate aficionados.

After everyone else had gone to bed, Peter hung back to talk to Caila and Chris. He told them he had lived and practiced on the family estate, which he inherited from his parents. His wife had passed away three years ago, and with no children, he had thrown himself into work. This morning he'd been on his way back from a callout when civilisation disappeared around him. Remarkably, he had known exactly where to go, and after picking up his chickens, he set off for Hever.

The roads outside this area had all gone, he told Chris and Caila, motorways were long wide stretches of dirt roads which, without human intervention, would soon be reclaimed by nature. Then he recalled that, although he couldn't be certain, he believed he'd spotted a person in a wooded area, somewhere near the Chilterns. Whoever, or whatever, he'd seen disappeared before he'd reached them, and he hadn't seen anyone else until he'd knocked on their door, this afternoon.

Peter sat back, and studied the woman in front of him, "Somehow, Caila, you look familiar to me. Have you ever been to Wales?"

"Chris and I discussed earlier that you look very familiar to us as well. We have been there once, on holiday, in Betws-y-Coed. Maybe that's it?"

"That must be it," Peter glanced at his watch. "Time to turn in, it has been a long day."

Just before he left the room, he turned around one last time, "Incidentally, we have more in common than still being around after this Event. I was also born in the Netherlands, somewhere in the south of the country. My parents always held me responsible for ruining their Dutch holiday. Goodnight."

A new dawn

Thursday 19 September

"No, it should be something pretty. Look at her little face. She is not a Terri, that's a name for a dog," Jenny put her foot down. "She looks more like a Rose, or a Lily. Or, what about, Iris?"

"Do I detect a pattern here?" Steve teased. "How about Petunia?"

"Don't listen to that silly man, sweetheart," Jenny reassured the unperturbed little girl, "we are not going to call you Petunia. Shame on you, Steve!"

"If I may make a suggestion. How about Aurora?" Peter proposed. "For a new beginning, after the Roman Goddess of dawn."

"I like that," Juliet smiled at the beaming baby. "This pretty little thing is a symbol of new beginnings, and Aurora sounds sweet. What do you think, Jenny?"

"Aurora?" since Jenny had taken on the role of carer and protector of the new-born, everyone recognised her right to have the deciding vote. "Yes, I like it.
What do you think, would you like to be called Aurora? Awww, she smiles, she likes it too. Good morning, little Aurora."

"That's settled then, Aurora it is. And maybe we can get a more or less exact birthday from Mateos." Caila looked around the table. "Before we go out today, I should explain a few things to you, but I'll keep it short. Chris, Steve and Richard heard this before, so, they can fill in the gaps.

Yesterday, I only told you that the world was reset by a species from a different planet. The Neteru seeded Earth with a variety of species, and recently they discovered that humans were about to destroy this little rock, with everything on it, in a rather nasty way.

This would have greatly upset our neighbours, by spewing chemicals into the Universe, so the Neteru had to intervene. They activated the twelve remaining direct descendants of the original human seedlings and asked them to choose seven companions each. I chose you, and that's how you got here.

To survive the Event, you all received an extra string of DNA; you are dormant Khered now, but you have a choice to become activated. This comes with benefits but also with obligations. Activated Khered will remain on Earth for 107 years, to help restart and supervise new human populations. To cover this time span they will live in Etherunian time, which basically means that, one century from now, they won't look a day older than they do today. The Neteru will help us stay healthy.

Activated Khered can use lectanimo, a form of mind communication, with Neteru and other activated Khered," Caila realised she'd forgotten to breathe throughout most of her speech and took a deep breath before concluding, "If you are activated, you will develop a spheream, a cloud-like haze to surround you. Chris, Steve and Richard chose to be activated. I am also activated, but as a birth Khered I had no choice in the matter.

Did I forget anything?"

"Just the baby thing," Steve brought up his pet subject, "but I believe that happens whether you are activated or not."

"Yes, that's right. In time, you will all have a child who will be a direct descendant of yours. It's going to be created in a safe way, on Etherun, and will be delivered ready to be fed and diapered. It works the same for both men and women and is safer than the traditional human method to produce babies. The Neteru are not keen on losing any Khered.

I realise you need time to think about this, so, have a bit of a ponder and talk to Chris, Richard or Steve; they are experts on this subject.

Later today, I'll introduce you to our Neteruian liaison," while she made that promise, Caila sensed Mateos had arrived and smiled as she turned to greet him.

"Why not now, Caila? There's no time like the present. I notice you are still using the castle's dining room."

"Yes, we are growing into it and it starts to feel like home," Caila made the introductions. "All, this is Mateos; Mateos, this is our team."

"Good morning, I trust you all settled in well. I hope you don't mind, but I would like to have a quick word with Caila first, it won't take long. Caila?"

With a, "By all means, old chap, lead the way," Mateos's Khered followed Mateos into the Inner Hall.

"A good morning to you, Mateos, how was your day?" Caila kicked her shoes off and pulled her legs up as she sat on the loveseat. "You seem contented."

"So do you, Caila. It's good to have a quiet moment, if I didn't have to attend another meeting in my life, I wouldn't complain.

Have you encountered any problems since the Event?"

"Nothing substantial, only about six kilos worth of complications."

"Fair maiden, fair maiden, thee speaketh in riddles."

"You are in a good mood!" Caila laughed, "Alloweth me to pray pardon me mine dearest brother mine."

Then she composed herself, "But seriously. Did you notice that cot, in the Dining Hall?" she rolled her eyes as Mateos shook his head, "No? … Typical! Men!

It's next to Jenny's chair, and there is a little baby girl contentedly asleep in it. We found her yesterday afternoon. Is this one of Black's accidental survivors? Peter mentioned that he thought he saw someone, on his way over here."

"That is one of the things I wanted to talk about. We believe that there are now two distinct groups of survivors. The first one is the group Black referred to earlier, they are still hiding in shelters which resisted the beam. At this moment, there is no way to locate them. The effect of the beam will last for 167 hours, and anyone exiting those shelters after that period will remain on Mesu until we reactivate the telumparticula, in 28 days. This poses a genuine threat to you, for the reasons mentioned by Black. But there is another unexpected group that remained on this planet; they are humans who were unaffected by the telumparticula. From our first analysis they appear to have accidently inherited partial inserts of Khered DNA. I estimate that there are approximately 100 of these partial Khered on this island, and your baby would be one of them. I will test her in a minute."

"You are not going to take her away, are you?" she hadn't considered this possibility earlier.

"Caila, I hope you know me better than that by now," Mateos looked genuinely hurt she could believe that of him. "This second group will remain, but please be aware that not all of them will be as innocent as that little baby of yours."

"I'm sorry, Sets, I know you won't hurt her," Caila regretted her rash remark, "it's just that we, and especially Jenny, have got rather attached to the little thing. We called her Aurora."

"That's fine, I understand, don't worry about it. And Aurora is an appropriate choice of name," Mateos wondered who'd thought of it, before he changed the subject.

"Some Khered requested a meeting, and from now on you will be picking up on these requests. Don't worry, you'll recognise it when they send one.

What you need to do next, is announce the meeting. Let's say, you would like to hold this meeting tonight at ten o'clock, which is thirteen hours from now. You send out the number thirteen while you form an image of your fellow Khered and your meeting room. Be prepared, because you will receive most of their replies almost instantly, that way you can reschedule quickly, if necessary. Then, when it's time for your meeting to start, you just imagine your fellow Khered in your meeting room, and that's all.

Would you like to try it now?"

"That sounds simple enough, and ten pm is fine by me," Caila stared at the wall of the Drawing Room while she thought of the number thirteen and imagined the other Khered in her cottage. "Wow, flip!" Caila startled as five replies came back almost instantly; she was better prepared when the other six arrived. "They all accepted. Blimey, I feel like a witch!"

"I'll get you a hat and a broomstick, someday, they will suit you," he teased her. "Is there anything else I can do for you, my little sorceress, before we re-join the others?"

"Yes, as a matter of fact there is, my dear wizarding teacher. Could you explain to me, please, who exactly Peter Overwood is? There is something incredibly familiar about him, Chris thinks so too. Why does it feel like I met him before?"

Peter's last words had kept Caila awake for a long time.

"Peter is your twin brother. I observed him throughout his life, he is a very kind man, you will like him. And he is the medical professional, you asked for."

"Why did you keep an eye on him? I never asked you before, how you knew he would be safe."

"For some incomprehensible reason, intelligence agencies believed that 'the curse', as they called it, was passed from mother to the first-born red-haired daughter. When they believed you were stillborn, they assumed the line ended there.
I kept an eye on Peter, because you were twins."

"That special bond between twins," Caila understood and smiled at her honorary Neteruian brother. "You are the best, Sets. Do you know that I may be the only one in this world to come out of this Event with more family than I started out with? You and Peter, two new brothers. I am still your honorary sister, right?"

"Always and forever. Come on, let's have a look at Aurora."

"Aurora was born 103 days ago and has indeed partial Khered DNA," under Jenny's watchful eye, Mateos had examined their baby, "she looks very healthy but let me know if you need any help. Although, I am sure, Peter will be more than capable to cope.
You have been taking very good care of her. Thank you, Jenny."

"My experience with human patients is limited, but I did some work for the Welsh Mountain zoo, treating their apes and monkeys," when he saw Jenny's worried face, he quickly added. "Don't worry, Jenny, I am only teasing you. I will make sure that I am well prepared to treat Aurora. I added medical books to my shopping list, and my education starts this afternoon."

"Mateos?" Juliet changed the subject. "We had a bit of a discussion while you and Caila were talking, and we decided that we would all like to be activated. Is that something you would like to do now, or should we see you later?"

"Juliet, allow me?" Mateos walked over to the slim dark woman and placed his hands on her back for a couple of seconds. "It's already done."

"Thank you, that was quick. And thank you for moving my animals safely to Hever."

The efficient former personal assistant then suggested, "Maybe you would like to activate Jenny next? She's the one who is most nervous about it. It's fine, Jenny, it is like Steve said, you won't feel a thing."

After he'd activated the rest of their group, Mateos claimed the chair next to Caila's and enquired about their plans for the day. He disappointed Jenny by declaring streaming was history but assured them they would still be able to play CDs and DVDs, at least until the re-activation of the telumparticula. Then he promised Richard to arrange for an engineer to visit him, to explain about their new source of energy.

However ambitious it was, Richard was determined to recreate the Etherunian method of generating clean energy, and with Luke and Chris to help him, Mateos believed it would be possible.

Caila's announcement, half an hour later, that it was time to go shopping was greeted with a heartfelt, "Oh, yes!" from Jenny, followed by a defensive, "Don't you all look at me like that, I just need some clean clothes!"

But clean clothes would not be the only thing Jenny and Caila would pick up that day.

A shelter in Essex

Twenty-four hours had passed since they'd lost all communication with the outside world.

Baldwin didn't know how long they would have to remain in this hellhole, but he was ready to go above ground and take control, as soon as it was safe to do so.

He would establish a fair society, a society where everyone was equal. As their leader he would take control of all common possessions, and everyone would share in his ideology. They would work for the common good.

And he, Prime Minister Baldwin, would lead them and educate them. They would follow him and look up to him.

He considered, he should rebrand the term of Prime Minister, it sounded too plutocratic, he would be a guiding light to his followers. Maybe he should insist on being called our Enlightened Leader, or our Guiding Guru. Or maybe, simply, our Dear Mentor Baldwin.

He looked at his heavily armed escort, and a barely visible smile lifted the corners of his mouth - let anyone try to argue with that. From now on, he was in charge. Then he glanced at Eleonor, who was busy writing out copies of his manifest. She would do for now, not the prettiest or the smartest of females, but she was loyal.

Best not to try and make another move on that pretty little soldier girl, the little snob; she probably fancied women anyway. He would find a suitable partner later, women loved and admired him, they always had.

Missing

They split up for their shopping trip.

Peter and Juliet went to Edenbridge, in search of medical supplies and equipment for their new combined veterinary and GP practice in the old Bed and Breakfast cottage, behind the castle.

Caila and the others took off for a day of foraging in Tunbridge Wells.

But their first stop was Jenny's old home, a terraced two-up two-down at the edge of town. While the others waited in their cars, Caila went in with Jenny, who lingered briefly at the pale blue door of the familiar house she'd called home for the last 21 years.

Before turning the key, she took a deep breath. Then she opened the door and stepped into the once welcoming hall.

Until now, Jenny had cherished a sliver of hope that her mother would be like Aurora, and that she'd hear her call out from the living room, reminding her to wipe her feet. But she was greeted with nothing more than an unwelcoming silence; her once warm home had become nothing more than a house, cold and dark, an empty shell which harboured mementoes from the past.

She slowly walked from room to room, stuffing her bags with keepsakes and pictures of her mum and brother. In the kitchen, the blueberries, dropped off by their elderly neighbour two nights ago, lay untouched in their glass bowl. Jenny swallowed hard before she climbed the stairs to her cosy room, where she changed from yesterday's office casual into something more practical.

Then she resolutely turned her back on her old life and walked out.

Luke was the only one who noticed the single tear running down her face, and when he offered her his neatly folded linen handkerchief, she accepted it with a grateful smile.

Caila looked up from her sandwich and out of the window. The old ABC cinema site had laid undeveloped for almost 20 years, much longer than it had taken the Neteru to decide it would be returned to nature. Like the others, she'd parked her car at a safe distance from Steve's truck, which stood surrounded by scratched and dented vehicles.

"We should find ourselves another lorry, this afternoon. It will save us so much time in the end."

"I don't think we have much choice," Richard followed Caila's gaze. "With Steve driving that monster, any smaller vehicles will be damaged beyond repair in no time at all."

"Oi!" his novice HGV driver husband objected. "I only scratched them."

"Yep. You're making progress," Richard assessed the damage, "you only scratched the ones out there."

"Yes, and he didn't total all of the others either," Jenny defended Steve while she was feeding Aurora. "Well, not completely, anyway. The only real write-off was the one in the parking lot, when he backed up against that wall."

"Thank you, Jenny, I think," Steve accepted the dubious compliment. "But there was no way anyone would have noticed that car, I'll let you know. And, who in their right mind would park their car between the back of a truck and a wall?"

"At least you will be able to tell us what to look out for, before the rest of us start driving trucks," Chris helped himself to another sandwich. "I think we made good progress this morning. We cleared out two baby…, what do you call them, shops, boutiques? And one toyshop.
We have bicycles and even more bicycles, and half the contents of the outdoor and camping shops. If we lose our utilities, we will at least be able to cook and purify water. And those shopping trolleys were really useful for clearing out the town centre pharmacies. What are we going to do this afternoon?"

"I was thinking that we should go clothes' shopping. We will need loads. They should last us at least until we mastered the process of requesting wool from a sheep, to crafting something resembling a wearable garment," all of Caila's attempts at fashioning her own attire, had failed that last requirement miserably. "Which reminds me, we should add sewing machines to our list."

"They taught us how to use those things at school," Jenny held up her right hand, presenting a small scar, "I ended up at A&E. Our teacher broke the needle when she tried to pull it out of my finger. That's when mum gave me my lucky charm. Since then, I never had a needle through my fingers again. But, then again, they also never let me near a sewing machine either."

"We should probably put you in charge of sheepshearing, just to be on the safe side," not too keen on the smelly animals, Richard was happy to delegate that task, "or until Peter has upgraded his degree."

"Sheep are cute, aren't they?" Jenny looked down at the baby in her arms. "Have you finished your bottle, Aurora? Look at you. You made a terrible mess, little lady. Oh, thanks." Jenny blushed as she accepted Luke's napkin.

"If I may suggest something, before we go out again?" Luke had been quiet during lunch.

"You most certainly may," hoping that Luke had an idea which would steer them away from Caila's plans for this afternoon, Chris was keen to hear an alternative, "we can postpone shopping for clothes if something else should take priority."

"No, this can wait until tomorrow," Luke smashed Chris's hopes. "This morning, I noticed the antenna for the wireless hotspot in the shopping centre. If we take it down, we could create our own wireless network, at home. We don't need much, just the antenna, the PoE and the router."

"And, with camera's and sensors, we could integrate it with an alarm system. That's brilliant," the idea of combining his old profession with his new role as head of security, excited Chris. "Let's make a shopping list tonight, and then we can start collecting the equipment tomorrow morning."

"That will score you guys some points with Mateos," Caila decided that asking what a PoE was, could wait until later. "But thanks, Luke, that's brilliant.
Are we all ready to go now?"

***

Peter and Juliet's first stop was the loading bay of the supermarket in Edenbridge, where they confiscated a large lorry; and after some to and froing, they agreed that Juliet should stick with their four-by-four, while Peter would drive the truck. Tomorrow, they'd find a second lorry for Juliet.
Together they methodically worked their way through the GP and dental practices in the town's centre, before visiting a small cottage hospital at the edge of town, where they wheeled their supplies out on hospital beds. As Peter inspected the contents of his truck, he remarked that they would have a fair semblance of a proper hospital soon.

Delighted with their finds, they decided to have an early lunch. And when they trolleyed, not only their lunches, but also the contents of the entire health isle out of the supermarket, Peter suggested they should enjoy their well-deserved meal on a bench overlooking the river Eden.

"I believe we achieved double of what we set out to do this morning," Juliet poured dressing over her salad, "those textbooks at the medical practice were a real bonus. And I never expected to find beds in that small hospital."

"Yes, we might consider skipping the vet's practice today. We have enough drugs and equipment to make a start at outfitting our clinic," while he stretched his long legs, Peter threw the curious ducks some bread. "But let's first enjoy our lunch, and the view."

"I like that bridge, it looks reliable and constant. Like it will always be there," Juliet studied the old stone bridge, which gave the town its name. Then she looked back at Peter and asked. "How long were you and your wife married?" When he didn't immediately answer, she added apologetically, "I'm sorry, I didn't mean to pry. You don't need to answer that."

"No, that's fine. I just reflected, how that seems a lifetime ago now," Peter looked at the old bridge. "Our lives have certainly changed unrecognisably, overnight.
Ellen and I were married for 21 years, she was also a vet. We were happy together, in our practice and in our private life; and I was devastated when I lost her after the accident. Ellen adored those chickens, that's why I took them with me, yesterday.
How about you?"

"My life, before the Event, you mean?" Juliet gave it some thought. "When I was younger, my parents wanted me to become an actress and find a husband. So, naturally, I became a personal assistant and stayed single.

I never missed a man in my life. True, when Caila talked about her life with Chris, it sounded attractive. But seeing those cheating city boys, I decided it just wasn't worth the risk. I was happy with my animals and my little veg patch, and I was saving up for an early retirement, as a self-sufficient smallholder."

Peter smiled, "I believe you got your wish. About the smallholding, I mean."

"I was aiming for something a little bit less ambitious than a castle, but it'll do," Juliet inspected Peter's salad box. "Are you going to eat those cucumber slices? …

No? … Would you mind if I had them? You can have my olives if you like."

While Juliet munched on Peter's cucumber slices, she reflected that life was still pretty good.

***

They'd made good time, cramming two trucks with a variety of practical clothes and shoes. Until Steve spotted a shop which stocked his favourite label. That's when sensibility was replaced by high end fashion. Steve had a ball, emptying rack after rack, until his treasured upmarket retail outlet ran out of his beloved brand.

"You look very handsome in that new outfit, Steve, but I think we should take advantage of the last daylight and collect some more essentials, before we go home," Caila pointed towards the exit, "Just down the road, near the station is a musical instruments' store. Could you guys go there, please? Luke will know what to take.

Jenny and I need to do some girls' shopping. Don't wait for us, we'll see you at home, in time for dinner. OOVII, could you go with them, please? Jenny and I need some privacy."

- I do not believe that to be a good idea, Caila. Mateos will not like it if we leave you behind. –

"Don't worry, he won't even miss us. We'll be back, long before Mateos comes home from his meetings. Besides, my lectanimo is better developed than Chris's, so I can easily reach you if there is a problem. Don't worry, I'll contact you if I need you."

- If you are sure about that? – OOVII was not convinced.

"Absolutely," Caila sounded confident. "Nothing bad is going to happen to us. Mateos said it himself this morning, we should be safe today, with the effect of the beam lingering."

"It should be okay, OOVII," based on past experience, Chris was happy to leave girls' shopping to the women. "Come on, let's go. Shall we take your trolleys?"

"Thanks, Chris. See you later, darling."

Caila smiled, as she watched them drive off. What was it, about the mere mention of girls' shopping, that send grown-up men running for the hills?

"Right, we have been very sensible and awfully practical so far. And, don't get me wrong, that is of course exactly what we need to be from now on. But I don't think it means we shouldn't have a bit of fun," Caila announced, "because, you know what happened to Jack, don't you?"

"Jack?" Jenny looked confused.

Caila laughed, "Sorry, bad joke, 'All work and no play …'? So, what do you want to go for first, make-up or lingerie?"

"Are you sure? Everyone in our group is so sensible, maybe I should give up on make-up."

"Sensible? Our label-loving lorry driver, Steve? Or me? I goofed up quite a few times, in the last couple of days. And, do you really believe that Chris, Richard and Luke actually need all those trainsets for their energy project?"

Jenny laughed when she was reminded of those three grown men, excitedly emptying out the model railway shelves at the toyshop.

"But all right," Caila conceded, "let's go for practical first: lingerie. We'll need loads, because that is going to be terribly difficult to produce ourselves when it's gone. And I can't imagine itchy woollen knickers being very comfortable. Is that sensible enough?
107 years at, at least six sets per year, that comes to 642 sets each.
What size do you think Juliet is? And Aurora will also need some, when she's a bit older."

They didn't come anywhere near the quantities Caila had estimated they needed; but Jenny firmly disposed of any feelings of guilt while they stocked up.

Make-up was deemed another necessity. As part of their history and culture, it would be indispensable course material for little Aurora's future history lessons.

"Forget about foundation, you don't need it," Caila assured Jenny, when the younger woman searched for the correct skin tone, "your skin is perfect, and when your activation is complete, you will look absolutely radiant. Trust me."

"And finally, last but not least, ..." Caila concluded, after assessing the remaining space in their vehicles, "... we need some appropriate clothes."

Jenny raised her eyebrows, "But we have lots of jeans, leggings, sweaters and winter coats already."

"I know, but that's practical, we still need appropriate," Caila explained. "We live in a castle, and we have a 17-foot dining table, and a grand piano in our living room, we should have clothes to suit our environment when we have a party or some kind of celebration. It will be Christmas soon.

This is Tunbridge Wells, we can find everything we need around here. And, ..." Caila grinned mischievously, "we'll finish up, at that posh suit shop, next to the station.

I'm sure our male companions will appreciate it, if we spare them the hassle of shopping for appropriate occasion wear. I made a note of their sizes earlier."

"They are going to hate us for this, aren't they?" Jenny laughed, as she viewed the large collection of suits covering their earlier purchases, "That's why you sent them home without us! Awww, I love it!" Jenny bent to adjust Aurora's car seat, "Aurora, pay attention please, this is your first lesson in handling the males of our species.
Oh, Caila. Those top hats are brilliant!"

As they were about to get behind the wheel of their cars, a dull thumping sound made them jump, and they scoured the area until they noticed a squirrel hopping from a roof onto a tree.

"This ghost town is beginning to get on my nerves," Caila laughed nervously. "Let's go home."

***

Peter and Juliet were busy unloading beds, when the four men arrived back from Tunbridge Wells.

"You had a productive day, by the looks of it. We are going to need a bigger castle, if we continue bringing in supplies at this pace," Juliet glanced in the back of Steve's truck. "That's brilliant, Steve, I believe you have all the raw materials to bake some fresh bread."

"And I notice, you also visited some pharmacies. Drugs should go down into the cellars, where it is cooler, you can use that trolley over there. Maybe we should add extra fridges to our shopping list," only then did Peter realise that their team was not complete. "Did you gentlemen, lose the ladies?"

"They got rid of us, to do some girls' shopping, but they promised to be back before dark," Chris noticed Mateos who'd appeared behind Luke. "Hi Mateos. How are you?"

"Where is Caila?" Mateos asked his, by now, familiar first question.

"Caila and Jenny needed to do some girls' shopping, they will be back soon," Chris explained for the second time. "Don't worry, we still have an hour and a half of daylight left." When Chris sensed Mateos's concern, he started to doubt the wisdom of their decision to split up. "Really, they'll be fine. Just give them another hour."

But when the sun set, at a quarter to seven, there was still no sign of Caila and Jenny.

Flock

At a quarter past seven, Mateos had had enough, "I'm going out to find them."

Chris instantly got to his feet, eager to help the Neteru, track down his wife.

"No, I'm going alone. I'll ask Dev to come over. Together we can scan the area and locate her over a larger distance than you can."

"Hi Mats, what's the problem?" Mateos's friend appeared almost instantly. "Don't worry, we'll find her. … I warned you, didn't I? I told you she'd be trouble."

Devyn's attempt to make light of the situation was lost on Mateos, "Let's just go. Chris, if she turns up, tell her to contact me or Devyn. She knows how to do that. Dev, you start here, I'll start from Tunbridge Wells."

It didn't take Devyn long to find them. They were moving painfully slow towards the castle, not far from Hever. Why the hell wasn't she using lectanimo, to let Mats know where she was, she was definitely well within range.

- Caila, it's Devyn. Let me know if you are in trouble, I can be there in a second, to help you. Together with Mats. –

Caila's response was not immediately forthcoming, and Devyn was about to contact Mateos when he heard her surprised voice answering him.

- Hi Dev, what are you doing here? No, we are not in trouble, not much anyway," was her cryptic response. "But we could use some help. Don't tell Sets, please. He'll just freak out. –

"Too late, he already knows," Devyn appeared next to Caila's van. "Mats asked me to come over to help him find you and Jenny. Why didn't you contact him to tell him where you were?"

"It's not that late," Caila checked her watch, "it's only been dark for half an hour or so. And I'm terribly sorry, I kind of forgot I could reach him. Don't, Dev, please wait, … Oh, you just did, didn't you? Oh, Dev!" Caila watched a very unhappy Mateos materialise next to Devyn. "Hi, Sets. You really did not have to come this far, we're almost home. Dev should have told you that we are fine, then you could have waited for us at the castle."

"Just tell me what's going on, Caila, we'll discuss it at home," Caila looked perfectly fine, so naturally, Mateos, who'd expected to find her injured or incapable to communicate, was furious. "And who is that?"

"What, oh that? That's Flock," Caila pointed at the horse which stood next to her car, but after one look at Mateos's face, she decided that now was maybe not the best time to tease him. "Sorry, bad joke. This young lady, sitting next to me, is Rebecca. We picked her up just before it got dark, together with her horse. There is something wrong with the animal's foot, so she can't ride it. We couldn't leave Rebecca behind in the middle of nowhere for another night, she's only 12 years old, but she refused to go anywhere without her horse. So, we got her into my van, and we had Flock follow us on a long leash, or lead, or whatever you call that piece of rope. We promised to take her, the horse that is, to a vet."

Caila looked at Devyn who tried very hard, but failed miserably to keep a straight face, which of course only aggravated Mateos's fury.

"Please, Dev, don't laugh," Caila pleaded. "I'm really, really sorry, Sets, really, I am.

I forgot that I could contact you, this lectanimo lark is still new to me. Please, don't be angry with me."

"Come on, give her a break, Mats," Devyn argued on Caila's behalf. "What else did you expect from someone with Cals's DNA? We've been through it all before."

Mateos was in two minds, between having a go at his best friend as well as at Caila, or taking the easy way out and giving in. He decided that the latter was probably quicker, and, in the long run, it would save him from being on the receiving end of an endless string of equine jokes.

"Okay, let's forget about it for now, next time just remember to contact me. Will you?" he was rewarded with a timid nod from Caila, who almost completely managed to hide that she was biting the inside of her lip, to stop herself from laughing.

Mateos ignored it, "Dev, can you please move that animal to the courtyard, for Peter to have a look at? I will accompany the ladies."

At that, Devyn vanished with Rebecca's horse, and Mateos got into Caila's van. Rebecca shrank away and sat as close to Caila as possible; she wished she'd never decided to go east.

Miss Riverton

When they arrived back at the castle with Rebecca, Caila and Jenny found everyone assembled in the small courtyard. Peter, with Juliet serving as his assistant, was examining the horse's offending hoof as Flock's young owner, casually strolled towards him.

"Hello there, are you a real vet? When can I have my horse back, please?"

"Good evening, young lady. My name is Peter Overwood. And yes, I am indeed a qualified veterinarian. May I assume that this horse belongs to you, Miss. …?" Peter wiped his hands.

The young girl ignored Peter's extended hand and replied with a huff, "My name is Rebecca, Rebecca Riverton. This is Flock, she has a problem with her foot. She will be fine in the morning."

"Is that your informed diagnoses, doctor Riverton?"

The girl blushed and, as her composure slipped, whispered, "I just want Flock back. And I want to leave, please. Those two are scary." She tried to inconspicuously point at Mateos and Devyn.

Juliet crouched before the frightened young girl, "Have you been alone since yesterday morning, Rebecca? Where are you from?"

"I'm from Malmesbury, Miss," was the unexpected polite reply.

"And you rode over here, in two days?" Juliet smiled reassuringly. "That is very brave of you. My name is Juliet, I am Peter's friend and assistant." Rebecca accepted Juliet's extended hand. "Peter is a very experienced vet, Rebecca, and he will take very good care of your horse. Won't you, Peter?"

"Yes, of course I will," Peter's hand was accepted this time around. "It is very nice to meet you, Rebecca. Your horse has a bruised hoof, it does not appear to be serious, but it would be best if you gave her a couple of days rest. She is a beautiful mare." Peter pointed at Luke, who appeared from the main hall, carrying a large bucket of water, "That young man over there, is Luke. I asked him to fill a bucket with ice water, for Flock's hoof. Why don't you let us take care of your horse, while you have something to eat? Juliet will stay with you."

"How about freshening up first? We have been out shopping for clothes today, and I'm sure we can find something you like. And then, I'll introduce you to the others, in the dining room."

As Rebecca followed Juliet closely through the double doors, she made sure to stay well away from the two alien looking cloud shapes.

"I don't think you made a friend out there," Caila walked back into the castle, accompanied by the two Neteru. "Thanks Devyn, at that pace it would have taken us ages to get that beast home."

"Don't mention it; always happy to oblige. Up north we have a very sensible bunch, with no horse dramas to speak off. But I should be on my way now, don't forget to invite me to your next show."

He was gone before Caila or Mateos had time to respond to his levity.

"Well, if I ever?!" Caila shook her head in mock disapproval before looking back at her honorary brother. "I hope you're staying a bit longer now, I obviously still have a lot to learn and I like having you around."

"Don't worry, I'm not going to say another word about tonight. So, you can drop the, 'I am so sincerely remorseful' act. I'm not falling for it, and your jaw will hurt if you try to keep it up for too long," Mateos hoped she'd be less impulsive from now on, but he doubted it. "Over the next few weeks I will indeed be here most of the time, to keep a close eye on you."

Caila pulled a face and laughed, "Yeh, right! But I meant what I said, Sets, I like having you around."

- Hi, Caila. Can you hear me? – Caila looked at Steve, who stuck his head around the door of the Dining Hall. - Just testing. –

- Dinner is served, Caila, – Richard demonstrated his partner was not the only one who had mastered the art of lectanimo.

- Receiving you both, loud and clear. By the way, your sphereams are developing beautifully, – she squeezed past Steve to see what was on the menu that evening. His newly formed spheream contrasted brilliantly with the dark panelling in the narrow passage to the Dining Hall. "Oh, delicious! Curry night!"

Then she greeted Jenny who entered the dining room with little Aurora, "Hi Jenny, Aurora looks gorgeous in that yellow dress."

"Yes, she does, doesn't she? I'll change her into her sleepsuit later, but we wanted to show off her new dress," as Aurora spluttered, Jenny handed the little girl her dinosaur toy. "Where are the others?"

"Right behind you," Peter walked in with Luke, Juliet and Rebecca. "Rebecca, I believe you haven't met Chris yet, and Richard and Steve. Steve is married to Richard, and Chris is Caila's husband. Caila is in charge of our little community."

- Am I? – Caila startled at the realisation that this was probably true, I guess I am, that makes me responsible for them as well. From Mateos's nod Caila understood he'd sensed her concern.

- You're doing fine. –

She gave him a grateful smile, before welcoming Rebecca to the table, "Hi, Rebecca. Sit down, please, and help yourself to food. I hope you like a curry.

Has Juliet explained what happened, yesterday?"

"Yes," Rebecca studied the labels with spice ratings, which Steve had helpfully left next to the dishes, "she told me that aliens took away all the people, because there was going to be a war. And that you are here, to start all over again." She tried to avoid looking at Mateos, who still scared her.

"That's about right. And you probably survived, Rebecca, because you inherited a bit of very rare DNA, just like baby Aurora. This here is Mateos," Caila looked at their liaison, "he is from a planet called Etherun and he is here to help us. Don't worry, he is not as scary as he looks. Out there, he was just a bit angry with me, because he was worried about us being late."

Over dinner, Rebecca came out of her shell, and announced she had decided to hang around for a couple of days, at least until Flock was fine again, maybe even a bit longer. Then she declared she'd promised to help Peter and Juliet at the clinic, and that she'd never broken a promise in her life.

A few minutes to ten Mateos nudged Caila, and she yelped, "Oops, I almost forgot. Thanks for reminding me. Bye all, I have a meeting, see you later in the Drawing Room."

Caila almost slipped as she rushed out of the dining room. And while she passed Christopher Columbus's bust on her way into the Library, she had no idea how important this meeting was going to be for the future of their community.

The chicken and the egg, and fish currys

Caila sank down onto the pink sofa, and while she picked up a cushion and looked up at the ceiling, she imagined herself with the eleven other Khered in her cosy cottage.
For the first time, she could see more than just the colours of their sphereams. Blue was a girl, a very young girl, younger than Rebecca, she guessed. And Pink Tiger, to Caila's enormous surprise, was a beautiful tall, blond woman.

"Hi, everyone, it's good to see you again. I would like to keep this first meeting after the Event informal; it is less than a week ago that we first met, and today is the first time, we can put faces to our sphereams. So, let's get to know each other a bit better, and then we'll talk about whatever we would like, or need, to discuss," Caila scanned the unfamiliar faces, before she introduced herself. "I'm Caila, and I live in the south of England."
Caila looked questioningly at Green.

"I'm Emily, and I live in Vancouver; that's on the west coast of Canada. It's good to finally meet you all properly," Emily smiled when she looked at the young girl on her left. "Hi, Blue. What's your real name?"

"I'm Anna, I live in Mount Magnet, in Australia," Anna shyly regarded the tall blond woman in the armchair, next to her.

Tiger gave her a reassuring smile, before she told the timid girl, "I visited Australia once, Anna. Mount Magnet that is in the mid-west, am I right?"

Anna nodded.

"Pleased to meet you, Anna. I'm Signe. I live on the other side of the world, in Sweden."

White informed them his name was Sahil and that he lived in Kerala, in India. Then Nicolas announced he'd lived in Luxembourg since his birth, 83 years ago; and Ang told them he was an engineering student, in Hong Kong.

When it was Black's turn, he introduced himself as Lucas, and Caila finally found out that Devyn's, '*up North*', was St. Johns, in Canada.

Alessa told them she lived under the Mexican sun, to which Violet responded by revealing she lived on the beautiful, but less sunny, island of Iceland. Yellow lived in Greece and went by the name of Sophia.

And finally, the orange William, made Anna very happy by divulging he also lived in Australia, be it across the country, on the east coast, in Sydney.

"I know this is going to sound very silly, but does anyone here know how to get eggs out of chickens?" Emily's question was greeted by a few seconds of stunned silence, followed by roaring laughter. So, she clarified, "I am a born and bred city girl, a Vancouverite in heart and soul.

Chickens are an enigma to me. Do we need a …, what do you call it again, you know, a man chicken?"

Caila bit her lip, stifling her laughter, before she replied, "I believe that's called a rooster, but that's the extent of my chicken knowledge. Anyone? Can anyone help Emily with this problem?"

Anna looked around the room, before she hesitantly raised her hand, "If your chickens are older than six months, they'll start laying eggs soon; but you don't need a rooster, unless you want chicks."

"Thanks, you're a life saver, I could hug you," Emily beamed, "I need fresh eggs, with my salmon."

"That sounds delicious. However, on a totally different note," Nicolas changed the tone of the meeting, "has anyone come across accidental survivors? Gronos, my Neteruian liaison, told me some of you had met some?"

"We found a chef who worked for one of the best restaurants in Hong Kong.
Or more accurately he found us. But, with all the skyscrapers flattened, that was not very difficult," Ang sounded delighted with the unexpected culinary addition to his group. "I have never eaten as good, as I have in these last couple of days."

When no one else responded, Caila told them, "Yesterday, we found a three-month-old baby, and today, we were found by a teenager on a horse. I don't think this group, with partial Khered DNA, is going to be a problem, but next week, anyone hiding in shelters, …" she looked at Lucas, "will be able to survive outside. And they may be armed."

"That means, partial DNA survivors could also become a problem, after next week," when Devyn had warned him about the potential threat, Lucas had discussed this issue with his group. "The ones leaving their shelters, could start recruiting them, if they meet. My group are preparing an alarm and defence strategy."

"That sounds terribly sensible, we should all consider doing something similar," Signe admonished herself for ignoring this matter. "What have you come up with, so far?"

When Lucas hesitated in his reply, Caila asked him, "How will you alarm the others in your group, when you believe there may be problems?"

"For our group of eight, we can use lectanimo. But we will also install a bell, and light signals for anyone who is not activated. When the alarm bell is rung, a series of lamps will switch on. If these lights are on, everyone knows they should go to one of the safe places."

"How about your defence strategy," Sophia wanted to know, "how do you plan to defend against weapons like guns?"

"We are still discussing that, but we talked about using sound or magnetism, in some way," Lucas's matter-of-fact remark impressed his fellow Khered, "and Ellie is teaching us how to make, and use, bows and arrows, and catapults."

"I had a catapult when I was a youngster," Nicholas smiled at the memory, "that thing was deadly. I regularly took a rabbit home, for the stew."

"Let's all discuss this with our groups. And call a meeting if we need help, or if any of us come up with the, metaphorical, silver bullet," Caila made a mental note to check out the bows and arrows at the castle. "Have your contacts explained how to contact me, if you want to request a meeting? … Yes? …

That's great. From now on, I'll try to organise non-urgent meetings at different times of the day, then we all get our equal share of interrupted sleep. You look beat, Sahil, what time is it in Kerala? Two, three o'clock at night?"

"Two-thirty," Sahil confirmed. "Do you have an inbuild world clock, Caila?"

"I have …, I had, a friend, who was from Kerala," Caila explained. "She told me the fish currys were delicious in your part of the world."

"She was right, our fish cuisine is the best in the world. I would invite you all, however, our local airport became defunct, a couple of days ago," Sahil yawned. "But you are right, I am beat. The past week has been terribly hectic."

"Sahil, you just gave me a brilliant idea," Signe almost jumped out of her chair. "This afternoon, someone mentioned to me, how much she was going to miss oranges, and mangos and kiwis. We can grow lots of stuff in Sweden, but tropical fruits are a bit of a challenge. And Sahil and

Sophia, you probably would like things from up north. Now, if we share, we can still have all of those things!"

"I hate to break it to you, Signe," Emily reminded her, "but as of yesterday morning, all international flights have been cancelled."

"Oh, but we have something far better now," Signe paused briefly to build the suspense. "Haven't your Neteruian contacts transported items for you?"

As Caila remembered how Devyn had moved Flock earlier that evening, it dawned on her what Signe's brilliant idea was, "Signe, that is wicked. But they'll never go for it."

"Why not?" Signe didn't appear to see the problem. "If we don't push them too hard to begin with, and if we start with something small. Something they can't refuse. Whose birthday is up next? Anyone in September? … October?"

Anna raised her hand, "I'll be eleven on the 23rd of October."

"That's brilliant," Signe beamed, this was perfect, no one could possibly refuse anything that was meant for this shy young girl. "Let's all think of a small birthday present to send to Anna, next month. Eleven gifts, for Anna's eleventh birthday!"

Everyone agreed to give it a try, and after a moment of companionable silence, they concluded it was time to go back home and catch up on some sleep.

But for Caila, bedtime would have to wait a bit longer.

Good night little sister

Caila checked the clock when she arrived back on the pink sofa in the Library; its hands had not moved since she'd rushed in at ten o'clock, earlier tonight. Apparently, they were still meeting in Etherunian time. She leaned back and closed her eyes, 'for just a couple of seconds,' she thought. Sahil was not the only one who was beat.

Caila fell fast asleep and did not wake until, more than an hour later, Chris walked in to fetch her.

"Mateos looked in on you earlier, darling, but decided to let you sleep. He told the others your meeting was running late. Almost everyone else has gone to bed now, I think the stress of the last two days is catching up on us. Peter is the only one who is still up, he would like to talk to you for a minute."

"Then I should tell him that he's my twin brother," Caila stretched and got up to follow her husband into the hall. "I didn't intend to fall asleep, but it was a great nap. I feel so much better now.
Sorry about earlier, I didn't mean to worry you. I completely forgot I could contact Mateos."

"Never mind, darling, Mateos probably gave you more than enough grief about that," Chris gave his wife's hand an understanding squeeze. "He wasn't too happy about us allowing you to stay behind either. Next time, I'll make you sign a disclaimer."

"He would keep me in a silver cage, if he could," Caila joked while Chris checked to make sure the heavy double oak doors were locked properly. "By the way, did he tell you he will be around most of the time, over the next couple of weeks?"

"You'd better be on your best behaviour then." Chris quickly kissed her on the top of her head, before they entered the Drawing Room.

"Hi Peter, I think we have some catching up to do."
Peter stood while Caila entered the drawing room, "Yes, indeed", he hesitated while he looked at Mateos and Chris. "I believe we do."

The latter got the hint, and requested, "Mateos, I believe I left my notes in the Inner Hall, could you help me find them, please?"

As Mateos followed her husband into the Inner Hall, Caila studied her new-found brother and pulled one of the smaller armchairs closer to the gently glowing fire, "I've been looking for a chance to talk to you too, but I don't really know where to start."

"I could not help but notice, Caila," Peter sank back into the larger wing chair, "that all your other Khered were known to you before the reset. And, as I get to know them better, I understand why you selected them," a frown appeared on his forehead. "You and I, however, were not acquainted prior to the Event. Would you mind if I asked you, how and why you selected me?"

"No, I don't mind. That is actually what I wanted to talk about. I did not select you," Caila admitted, "Mateos did."

The deepening frown in Peter's forehead betrayed his growing curiosity.

"Peter," Caila combed the hairy hearth rug with the tips of her toes, "did your parents tell you anything more, about the circumstances of your birth? I mean anything else than that it happened in the Netherlands." This would be so much easier to explain if Peter already knew he was half of a set of twins.

"Not really, my relationship with my parents was not intimate. I was mostly cared for by a nanny, until I was sent to boarding school, at the age of eight.

The most interaction I had with my parents was in my late teens, when they attempted to dissuade me from a career as a veterinarian, and in my early twenties, when they disagreed with my choice of partner," he paused for a moment. "I learned more about my parents after they passed away, than during their lifetime. My father was an avid diarist and recorded every one of his many engagements and opinions, in painstaking detail. I simply archived most of these diaries after his death, but I read the one which covered the period of my birth.

If I remember correctly, the hospital where I was born was in the south of the country. My mother was pregnant with twins, but my younger sister was stillborn."

"And the name of that hospital was, the 'Diakonessenhuis'," Caila completed the picture for him, "and you were born on Friday the 7th July 1967, early in the morning."

"Please, continue," Peter invited.

"At that time, intelligence agencies kept your family under close surveillance. They believed that a first-born red-haired girl in your family would inherit a 'curse' which made her part of an alien conspiracy to invade Earth. They were ready to weed …" Caila, inadvertently, used the same word Mateos had used earlier, "… ready to remove her from your parents. And if it hadn't been for Mateos, they would have succeeded."

She paused for a moment, struggling to find the right words, "Peter, your sister was not stillborn, but the child of another couple in that hospital was. Mateos switched the two girls, and your sister was assumed dead by the authorities, and therefore your family was no longer considered a threat to the security of Earth."

"First-born red-haired girl? Are we talking about twentieth century intelligence here, or fifteenth century Malleus Maleficarum? Red hair does occur in our family, but it skips generations. My grandmother had beautiful soft auburn hair. A bit like yours."

Then it dawned on Peter what Caila was trying to tell him, "Exactly like yours. Are you my sister, Caila? My twin sister?"

"Yes, I am. Mateos told me this morning. Last week, he offered to select my seventh chosen one when I told him that I was looking for someone with medical skills. He looked rather smug when I said that, but I think he would have selected you even if I'd asked for a, uhm …, an insurance underwriter."

"So, you are my little sister? That is a shock. A good one, but it is still a shock," Peter studied the woman, searching for a hint of family resemblance. "We don't look very alike, do we? I am about a foot taller than you are. Did your parents feed you properly?
But your eyes; that is why you look so familiar." He stared into his sister's bright green eyes, "We have the same eyes."

"Yes, it is a shock, isn't it?" Caila remembered how she'd felt after Mateos told her she had a twin brother. She wished she could read Peter as easily as she could read Mateos, who was an open book to her now. "But I'm glad you're here, even if I wished I'd got to know you earlier."

"And I am happy to be here," Peter smiled, "and I would not have minded having you around when I was younger, to help me fight my corner against my, …, our parents."
He glanced at the door, "I believe your husband and Mateos would like to know how we got on. This is the third time, they attempted to discretely look in on us."

Caila looked over her shoulder and caught a glimpse of Chris, nonchalantly strolling away into the Inner Hall, "Chris, you and Mateos can come in now, the surprise is over."

When Mateos apologised for separating the twins at birth, Peter assured him that, given the perilous situation, he'd have done the exact same thing.

With another glass of wine, they went on to discuss practical matters. Peter suggested, he should continue his search for medical equipment, together with Juliet. And he agreed to take Rebecca with him since she seemed to trust him and Juliet more than the others. In the afternoons, while he and Juliet worked on their new hospital, he would set homework for the 12-year-old, who'd expressed interest in becoming a doctor.

Later, as they entered the Edwardian Wing, Peter briefly embraced Caila and whispered, "Goodnight, little sister".

A shelter in Essex
Sunday 22 September

It had been four long days since the disaster, and Baldwin was getting sick and tired of the dimwits he had to spend his days and nights with.

On the second day, one of those oversized action-men had suggested going outside to explore the situation above ground. Pleased with himself that he'd anticipated such a development, Baldwin had put a stop to it. Without his guidance, these ignoramuses would undoubtably have been stupid enough to poke their heads out of the door and kill themselves in the process. They would willingly stick their hands into a flame, to check its temperature!

'Recognisance', that's what they called it; as far as he was concerned, it was plain and simple stupidity.

There were four other AC3 bunkers like this one, and all of them filled with decidedly expendable Guinea pigs. Three days ago, he'd called the first one; he told them he and his men were above ground and it was safe for them to venture out. He'd also informed them he had sent a security detail, to meet them and escort them back to London. Then he asked for confirmation that their transport had arrived safely.

After he'd heard them open the door to their shelter, all communications had ceased. As had their lives, he assumed.

'No big loss,' he thought, he'd never been a royalist anyway.

Tomorrow he would try again.

George and Gemma
Wednesday 25 September

When they were awoken by a series of clicks, followed by a high-pitched beeping sound, Gemma was the first to catch on, "George, wake up, we overslept. It's been seven days, the door is open, anyone can come in now."

George leapt out of bed and stared at the sliver of sunlight entering their stuffy quarters, "Well they don't appear to be in too much of a hurry to release us from our involuntary, yet not too unpleasant captivity, my darling." He lifted the 16-kilogram bag of flour, which they'd decided would make an adequate door wedge to keep the triple-enforced-steel-alloy obstruction, otherwise known as a door, in place, as soon as it decided to unlatch.

To doubly ensure that the wretched thing would not accidently lock them in again, he also secured the door, like Smickolth had demonstrated one week earlier. Only then, did he satisfy his curiosity, and look outside.

Shocked, George took a step back into the shelter, and looked over his shoulder at Gemma. He rubbed his eyes and looked out again. No, he had not been hallucinating, and there was nothing wrong with his eyes.

While he tried to make sense of what he'd seen, George turned around to face his fiancée, who was frantically trying to gather her clothes and get dressed at the same time.

No, there was definitely nothing wrong with his eyes, "Don't hurry, darling, I don't expect anyone to arrive, anytime soon," he inspected the alien looking landscape one more time. "Something happened while we were in here, something bad. … There is nothing left out there, Gemma, everything is gone," his voice sounded hoarse as he faced his fiancée. "It's all gone. Everything has vanished."

"Very funny, but I believe we would have noticed if a bomb had been dropped while we were in here," Gemma normally loved her fiancé's sense of humour, but this time it was misplaced and ill-timed. "Get dressed, please. You don't want to adorn the frontpages of the tabloids dressed in only your underpants," she inspected her fiancé's current state of undress, "or less."

Quietly, George took her by the arm, and gently led her to the door.

"George, I need my …."

As the fresh air touched her bare skin, Gemma fell silent.

"No palace, no London, no tabloids, no cameras. Only you and I, and this ruddy shelter."

They stood silently on the doorstep of their metal-enforced concrete home, observing the vast expanse of nothingness, until Gemma found her voice.

"Do you think it's just London? And is it safe to be outside?"

Apart from the absence of civilisation, Gemma didn't see or smell anything out of the ordinary. She had no idea what the aftermath of a nuclear disaster looked like, but she surely did not expect it to be like this. This was too fresh, … too clean.

George felt, that with his military background, he ought to have some idea what to do next, but this was not like anything they had ever prepared him for, "I don't know, Gemma, I really don't know. I believe nuclear weapons would have destroyed the trees as well. This looks almost, …, almost alien. Maybe we should get dressed and find out. Let's change into something comfortable and pack some supplies."

"May I remind you, my darling, the only clothes we have left are the ones we wore last week, when we went into this shelter. The clothes we have been wearing all week. You'll look horribly overdressed in your suit and tie.
Jeez, I'm so glad I didn't change into my heels just yet," Gemma wiggled her feet into her comfortable trainers. "Where shall we go? Maybe we should go and find your family?"

"That would be a good plan, if I had even the faintest idea where to start looking. But they told me absolutely nothing; they simply left, without telling anyone where they were going," he could not believe they would have left for a shelter, leaving him and Gemma behind in London, leaving them behind to …, he didn't even want to consider that possibility. There had to be another explanation for their sudden departure. "There is of course a chance they will come back to London. What I do know, is that we can't stay here and wait for them, we'll run out of food soon," George eyed the meagre supplies left on the shelves in their shelter: biscuits, sweets and bottled water, and more flour. What the hell had his brother intended to do with those quantities of plain flower? "But I haven't a clue where we should go, we might as well flip a coin."

Despite the bizarre situation, Gemma laughed, "George, darling, I did not remember to take my purse last week; I am flat broke. So, unless you have some spare change in your pocket?"

"Please, take me seriously, woman," George teased her, "I am a professional, trained to deal with these kinds of situations." He scanned the room, "You packed our backgammon set, didn't you?"

"Well, yes, I did. It's sentimental, I thought it would be a nice keepsake, to remind us of our premature subterranean honeymoon," Gemma defended her move to pack the rather bulky box. "Oh, I see what you mean. The dice! 1-2-3-4 for north-east-south-west? Five and six for try again."
She got the dice out and threw a six, "Your turn."

With a casual flip of the wrist, George sent the dice flying, "Three! We're going south. Let's hope there are some people or buildings left out there. But even if there aren't, we are better off in the countryside than in the remains of the city."

***

They walked for eight hours until, just south of what they assumed had been the M25, they spotted signs of habitation. Ducks were noisily grazing between a herd of deer on a green beside a village pond, and although the couple were disappointed to find Godstone deserted, it seemed like a good place to spend the night. After their long hike on dirt roads through untouched countryside, the chocolate-box village felt like the ideal place to spend the night; the hotel was warm and cosy, with its fridges and cookers still in perfect working order.

After finishing their first hot dinner in a week, they settled on a comfortable sofa next to the fireplace, to sample a variety of ice creams and local cheeses.

"At least it's progress," Gemma leaned against her fiancé and yawned, the food and the open fire made her drowsy, "there is left more of this one little town than there is of the whole of London."

"That's right," George emptied his second bowl of ice-cream, "but I would feel better if we could find out what happened last week. It is curious that the gas and electricity are still working. There's no emergency generator, and I can't imagine that someone is still keeping the power stations running."

"We may never find out," again, Gemma wondered if her parents were still alive, "but let's leave the worrying until later. For now, I'm glad we found some proper food and a roof over our heads. What shall we do tomorrow?"

"I think we should explore this build-up area a bit further. See where the boundaries are and look for other survivors. It's best of we do that in a methodical manner, working inwards from the boundaries."

"Or, we could take a day off and do something fun. I saw two bicycles outside. We could visit this place here," Gemma showed George a leaflet she'd found earlier. "Hever. If it's still there. It says that it is Anne Boleyn's childhood home; a romantic double-moated castle, with magnificent gardens and fresh, locally sourced food in the restaurants. They recommend a picnic on the beautiful lawns."

"So, you want to visit the family home of the wife of my great, great, lots of greats, great uncle?"

Gemma slapped his fingers, as he stole some ice-cream from her bowl.

"Why not? Our calendars are clear, and you haven't seen that much of England yet.
Are you sure, you want to ride a bicycle? We could take a car, I tried starting one earlier, and they still work."

"You are not getting me into a car any time soon, my darling, I love the fresh air after a week in that metal prison cell. It's only ten miles, that's no more than an hour. At most."

***

"It's beautiful, isn't it? No wonder they call it the Garden of England. I like those trees overhanging the roads, they are like green tunnels. Do you have any straight roads, here in this country?" the next morning, after a good night's sleep, Gemma enjoyed her bike ride through the Kentish countryside. "Shall we get something to drink? I'm thirsty." They'd parked their bikes against a table while they were having a rest on the terrace of a supermarket.

"Why not?" George pulled Gemma up, from the metal chair. "Let's see what they've got."
While the doors slid open, welcomingly inviting them into the store, George wondered again who kept the electricity going.
Then, as he noticed the empty fruit and vegetable isles, he stopped abruptly and held Gemma back, "It looks like we are not the first ones to go shopping at Waitrose.
Let's quickly get what we need and then go back outside. From that terrace we have a good overview of the area."

"So, we're not the only ones left in the world," Gemma was partly reassured, partly worried. "Let's hope the natives are friendly."

"Careful, darling, I am one of those natives," George made a playful grab for his fiancée. "But let's be careful from now on, I don't fancy running into the armed neighbourhood watch. Do you still want to cycle to Hever?"

Gemma punched him in the shoulder, "Of course, I do; with you as a bodyguard I have nothing to fear. Come on, let's get that orange juice and head for the late Ms. Boleyn's home. She's the one who was beheaded, isn't she?"

Lab rats

"Caila!" Rebecca's volume was impressive, "Caila!"

Caila watched the waving teenager, perched on a bench outside the castle, surrounded by textbooks. She had adjusted perfectly to her new life at Hever, even throwing the odd tantrum now that she started to feel at home. And she appeared to get used to Mateos. They'd discovered that Rebecca could only see him when he masked as a human, but as a Neteru, he was nothing more than a ghostly haze to her.

"Hey, Caila! Look, over there!" Rebecca pointed in the direction of the information booth. "A man and a woman, on bicycles."

'Perfect timing,' Caila put her heavy basket filled with apples on the drawbridge and rushed towards the excited teenager, "Rebecca, go to Peter and tell him to be ready, he'll know what to do. And ask Turgon to come over to me. You stay with Peter, please," Caila saw a, 'but', coming. "Now, Rebecca. Quick as you can."

Caila was happy that Turgon was still around. The Neteruian engineer had stopped by to give Peter a hand getting a scanner up and running, in their new cottage hospital. Everyone else had left for another day of stocking up, in East Grinstead. And she had no idea where Mateos had gone to, she only knew that he was out of reach until sometime that evening.

It didn't take long for Peter to contact his sister, informing her that he and Rebecca were in place, - Caila, we've got you covered. Don't take unnecessary risks. –

- It appears to be only the two of them, – OOVII circled the castle, - but I sent corvids out to investigate if there are any more unidentified humans in the area. Don't take any risks, Caila. –

As Turgon joined Caila outside the drawbridge, she repeated Peter's and OOVII's caution, not to take any risks.

- Thank you all, what did you say about taking risks, – Caila fired back while she watched their visitors dismount, - I didn't quite catch that. –

"Good morning, can you tell us what happened, please? You are the first person we've seen in a week," George got straight to the point.

"Apologies for my fiancé's lack of manners, it's probably the shock," Gemma, sensing Caila's reservations, dropped her bike, and with an extended hand and a smile, she stepped in. "My name is Gemma, and this is George."

Caila shook her hand.

"We came from London. Do you have any idea, what happened?"

'Gemma and George? Of course, George and Gemma!' now that Caila recognised them, she believed that the odds of both of them having partial DNA were a bit too small, and if they had survived in a bunker, they were bound to be accompanied by at least some bodyguards of sorts, "Nice to meet you, Gemma, I'm Caila. You said that you hadn't seen anyone in a week. Is it just the two of you then? How did you survive?"

"Come on, Gemma," George felt uneasy, this wasn't the warmest of welcomes, and he'd seen the other girl run back into the castle, probably to alert others. "Maybe we should move on," he picked up his backpack and reached for the zipper.

"I wouldn't do that, George. Put your bag down, please," Caila warned him, and when the man hesitated, she added more urgently, "Now! … Unless you want to be used as an archery target."

George carefully placed his bag back on the ground and held up his hands. "See? Empty. I was just getting my cap, Caila."

Then deciding to err on the side of caution, he answered the woman's earlier questions, "One week ago, I was asked to sign off on a panic room for my brother, and, as part of the sign-off process, we were requested to test the locking mechanism. For some unfathomable reason, my brother had ordered a feature that keeps anyone locked in for a week, if the internal PIN is not immediately followed up by an external release code. After we locked ourselves in, the contractor failed to respond to our requests to release us and we were not freed until yesterday morning, exactly one week after being confined.

When we opened the door, London was gone, and then luck of the draw sent us south."

- They don't have any Khered DNA, – Turgon had examined the couple, - I would like to have a look at that bunker, but I need a location. –

- I have a fair idea where you can find it, – the Neteru's idea sounded sensible to Caila. - If I send you an image of the rough location, then could you go and see if the amount of waste corresponds to no more than two humans, please? I'll keep them busy. –

Turgon accepted the image of Kensington Gardens and left instantly, without answering.

- Corvids are reporting no additional human activity in the area, – OOVII returned and perched on the railing of the drawbridge, close to his human Khered.

Reassured, Caila smiled at their unexpected guests, surely, no one would invent an absurd story like that, "That story is almost too crazy for anyone to make up. How did you find us, here at Hever?"

"Last night we slept in a hotel, in a village called Godstone, where we found some tourist brochures. I let Gemma decide," George scanned the castle for signs of the woman's armed friends, "and she selected Anne Boleyn's erstwhile abode. We were looking forward to a picnic on the lawns."

- Just enough waste for the two of them, and the DNA profiles fit these humans. –

Caila's mouth dropped open while she stared at the Neteru, who'd returned an reported her findings. She definitely did not want to know how Turgon had compared those profiles, - Thank you, Turgon, that's eh, … brilliant. –

- Peter, – Caila remembered to give her brother the all clear, - they checked out. Could you come down, please, and take Rebecca with you? You are not going to believe who they are. –

"Then you should probably have one," Caila returned her attention to her guests, "a picnic on the lawn, I mean. Do you have enough food? You are welcome to stay. You can leave your bikes out here, and if you decide to stay a bit longer, then you can put them in the shed with the others. Oh, and George, it is safe for you to pick up that bag now."

At that seemingly mercurial change of heart, George regarded his host suspiciously, he hadn't spotted any bowmen yet, but he also hadn't seen any signs of Caila calling them off, "We shouldn't impose on you any further, Caila. We'll have a picnic and then we will be on our way again." He turned to pick up his bicycle.

"But where would you go, George?" a vaguely familiar voice asked. "The current options are exceptionally limited, if you are looking for human company."

George looked back up, and regarded the man who'd appeared on the drawbridge behind Caila in amazement,

"Peter? … Peter Overwood? How the hell did you end up here? Gemma, this is Peter, I told you about him. He is the one who declined our wedding invitation and sent us the toast rack. Remember? That broken toast rack.
Peter, it has been a long time."

"Three years, and you broke that toast rack yourself. Remember? Fifteen years ago. I am delighted to finally make your acquaintance, Gemma," Peter greeted them warmly. "This overly excited young lady over here, is Rebecca. I barely managed to restrain her, George, she was ready to shoot you when you reached for that bag. I apologise for that, but we need to be careful out here. And the little one, is Aurora, we are on babysitting duty while the others are out shopping.
Please, do come in and join us in the Drawing Room."

To Rebecca's displeasure, Turgon's bright purple cloud, followed them back into the castle. But her excitement about their noteworthy visitors, banished her trepidation of the nebulous Neteru to the background.
Inside the comfortable Drawing Room, George repeated his story about the bunker and added that, ten days ago, his father and brother had unexpectedly left London, with their families.

To fill in the blanks, Peter gave an account of the reset Event, but hesitated before adding, "I seem to recall that in the event of a disaster, the five most senior members of your family are to be taken to a high security shelter. That is probably where your family went, they were most likely not left any other choice. They may well be alive today."

"Gran, father, my brother and his two children," George counted them out on his fingers, "I guess those shelters aren't built for large groups."

He sounded bitter, and Gemma gave him a hug, "We are still here, together, and we found new friends." Her hopes, that this was a local event, and that her own family were still safe, had been dashed when Peter explained that the effect of the reset was worldwide, "Have you ever met any of these Neteru, Caila?"

Rebecca huffed, and Caila smiled, "Rebecca is still getting used to our visitors from outer space. Yes, we have our own contact, he is called Mateos, and he will be back later today. You won't be able to see him though, just like you can't see Turgon, who is here in this room with us, right now. We survived because we have a little bit of alien DNA, that is what allows us to see the Neteru, and communicate with them.

Why don't you stay for a while, meet the others and then decide what you want to do?"

She felt sorry for them, Gemma was stuck in a strange country, far away from her family. Caila had seen the glimmer of hope in Jenny's eyes, before the girl had entered her old home; visiting the place where she'd grown up had been painful, but it had helped her to accept the current situation. Gemma would never have that chance.

And George? Well, finding out that you had been left out of the family shelter when they knew the world was about to end, would be pretty hard to take.

"We could use someone with your background, George. Except for Peter, we all come from cosy office jobs; with your training you could be a great help for Juliet, digging the beds to prepare them for planting in spring."

When everybody laughed at her clumsy sales pitch, she quickly added, "And of course, because you are both really nice people."

"I bet, that office job of yours didn't involve any marketing?" still laughing, Gemma looked at George, who nodded. "But, yes, we'd love to stay for a while, and help out."

Peter looked at Turgon and got up, "And I would love to stay and talk, but Turgon and I have a scanner to install. I'll see you all later, for lunch," he turned to Rebecca, "Becca, are you sure you don't want to join us?"

"No, I'll keep watch, out front. Besides I need to study," then, she clarified to the newcomers, "I am studying to be a vet and a doctor. Peter is teaching me."

After Turgon had returned to Signe in Sweden, early that afternoon, Rebecca was happy to re-join her mentor at the hospital.

Caila and Peter, helped George polish off a bottle of wine, while Gemma and Rebecca washed their picnic away with orange juice. Rebecca protested in vain that, if she was old enough to study medicine, she was surely old enough for a glass of wine.

"No, Becca, one of us needs to stay sober, in case we have a medical emergency this afternoon," Peter winked at Caila, while he got up. "Follow me, my abecedarian. There is work to be done, and lectures to be attended.

George and Gemma, I'm sure my sister will keep you occupied for the rest of the afternoon. She promised us roast potatoes for dinner."

"Sister?" George raised his eyebrows, as far as he knew, Peter had always been an only child.

"Yes, I am Peter's sister, his twin," Caila watched her brother walk away. "I'll explain later, while we peel those potatoes. We need enough to feed eleven. We also have lovely, freshly harvested parsnips to prepare. And we have sausages.

You're not vegetarians, are you?"

***

That evening, the others accepted Gemma and George unconditionally, and Jenny, who was pining for a party, proposed they should let the wedding go ahead, as planned. Chris suggested, that a Neteru style partnering ceremony might be appropriate, which, as he had been informed by a reliable source, was an intimate and relaxed affair. His wife had the good grace to blush, as he gave her a pointed stare.

While the others got busy planning the upcoming nuptials, Chris whispered, "I hope you didn't take any risks, when they arrived this morning. Mateos will kill you, if you did, and I would be right behind him, one-hundred percent."

"Have you ever known me to take unacceptable risks?" Caila was not worried, and when she noticed that her husband was not convinced by her selective memory, she added, "No really, darling, I was very careful. Peter and Rebecca had me covered, Turgon was right next to me, all the time, and OOVII's army scanned the area for extra visitors. Not even Mateos can find fault with that."

So, naturally, when Mateos finally arrived, he glared at the newcomers across the table and demanded, "Why did you meet them outside, Caila, alone? Turgon told me about it."

"And a good evening to you too, Mateos. I'm sure that Turgon also told you that she was with me from the start, and that I had two ace archers covering my back," Caila retorted, she'd been perfectly safe. "And do you realise that George and Gemma can't see or hear you? It must look like I'm talking into thin air."

- Turgon said that they had no Khered DNA at all. Could you double check, please? –

"George and Gemma. Mateos is back," Caila informed their guests, "he knows you can't see him, but he says hello."

- There are three of them, this one is expecting a child, – while   he   examined   Gemma,   Mateos   made   the announcement to the assembled Khered, - it's probably about seven weeks. –

Jenny, dumbfounded by the unexpected bit of news, gasped and coughed, covering little Aurora in a hail of chocolate crumbs.

"What did I miss?" Rebecca poured Jenny a glass of water.

"It's nothing, it was just Mateos, making an observation," hiding her irritation with the Neteru, Caila pushed her chair back. "Let's all go to the Drawing Room. Gemma, could you give me a hand, please? I need to get some extra throws from the Library, the Drawing Room is getting kind of chilly around this time."

While the others filed into the Drawing Room, Mateos followed Caila and Gemma into the Library.

"Gemma, would you mind if I asked you an indiscrete question?" Caila posed the obligatory yet obsolete question before diving in headfirst. "Are you pregnant?"

When Gemma's only reply was a speechless stare, Caila explained, "After he arrived home, Mateos examined you and George for Khered DNA. He didn't find any, but he discovered that you are pregnant. That is the observation I told Rebecca he'd made. Unfortunately, he broadcasted the announcement to the entire room. You, George and Rebecca were the only ones who couldn't hear him." Caila raised her eyebrows at Mateos who, with his back to the two women, was studying the portrait of Johann Jakob Astor above the fireplace. "Mateos is here in the Library with us, so if you want to give him a piece of your mind, be my guest."

Gemma didn't take Caila up on that offer, as she simply declared, "Yes, I am pregnant, I think it's about six or seven weeks. George knows and he is very happy about it, but we didn't tell anyone else yet, his family might have had reservations, about the timing."

"Yeh, I can imagine that wouldn't have gone down well," Caila scooped up an armful of blankets, "but I don't think anyone in our group will have a problem with it. Why don't you and George confirm it to everyone, now that the cat's out of the bag? I'm sure Peter will want to brush up on his midwifery skills. Unless, of course, you'd rather wait a bit longer, then I'll tell them that Mateos spoke out of turn."

"No, that's fine," Gemma looked around, not seeing anyone else in the Library than Caila, "and thank you, Mateos, for confirming it, we only did a home test."

"It's fantastic news, Gemma, everyone will be so pleased for you and George. And Mateos apologises for his indiscretion."

The Neteru scowled, while his fibbing Khered handed Gemma an armful of throws, "Could you take these to the Drawing Room, please? I need to have a quick word with Mateos."

Caila waited until Gemma had left the room, before she faced her liaison, "Thanks for using the P.A. system to announce that little bit of highly personal information. You made Jenny waste the last bite of her brownie."

"It is just a pregnancy, and it is still early days, no more than seven weeks," Mateos moved over to the writing desk and studied the titles of a series of books before he faced his Khered, "you shouldn't get too excited about it."

"And that is exactly what I would like to discuss," Caila hoped he would understand, but his demeanour was not promising. "In the excitement, no one remembered the repeat Event. But I'm sure that they will, eventually, and they will put two and two together. With no Khered DNA at all, those two are not going to survive the reactivation of the telumparticula, are they?"

"Caila, their survival was a fluke …" Mateos did not get far, before Caila interrupted him.

"But they did survive, didn't they? And they are not the army, armed to the bloody teeth, ready to take us out. Gemma and George are an ordinary couple, who would fit in perfectly well with our group. And honestly, we could use some muscle power.
So, how would you like us to handle this? Do we need to escort them back to their London bunker, for a week, or will you adjust their DNA?"

"Their shelter has been destroyed, it posed a security risk. And you know that I cannot adjust them," Mateos tried to reason with his impatient honorary sister. "You have your seven chosen ones, that is the maximum I can give you."

"I am very well aware of the fact, that I am allowed only seven 'activated' Khered, and I am not asking for more. I am only asking for Khered DNA, or simply enough partial DNA to allow them to survive the next blast.

I went along, and I agreed with to reset. ..."

Mateos made as if to interrupt her.

"No, Mateos, wait. Hear me out, please. I realise it was the only option. I saw the alternative. Remember? But I am still human, and seeing all humans disappear because of an Event I approved, was not easy. How would you feel if you were given the same choice about the Neteruian population? Gemma and George are lovely, and their baby is a symbol of hope in this crazy situation.

This is where I draw the line. You are not removing George or Gemma or their baby, or any other innocent survivors who come our way. Just raise this at your Assembly, I'm sure you can convince them."

"Be reasonable, Caila, it was extremely difficult to convince them to give humans a second chance, in the first place," Mateos objected calmly. "They won't allow me to increase the numbers of human seedlings any further."

Caila was stunned that he could be so matter of fact about this, so cold, and before she could help herself, she replied icily, "The number of lab rats, you mean?"

"Caila, that is not fair," Mateos was perplexed, he'd expected a tantrum, or shouting, but not this detached and cold response. "I don't believe that I deserve that. You are certainly not lab rats to me, and I never treated you as such."

"No, I can't deny that, you have been very civil about it all, about restarting your experiment. But, Mateos, …" Caila took a deep breath, "if you are not going to help me with this, then I will do it myself."

"You can't," there was no way she would be able to do that, "that's impossible, only Neteru can adjust humans."

"Are you absolutely sure about that? I can mask and cloak; and remember how I adjusted Chris. After all, you yourself asked me to be discrete if I practised my Neteruian tricks. And believe me, Mateos, I have been practising," Caila hoped he wouldn't call her bluff. "Ten days. That's it. If you haven't done it by then, I'll do it myself."

Not waiting for an answer, Caila turned on her heels and walked out of the Library, shutting Mateos out completely. Ready to keep that up for the next ten days, if necessary.

A shelter in Essex

Wednesday 2 October

Baldwin had tried again on Monday, the fifth day after the disaster, with the same result as his first attempt. He had been locked up for two weeks now and was ready to give it another go. There were only two cages of bunny rabbits left, if this next one didn't work, he would wait at least another month, before opening the last one. It was a shame about the second load, all military, he could have used them.

"Good morning, this is acting Prime Minister Baldwin Thurogood speaking. Four hours ago, we opened the door to our shelter. We found that it is now safe to exit, and we sent out a vehicle to meet you. Can you please confirm, that this vehicle has arrived at its destination? You will be escorted back to London to assume your duties."

Eleonor had come into the little office space, and was excitedly listening in.

'Stupid woman,' he thought, he'd explicitly instructed her to keep watch in the hall.

Last time he called, he thought he'd heard someone at the door, and today he'd found the phone disconnected and drained. Thank goodness, he'd had the foresight to pocket himself a spare lead. Traitors. Probably that pretty soldier girl, Emily, the vengeful bitch. He'd seen her whispering with her two friends, and he made a mental note to get rid of the morons as soon as they'd outlived their usefulness.

"Affirmative," a male voice on the other end of the line demanded his attention, "standby for confirmation." Baldwin heard a door being opened and held his breath. Good, he could still hear them talking. Then a shout was followed by total silence.

"Apologies for the delay, Sir, …" the man's voice faltered, "… Mr Prime Minister. We were not prepared for this sight. There is nothing left out there, nothing but wasteland as far as the eye can see. And there is no sign of your vehicle."

"I do apologise, I should have warned you about the situation above ground. Please, confirm your position, then I will check with your escort."

"Newport, Wales, that is 51° 35' 9.51" N, -2° 59' 32.41" W; I confirm, Newport, …"

Baldwin tuned out, if those guys were in Wales, and there was indeed nothing left out there, then it would take them days to march back to London.

"Newport? Baldwin here. I contacted your driver, he informed me that his Land Rover broke down. He will abandon the vehicle and return to London by foot.

Newport, please make your way to London, I will receive you in Downing Street. Failing that, make your way to Edenbridge, in Kent, 51° 11' 0" North, 0° 40' 0" East.

Newport, how many in your party?"

"Mr Prime Minister, we confirm that we will meet you in Downing Street, London. Failing that, we will make our way to Edenbridge, in Kent, $51° 11' 0''$ North, $0° 40' 0''$ East. There are six in our party, five male, one female. We estimate, that we will establish contact in London in 72 hours."

Only six. That was not much, but if they were fit enough to make it to London in three days, they would be useful. Probably military, "Very good, Newport. Over and out."

"Oh, Baldwin, isn't this exciting. We can go back to London now. You will be Prime Minister, and I will be your Chancellor," in idolatry admiration, the dumpy woman looked up at her lifelong hero.

"Let's be on our way then, Eleonor," Baldwin was flattered.

Eleonor held the door for him, as they walked into the large open space at the centre of the bunker. The eleven men and two women stopped talking when they entered.

"Comrades, you can open the door now," the Prime Minister's accent, had lost its upper-middle-class edge, "The sensors on shelter three, indicated that it is safe to do so."

Baldwin didn't notice the glance that was exchanged between Emily and her two friends.

"Sensors?" she mouthed at Gary.

"Sir!" Noah, labelled 'Action Man Number One' by Baldwin, obliged instantly, "All clear, Sir." Ramrod straight, he stood aside to let his Prime Minister pass.

"No, soldier, you go first. You earned that privilege," Baldwin stepped back. 'And it will be your head that's blown off if there is anyone out there,' he thought, 'not mine.'

"Please proceed, comrade."

"Sir?" Action Man sounded unsure when he called out to Baldwin, "Mr Prime Minister? There is nothing out there. No buildings, no roads, no cars. Nothing. There is nothing at all."

Pushing Baldwin aside, Eleonor rushed out to join Noah, "Baldwin, he is right. There is nothing," she looked up at her icon, who'd also stepped out into the alien landscape. "Do you think we travelled back in time, to the middle ages?"

Baldwin regarded the woman with contempt, "Eleonor, could you for once attempt to use whatever little brains cells you have? Of course, this is not time travel. We were nuked by a bunch of aliens. And I know just where to find their redhaired witching accomplice. We are going south, to pay them a visit; to introduce ourselves and show who is in charge."

A day to remember
Thursday 3 October

It hadn't taken the others very long to catch on. Chris had asked her that same evening how George and Gemma were going to survive the reactivation of the telumparticula. And Peter, Juliet and Luke asked her the next morning. Caila had told them all the same thing, with a lot more conviction than she actually felt, "Mateos will take care of it." When Juliet offered to tell the others, she was thankful, it would take some of the heat away from her.

Devyn had visited Hever on Monday morning to explain that, what she'd asked for, was impossible. And, when she gave him the same ultimatum, she'd given Mateos, he'd asked her if she'd completely lost her mind.

She had simply told him "No", before masking as a crow and flying into the nearest tree.

Fortunately, Devyn was completely stunned by her little stunt, and left instantly, so that he didn't witness how Caila clumsily crashed down from the low branch on which she'd landed and painfully twisted her ankle.

Two days ago, Chris asked his wife what was going on between her and Mateos, but Caila had told him that it was just a brother sister thing. There was no need to worry her husband, not just yet.

Caila looked at herself in the full-length mirror. Today was the day of the wedding, and she felt like crying. She hadn't heard from Sets since their fight, last week, but still felt the same way. There was no way, she was going to let that second beam take George and Gemma away from them. But she missed Sets, why didn't he understand how important this was to her?

Oh, flip, in only a couple of minutes, she would have to go down to join the others. How could just thinking about crying bring about more tears? This was going to ruin her make-up, again, and she'd run out of tissues.

A knock on her door brought Caila back to reality, and while she took a wild swipe at her tears, she called out, "Come in."

Steve took one look at her before pulling out an enormous white linen handkerchief.

"What's wrong, Caila? You haven't been yourself since you had an argument with Mateos, last Thursday. No, don't deny it, you were thick as thieves, but now you haven't spoken or even looked at each other for a week. Stay still, I don't want to smear your mascara."

While he carefully wiped the stains under Caila's red eyes, Steve was rewarded with a watery smile.

"That's better, young lady. Now, I don't want to take sides, but if you need someone to beat some sense into that alien half-brother of yours, I'll be happy to oblige. I don't know if you've noticed, but with all that manual labour I have become very muscly," Steve flexed his barely visible biceps. "I'm sure I can do him some harm, before he whisks me back to my room."

"Oh, Steve, you're the best," Caila laughed. "I'm sure that Mateos and I can sort this out, but I'll keep your offer in mind." She scrutinised his appearance, "You look stunning in that suit. I've never seen you dressed up like that."

"And you look beautiful in that gown, turquoise is a good colour for you. It is a lavish affair for a quickie wedding, isn't it?" with an elegant swirl, Steve offered Caila his arm. "Lush!"

"It certainly is," Caila rested her hand on his arm, and let herself be led out of the room, "and we are going to make it a day to remember."

The Drawing Room looked like something out of a fairy-tale, decorated with a wealth of flowers from the garden, and white ribbons everywhere. Even the low autumn sun did its utmost to make the space look perfect, as it shone in, bright, warm and romantic.
Luke played Wagner's wedding march when Gemma and George entered the room together. Then, holding hands they faced each other in front of their friends.

"George, we have long looked forward to this day. We started planning our perfect wedding over six months ago. We had the church booked, the reception planned, and we invited hundreds of guests.

And then, unexpectedly, we spent our hen and stag dos together, in a shelter, just the two of us; with lots of sweets and endless games of backgammon. And it was perfect.

Now, we stand here at Hever, still together. Not the wedding we had planned, in a large church, with hundreds of guests. But an intimate partnering ceremony, in a drawing room, just the two of us and ten friends. And it is perfect.

I love you, George, and I promise to share the rest of my life with you. As your partner." George was visibly moved, and Gemma smiled at the man she loved so much.

"Gemma, when I met you, I believed you might be the one. … That one woman, who I could spend the rest of my life with. And when I got to know you better, it didn't take me long to realise that you were truly that one woman for me. You made me unspeakably happy when you told me you felt the same, when I asked you to marry me. I thought, I could see how our life would be; us working together, starting a family and growing old.

And then came that moment, the moment I opened that door. The door to our new future, a future that we did not foresee. But I still want us to work together, start a family, and grow old. Build a better world, for us and for our children.

That is why I stand here with you, Gemma. To pledge my love to you, to promise you that I will spend the rest of my life with you, as your partner. I love you, Gemma."

"George and Gemma," the couple had asked Peter to officiate the ceremony, "all in this room, have borne witness to your vows. From this day forward, you are partners for life."

Caila sensed Mateos's presence while the couple exchanged their vows; there was a deep sadness about him. But when she felt how he tried to connect to her, she resisted, this was not the moment. Instead she moved closer to Chris and whispered that she loved him.

Partners for life. She hoped it meant more than two weeks for this couple. A tear slipped down her face. 'No,' she vowed silently, she would make sure that life was longer than two weeks for them.

Mateos left the Drawing Room before the end of the ceremony, but Caila sensed he was still somewhere in the castle. Something didn't feel right. She ignored her feeling of unease as she followed the others into the Dining Hall, for George and Gemma's wedding breakfast. This was their big day, and nothing should spoil it.

The newlyweds scrutinised their presents, which had been piled high onto a side table.

The card had been the largest they could find, and it was signed by everyone, even, with a little bit of help from Jenny, by baby Aurora. Peter had found Gemma and George a beautiful paperweight, and told them that the Asters inside, symbolised deep emotional love and affection. Juliet got them two crystal champagne glasses, and a bottle of bubbly, for them to share after the baby was born. From

Jenny and Aurora there was a dainty little heart shaped statue, and Luke had found them a beautiful pen and a diary. Rebecca's gift, of a book with photos of the United Kingdom how it used to be, was a brilliant find. Caila and Chris gave them a pair of matching soft bath robes, for the long winter months, and they had filled a picnic hamper with the couple's favourite foods. Steve and Richard pooled their resources, which meant that Steve had found them an enormous tiered cake stand, and Richard had stacked it high with home baked cakes and biscuits.

While everyone was busy admiring gifts, Caila sneaked out of the room. It was impossible to ignore Mateos any longer, something was not right.

She found him in the study, at the far end of the Library, staring out of the window.

"Sets, what's wrong?"

When he didn't turn around, Caila attempted to scan his memories. He noticed it and tried to stop her.

"Don't," but he was too late.

"I'm sorry, I had to know, it hurt too much," she apologised. "It's Tia, isn't it?" Caila walked over to him. "Was that the last time you saw her? On her wedding day?" Just as she thought that her honorary brother was not going to respond, he opened up.

"Tia's partner was from a different planet. He refused to become Neteru, and Calia decided to transform to his species. I could have prevented it, I should have stopped her. She was killed one day after their ceremony."

"I'm so sorry," Caila stared out at the trees, laden with apples, "I didn't know."
As they stood there, quietly side by side, they didn't notice OOVII, who watched them with concern.

Then Mateos resolutely turned away from the window, "Don't you have celebrations to go back to, Caila? You look beautiful in that dress, I'm sure your husband wonders where you are."

"Yes, I should," Caila sighed, "probably." She did not want to leave Mateos alone in the study. "Yep, I should probably go back."

"Maybe, I should go with you?" Mateos surprised Caila with his offer. "I have a present for the newlyweds."

Caila's face fell, when he showed her a fascinating translucent sort of stone, which displayed a beautiful image of Etherun, "That is gorgeous."

Studying her face, he wanted to know, "Did you expect something else?"

"No, it's gorgeous, Mateos, really, it is. They will love it," Caila smiled at him, she didn't want any more fights, not today, not ever. If it wasn't sorted in time, she would take care of it herself, she was sure she could do it. This shouldn't be Sets' responsibility.

"Are you sure you wouldn't rather they became Khered, so that their, 'forever after', will last a bit longer?" Mateos pushed her.

"Did you? Really?" with tears in her eyes, Caila hugged Mateos. "Oh, I love you, Sets. I knew you would understand. How did you do it?"

"You did most of the work, when you convinced Devyn that this was a good idea. He is the one who proposed it at the assembly," Caila bit her lip, she hoped Devyn hadn't told Mateos how she'd changed his mind. "He has a better rapport with the leaders than I have; all I had to do was second him.

We can now use our discretion, to insert partial or full Khered DNA into humans who were unaffected by the telumparticula, or who survived in a shelter. Mind you, we are still not allowed to activate any more Khered."

"That's fine, it will be their best present ever," Caila was over the moon. "What will you do, partial or full?"

"I believe full would be a good idea, to avoid situations like we have with Rebecca. She is petrified every time I am not masked," Mateos had become annoyed with the girl's startled little shrieks, every time he came near her, "if she agrees, I would like to restore her partial DNA to full."

"I'll talk to her, I think she'll like it. Come on, let's get back to the celebrations," but then Caila eyed Mateos worriedly. "Are you sure you want to go, Sets? I can excuse you and tell them about your gifts."

"No, I would like to be there."

But in the Library, he stopped and held Caila back, "I don't know how you managed to morph into a crow, Caila, and fly, but please, be careful.

Tia tried to morph into some bird once and fell ten floors down, it took her weeks to recover. However efficient it was, you scared the hell out of Dev, and I noticed you were limping that evening."

"I won't do it again. I just wanted to show Devyn that I was serious about this, and it was only a very low branch. I couldn't keep it up for very long though, and I slipped when I climbed back down. It was nothing more than a twisted ankle," she noticed that Mateos was about to interrupt her, so she quickly reassured him. "No, really, Sets, I won't do it again, I promise. Could you tell Devyn too, please? And tell him I apologised?"

"Don't stare, it's just Mateos and me," Caila felt uneasy when everyone looked at them as they entered the Dining Hall together. "George, Gemma? Can we steal you away for a tiny little minute, please?"

Hand in hand, the newlyweds followed them back into the Drawing Room, where Caila explained, "I'm really sorry about this, but in a minute, you will see why I wanted to do this as soon as possible.

Do you remember when I told you about that extra bit of DNA, that the rest of us have?

And, I believe the others explained the difference between the various types of Khered DNA.

Well, Mateos cannot activate any more Khered, I was allowed to select only seven, but he is now authorised to add dormant DNA to survivors, so that they become Khered.

That may not sound like a major thing, but the issue is that in less than fourteen days, the beam that was used two weeks ago, will be reactivated. Anyone without Khered DNA will disappear, and we don't want that to happen to you. That's why, we would like you to have your DNA adjusted. It will not only mean that you are unaffected by the telumparticula, but you will also be able to see the Neteru and communicate with them."

"No one told us, that beam would be fired again," George sounded surprised.

"We didn't want to worry you, before your wedding day," Caila explained, "and we knew that Mateos could get this sorted in time."

"I'd be happy to have my DNA adjusted. It beats another week's confinement in that ruddy shelter," George agreed without hesitation. "How about you, Gemma?"

"Will the baby be safe?" his partner frowned.

Caila looked questioningly at Mateos.

- He will be fine, he will be adjusted as well. –

- He? – Caila smiled surprised, and Mateos nodded.

- Yes, it is a male child. –

"Oh, I'm so sorry, I was distracted for a moment. I didn't mean to worry you. The baby will be fine, it will also receive Khered DNA. It's just that Mateos told me the gender of your baby. Would you like to know what it is?"

"If it's safe for the baby, then I'll be happy to have my DNA adjusted. I don't really mind if we have a boy or a girl, as long as it's healthy," Gemma looked at George, as if to gauge his opinion, and when he nodded, she requested, "Yehhh, go on. Tell us, please?"

"Good morning, Gemma, it's nice to meet you," Mateos stepped away from Gemma's back, "you should be able to see me now. Your baby is a very healthy boy."

"That is wonderful news," George inspected the Neteru, "and it's good to finally meet you, Mateos. Why is Rebecca so skittish around you, you look perfectly …", he hesitated, "human to me."

"That is because, at this moment, I mask as a human, but it takes too much energy to keep that up permanently," Mateos explained. "Congratulations on your partnering, I brought you a present, it is from my planet, from Etherun."

"That is beautiful!" Gemma exclaimed as she studied the image. "Is that what Etherun looks like?"

"Yes, it is. I am very proud of it."
While Mateos was happily chatting about his home planet, Caila shepherded them back to their guests in the dining room.

Later that day she had a quick word with Rebecca, who agreed to receive full Khered DNA. But not because she was afraid of Mateos, she declared, it was only because she believed it would not be right for her to be the only one with only half a string.

Little did the 12-year-old suspect, that it was not her DNA that would prove to be of importance to her future, but one decision she took two weeks earlier, on the day she arrived at Hever.

Couples' night

"That was romantic, wasn't it?" the half-moon gently illuminated the square outside the castle, and Caila could easily make out Chris's face as she snuggled up closer. She looked up at the sky and recognised The Plough and the North Star. "It's not much of a honeymoon though, but they looked so happy together. Do you think they'll be as happy as we have been? Still are?"

"I'm not sure that's possible, darling, but I'm sure they'll give it a try," Chris pulled Caila closer. "You also look happier, now that you patched things up with Mateos. That was a serious fight. Who won?"

"I do feel a lot better. And, you know? I believe neither of us won or lost. But we got to know ourselves and each other a little bit better."

"That is way too philosophical for a romantic evening like this one, Caila dear," hand in hand, Steve and Richard strolled towards them, "But I'm glad you didn't need to take me up on my offer."

"And, what offer would that be?" Richard looked bemused.

"Your husband, offered to beat some sense into Mateos, using his now well-developed biceps," Caila stroked Banjo's soft fur as the cat brushed up to her legs.

Richard and Chris exchanged a quick glance, before Richard burst out laughing.

"Steve, I'm looking forward to examining those well-developed biceps of yours, later tonight. But, let's take a walk first. See you later, guys."

"I'll let you know that …" Steve's voice died down, as they disappeared into the gardens, followed by their cats.

"What was that all about, little sister of mine?" Peter had gallantly offered Juliet his arm, for a late evening stroll through the gardens.

"That was about Steve's well-developed biceps," Chris enlightened his new brother in law.

"I will have to read up on anatomy then," Peter frowned, "I have always been under the impression, that biceps were muscles in the brachium, but I never observed any signs of muscle tone in Steve's upper arms."

"Peter, shame on you," Juliet chastened her companion. "Steve has, well he …., well, a few more weeks out in the gardens and he will develop some serious muscle tone. I'll make sure of that."

"How are the gardens shaping up?" Caila wanted to know. Juliet had taken responsibility for the animals and the vegetable garden, now that Rebecca assisted at the surgery.

"We are making good progress, certainly with George helping us out. I'm glad those two declined our offer of a couple of days honeymooning. There is a lot of work to be done this time of year."

"Absolutely," Caila agreed, "and with most of the shopping done, we can all start helping you prepare for winter. How's Rebecca settling in?"

"Feeling more confident, now that she can see Mateos properly. She is a pretty smart girl, I don't remember being this quick at chemistry when I was at school. She told me that she is determined to be my associate before her sixteenth birthday, and at the rate she is picking up new subjects, I would not be surprised if she managed to do just that. She is brilliant.
Come on Juliet, let's take a quick walk around the Italian gardens. Do you have your flashlight? Goodnight, Chris. Goodnight, little sister."

"We should have found ourselves a quieter place, this spot is busier than London Victoria at nine o'clock in the morning," Caila exaggerated.

"Well, you are very close to the door, and it is an awfully nice evening for a walk," Jenny strolled out next to Luke, who pushed Aurora's new state-of-the-art pram.
"I wonder when we'll have our next wedding?" Jenny watched Peter and Juliet's silhouettes disappear into the dark gardens, "Luke, shall we go left or right?"

"Right, please," Luke adjusted Aurora's blanket, "I need a new pen, from the shop."

"Bye you two, see you in the morning," Jenny gave a quick wave, before they disappeared between the ghostly contours of the topiary figures, which lined the path leading to the entrance. "Say goodnight, Aurora. Oh look, Luke, she smiles."

"Let's go inside, before they all come back again," Chris watched how the glow of Luke's green and Jenny's purple sphereams, disappeared into the distance, "and I believe I owe you an apology, my darling. I told you Jenny would drive Luke mad, but they seem to be getting along quite well together."

"Yes, they are, aren't they? And Jenny is an absolute star with Aurora," Caila frowned as she peered into the distance. "Perhaps we should organise some extra target practice."

"Did you see something out there?" Chris followed her gaze but saw nothing.

"I'm not sure, I thought I saw a flash of light," Caila shivered despite the unseasonal warmth, "it was probably my imagination."

"Maybe," Chris stared into the dark woods, "but we'd better not take any chances. With Luke also having spotted changes on the supermarket shelves, we should keep an eye out and beef up security. They could be partials who are reluctant to make contact, but we can't be certain that they are not hostile. I'll be glad when that second beam has been fired."

Inexplicable darts

Saturday 5 October

"It's Caila's turn," Chris warned the others, "take cover everyone!"

Ignoring her husband's remark, Caila bit her lip in intense concentration while she tried to raise her bow and draw in one fluid motion, like Peter had shown her earlier. She aimed, squinted her eyes, and released.

"Caila, mind our goats!" Juliet called out. "That arrow is supposed to go in the direction of that big round colourful disk, right in front of you."

"Would you like me to show you?" Rebecca put in her two cents' worth. "You're not holding the bow correctly."

"Thanks, Rebecca, but I think that's it for me, this is like darts."

The group roared with laughter.

"Dear god, I hope not. That would suggest, it is not even safe to hide behind you, while you release," Peter took a step back. "It was no mean feat, hitting the door behind your back, yesterday evening."

"Thank you, dear brother. Anyone else?"

"Well, since you asked," Mateos, her other sibling, chipped in. "You could use a trumpet, instead of a bow and arrow. It would see any enemy off in seconds, and it would be safer for the rest of us, as long as we wear earplugs."

"Remind me. Why did I ever wish for a big brother?" as she raised her arms in despair, Caila's bow got stuck in a rose bush. "Rebecca, it's your turn," she pulled her bow free from the obnoxious scrub and stepped aside to allow their ace archer to take her place.

The teen elegantly took aim and hit the target dead centre. While the group applauded her achievement, Rebecca took a little bow, "Thank you, it was nothing."

That morning they had decided to prioritise security over foraging. In the past couple of weeks, they'd collected every vegetable seed, bulb and plant they could find; their kitchen shelves were bulging with full, and yet to be filled, storage jars, and they would not have to worry about producing their own clothes for quite a few years.

From now on, until the repeat Event, they wouldn't leave the castle grounds, while two guards would be manning the tower constantly. And they were going to perfect their archery skills. Skills which were non-existent in Caila, and therefore a constant source of amusement to the others.

"Jenny? Why don't you have one last go?" Chris handed her another arrow, "Then we'll have lunch before George and Gemma relieve Steve and Richard from guard duty."
Jenny wasn't as good as Rebecca, but she hit the target comfortably.

"Great job. Lunchtime!" Caila was happy to give archery and her random aim a rest. "And, for some extra exercise, we will all be assisting our head gardener this afternoon."

***

"If Juliet is our head gardener, then I vote that Richard and Chris should be our head chefs," Jenny grabbed the last piece of carrot cake, one of Richard specialties. "This is delicious, and Chris's egg curry is simply to die for."

"And we ..." Caila stopped mid-sentence to listen to a lectanimo from the guys in the guard tower, "that was Richard. Three men are approaching the castle, they just walked past the Guthrie Pavilion. Everyone. Get into position, please."

"Wait for me," as Caila started walking out, towards the drawbridge, Mateos was right behind her, "don't take any risks."

"I won't. And with you and Rebecca to cover my back, I don't really have anything to worry about, Sets. I still think it's funny that you didn't classify those bows and arrows as weapons, but as a game."

"So far, I have only been able to classify them as dangerous when they are in your hands, Tia. Khrhhsh evacuates the grounds, every time you approach the practice area."

"Very funny, Sets."

Yes, those were three men, all right; Caila watched them approach, but they didn't look very military; none of them had the straight and stiff posture she associated with soldiers. She allowed them to proceed until they reached the middle of the square.

"Good afternoon, gentlemen. Can I ask you to stop right there, please? My friends and I would like to make sure that you come in peace," Caila had prepared a little speech after the arrival of George and Gemma last week. "Do you carry any arms? Any guns, or knives?"

The elder of the three visitors replied in a soft voice, "Good afternoon, miss. We only have the knifes that we use to prepare our food, they are in our bags. We have nothing else."

He appeared nervous, but harmless enough. And, whilst the younger boy eyed Caila curiously, the man on the right avoided all eye contact.

"Then could you place your bags on the floor, please, in front of you? And remove your coats?" Caila watched how a cloaked Mateos inspected their callers, while they did as they were asked. "Yes, that's fine. Thank you. … And now a slow twirl, please?"

Mateos moved back to Caila, - No weapons. –

"Thank you, gentlemen. How did you survive?"

It was the older man again, who answered, "I'm not sure. I walked out of the butcher's, when, all at once, the world disappeared around me.

Jeff here, I'm Barnaby by the way; Jeff told me that he was on his way to work when it happened. And young Mike, he just arrived at school.

I met Mike south of Nottingham, and Jeff north of London. I'm from Manchester myself. We came down to London, to find some kind of Government. But London is also gone," Barnaby shook his head, as if he still couldn't fully comprehend what had happened.

"I'm afraid that this is all that's left of the UK, Barnaby," Caila confirmed. "I'm Caila. Why don't you come in? We were having lunch. Luke and Juliet will follow us in with your belongings."

- You can all come down now, – Caila used lectanimo to give the all-clear, - Luke and Juliet, could you pick up their coats and bags, please, and take them inside? Feel free to have a quick peek. Richard and Steve, can you hand over watch duty to George and Gemma, please? –

"Is that all of you, then?" Jeff, a handsome young man of around thirty, spoke for the first time as they crossed the courtyard.

"No, it is not."

Caila warned the others, not to give too much away, she wasn't sure why, but she didn't trust this guy, "Did you meet anyone else, on you trip down south?"

"Mike believes he saw someone, but they ran," it was again Barnaby from Manchester who responded. "That was probably near Leicester, although it's hard to tell now that all the road signs are gone."

"I assume it can be a bit scary, to meet strangers in these circumstances," Caila looked at the boy, whose well-worn school uniform bore the signs of his long track south. "But well spotted, Mike. Where are you from?"

"I'm from Wath-upon-Dearne, miss, that is in Yorkshire," Mike looked older than Rebecca, but he lacked her ballsy attitude.

"Caila will be fine, Mike, everyone calls me Caila. How old are you?"

"I'm sixteen, I passed my GCSE's last year."

"Then maybe you can help Rebecca with some of her subjects," Caila suggested. "Are you hungry?"

The skinny young man nodded.

"This is our dining room. It's just sandwiches, but the bread has been freshly baked. Please, sit down and help yourselves," she invited them. "Oh, hi Chris, come and meet our guests. This is Barnaby from Manchester, Mike from Yorkshire and Jeff from …, where are you from, Jeff?"

"I'm from King's Lynn," Jeff shook Chris's hand. "How do you do, Chris? Are you in charge of this little community?"

Chris raised his eyebrows towards his wife, who shrugged, "No, I am not. If anyone is in charge here, it's Caila."

"Pleased to meet you, Chris," Barnaby sensed the awkward situation. "We arrived in the area late last Thursday, but we waited a couple of days to see if it was safe to make contact. Caila, would you mind if I stayed here for a while? We have been on the road for a long time, and it would be good to be part of a community again. We will of course reciprocate. Just put us to work, wherever you need us. I am not as young as I was, but I'm still dead fit. I used to be a binman, that was before they started calling us refuse collectors."

"We'd be happy to have you, Barnaby," Caila looked questioningly at the other two. "Mike, would you like to stay as well?"

"Yes mi…, Caila. And I can help too. I helped my father in the garden, we grew our own vegetables."

"That's perfect, you should talk to Juliet then, she is our head gardener," Caila turned to the last of the three men. "Jeff, how about you?"

"We were actually hoping to find a more formal form of authority," Jeff appeared reluctant, "however, if the others are staying, then I might as well do the same, temporarily. I must warn you though, that I am not used to manual labour, I worked as an executive. Strictly brains, my dear."

"Don't worry, Jeff, most of us have a background similar to yours. The office job, I mean, none of us can lay claim to having reached executive level. Mike and Barnaby have the advantage over us pen-pushers now, whose only form of exercise was lifting our typing fingers. Why don't you give us a day or two? And if it's not for you, you can always move on."

Jeff scrunched his eyes, not certain if Caila had just paid him a complement or put him down. He decided that, from such an obscure little woman, it had to be the first.

Steve and Richard showed the newcomers their rooms, where they freshened up before joining the others in the gardens. To Jeff's chagrin, Barnaby resolutely declined Caila's offer of an afternoon's rest before being put to work by Juliet.

Mike and Barnaby proved skilful with a spade, sticking the implement into the ground and turning large scoops of soil; Jeff's expertise was sticking the gardening tool in the ground and leaning on it whilst complaining about his aching feet and back.

He would have to adjust significantly if he planned to make his home at Hever, Caila thought, or maybe he would move on, after he found out there were no vacancies for execs here. Then she chided herself for not giving the man a fair chance, maybe it was all just an act triggered by the unexpected and bizarre situation he'd found himself in, after the Event. Maybe he would change when he felt better at ease.

***

And change he did!

That evening, when Gemma and George joined the others, after being relieved from guard duty by Chris and Caila, Jeff stopped whining and started gushing.

Until Gemma, who felt the tension grow in their normally relaxed group, resolutely put a stop to it, "You are so right, Jeff! George is an absolute marvellous cook. He is completely and utterly brilliant, at everything he turns his hand to. That's why I married this amazing and handsome man." In an over-the-top performance, she clasped her hands and viewed the object of her affection with big doe-eyes, "Isn't he the picture of absolute, wonderous and glorious perfection?!"

"Hear, hear!" after the laughter died down, Juliet seconded Gemma's declaration of admiration. "And that, my dear, is why your perfect George will be our head-digger tomorrow morning. And I was hoping I could put you down, Gemma, for sorting our seeds and making an allotment calendar."

"That's fine by me. But don't be surprised," George warned her, "if you lose most of your Brussel sprouts' seeds if you leave Gemma alone with those things."

"Don't worry, I counted every single one of them," Juliet laughed. "Now for the rest of you. Caila and Chris, will be digging the near bed. Rebecca and Mike, you two are on weeding duty. Barnaby and Jeff, digging the far bed …"

"Juliet," Jeff interrupted, "with my back injury, I don't believe I will be able to do any digging tomorrow."

After Jeff rejected all other activities suggested by Juliet, on the grounds of diminished back, elbow and ankle power, sensitive skin and allergies, their head gardener despaired.

"Then what can you contribute to our agricultural activities, Jeff, without doing injury to yourself?"

"With my background in management, my dear," Jeff thought the answer was obvious, "it makes sense, for me to relieve you from the organisational and administrative elements of this operation. I am well versed in organising complex projects, and it will free you up to take a more active role in the practical aspects of our food production."

"Jeff," George's voice was deceptively calm, "Juliet is highly experienced and skilled in the organisation of complex projects. Furthermore, her knowledge of all matters related to agriculture is unsurpassed. Juliet is, and will remain, our extremely talented and highly respected head gardener. I would urge you, to not ever challenge Juliet's position in our group again. Is that understood?" George didn't wait for Jeff's response, "And tomorrow, you will be on the digging squad with me. Like Juliet proposed in the first place."

After a reluctantly mumbled agreement, Jeff kept a low profile for most of the evening. Until Jenny got up from the sofa to check up on Aurora, who had woken up with a high-pitched squeal. When Jenny lifted the baby out of her cot, a shrill whistle pierced the silence and Jeff smacked his lips,

"I wouldn't mind having such a good little yummy mummy picking me up. How about it, Jenny?"

"Oi! Douchebag!" while Jenny held Aurora protectively and stomped back to the sofa, a fuming George shot up from his chair, "What the hell!? Listen, and listen carefully, Jeff, because I am only going to say this once.

We do not tolerate this kind of lewd behaviour here at Hever, we respect each other, in word and in deed. If that is not acceptable to you, then you don't belong here, and I would advise you to leave, sooner rather than later. Do we understand each other, Jeff?"

"My sincerest apologies, George," Jeff shrunk away as he attempted to placate George, "I merely meant to complement Jenny on her good looks."

"Maybe you didn't understand me correctly, Jeff," George was not impressed by the man's insincere apology to the wrong person, "There is no excuse for what you did and said to Jenny. Is that crystal clear? Now apologise to Jenny."

Aggrieved, Jeff declared that he understood, and his weak excuse of an apology was accepted by Jenny. But the atmosphere was spoiled and remained tense for the rest of the evening.

Oblivious to the incident, and altogether unaware that it was not the enemy without but the enemy within who would soon demand their attention, Caila and Chris spent a quiet night in the tower, scanning the castle's deceptively peaceful surroundings.

Mayhem
Sunday 6 October

When Caila walked into the entrance hall, a piercing scream ended the early morning tranquillity. The door to the Dining Hall was closed, and when she opened it, she was greeted by a scene of mayhem. A shirtless Jeff held Rebecca in an iron grip, while he brandished a belt in his other hand. All the while, the frantic 12-year-old was kicking, and screaming at the top of her lungs.

The moment Jeff noticed the woman at the door, he let go of the girl and growled, "That child is deranged. She needs to be taught a lesson."
Rebecca ran towards the open door and clung to Caila.

"I find you in here, shirtless, with a belt in your hand, grabbing a 12-year-old girl, and you tell me that she is deranged?! You'd better have a damn good explanation for your behaviour."

Rebecca started sobbing, "He told me to mend his shirt. And I told him where he could find the sewing things. … And then he called me an insolent little bitch. … He said, that I should be taught, … a lesson. … Then he grabbed me, and, …, and, …" Rebecca hiccupped, "I was so scared."

While she used lectanimo to alert the others, Caila kept an eye on Jeff, then she told Rebecca to go and fetch Peter.

"But, …" despite her fear, the girl did not want to leave Caila alone with this man.

"Now, Rebecca," Caila gently pushed Rebecca towards the door, safely away from Jeff, calmly urging her, "Don't worry, I can handle this."

After she'd let go of the girl, Caila heard her running footsteps disappear in the Outer Hall, "Jeff, I am going to give you one chance, and one chance only, to walk out of that door in one piece. Then you keep walking until you are well away from this area. You don't ever come near this place, or near any of us, again. Have I made myself clear?"

Jeff sauntered menacingly up to the smaller woman, "Or what, my dear? Am I supposed to be impressed by a midget like you?" He made to grab Caila's arm, but she'd anticipated his move and kicked out.

Jeff doubled over.

"I asked you, if I'd made myself clear, Jeff?" the midget repeated herself. "What? Have you lost your voice? Then just listen to me. If I ever see you again, I will make your little speech problem permanent. Extremely permanent!"

When Caila heard the reassuring sound of footsteps running towards the Dining Hall, she turned around and asked, "Can someone put the trash out, please?"

"I apologise, Caila," Barnaby felt responsible for introducing Jeff into their group. "If I'd known what kind of a monster he was, I would never have asked him to join young Mike and me."

"Don't give it another thought, Barnaby, it wasn't your fault," Peter put the older man's mind at ease, "even if Jeff was not the most agreeable of men to begin with, no one could have predicted his abhorrent behaviour."

"I agree with Peter. Wouldn't it be useful, though, if men like that wore a big sign: 'Don't approach, I am a snake in disguise'? And you did well, Rebecca," Gemma winked at the girl, "from what Caila told us, you screamed loud enough to give him a headache as well as a hearing problem, before she matched it with a speech disorder."

"Yeah," Rebecca felt safe with Peter's arm around her, "and don't forget his bad back and aching feet." She looked at the door, to see Chris and George returning.

"I trust, the malfeasant has been appropriately disposed of?" Peter noticed the men's bruised knuckles.

George hid his hands, "He is still alive."

"Which is more than he deserves," Chris shrugged.

"How about breakfast?" last night's biscuits were the last thing Caila had eaten. "Luke and Jenny had something to eat, before they relieved us from guard duty. But I am famished."

"Yes, and then you should probably get some sleep," her brother advised, "you have been on your feet since yesterday morning."

"Is that your expert opinion, as my GP?" Caila teased Peter. The confrontation with Jeff had left her tense as a bowstring, but his old-fashioned advice of a cup of hot, strong, eye wateringly sweet tea had helped surprisingly well.

"That is my expert opinion as your GP, Caila, and my advice to you as your concerned brother," Peter got to his feet, "but, let's have some breakfast first."

"Where is Caila?" after hours of meetings on his home planet, Mateos felt drained when he arrived back at the castle.

"Hey, Mateos. How are you?" Steve tried to sound matter-of-fact, but he was a frightfully bad actor and his performance fell flat. "Caila is fine, don't worry. She was on night duty with Chris, and they need their little beauty sleep. Could you join us for a moment, please?"

"What's going on, and what happened to that third man who arrived yesterday?" one look at Steve was enough to tell Mateos something was wrong. "I saw Gemma outside with the other two. But the annoying one, wasn't with them."

Gemma had taken Barnaby and Mike, who were still oblivious of the background of the Event, for a tour of the grounds to give the others a chance to bring Mateos up to date.

After assuring the agitated Neteru once again, that Caila was fine and really needed her sleep, Steve presented Caila's honorary brother with a toned-down account of what had happened in the Dining Hall, earlier that morning.

"Jeff was terribly scary, look …" Rebecca upped the tone as she showed Mateos her bruised arms and added helpfully, "but Caila kicked him right in the …"

"Right where it hurts us men the most," Steve interrupted Rebecca, and finished her sentence for her, "he will be singing soprano for a while. And then, Chris and George escorted him out of the area. Right, George?"

Hiding his bruised knuckles under the sleeves of his sweater, George simply nodded.

"Let's hope we've seen the last of our executive from King's Lynn," Peter concluded, "our other two guests are agreeable enough. Juliet had a chat with Mike, this morning, and he is eager to help us out in the garden. And Luke had a long conversation with Barnaby. Right, Luke?"

"Yes," Luke answered the question, but only realised they wanted to hear more when he noticed everyone staring at him. "Barnaby is an angler. He believes that there is quite a lot of edible fish in the river Eden. So, I told him about the fishing gear we picked up from that store in Tunbridge Wells, and he is keen to give it a go."

"Mike is quite knowledgeable about gardening, he told me he always wanted to be a farmer," Juliet contributed. "He also helped his parents conserve fruit and vegetables, and that'll come in handy with all those apple and pear trees out there. I wouldn't mind if he stayed with us for a very long time."

"And he promised to help me with my studies. He sat his GCSEs last year, you know. I really think we should ask him to stay."

"And that would have nothing to do with the fact that your potential tutor is tall, dark and handsome?" Richard teased the young girl.

"I'm sure, that I have no idea what you are talking about," Rebecca huffed. "I just believe that maybe we should tell Mike everything, we don't want him to leave because he thinks this castle is haunted," she threw a sneaky little sideways glance at their Neteruian liaison.

"Thank you, Rebecca, for that caution," Mateos replied drily, "I'll try not to spook your Mike."

"Becca, I believe it is time for your lessons. Now, we can still just about fit in two hours of chemistry before lunch. Maybe you should ask Mike to help you with your homework tonight?" Peter advised his pupil. "Mateos, could you raise the issue of Barnaby and Mike with Caila and Chris please, after they've woken up?"

Rebecca gingerly lifted the contently purring Bluebell from her lap, before reluctantly following Peter to the clinic, mumbling, "I had a horrible shock, this morning. You should be nice to me."

"I will tell them, and if everyone is happy with full DNA, then so am I," Caila agreed with Chris and Mateos, while they waited for the others to join them in the Drawing Room, after lunch.

"Hi, Jenny. Have you had anything to eat?"

"Luke is filling up some plates with leftovers. We'll have them in here during the meeting, but I wanted to feed Aurora first," Jenny sat down next to the fire and lifted the baby out of her carrier.

"You are doing an amazing job with her," Caila was astonished at how much the infant had changed in less than three weeks. "Is it my imagination, or is she starting to make funny noises?"

"I think she is trying to imitate sounds, and she wriggles a lot more than she did at first," Jenny looked proudly at the spluttering little girl in her arms. "Peter says she's making good progress, she is growing nicely, typical for a three to four-month-old."

She looked up at the handsome man, walking towards them, "Luke is very good with Aurora too, she giggles every time she sees him."

The Drawing Room slowly filled up, and when it looked like they had a full house, Caila asked, "Are we all here now? … Yep? …

Mike and Barnaby, welcome to your first official Hever meeting. This one was called in your honour. Your ears must have been buzzing to no end this morning, because we've all been talking quite a lot about you. But, before it's my turn, I would like to ask you both if you like being here with us, at Hever?"

"I can't speak for Mike, of course, but I'm dead happy here. I would like to stay indefinitely, if you will have me,"

Barnaby liked the companionship, his comfortable room and the good food. "What do you say, Mike?"

"I would like to stay as well, please," Mike was glad to settle down.

"That is brilliant, because all of us, would very much like you to stay. But first, let me explain what happened to the world, three weeks ago, and why we are still here. I'll give you the short version, and then I would like you to make a choice."

While Caila explained the course of events and the intricacies of Khered DNA for the so many-th time, she felt she'd missed a trick when she hadn't recorded it the first time around. Then all she would have had to do now, was hit the play button.

Barnaby and Mike were happy to have their partial Khered DNA converted to full. And when the easy-going Mancunian caught sight of Mateos's grey spheream for the first time, he delightedly informed the Neteruian, that he was dead happy to meet a visitor from outer space in his lifetime.

Their peaceful get-together didn't last much longer, however. About ten minutes after Mateos had adjusted their newcomers' DNA, Peter warned them that a group of thirteen armed men were approaching the castle.

And for the first time since the Event, Caila was truly worried when she instructed the others, "To your stations, please. Barnaby, you go with Jenny. Mike, you follow Luke.

Come on, Sets. Let's meet them."

A visit from the PM

With 13 guns aimed at their home, Caila took no chances and remained in the relative shelter of the gatehouse. When she called out, "We know that you are armed. Drop your weapons. We have you covered, and we will not hesitate to shoot," her well-intended advice fell on deaf ears.

"There is no need for violence, my dear lady," satisfied he had the upper hand, Baldwin straightened his back. "My name is Baldwin Thurogood and I am the Prime Minister of the United Kingdom. I am here to lead our battered and bruised country into a new future. To help heal the trauma caused by the disastrous events of these last few weeks, and to give comfort and support whilst we rebuild our society. A new, and fairer society.
This is Eleonor, she is my Deputy and Minister of New Order. And these guards are all members of my new cabinet, they are armed for our protection only. They will protect you too, if you pledge your loyalty to my Government."

"Baldwin, you have no authority, and your Government has no legitimacy," Caila denounced the Prime Minister and his armed parliament. "You and your men are welcome to join our community, but your weapons are not.

All of you, please, listen to me. This world was destroyed by politicians, by their greed, their aggression and hunger for power. Don't allow Mr Thurogood to repeat past mistakes.

You have seen what happened to England, and to the world. Earth is now under the supervision of its creators, the Neteru. To protect this planet, they were forced to remove most of the human population, and they won't hesitate to remove what's left of it, if we don't mend our ways.

We arrived at a cross roads, and we are faced with a choice. We can restart society using the old ways and, ultimately, be wiped out completely.

Or, we can choose to build a new world, where we live peacefully in a restored environment; where we work with our creators to find our own, unique, place in the Universe. We, in this little enclave, chose the second option. We invite you all to do the same. Please, drop your weapons and join us."

Caila felt a glimmer of hope, when she noticed how one of the men slightly lowered his gun, but Baldwin spoke again.

"Don't listen to this traitor. She sold our country, and indeed our world, out to an alien force. Will you put your trust in me, or do you trust this collaborator to a hostile foreign regime? I fed you and I kept you safe, while this woman assisted in the destruction of our country."

- Caila? – it was Jenny, - George says that he recognises two of the soldiers. They fought with him in Afghanistan. Their names are Gary Miller and Rory Quinn.

Rory, or Clover, owes George, or Spice, majorly, just mention bananas, he says. –

"This hostile foreign regime, that Baldwin so callously dismisses, is the regime that gave life to this planet. They gave life to us all.

Baldwin has no right to demand your support. He was never elected as the leader of this country, he appointed himself.

Gary and Rory, Baldwin despised you for the work you did in Afghanistan. But Clover, Spice would love for you to join us, he tells me to mention bananas."

Caila noticed how the three guys on her right now lowered their guns completely.

But she wasn't the only one, Baldwin noticed it too, "Traitors, shoot them!" he instructed his loyal cabinet members to take out the defectors.

Parliament in session, took on an entirely different meaning as the combative politicians took aim at their colleagues.

When one of the men on Caila's right clutched his arm and fell to the ground, his two friends instantly dropped to the floor. They raised their guns and took aim at the opposition, left and centre.

While Baldwin was pulled behind a topiary column by one of his guards, Eleonor was left to her own devices and scrambled back over the bridge to take cover in the wooded area.

Then, one of the men near the maze, on Caila's left, unexpectedly provided cover for Clover, allowing George's friend to pull his injured mate behind the giant yew corkscrew.

But the men in the centre, who had been closest to Baldwin, remained loyal to their Prime Minister and took aim at both sides.

The gunman next to Clover took out one of them and wounded another. But that still left four gunners, and Caila heard Chris ask their archers to take aim at the men in front of the castle. When one of Baldwin's remaining guards fell, hit by an arrow, someone shouted, "Retreat!" and the remnants of Thurogood's new cabinet fled, whilst providing cover for their leader.

As they disappeared into the distance, the instance silence cast a dark cloud over the post-Event tranquillity.

- Jenny, could you send George down, please? We need him to meet his friends.

Steve and Luke, could you come down as well? Peter, we'll need you and Rebecca too.

Chris, everything appears to be safe, but could you and the others stay in position to cover us? Just in case. You've got the best view up there, so I'll leave it up to you to decide when it's safe to come down. –

Caila realised they should go out onto the square to help the wounded, as soon as possible, - Sets? – She looked over her shoulder, searching for the Neteru, but he had disappeared, - Sets, where are you? I need to know that it is safe to go out. –

- They appear to be leaving the area, but I'll let you know if they return. And don't go out yet, they still have their weapons, – Mateos warned her. - I contacted Dev and asked him to come over and help us. –

Caila nodded vaguely and, while Devyn appeared outside, she shouted, "You three, collect all your weapons and throw them into the moat. Knives as well as guns, everything. After you've done that, we can come out and help you with your wounded."

"Do as she asks, Clover," George joined Caila in the gatehouse, "get rid of all your weapons. What is the situation out there?"

While Clover started collecting weaponry, he yelled back, "Gary was hit in the arm, he needs a medic, asap."

"Wilson is a goner," the soldier on the left checked on the three men on the ground, "Hobson is also dead. … Peyton is still breathing, but he is badly hurt."
He collected all their weapons and chucked them, together with his own little arsenal, into the moat, before joining Clover, who had done the same.

Caila watched how Devyn checked the last of the six men, - All clear, Caila. –

"Could you lower the drawbridge and open the portcullis please, and then follow me outside?" Caila was glad to have Steve and Luke with her. "But don't take any risks, be ready to run back inside at the first hint of trouble."

- Mats would like you to stay inside, until he is back, – while Steve made to open the portcullis, Devyn materialised inside the gatehouse to remind Caila of his friend's warning,

- Hi Devyn, I'm so glad you're here to help us, and I wouldn't mind waiting for Mateos if there weren't people out there who were badly hurt and need our help. If you are certain that they are disarmed, then I think we should go out, as soon as possible. –

After Devyn confirmed that he was sure they were all unarmed, Caila checked with George, "Then we should go out, if George also believes it is safe to do so?"

"I believe the situation is stable," George confirmed, "but as you mentioned before, stay alert and be ready to retreat. Stay close, Caila. And, Steve and Luke, stay behind us."

"Clover! Good to see you again," George greeted his friends, "Gary, how are you?"

"Seriously bloodied up, mate, but I'll live," Gary cradled his injured arm, while he was supported by his other colleague, who Caila had earlier believed to be a man. "This is private Lindsdale; Emily, for short."

"Sir!" Emily saluted George.

"At ease, soldier," he replied, "it's strictly civvies here. This is Caila, she is in charge of this community."

"Good afternoon, ma'am," Emily greeted Caila. "Do you have a first aid kit on the premises? We need to bandage Gary's arm."

Caila smiled at them, "Hi Emily, it's just Caila. And I believe we can do better than a first aid kit. Our doctor will have a look at your arm in a moment, Gary. Hey Rory, nice to meet you." Then she looked at the last of the four soldiers.

"Ma'am! My name is Captain Noah Greyhound, we have two dead, and one critically injured."

"Nice to meet you, Noah," she glanced at George, and when he nodded, she called out, "Peter, could you come out here, please? You probably want to have a look at this man over there, before we carry him in." Caila turned back to Noah, "What did you day his name was?"

"That is corporal Charlie Peyton, Ma'am," his voice was clipped.

Peter joined them, and crouched down next to the unconscious Charlie, "We should get him inside, as soon as possible. Steve, can you get me a trolley, please? Rebecca can show you where to find one. Ask her to wait for me in the hospital." Peter then turned his attention to the other wounded soldier, "Gary, are you good to walk to the hospital?"

Caila scanned the gardens, everything appeared peaceful, as if the last half hour had not happened. Then she looked at the two men on the ground, next to the wooden bridge that crossed the outer moat. They'd survived in the most unlikely of circumstances, and to die right here and now seemed so senseless to her. Why couldn't they stop fighting?

- Chris? – with a lump in her throat, she contacted her husband, - I think we are secure here. We can't leave those two men out there, on the ground. We need to bury them. –

- It looks secure from up here as well and Mateos just gave us the all clear, I'll be down in a minute. We will move the casualties to the cellars, and then we'll have a funeral for them later. –

- Thanks, I'll help you, – Caila looked back down at the two dead soldiers. One of them looked so terribly young, barely out of his teens. Why?

- I believe I asked you to wait for me, Tia, – Mateos was back, but Caila really wasn't in the mood for an argument.

- Not now, please. Devyn checked them for weapons, and we would have turned back the second you'd told us that those jerks had turned around. I put my trust in you and Dev, you never let me down before. We had wounded men who needed help, – she swallowed and blinked, before she looked him in the eyes. - I don't want to fight with you, not right now. Do you mind if I get this bunch sorted first? Then we can talk later, in the Library. –

- No, that's fine, – Mateos noticed how she fought back the tears, - but I am staying with you. –

- Of course, – then she continued, including all the activated Khered in their conversation. - I'm taking our guests to the Dining Hall. Could you all come down to meet them? I believe it's best not to talk about Khered, DNA or Mateos, until it's safe to do so. Could you tell the others as well, please? … And, thank you all.

Are you ready, Sets? –

Caila showed Rory and Noah into the castle, where she introduced them to the others, before she went back outside with Chris and George to move the dead men into the cellars. Afterwards the three of them stood together, silently paying their respect to these two young men.

**

Two hours later, Caila finally found the time to meet up with Mateos and Devyn. She closed her eyes and leaned back into the sofa. All she wanted was a moment alone, to cry. But instead, she let out a deep sigh and bit the inside of her lip.

Devyn nudged Mateos to hold back, and when Caila opened her eyes, the two Neteru were regarding her so patiently, that she couldn't help but smile, "Thanks, Sets. I was convinced you were going to have a go at me, for disregarding your advice earlier."

"I was, until Devyn reminded me, that was the last thing you needed right now," as he observed Caila's drawn face, he realised his friend had been right. "So, what are we going to do about this situation?"

"Well, we have, what …? Ten days to go until the telumparticula is reactivated. And, in the meantime, we have one madman on the loose, who may be plotting revenge," Caila summarised their situation. "He is accompanied by four heavily armed and trigger-happy troopers. Possibly by six more, if they make contact with the Welsh bunker bunch."

Rory had told them, how Baldwin had asked the Welsh survivors to join him in London.

"And," Devyn added, "we have an equally dangerous situation up north. Possibly also in several other locations. I believe, we should request that the telumparticula is reactivated early. It should happen as soon as possible."

"Don't look at me, to broach that subject with our leader," Mateos sounded defensive, "you know I don't have much credit with him. And I believe he is getting suspicious of Caila. I don't want to draw any more attention to her, than is strictly necessary."

"No, I should be the one to raise it," Devyn agreed, "I will request an emergency assembly; this issue needs to be addressed without delay."

"And we should increase security down here, I'll discuss it with Chris. No one should go out alone or leave the grounds. We also need to keep a close eye on our newcomers, possibly even guarding the halls at night, to catch any nightly snoopers," Caila hoped she was overreacting, but today, the reality of her new responsibility had hit home. "Does that sound reasonable to you?"

"That sounds very sensible, and with Mats almost constantly on-site, you should be fine," Devyn reassured her. "And I will, of course, come over the moment you need me. I'll also ask Turgon and Athyc to stand by, in case we need an extra pair of hands."

"Now, what would you like to do about your new guests?" Mateos was keen to avoid another fight, like the one they'd had over George and Gemma. "I heard you asked the others, not to mention DNA or Khered."

"Yes, I'd really rather leave them in the dark, until we are certain we can trust them," Caila thought for a moment. "George knows two of them, and one of them owes him majorly. They don't seem too keen on Thurogood, and Emily isn't a fan either. I believe she was among other things, not too charmed by some less than charming amorous advances Baldwin made towards her. But we don't know anything about the other two.
We still have ten days, until the reactivation of the telumparticula, hopefully a bit less. So, as long as I can count on Mateos to adjust them, if and when we decide it's safe to do so, then I would prefer to wait and get to know them a bit better first."

"You can count on me," her liaison was quick to agree.

"See, that was easy, I don't understand why your leader has such a problem with you. You are perfectly reasonable." Caila was almost instantly hit by a wall of pain. And by something else, which she was sure, Mateos had not wanted her to pick up on. "Sorry, Sets. None of my business."

"It's fine. I'll tell you about it, someday," Mateos responded softly, before he looked at Devyn, and concluded. "Right, Dev, we won't keep you any longer, they are probably waiting for you up north. Thanks for coming over, at such short notice."

"No worries, Mats. Just let me know if you need me. Stay safe, you two."

With that Devyn disappeared.

"There is nothing you could have done to prevent this," Mateos moved closer to Caila, and she felt the connection when their sphereams touched. "You know that, don't you?"

"I know, but one of them was just a boy, he can't have been much older than Mike. Why did he have to survive the Event, just to be killed? Now? Barely two weeks later? He still had his whole life ahead of him." In her mind Caila realised that Mateos was right, but it still felt wrong. So incredibly wrong.

"I know, Tia," Mateos vowed to stay close, and not let her out of his sight until after the repeat Event had been triggered. Even if he could not undo what had happened that afternoon, he could still do his utmost to make sure it did not happen again.

Doctor Riverton

As Peter led Gary into the clinic's spotless treatment room, his young assistant rushed to cover the examination table with fresh paper.

"Rebecca, go and help Gary remove his jacket, please," Peter requested. "Steve and Juliet, stay with Rebecca, I'll be with you in a minute."

His eager student, who'd already donned her scrubs, was keen to get some real-life practical experience and instantly reached for a pair of scissors. When her mentor raised his eyebrows, the young apprentice got the hint and politely introduced herself to her victim.

Peter turned his attention to his second patient, "George and Emily, get Charlie in the operating theatre please, it's through that door. And keep applying pressure to that wound. I won't be long."

He was just putting on a pair of gloves, in the adjoining scrub room, when he heard a dull thud, "What's going on over there?"

"It's fine, Peter, I can handle it," Rebecca shouted. "Juliet, elevate his legs and don't let him get up too soon. It's just Steve, he fainted, Juliet is taking care of him."

When Peter walked in, Steve was still on the floor with Juliet kneeling beside him, "He is already coming around. I'll let him recover for a couple of minutes, before I get him out of here. You attend to Gary."

Rebecca had cut Gary's jacket away, and was now examining his arm, "Doctor Overwood, the patient's hand is warm and well-perf...f..., ... well it is not white, the blood-flow to his hand looks fine. The amount of blood loss does not indicate any major arteries were hit. The patient can still move his arm so, there are probably no broken bones. And I think the bullet went straight through, because there are two little holes, one on each side of his arm."

Gary gaped at the 12-year-old, while Juliet enquired, "Would you like doctor Overwood's assistance, or will you treat the patient yourself, doctor Riverton?"

"I would like doctor Overwood to confirm my diagnoses, please. If I am correct, then I propose disinfecting the wound and applying a pressure bandage. I would like the patient to be kept under observation to make sure that the bleeding stops properly," Rebecca sounded confident, and concluded with a triumphant, "Oh, yes, and keep his arm elevated for a while, of course!"

Peter supressed a smile, as he walked over to the speechless Gary, "Allow me, please, Rebecca. Why don't you quickly clean your hands again, and grab another pair of gloves?

Would you like me to examine you for a second opinion, Gary?"

"I would not dare to doubt your colleague's diagnoses, but yes, please," and when Rebecca was out of earshot, he whispered. "How old is she?"

While Peter examined Gary's hand and arm, he assured his patient, in an equally soft voice, "She is twelve, but I trained her for almost a month now. Don't worry, you're in safe hands." When Rebecca walked back into the treatment room, he continued at a normal volume, "Let me just check your blood pressure.

Rebecca, you were right on the mark. Could you give me a hand, please? Fetch that antiseptic solution, over there. ... yes, that's the right one.

Gary, we are going to flush your wound, to remove any debris and reduce the risk of infection. In different circumstances I would offer you a local anaesthetic, but our medication is rationed, and I need to attend to your colleague, rather urgently. Tell me if the pain gets too much for you.

Right, Rebecca, here. ... No, more, really flush it. You don't need to worry about spilling."

Young doctor Riverton proved that she had no problem following orders, and instantly soaked the floor and Peter's shoes, as well as Gary's injury.

"Exactly, that is how it's done. Now, get me those... Oh, thank you Barnaby."

Barnaby, who'd volunteered to replace Steve, had already moved the trolley with bandages over to Peter's side.

"Rebecca, hold those gauze pads in place, please. That will keep the wound clean, and this tape will pull the edges together. In this case we don't need suture. And now, you finish off with those stretch bandages.

Barnaby, could you keep an eye on Gary for a while? Call me if you need me. …

Rebecca, if you feel up to it, you may scrub in and join me in the operating theatre when you are finished here. … Juliet? Follow me, please."

Peter walked out to see to his next patient, not long afterwards followed by his eager young protégée.

**

"Peter was totally brilliant," Rebecca finished her graphic description of Peter's surgical skills, "and he let me help during the surgery. I handed him the instruments and I removed the hemostat. Next time, I will be doing the stitching. Peter is going to get me some kind of fake arm, to practice on. Right, Peter?"

"Absolutely, Rebecca. But I believe, it is bedtime for you now."

Rebecca opened her mouth to protest.

"You had an eventful day, and I need you alert and fit in the morning, to do the rounds with me," he winked at Juliet.

"Peter is right. Come on let's go, I was so proud of you. You were very professional," Juliet got up and extracted Rebecca from the mountain of cushions, which surrounded her on the sofa. "Goodnight, Chris and Caila. You look like you could also use some sleep. Don't stay up too late, all the guards are in place and I believe Mateos is doing double overtime."

"She is a precocious little girl, isn't she?" Juliet picked up the stethoscope which Rebecca had left on the hall table. After delivering the dynamic teenager to her room She and Peter had stopped to talk in the hall outside Juliet's door. "And she is very fond of you."

"She is incredibly smart. Of all the people to land on our doorstep, I could not have wished for a better student. I would like to think that, if Ellen and I'd had children, they would have been like Rebecca," Peter admired the gutsy and inquisitive teen. "She is very fond of you too, and ..." he hesitated for a moment, "have you noticed that she tries to discretely move us next to each other, whenever she has the opportunity to do so?"

"Not always very discretely." Juliet laughed, "I believe the others are starting to notice it too. I heard Steve joke to Richard, about our little matchmaker."

"You don't mind, do you?" Peter looked alarmed.

"No, of course I don't," Juliet quickly reassured him. "And I hope you don't mind either."

"I certainly don't. Truth be told, I very much enjoy your company. That little cupid has hit us with her golden dart, and I believe it is time for us to surrender," Peter pulled

Juliet into his arms and kissed her softly on her lips. "Goodnight, Juliet."

Pea plants and other confessions

"How are you, darling?" Chris and Caila were happy to be on their own, in their cosy room in the Edwardian wing. Chris shifted a pillow as he put an arm around his wife's shoulders, "I was terrified, when you were down there, talking to that piece of slime."

"It was no great pleasure, talking to that toad. He always looked bad on television, but he is even worse in real life," the red copper fireplace reflected the light from the lamps on the dressing table, it was a warm shade of red, nothing like … Caila stopped her reflections from taking her back to that afternoon, instead she pulled Chris's arm closer around her. "Do you think he'll stay away now?"

"I hope he will," but her husband sounded doubtful. "We'll need to be careful over the next ten days, so, I'm afraid that preparing the garden will have to be put on hold."

"That's fine. Juliet won't mind," their pragmatic head gardener had already assured her that turnips were only nutritious, if you were still alive to enjoy them. "What do you think about the new guys?"

"I think we can trust most of them. Rory, definitely. I believe he is very happy to be rid of his right honourable Prime Mistake."

Caila laughed, "I believe you're right. Let's just wait and see how they work out."

"Caila?"

"Hmmm?"

"Talking about Juliet, and the garden. Do you know how many pea plants Juliet is planning?"

"What, pea plants? No. Is that a problem?"

"We have freezers full of frozen peas, we have a store full of canned and potted peas. Peas are kids' food. We need broad beans and parsnips and beetroot, something with a bite. Not more fluffy, mushy peas."

"Did you talk to Juliet about that?" Caila realised Chris was trying to distract her from today's events, and she gratefully let him.

"She told me that peas are brainfood, and that they will help us develop our new energy source quicker. So that she can ..." Chris paused for maximum effect, "grow more cucumbers in the greenhouses!"

Caila shrieked with laughter, the one thing worse than peas, for Chris, were cucumbers, "I think she was teasing you, I told her once how you feel about cucumbers.
But I'll talk to her, I wouldn't mind some extra broad beans either, and they freeze well for winter."

After that minor veggie drama, they sat in silence, until Caila asked, - Can we go into lectanimo, please? I need to talk to you, privately. –

- That sounds ominous. –

- I just want to talk to you about my conversation with Mateos and Devyn. It's not terribly shocking, but it needs to stay between us, for now. They are going to ask the assembly on Etherun if the telumparticula can be activated early. –

- Very sensible, – Chris agreed, - with those nutters on the loose, things could get hairy. And the sooner those weapons are removed, the better.
But what about our new guys, they have no DNA to keep them safe. You didn't have another fight with Mateos, did you? –

- No, of course not, no one would want a repeat performance of that incident. Least of all, Sets and I, – Caila pulled a face. - No, Sets will adjust them, if and when we ask him to do so. It's just that the leader of the Neteru got wind, that I am a bit peculiar. –

- Well, that's nothing new. Everyone knows that you're a bit weird, my darling. Ouch, – Caila nudged him painfully with her knee, - careful darling, I'm not ready to see doctor Riverton, just yet. But all joking aside. Is that bad? –

- Mateos and Devyn are not happy about it. And frankly, neither am I, – Caila hesitated.

- Come on, you might as well tell me everything now, – Chris encouraged her to continue. - What is it? –

- I picked up on some of Sets' memories, when I asked him about the leader. …
No, it was accidental, Chris, really it was. And I don't think Sets noticed it this time around. He was too upset. It has

something to do with his sister, Calia. There is a lot of pain and anger there. We need to tread carefully.

If this comes to a confrontation, we might be in big trouble. I almost asked Devyn not to request that special meeting, but I didn't want Sets to know what I picked up on. We don't want to have to fight Guvnor, at the same time we're being attacked by the Baldwin bunch. –

- You're right, it is probably best to concentrate on one thing at the time. Besides, fighting Baldwin is one thing, but I don't think we are ready to take on an angry Neteru, – Chris frowned. - Are you sure that you can't discuss this with Mateos? Or is there more to this than you are telling me? –

- No, I really wish I could discuss this with him, but I can't, – Caila sighed, - and yes, there is more, but I don't know everything yet. I need to piece a few more things together, before I have the complete picture. Calia's memories are coming thick and fast now, – she rubbed her eyes. - It really wasn't fair of me to dump this on you, darling. There is nothing anyone can do at this moment, but thanks for listening.

- Always happy to be of assistance, my dear. But seriously, let me know if there is anything else. I'd rather know what's going on, even if I can't do anything about it, – Chris pulled her closer. - Could we get out of this lectanimo mode, please? It is exhausting. –

His wife gladly obliged and buried her face against his shoulder, while she mumbled, "Do you know how much I love you, Chris?"

Later that night, she briefly woke up when she heard voices further down the hall, followed by a door closing; Caila wondered what was going on, but she was too tired to get out of bed and find out.

Moles

Tuesday 8 October

"Peter!" Caila turned the corner into the passage which connected the Edwardian Wing to the castle and ran to catch up with her twin. "How are your patients?"
Yesterday had been a quiet day, but today she felt restless, after Mateos had left for the emergency assembly on Etherun, last night. A meeting, from which he still hadn't returned.

Peter studied a painting of mountain goats, on the wall beside him while he waited for Caila to catch up. The landscape reminded him of Wales and his old life.
"They are both doing well. Gary's arm is healing nicely, he is a nice chap and a good patient. Although he had some doubts when I told him he had a choice between a 12-year-old first-month medical student, and a veterinarian for his check-up.
Charlie is recovering exceptionally well from his injury. His recuperation is a great deal faster than I expected it to be, I even caught him out of bed this morning, in the halls. He told me he was looking for the loo."
"But, aren't those rooms en-suite?" Caila furrowed her eyebrows, this sounded familiar.

"Indeed, they are, and, last night, he professed he was too weak to even sit up. After that hall incident, Juliet and I have taken turns to keep an eye on his door. I am not convinced we can trust him, Caila, and I was on my way to find Chris to discuss this matter."

"How bad was Charlie's injury, actually?" Caila tilted her head, she should have asked this earlier. "I know what Noah said, that he was badly hurt, but how badly was it really?"

"Do you think he is …?" Peter didn't finish his sentence, while he let the idea sink in.

Caila nodded, "Noah was caught as well, when he tried to leave his room, Sunday night. And he used the same excuse, he said he got confused, searching for the loos. Chris assigned constant companions to our new guests. Just to be on the safe side. Steve is with Noah, but we believed Charlie was too ill to leave his bed."

"You know, Caila? If Noah is a trained sharpshooter, then he is a rather poor one. From that distance he could have easily taken out half of those guys, but he didn't hit a single one. And Charlie absolutely needed medical attention, urgently, but he was not as badly hurt as Noah led us to believe," Peter smiled at Caila's husband as he walked in from the Inner Hall. "Good morning, Chris, we were just discussing Charlie and Noah."

"I haven't seen much of Charlie, so I don't know about him, but I don't trust Noah. He tried to give Steve the slip earlier this morning, and he is a bit too interested in our defence strategies for my liking," Chris looked at his wife. "Caila, Devyn is in the Library, with a Neteru called Yawaog. They would like to speak to you."

"And Mateos?" Caila was disappointed when Chris shook his head. "Peter, could you update Chris on Charlie, please? And Chris, I may be busy for a while, but don't worry."

Caila turned and rushed off. But in the Entrance Hall she paused, next to the heavy iron-lined postilion's boots, this was no time to rush in, she needed to keep her wits about her. Touching the cool leather straps focussed her mind. Then she determinately stepped into the Library.

Swan poo

"Devyn, how are you? Chris told me you'd arrived," Caila gave Devyn a polite smile and a nod, before she introduced herself to the unfamiliar Neteru. "Good afternoon, I am Caila."

"Caila, this is Yawaog, he is your new contact," Devyn introduced the speechless and motionless shape while he placed a figurine of three little monkeys on the writing desk, "Our assembly leader personally selected him, especially for you." He hoped Caila would get the hint, and not ask any questions in front of the other Neteru.

"That is ever so considerate of your leader; I would love to meet him some day, to thank him personally. And I look forward to working with you, Yawaog. Would you like to have a look around the castle, while I see Devyn out?" Caila tried politely to get rid of her new minder. She was worried about Mateos and needed to speak to Devyn alone, to find out what had happened yesterday.

"I will accompany you," Yawaog voice was emotionless and authoritative, "my instructions are to stay close to you, at all times."

"That is so very considerate of you, and prudent, in view of all that happened here earlier," Caila smiled sweetly, while she thought she could happily strangle the stiff, "but I am afraid that you caught me at a rather awkward moment. With all these goings-on, I haven't had time to bathe since Saturday night, and I'm afraid I am exuding a rather obnoxious whiff, by now," Caila screwed her nose. "Would you mind terribly if I took a bath? I really smell like *swan poo*."

Caila emphasised her last two words, before resolutely turning around to walk in the direction of her room in the Edwardian Wing. But subtlety was lost on Yawaog, as he followed her dutifully.

"What Caila is trying to tell you," Devyn clarified patiently, "is that she needs to remove her clothes to bathe. Humans require privacy for their bathing ritual."

"But I don't mind if you wait outside my door," Caila assured the single-minded Neteru. "In fact, it would make me feel so much safer; I won't need much more than an hour. Goodbye, Devyn," she wiped some invisible dust from her skirt, "and thank you so much, Yawaog."

Firmly closing the door behind her, Caila left it to Devyn to emphasise the importance of modesty to female humans.

"I hoped you'd get the 'swan poo' thing," a couple of minutes later, Caila greeted Devyn in the souvenir shop.

During one of his earlier visits, she'd had a clumsy moment, slipping on an offensive heap near the information booth, and the Neteru had gallantly offered her a wet towel from the shop to clean her skirt.

"Listen, we don't have much time, with that robot waiting outside my door. Just give me the short version, please. And then I need to ask you some questions."

"Caila, you shouldn't be able to use anima migro," Devyn was taken aback by the sight of Mateos's Khered, who'd materialised in front of him in the shop, "Khered can't do that, only Neteru can."

"Anima-what? ... Oh, you mean the 'Spocky beam me up' thing! I picked that up when ..., well never mind that, quite early on, actually," best friend or not, Caila was not keen on anyone finding out she'd picked this up from Mateos, "It's not that difficult anyway. Now, tell me what happened?"

"During yesterday's emergency assembly, they flat-out refused to reactivate the telumparticula earlier than planned. Mats lost it massively and got into a heated argument with our leader. He was sent out of the meeting and replaced by Yawaog. Our leader referred to the recent unrest at this location, to justify this move," Devyn hesitated, "and, ..."

"Oh, f...flip, Dev, just tell me!" Caila impatiently urged him on.

"Mats doesn't know this yet, he was sent out before it came up. They are considering removing you, or maybe even all humans, after all," Caila could sense Devyn's desperation. "I will do whatever I can, to convince them to re-think that course of action. It will destroy Mats, if that happens."

"Not only Sets," Caila replied dryly as she thought of Chris and the others, before looking back at Devyn. "Don't worry, I know that there is not much you can do about it." She smiled at the Neteru.

"But it won't happen," Caila impassively observed her image, in one of the many mirrors in the shop. "We won't let it happen. …

Dev, if I ask you some questions, then could you just answer them for me, please, and not ask anything back?"

"You are taking this very calmly," Devyn eyed Mateos's Khered and her frowning mirror image suspiciously. "What are you intending to do? This is not a game."

"I am very well aware that this is not a game," Caila assured him, "but I also know that I cannot make this situation any worse than it already is. The chance of you changing the leader's mind is almost non-existent. Am I right?"

"Yes, you are," Devyn admitted. "What would you like to know?"

"Is your leader's name Guvnor?" Caila started her interrogation.

"Yes, it is," Devyn frowned.

"Were you away from Etherun, in the time leading up to Calia's partnering ceremony?"

"Yes. Yes, I was."

"Does Sets blame himself for Calia's death, because he could not prevent her from converting to her partner's species?"

"Yes."

"Do you know what, '*donkey ears*', means?"

"No."

"Do you know who Gunf is?"

"Yes, Caila, but …" Devyn didn't like where this was going.

"Thanks, Dev. That's all I need to know," Caila cut him off abruptly. "There is one last thing I would like you to do for me," she hesitated, "but I don't want you to be implicated, if what I am going to do goes wrong. You can say no, I don't want you to take any unnecessary risks."

"Just ask. I'll see what I can do."

"Send me a message when that daft sod outside my door has finally told Guvnor that I disappeared. And," Caila stared into the mirror again, they would face this together, "if I don't come back, could you, please, keep an eye on this bunch over here? And tell Chris and Sets that I love them." With those unsettling last words, Caila and her mirror friend disappeared.

Allies and adversaries at Chartwell

"Thanks, Jock, I needed that," she stroked the purring marmelade feline on her lap and gave him another one of the cat treats, which she'd found in the kitchen.

"No wonder, he loved this house so much," Caila sat cross-legged on the wooden floor in front of one of the high arched windows, in the dining room of Chartwell. The view of the gardens and the gently sloping landscape was stunning.

"I'm really sorry I gave you a fright, but this anima migro thing is a lot faster than walking, and I am a bit short of time," she'd had a good cry, and Jock had comforted her, or maybe he'd just asked for more treats. Whatever it was, the effect was the same, Caila felt comforted, and as prepared as she could possibly be.

"Ironic, isn't it, Winston?" she studied Churchill's picture. "You were famous for your speeches, and I am a chronic mumble-er. And yet, …, if I want to pull this off, I will have to deliver some pretty convincing lines, in this beautiful home of yours. That is, if I can even convince him to come over. And if he doesn't take me out, before I have a chance to so much, as open my mouth.

The man I'm going to meet is much like the man Field Marshal Alanbrooke described in his diary: 'Never have I admired and despised a man simultaneously to the same extent. Never have such opposite extremes been combined in the same human being'.

The difference is that that man was human, and it was you, Winston; the man I am going to meet is Neteru, and he is my ...."

- Caila, he knows, – Devyn interrupted her one-sided conversation with one of England's most famous Prime Ministers.

"It's showtime, Winnie," Caila let go of the cat and got up, "in your basket, Jock, and keep your head down."

Nervously, she sat down at the large round dining table and, forgetting all about the beautiful Kentish landscape surrounding her, concentrated whilst resting her hands on the pale table top. This had to work.

"Guvnor!" he should be picking this up, together with her location. When he did not immediately appear, Caila repeated her call, "Guvnor, get over here to explain yourself; or I'll give you *donkey ears*."

Caila looked the steel-blue-grey figure, who materialised between the two doors at the far end of the room, straight in the eyes. She flinched, it all fell into place now.

"I don't need to explain myself to the likes of you, you forget who is in charge here," Guvnor raged. "You forget who you are. You are an anomaly, an abomination, and as such you should never have been created, you have no right to exist."

"Why don't you look at me?"

After the brief glimpse he'd caught off her, when he arrived, Guvnor had avoided looking at Caila.

"They say that I look like her. Like Calia.

You do remember Calia, don't you? And her partnering, to a man who didn't love her?

No, he did not love Calia, he accepted her, because his father threatened to disown him, but he despised her, and you knew it.

Remember, how you convinced her to convert to her partner's species?

And then, the next day she was killed. Murdered. Remember?"

Guvnor furiously turned around to confront Caila, but he stilled at the sight of her bright glowing spheream.

"How would Calia feel, if she knew that you let her brother believe that he was the one responsible for her death, because he could not prevent her from converting to her partner's species?" Caila took a couple of steps toward the Neteru. "I can tell you, Guvnor, how she would feel. She would feel angry and ashamed. Ashamed that her father, her Gunf, could do that to the brother she loved more than life itself."

"How did you know about '*donkey ears*'?" Guvnor, as if hypnotised, now just gazed at Caila. "I noticed that you scanned my memories, when I arrived, but you mentioned 'donkey ears' before that. When you first contacted me."

"You should know the answer to that," Caila replied, as she took another step closer to the Neteru. "If you know what kind of an abomination I am, then you also know that I have Cali's memories. '*Donkey ears*' was your little secret. Even your partner didn't know about it."

"Don't call her that," Guvnor snapped.

"What? ... Cali? ... Why not? It was your nickname for your daughter, and she loved it," Caila took one step closer, "she loved you." Another step, "And you loved her. Why did you let her partner with that creep?" Another step.

"Listen, the ..."

"I'll listen to you, Guvnor, if you call me by my name. My name is Caila. You call me Caila, or it will be 'donkey ears' for you," Guvnor hesitated, so she assured him, "I was able to call you back from Etherun; giving you 'donkey ears', should be child's play."

"Listen... Caila. Calia was stubborn, and she loved him. There was a war going on, and this partnership had the potential to bring peace. Calia was lovely, he would have come to love her, eventually. And then I could have convinced them to convert back to Neteru.
No one could have predicted Cali's d...," Guvnor wavered, "what happened to Cali. I would never have allowed this partnering, or her conversion, to proceed if I believed that she was in any sort of danger.

I loved my daughter, and I have lived with the remorse for what happened, ever since the day she passed away. And I will never forgive myself, not until the day I die."

"I believe you," Caila softened her tone, she believed that Guvnor was sincere in his regret and in his love for his daughter, "but, why did you allow your son to believe that he was responsible for Calia's death? Mateos adored his sister, and she adored him."

"When Mateos blamed himself, I did not disagree. In a way, it partly released me of my own feelings of guilt," Guvnor admitted. "Then, as time passed, I could not allow him to find out what had really happened. I love my son, and telling Mateos what really happened, would have alienated him from me forever," he noticed Caila's doubtful expression. "Whatever you think of me, Caila, I love my son dearly.

And I am proud of him, he is a brilliant scientist. Although I always hoped he'd follow in my footsteps, as a diplomat. But he followed his passion for science, and he has excelled in his chosen profession."

"You wanted Mateos to be a diplomat?" Caila was stunned, and briefly lost track of what she was here for. How could anyone with an ounce of common sense, ever believe that Sets could be a politician? "If he had chosen that path, then …, well …, then you would have had to dispose of the crumbled remains of this Universe a long time ago. In a very small bin. I'm sorry, Guvnor, if this wasn't so serious it would be hilarious. Even when he was a child, you'd have been hard-fought to find anyone less diplomatic than Mateos.

Devyn? Yes, he was able to settle any dispute. But you could always count on Sets, to make any bad situation, even worse."

"Caila, did Cali blame me, in the end? For what happened to her," Guvnor needed to know, and this female with his daughter's memories, was the only one who could tell him.

'He starts to resemble the father I've seen in Calia's memories,' Caila thought, and she explained, "I only have her memories until the moment she left Etherun, right after the ceremony. That is when Mateos took her DNA.

Maybe Calia had a twinge of doubt when she saw Devyn, just before her ceremony. She had a serious crush on him, before he left Etherun. But she loved her partner, and she had no idea how he felt about her.

And when she told you that she loved you, when she said goodbye, she meant it. She loved you and she trusted you, and she vowed to wear that silly bracelet you gave her, forever."

"This is very hard for me to hear, Caila," Guvnor replied, "if I had prevented this partnering, Cali would still be with us today. Devyn is like a son to me, he might have been her partner. Now he is the only remaining link between Mateos and me."

"Guvnor, I am not going to plead with you to change your mind about removing me. Sets should never have used

Calia's DNA. I don't agree with your description of me as an abomination, however, part of me should not have existed.

But, please, don't punish all humans for this one mistake. And that is all it is, a silly mistake made by a young man who grieved for his sister," Caila swallowed. "And please, tell Mateos the truth. You can never undo what happened to Calia, but you can help Sets. Most of his life has been clouded by this guilt, that he felt for what happened to his sister. You are the only one who can change that."

"Do you realise what you ask of me, Cal …, Caila?" Guvnor corrected himself. "I will lose Mateos forever and, most likely, Devyn as well."

"Maybe," Caila agreed. "I know how angry Mateos will be when you tell him, and it will be a terrible shock to Devyn too. But you already lost Mateos, you can't make that any worse, only better.

Please, help him get rid of some of that pain. Sets is the only one who could not have changed the course of events.

If Devyn had told Calia, how he felt about her, before he left Etherun, then maybe she would never have fallen for that creep.

You could have told Calia, about that creep's true feelings for her.

But in the end, I don't think any of it would have made any difference. Calia was stubborn and she was in love, she would not have listened to you, or to anyone else," Caila took one last step towards Guvnor. "If nothing else, tell

Mateos the truth as a last gift to Calia. She loved her brother, she would never have wanted him to suffer like this. She'd have given you *donkey ears*."

"You are very much like her," Guvnor reached out to touch the Khered's auburn spheream, "you are what she might have been, if she had lived. Cali was so protective of her brother."

"Please, just tell him that you love him," Caila touched the Neteru, while a single tear ran down her face, "and then tell him the truth. That's all I ask of you."
Caila felt him pull away from her, and then she was alone again, in tears on the rough wooden floor of the dining room.

After a while, Jock nudged her legs, and Caila looked back up at Churchill's picture. "How about that, Winston? That was probably the almightiest incompetent piece of rambling, you ever witnessed.
Calia loved her father so much, and her memories were so strong when he was here, that it was hard to stay focussed. I just want the others to be safe, and I want Sets to be happy again. That's not too much to ask for, is it?" Caila dried her tears. "What do you think, Jock? I'm sorry for getting you wet again."
She shifted her attention back, from the cat to Winston's picture, "It's been an honour, Mr Churchill. You have been an enormous support, and a great inspiration. I'm sorry if I disappointed you.

But I should be getting back home now, I've been gone for hours and they'll be worried about me. And, I want as much time with everyone as possible, before …. Well, you know before what.

Would you mind if I took your glasses, from your desk in the study? I have a friend who is a great fan of yours. He will cherish them.

And Jock, would you mind if I took him to Hever? He'll have some company there, and all the snacks he could possibly wish for."

Caila smiled at the marmelade cat and stroked his thick soft fur lovingly. "Would you like to come back home with me? I promise not to get you wet again."

Caila got up and collected Churchill's glasses, his picture, and one of his paintings. Then she picked up a cat carrier and bagged a few boxes of Jock's favourite treats. "Hold on tight, Jock, and say goodbye to Chartwell."

Cats bearing gifts

Caila returned to the same shop at Hever where, at this time of day, she did not expect anyone to witness her alien-inspired arrival.

"Caila, are you okay?"

"Devyn?!" Caila jumped. "I will be, once I recover from that heart attack you bloody nearly gave me. I was just about to let you know, that I am still alive."

"You've been crying. What happened?" Devyn eyed her worriedly. "Guvnor just cancelled all meetings, and all decisions regarding Mesu have been put on hold. What is going on?"

"I went to see a great man for inspiration. I don't know if it did any good, but at least I'm still alive," Caila noticed Devyn's worried face. "No really, don't worry, I'm fine. It's late, I should go back to the castle. Is Yawaog still hanging around?"

"Yes, he is on your partner's tail now. But, Caila, …"

"No, I'm sorry, I can't say anything right now," Caila interrupted him curtly. She wished she could tell him, but first, Guvnor should have a chance to explain himself to his son, and to Devyn.

Unable to handle a, possibly permanent, farewell, Caila turned away from the Neteru. "Let's just say goodbye, Dev. I'll see you later."

"Caila! Where have you been? No one knew where you'd gone. And I had him ..." Chris lowered his voice and nudged towards Yawaog, "following me around, ever since he found out that you were not taking a bath."

Chris closed the door, before he hugged his wife and whispered, "Where is Mateos?"

"I've been out shopping," Caila put her bags and the cat carrier on the floor as she cursed the persistent Neteruian minder. "This is Jock, Jock VI, he is moving from Chartwell to Hever, and those," she pointed at her bags, "are his special cat treats.

Yawaog!" Caila jumped, when she turned around to find the Neteru only one step behind her. "Could you go to the tower, please?"

Unmoving, Yawaog informed her, "I have strict instructions, to not let you out of my sight."

"Yes, I am aware of that. But I believe your first instruction, is to prevent further escalation of the problems at this colony? And you were advised, that not letting me out of your sight was the best way to achieve that goal. Am I right?" convinced she would not get a reply, Caila didn't wait for one. "Well then, Yawaog, I received reliable information that an attack is imminent.

We as humans don't have very good night vision, but your vision is perfect, at all times. We need you to scan the area to prevent an attack, and subsequent escalation at this location. Does that make sense?"

Yawaog hesitated, and sensing she had all but convinced him, Caila pushed him, "Come on, you don't want to mess up again, do you? I'm sure Guvnor wouldn't like that. Chop-chop, on your way to the tower, please."

"Impressive," Chris grinned as the Neteru vanished. "Do you want to talk? Or would you like to eat first? We waited for you in the dining room."

"Then I would like to eat first. I'll tell you what happened when we are alone in our room," Caila turned towards the Dining Hall. "Is everyone in there?"

"Everyone, except Rebecca and Peter; they are on guard duty. I'm sure they will appreciate you sending Yawaog up to the tower, to help them. I thought he'd never go away."

Chris quickly kissed his wife, before they joined their friends, "Look, who I found wandering in the hall. She's back and she's hungry."

"And she will stay that way, if you don't let go of her, to let her sit down and eat," Steve looked over his shoulder. "What is that, Caila?" He pointed at the cat carrier, which emitted a soft meowing sound.

"This is Jock VI, and I think he's trying to tell us that he smells salmon. He brought some extra special treats, for Bluebell and Banjo," before Caila sat down, she bribed her friends' cats with the snacks, when they came to investigate their new feline companion. "And I got you a present as well, Steve. Why don't you come up to our room, later tonight, to pick it up?"

She looked around the table. "This is the first time we used all our chairs. Hi, Charlie, I'm glad you felt well enough to join us. How do you feel now?"

"Very well, thank you," he sneaked a barely visible glance at Noah, "so good in fact, that I believe I no longer need a constant carer, I feel guilty for putting a strain on your scarce resources. Maybe I can even take up some light cleaning duties, while I recover further."

"Oh, dear no, Charlie," Caila sounded horrified at his suggestion, "less than two days ago, you had major surgery, performed on you by a first-month medical student and a vet. We are going to watch you like hawks for the next couple of weeks; we want to nip any possible complications in the butt.

But if it makes you feel any better, and if Peter agrees, then I have no objections to you taking up some light cleaning duties. We have a lot of surface to cover here. Thank you ever so much for your kind offer."

***

"That was sneaky, my love," Chris called out from the bathroom, "even for you."

"I'm sure I have no idea what you're talking about, my darling," thinking back of Charlie's shocked face, Caila tried to sound innocent but gave up. "Well, if Charlie is a spy, then the least he can do for us is mop some floors, to pay for his room and board, and for the information he is trying to steal. What do you think of him?"

"He knows he is under surveillance and he tried to give Steve the slip today, twice. Richard is with him now. George is with Noah, who has been coming up with all sorts of excuses to go out alone." Chris slipped onto the sofa, next to his wife, "Juliet is keeping an eye on Emily, but I think she's okay. I trust Rory and Gary, George vouched for them, and they have no problem with us following them around. Luke is guarding the halls tonight," he rushed through his security update, before he changed the subject to what really interested him. "Now, darling, tell me what you were doing at Chartwell, this afternoon."

- I needed some privacy, to meet Guvnor, – Caila responded, using lectanimo, - he is the leader of the Neteru. Devyn told me that the emergency assembly on Etherun went horribly wrong. To start with, they did not allow them to bring the repeat Event forward. Then Mateos lost his temper and was taken of the project, – Caila hesitated for a moment, but she did not want to keep anything from her husband. - And Guvnor threatened to remove all humans; Devyn told me, that he didn't believe he'd be able to change his mind. –

- Why would he want to do that? – Chris was dumbfounded. - After all those meetings and consultations?
–

- I'm afraid it had to do with me and Calia's bit of DNA, – Caila looked at Jock, who'd fallen asleep on their bed. - So, I went to Chartwell this afternoon and I called Guvnor to Earth. I used Calia's memories to convince him to come over. When he arrived, I scanned his memories to fill in the gaps.

Guvnor is Mateos and Calia's father, so he was obviously not happy when he found out about the origins of my extra bit of DNA. From Guvnor's memories, I found out that he allowed Mateos to believe he was responsible for Calia's death.

He was quite angry with me at first, but we talked and, overall, I believe it went well; I convinced him not to remove all humans, – Caila hoped that part was true, - and I also asked him to tell Mateos what really happened to his sister. – She trailed off, and as she watched the astonished look on Chris's face, she could not bring herself to tell her husband she might still be removed on her own, - Well, that's kind of it. –

- I don't know what to say, – Chris was astounded. - Why did you go alone? I could have gone with you. Helped you. You took an enormous risk. Apart from meeting with that vengeful Neteru, you could have run into Baldwin, – Chris's concern for his wife turned into annoyance. – And we agreed that no one should go out alone; or leave the grounds. How did you contact Guvnor? You need OOVII to contact Mateos, when he is out of reach. –

- I'm sorry. I should have told you where I was going, but there wasn't time, I used anima migro to go to Chartwell, that's how the Neteru travel around. I learned how to do that when Mateos took me to Victoria.

I also learned how to make contact over larger distances, but I didn't want anyone to notice how different I really was, that's why I still used OOVII to make contact, – then she decided to come clean completely, and confessed. - And I am also rather good at scanning memories, but only with the Neteru; and I only do it when it is absolutely necessary.

I'm really sorry, Chris, I wish I could have told you, or taken you with me to Chartwell, but it was simply impossible. –

- All right. Let's forget about it, – it was too late to change it anyway, - but next time, when you intent to do something crazy like that, please tell me about it.

Do you think he'll let Mateos return to us? And how can you be sure that Guvnor will tell him the truth? He doesn't exactly sound like the perfect father. –

- He's not that bad, Calia loved him, – Caila was surprised by the intensity of her feelings as she defended Guvnor. - He made some terrible mistakes, but I am convinced he loves his children. Of course, I cannot be absolutely certain that he'll tell Mateos the truth, but I am sure that he will, and in the unlikely event that he doesn't, I have a backup plan. –

Caila noticed Chris's suspicious face, so she quickly clarified, - Don't worry, it doesn't involve anything dangerous, or crazy. I just wrote Mateos a letter. I'll ask Devyn or Turgon, to deliver it. –

Chris didn't understand how his wife could trust someone like Guvnor, and he was not convinced that Mateos would be happy about it either, but for now they had other things to worry about.

He sat down next to Caila and quit the exhausting lectanimo, "About that spy business. I asked everyone to stay inside, as much as possible, and to report to each other regularly to confirm that we are all still safe."

"No worries," Caila assured him, "when I'm not with you, I will contact you at least once every half hour. Will that do?"

"That's fine. Maybe it's overkill, but I'd rather not take any risks. It'll only be for the next ten days anyway," Chris was distracted by his wife, who squeezed his upper arms. "What are you doing?"

"Examining your biceps, darling, you are a very professional security officer," she nodded, and crunched her mouth and eyes, in mock appreciation, before she fell back onto the sofa, laughing helplessly. "No, stop it. Chris. Please. Don't tickle me."

Later that night, while Chris watched his wife sleep, he wondered if they shouldn't lock Charlie and Noah up for the next ten days. Then he dismissed that idea as too extreme; it was a decision he would come to regret very soon.

An extra pair of eyes
Wednesday 9 October

"A kingdom, for the first person to tell me what is happening!"

"Turgon! What are you doing here? How is Signe?" Caila couldn't believe her eyes when the chatty Neteru appeared in the Library. "Richard didn't tell me that you were coming over. I believe he's on guard duty, and so are Luke and Chris."

"No one told me that I was going to stay with you either, until ten minutes ago," Turgon's tall purple shape, leaned relaxed against the ornate fireplace in the Library. "This morning Devyn showed up unannounced, and he instructed me to pack up and relieve Yawaog, here at Hever. So, here I am.

Athyc is temporarily taking over from Devyn, and they replaced Athyc and me with a couple of lightweights. Apparently, my colony is dull and stable compared to yours. Devyn said he was called back to Etherun, urgently, and he made me promise to make sure nothing happened to you. He also asked me to tell you, that it was fallout from yesterday. Now, does that make sense to you?"

"I'm not sure actually," Caila picked up a porcelain figurine of a dancing woman and turned it in her hands, as she evaded the question, "but I'm so glad you are here. Yawaog is not a good one for gossip. Now, what is the latest news from Etherun?"

"So, it's true then?" Turgon caught the statuette as it tumbled of the mantelpiece when Caila replaced it too close to the edge. "I heard rumours, after the last assembly. About an attack on this place, and about you and Mateos, and about uhm … What is going on?"

"I really couldn't tell," Caila noticed Turgon didn't believe her. "I don't know where Mateos is, or why exactly Devyn was called back. … No, really! All I can tell you is that we had an armed attack from a self-pronounced Prime Minister and his band of barbarians, and he may try again. That's why everyone here is almost constantly on guard duty. Chris coordinates security."

"Can't tell, or won't tell?" Turgon prodded, and Caila shrugged while she gave her an apologetic smile. "Right, then I won't push you for more information. Just tell me what I need to know, and what you would like me to do."

***

"Caila, you have been terribly lovey-dovey these last few days. I lost count of the number of times you told me you love me. You are not planning something crazy again, are you?" Chris eyed his wife suspiciously, before he continued to lay out cutlery.

"Of course not. It's just that after that horrible attack, and after Guvnor's threat, I realised even more how much I love you," Caila bit her lip. "Sorry, darling, I won't say it again."

"Don't ever apologise for saying you love your partner, Caila," Turgon advised, when she dropped in. "Just accept that your wife is smitten with you, Chris. …
Oh, and your idea worked perfectly. I followed Gary, Rory and Emily around all day and I am convinced that you can trust them. I would be careful about those other two new guys though. Emily suggested to Rory and Gary they should ask you to search their rooms. Noah was apparently very close to, …, what's that minister guy's name again?"

"Baldwin," Chris reminded her. "Yes, Rory suggested it to George, who then mentioned it to me. Steve and I had a good rummage around in their rooms this afternoon, but we couldn't find anything out of the ordinary. I wouldn't mind if you double checked, or have you already done that?"

"Yes, I thought I'd use my under-utilised initiative for once, but I couldn't find anything either. Not in their rooms and not on their persons," convinced that they were hiding something, Turgon had been disappointed at not finding anything incriminating, "Would you like me to keep an eye on those two, from now on?"

"Yes, please, and thanks," Chris heard the sound of approaching footsteps on the wooden floor of the entrance hall. "That will be the others, for dinner."

The Neteru vanished, and after a second search of Charlie and Noah's rooms once again proved fruitless, she hid in the minstrels' gallery, high above the Dining Hall. When she noticed how Noah and Charlie exchanged a nod and a conspiratorial glance, Turgon wished she could read minds.

The coordination centre
Thursday evening 10 October

"Caila, you really should get some proper sleep," Peter found Caila dozing at the writing desk in the Library, "you hardly slept since Mateos was recalled to Etherun."

"Oh, hi, Peter. Don't worry, I'll go to bed in a couple of minutes, I just need to finish this first," Caila yawned and stretched, her brother was right, she felt dead tired. "I saw you and Juliet in the hall, a couple of nights ago. Are you two getting serious?"

"Are you changing the subject, my little nosey sister?" Peter reproached his younger sibling. "But yes, I like Juliet very much, and the feeling is mutual.

Now, what is this?" Peter picked up the wooden cat figurine that Caila had been working on and weighed it in his hands. "Is this one of those puzzle-lock boxes? How does it open?"

"That's a secret, of course. I hollowed it out and put a message inside. Mateos will know how to open it," Caila inspected her handywork, the wooden cat's right paw was raised, as if waving to catch her attention. "I just need to finish this, and then I'll go to bed. I promise. Tomorrow, I'll give it to Turgon to deliver to Mateos."

"All right, then. But let me know if you need something to help you sleep," he raised his hand when Caila opened her mouth to protest, "nothing to knock you out, just something to help you fall asleep quickly. Good night, Caila."

"Night, Peter," Caila smiled at her brother, she'd come to love her twin.

"Caila," his tone of voice was glacial.

"Devyn?" Caila startled, she hadn't noticed his arrival in the Library, and didn't know how to respond; she hadn't seen him this stand-offish since they'd first met, on their way to Hever. "What's wrong? Could you please say something?"

"What would you like me to say?" Devyn's demeanour was devoid of all emotion. "Would you like me to ask you, why you didn't tell me about your little chat with Guvnor, when you arrived back at Hever, two whole days ago? Or, why you waited for Mats' father to tell us? Or maybe, you would like me to ask you, why you even trusted Guvnor to tell Mats the truth, after all this time? Were you ever going to tell us? Or were you going to keep it to yourself, as an insurance policy?

We trusted you, and I have never been so wrong about anyone, in my entire life." Devyn stopped Caila before she could reply, "No, Caila, I don't want to hear it.

I am only here to tell you, that the telumparticula will be reactivated 48 hours from now.

All Khered, including you, will be unaffected, and you have been allowed to keep your new source of energy. Congratulations, you've got what you wanted.

Mateos is up north with me; he asked me to tell you not to try and contact him. You will be assigned a new permanent liaison by the coordination centre on Etherun, and you won't hear from either Mateos or me again."

"Devyn, wait," Caila pleaded. "Please? Give me one minute."

Devyn didn't respond, but he didn't leave either.

"You are right, I could not be certain that Guvnor would tell Sets, or you. But I had to give him a chance, he was Calia's father too.

I don't expect you to understand this, but with Calia's DNA came her memories, and with those memories came her feelings. She loved Sets and would have been furious with their father, for what he did to her brother. But she also loved her father very much, and Guvnor loved his Cali, just like he still loves Sets.

I had to give him a chance to make it up to Mateos, not just for Mateos, but also for Calia," Caila hesitated. "I promise, I won't contact Sets, if he doesn't want me to. But he needs to have this. Will you please give it to him?"

Caila walked over to Devyn, to hand him the waving wooden cat.

Devyn inspected the figurine and turned it in his hands, "Really, Caila?" he looked her straight in the eyes, "Could you possibly sink any deeper?"

Then he was gone.

Noah's prize

Friday morning 11 October

"Caila, wake up!" while Steve remained at the door to keep an eye on the hall, Chris shook his wife urgently. "We are on full alert, we need you out there. How much sleep did you get? You look awful!"

"It was just a bad dream. What time is it?" Caila forced her eyes open and tried to lose the image of Devyn, shouting at her that she'd killed Mats. "What's happening?"

"It's a quarter to six. OOVII noticed Charlie signalling from his window, light signals, and a bit later there were replies from the woods," Chris handed Caila her clothes. "Turgon has gone to investigate. Also, Noah seems to have disappeared. When you didn't react to the alarm, we were afraid he'd got to you."

Caila was wide awake now, "Do you have everyone in position?"

Chris nodded.

"Then I'll go to the gatehouse, just in case he's prepared to talk, and if he is not, then I'll come back up to you, in the tower. Don't worry, I'll stay close to Turgon."

"That's fine, but don't take any risks, and stay in touch," Chris impressed on his wife. "And, please, keep an eye out for Noah, he could still be somewhere inside the castle. It's strictly two's from now on, I will be with Steve."

"Twelve men, ten of them heavily armed," Turgon interrupted them.

"That's one less than last time," Chris noted, "but then we didn't have two traitors inside. At least Charlie is out of action."

Caila gave her husband a quick kiss and a reassuring smile, before she invited the Neteru, "Are you ready, Turgon?"

"Stop right there, Baldwin," she could barely make out the self-pronounced Prime Minister and his men on the dark square in front of the castle, as she shouted out from the gatehouse. "What do you want?"

Baldwin presented his carrot instantly, "We are prepared to give you a second chance, Caila. There is no need for violence. We don't want anyone to get hurt. Join our new order and we will protect you and everyone else in this castle, from attacks. I will personally guarantee your safety. Join us now, and we will pardon you and your men for the murder of private Hobson."

"Protection? … From your own attacks? … That sounds like a bit of good old-fashioned protection racketeering," Caila was not impressed by the Prime Minister's offer. "Did you inform your men that they are no longer soldiers for good old England, but crew to the mafia? Or should that be, crew to the Baldwin Firm?"

"I am a patient and understanding man, my dear lady," Baldwin was offended that his ethics were called into question, "but I will not have you insult me, or my comrades, in such a manner. I demand an apology."

"You leave me speechless, Mr Thurogood. You turn up in the dark with an armed posse, you threaten me and my friends. And then you demand an apology? From me?" Caila paused briefly. "All of you, please listen to me. It is clear what kind of a man Mr Thurogood is. Leave him and make a new start. With, or without us."

A shot rang through the gatehouse, and Caila ducked.

"Baldwin, you should invest in a practise range. The aim of your soldiers is abysmal."

- Flood the area and return fire. – While Turgon pulled her out of the gate house and onto the spiral staircase, Caila heard Chris give the order to attack. Then, as floodlights illuminated Baldwin and his men below, all hell broke loose.

"Ouch," Caila stumbled on the uneven stairs. - How are we doing, Chris? –

- We have three men down and two on the run, but still five shooters left standing. The PM and his shadow just ducked out, – Chris updated his wife. - No, that is four down now. –

On the first floor, when Caila stopped off in the Queens' room, to peer out of one of the little windows, she had an idea, - Chris, could you hold your fire, please? I'll see if I can tempt Baldwin out of his hiding hole for you. –

She waited for her husband to give the order, before pushing the window open and calling out, "Oi, Baldwin. … I thought you stood for equality, and for the working man. Why are you hiding behind their backs, you coward? Why don't you show that you are a man of your word, and lead from the front?"

The gunfire stopped briefly while Caila challenged the self-pronounced Prime Minister.

"That window, up there on the left! Get the witch," Baldwin, heard but not seen, was obviously more a man of 'the' word, than a man of 'his' word.

Caila ducked and rushed out of the room, it was time to join the others, - Sorry, that didn't work. I should have known. –

- No, it was rather a long shot, – 'a politician sticking his neck out,' Chris thought, 'was an oxymoron.' - But we got the one who got up to have a shot at you. Only three more to go … No, make that two, – he kept count.

- Keep at it, they are blinded by those floodlights, but in less than 15 minutes we'll lose that advantage, when the sun rises. I'll be with you in a minute. –

- Chris, we have a problem in the Long Gallery, – Jenny, who was on the first floor with George and Gemma, warned them, - Noah has a gun on Gemma. –

- Where is he exactly, Jenny? – Caila needed to know. - I'm just around the corner. –

- Noah is at the far end of the Gallery, – Jenny gave Gemma a barely visible nod, - in the alcove nearest to the orchard. –

- Chris, I'm on my way there now. Could you ask Peter to come down on the orchard side; and Richard with Becca on the side of the maze? Peter and Rebecca are our best archers, but tell them to stay out of sight, until they can get a clean shot. We need Richard to communicate with Becca. Jenny, I'm almost there now. –

Caila descended the last narrow set of stairs, only six steps to go, and the door on her right was open.

Her arms raised slightly, to show she was unarmed, she walked in slowly, careful not to startle their treacherous house guest,

"Noah, it's Caila. Why are you doing this?"

George was sat on the floor, in front of the middle alcove, his bow well out of reach. And Jenny, who used lectanimo to keep the others updated, watched her from the far side of the Gallery, also disarmed. Noah stood in the alcove nearest to Caila, he had his arm around Gemma's neck and a gun against her head.

"Well, well, if it isn't Benedictina Arnold herself," he drawled. "Listen lady, I want you to order everyone in your little group of quislings to drop their weapons. Then they are to go downstairs, open the gates, and surrender to Prime Minister Baldwin.

You don't stand a chance this time around, you lost this battle, even before it began."

It was obvious, that Noah had no idea what was happening outside; from this side of the building, it was impossible for him to see.

- Caila, don't tell him about their losses, – Chris instructed, - we don't want him to panic. –

- I'll try to lure him out of that alcove, before Peter and Rebecca arrive, and I'll see if I can get him to let go of Gemma. –

"Noah?" Caila did her best to control her nerves, she had never seen a real gun aimed at anyone before and was terrified of making a mistake. "Why don't you let Gemma go? Or, at least let her sit down for a while, with that arm she is not going anywhere, and she is obviously in pain. Is it broken?

Just let her go for a moment, please. You have the gun. You are in control."

"Why don't you take her place, if you're so worried about her?" Noah challenged Caila, as he saw an opportunity of a bigger prize to hand over to Baldwin. "Keep your hands where I can see them and walk over here. Then, I will let your friend go."

- Stall him, – Richard advised her, - we're almost there. –

"I will come over to you, Noah, but you will have to let Gemma go first," Caila tried to reason with him. "You know that I am worth a lot more to Baldwin, than Gemma is.

Let me see that you release her, and then I will take her place."

Noah took a small step forward, pushing the injured Gemma in front of him.

'Just a little bit further,' Caila thought, 'and then Rebecca will have a clear shot from her position at the other side, when she arrives.'

"Come over here now, Caila, slowly," Noah coaxed her, "then, I'll let Gemma go."

- Don't go any closer, – Turgon warned her Khered, – Peter and Rebecca are almost here. –

"No, you know the rules, Noah," Caila reminded him, "you need to let go of Gemma first."

Noah took another step closer to the door, he was almost out of the alcove now, "This way, Caila. Nice and easy," he changed the aim of his gun from Gemma's head to Caila's, before he pushed Gemma to the floor.

Then chaos erupted, and everything seemed to happen at the same time. The rising sun flooded the Long Gallery with light, and the deafening sound of an enormous explosion filled the air. Peter tried to catch the door as it slammed on him.

And, while Noah took another step forward and raised his gun to take aim, Caila dived out of the way. From the corner of her eye she saw Rebecca appear on the other side of the Gallery, just before she felt a hard push in her stomach.

Then everything went black.

Doctor Riverton revisited

Noah lay on the floor near the alcove, Rebecca's arrow skewering his head, only a few feet from the motionless Khered.

"Caila!" Peter ignored the pain in his right hand as he ran towards his sister. "Richard, we need to get her down to the hospital, go and get a stretcher. Rebecca, come over here, I need you." - Chris, meet us at the hospital. –
With his left hand, Peter clumsily tore away Caila's bloodstained jumper, "What the …?!" He observed how two small bullet wounds close before his eyes.

Turgon, who was crouched beside him, mumbled, "That is impossible. Khered should not be able to do that, we need Mateos here." The Neteru zoned out instantly to alert Caila's original liaison, - Mateos, I need you here, now. –
She waited only a couple of seconds, before repeating her request for assistance more urgently, - Mateos, Devyn. I need you here, with Caila! Now! –

This time Mateos responded, but with a detached voice he informed her, - Turgon, all matters regarding the red colony are now to be referred to the coordination centre on Etherun. Caila was made aware of this situation yesterday evening. Don't contact us again, please, contact the coordination centre. –

Momentarily stunned, Turgon stared at the floor, but one look at Peter and the pale Khered, projected her back into action. If the rumours were true, then there was only one other person who could help her, "Get her down to the hospital, Peter. Carefully. I'll get help, you are going to need it."

She braced herself, she'd never contacted one of the leaders before, and this one had a reputation for being very unapproachable indeed, - Guvnor, I have an emergency at the red colony. It's Caila, she has been shot, I believe she is part Neteru, she … –

"Leave her!" Turgon and Peter jumped back as Guvnor arrived next to Caila. "What happened?" he snapped, while he knelt beside the unconscious woman.

"She was hit by two bullets, in the stomach area," Peter inhaled sharply, his right hand burned with pain, "when I examined her, the entry wounds were closing up."

He felt Caila's stomach again, "Her abdomen feels tight and swollen and she displays all the symptoms of shock. She is bleeding internally, we need to get her downstairs as soon as possible, she needs surgery."

"Do you know the location?" when Turgon nodded, Guvnor looked back at Peter, "Are you the surgeon?"

"Yes. But, …" Peter doubted how much use he would be, "… Rebecca will need to assist me, I can't use my right hand."

"We'll take care of your injury. Now, go to the hospital. We will be there with Caila when you arrive."

While Peter and Rebecca ran out into the hall, Guvnor turned to Turgon, "Hold her carefully, and send me an image of the destination, I will make sure that Caila receives it. Just follow my lead."

Peter had shown Turgon around the hospital earlier, and she aimed for the operating table in the middle of the theatre.

Chris was already there and shouted his wife's name as he ran towards her. But Turgon caught Caila's distraught husband before he reached the table, "Chris, she is badly hurt. Guvnor will help Peter with the surgery. There is nothing you can do for her at this moment."

While he held Caila's hand, Chris softly brushed her hair out of her face, "Caila, darling, you promised me you'd be careful."

"Chris," Guvnor turned his attention from Caila to her husband, "we will get Caila back to you. I am going to work with your surgeons to heal her, but I need you to remain as calm as possible. You and your partner are emotionally very close, it will hamper Caila's healing capabilities if she senses your anxiety."

Then Peter rushed into the theatre while Rebecca called out that she was going to scrub in.

"Chris, we are going to operate immediately. We need you to wait outside," Peter lay his left hand on Chris's shoulder. "Come on, Chris. Steve and Richard will stay with you." He gently led his brother-in-law in the direction of Steve, who took over and sat Chris down on the sofa in the waiting room, between Richard and himself.

"Give me your hand," Turgon grabbed Peter's hand before he had a chance to respond. "I can start the healing process, but it will take at least half an hour for the damage to be restored completely."

The pain disappeared instantly, but his hand felt stiff and numb. Peter looked at the Neteru, who Turgon addressed as Guvnor.

"Can you operate, Guvnor?"

"No, I can only assist with the Neteruian healing method. You and your assistant will have to perform the human techniques. Do not use an anaesthetic, I will help Caila stay pain free, she needs to remain alert to heal herself, after you removed the bullets."

"I can't do that," no one had noticed Rebecca coming into the operating theatre, she was wide-eyed and terrified, "I can help you, but I cannot operate."

"Rebecca, darling, listen to me," Peter looked at the 12-year old and realised that this was an impossible situation, but he had no choice, "I am going to scrub in, and then I will tell you exactly what you need to do. And, whenever possible, I will guide your hands." He took a marker and circled the area where the bullets went into Caila's stomach,

"We first need to do an X-ray to locate the bullets. Becca, can you set it up, please, while I scrub in?"

Rebecca went on autopilot, and when Peter came back into the theatre, she nervously asked if she'd done it right.

"It's perfect," he smiled encouragingly at the frightened girl. But when he examined the results of the X-rays, he cursed, "We need to operate immediately. This is even worse than I thought.

Yes, that's fine," he dismissed Juliet who had been disinfecting Caila's skin, with an iodine solution. "Thank you. Guvnor, are you ready?"

Guvnor laid his hands on Caila's head and nodded while he used lectanimo to communicate with her, - Caila, darling, listen to me. I know you can hear me. You only need to numb the pain. Concentrate on me, and on numbing the pain, nothing else. You can do it, just numb the pain. Yes, that's it ... –

Peter turned his attention to Rebecca, "On this side, please. You first need to make an incision, from this point here, to there. Hold out your hand. Here is a scalpel.

Place it at the start point, then you press, and pull in a straight line. Just like you saw me do earlier. Take a deep breath, Becca, remember the angle, I know you can do it. ... Yes, that's it. That's perfect."

Rebecca had made a perfect incision, and Peter exhaled a sigh of relief; but before he could instruct her how to continue, the incision healed before their eyes.

Again, Guvnor tried to persuade Caila to concentrate on only numbing the pain, and stop her from healing the incision, - Don't resist, they only want to help you. Let them do their job. – He looked up at the surgeons, "Try again when I say, 'now.'"

- Don't resist, my darling, trust me. Let Rebecca do her job. –

"Now."

- Relax, Caila, don't resist, they will do the work for you. –

When Caila closed the incision again, Peter interrupted Guvnor, "This is not working. We need to try something else."

"Apart from Mateos, there is only one specialist who knows enough about both Neteruian and human anatomy," Guvnor didn't hesitate to call him over, - Gollosnor, I need you here, on Mesu. Urgently. –

"Guvnor?" a cobalt blue Neteru materialised almost instantly.

He glanced at the table and asked, "She is an activated Khered?"

"Yes, she is, but she has additional Neteruian DNA. Caila will need help healing herself," Guvnor pointed at Caila's X-rays, "after those projectiles have been removed, but she resists human intervention."

"Can we use laparoscopy?" Rebecca's voice trembled as she suggested it, and she blushed when the three men looked at her. "Caila cannot close her wound, if the instruments are keeping it open."

"That might just work," Peter nodded thoughtfully, "but it may be difficult for you to get a grip on those bullets."

He looked at Gollosnor for advice, and the Neteru simply instructed him, "Set it up. Guvnor, do you remember how you helped Calia, after she'd fallen?"

Guvnor remembered it vividly, "Yes, but Caila is not a full Neteru."

The blue Neteru ignored Guvnor's remark, "I'll show you what you need to project to her, after her human surgery." Then he turned back to Peter, "Are you using an anaesthetic?"

Peter assured him that they were not, and that Guvnor had told him he would be taking care of pain management.

"Is she going to operate?" Gollosnor noticed how Rebecca was closest to the table.

"I hurt my hand," Peter unsuccessfully attempted to move his fingers, "I can't use it yet. There is no one else, unless you can do it."

Gollosnor had the irritating habit of ignoring any questions or remarks which he found irrelevant, and he instructed Rebecca, "Right, girl. I need you to get those bullets out, as soon as possible. Get started."

"Right, Rebecca, there we go. You make the incision, then I'll push the instruments through, while you make the cut. That's right, the Veress needle, we are going to need to insufflate the abdomen first," Peter looked from Rebecca to the screen. "Well done. Keep looking at that monitor, …. Remember where you want to go and go slowly. Easy does it. Very good. … Hold on, there is the first one. … Steady! … Now, grab that bullet. … Excellent! … And back out, slowly."

They all heard Rebecca's sigh of relief, when she dropped the bullet in the metal tray.

"And, one more time for the second one. Juliet, hand me those retractors.

I am going to use these to keep the incision open, Becca, after you've removed the instruments. The gas needs to escape, before Caila closes the incision.

That's right, do exactly what you did the first time. … Keep your eyes on that screen. This bullet is in a very difficult location, the bleeding could get a lot worse when you remove it. Try to do it as gently as possible. … Right, careful. And pull it out slowly. Yes, that's it, well done. You can remove the instruments now. …

Take hold of these retractors for a moment please, my hand feels like jelly."

"She's pulling at the retractors," almost immediately, Rebecca called him back to the table.

With his left hand, Peter examined Caila's stomach, "Unbelievable! You can remove those retractors, she expelled the CO_2 and is trying to close the wound."

He turned to the Neteru, "Gollosnor, she is all yours, but you'd better be quick, her blood pressure is dangerously low."

Guvnor concentrated on Gollosnor, who had been studying the screen and the X-rays, and only seconds later he nodded and focused on Caila, - Caila, darling, now it is your turn, I know that you can do this. I am going to show you an image; this is how it should be. Let Cali's memories guide you, she knows how to do this. Stay calm, we have lots of time. I am here, right beside you. Just follow the image, I'll help you. –

For more than twenty minutes they stood together, silently watching how Guvnor guided Caila, until Rebecca cautiously pointed at a monitor and whispered, "Her blood pressure; it's increasing."

From that moment on, Caila kept improving, but it still took more than three hours before she made a soft moaning sound and opened her eyes.

"That hurt like hell. What happened?"

"You really had us worried there, little sister," Peter checked his twin's pulse. "That's more like it." He turned to Juliet, who'd kept Chris updated on Caila's progress during the last three hours, "Could you go and see Chris again, please, and tell him that Caila regained consciousness. We'll move her to a ward, as soon as possible."

Peter then faced the two Neteru, "All I can say is, thank you. Although it seems hardly adequate, after what you did for Caila, and for the rest of us."

"Guvnor?" Caila turned her head. "I thought you were there. You were guiding me." She tried to sit up.

"Take it easy, young lady," Guvnor cautioned her, "you should rest for a while, we can talk later."

Caila had already given up on her attempts to sit up, "You are probably right, but this bed is not very comfortable," she wriggled around on the stiff mattress of the operating table. "Where is Chris?"

"If you promise to stay still for a little bit longer, we'll move you to a real bed on the wards," Peter shook his head and walked towards the door. "Your husband is in the waiting room, with Steve and Richard. I'm going to talk to him right now, and then you'll see him in a minute."

Chris shot out of his chair the moment Peter walked in.

"Chris, your wife will be fine, in a minute you can go and see for yourself. Caila is wide awake and she asked for you, but she still needs rest."

Then Peter turned to Steve, "Could you get a bed in here, please? From the single ward."

"No problem," Steve let go of Richard's hand and was already out of the door when he yelled, "I won't be a minute."

"Gemma, what seems to be the problem?" Peter noticed that he had another patient waiting for him. George had an arm around Gemma while she cradled her limb left arm. "Oh dear, that does not look good."

"I think it's broken," Gemma stated soberly as she looked at her painful arm and grimaced, while Peter crouched down to examine it, "Noah hit it with one of those metal barrier poles."

"Don't worry, we can fix that," Peter stood and stretched. "Please, give us a moment to clean up and get Caila settled. Would you like something against the pain?"

"Maybe later," Gemma's hand stroked her stomach, "I don't want to take anything that could harm our baby."

"I understand, we'll be careful of your little one," Peter reassured her.

"That's quick, Steve. We need it in there, please."

When Steve hesitated at the door of the operating theatre, Peter remembered his earlier response to blood and suggested, "Or maybe you and Richard should go and check if Caila's room is ready. Chris and I can take over from here."

Impatient patient

"May I come in, please?" Guvnor glanced into Caila's room.

Caila had been alone with Chris for more than an hour now, and she was driving him to distraction, ignoring all advice left by Peter and Guvnor, to rest for a while longer. So, with a sigh of relief Chris invited the Neteru into the ward, "Of course, Guvnor. Please do come in. And could you, please, tell Caila that she can't get out of bed yet? She is the worst patient ever!"

Mateos's father was not half the Ogre he'd imagined him to be after his chat with Caila, two nights ago. He'd helped save Caila's life and seemed to genuinely care about her.

Guvnor looked from Caila to Chris, "I believe she is probably on a par with one other, very bad, patient I knew. Chris, would you mind if I spoke to your partner alone for a moment? I promise I won't get her too excited."

Caila smiled at Chris and nodded.

"That's fine, and it will give me a chance to change into some clean clothes.

I'll be back soon, darling," Chris kissed his wife and impressed upon her, "behave yourself."

Thoughtfully, Guvnor watched Chris leave the room, "You have chosen a perfect partner, Caila. He loves you very much, and he is very protective of you," he moved closer to her bed, before he asked, "How do you feel now?"

"Pretty good actually, considering what happened," Caila said. "Thank you, Guvnor, for everything you did for me. Is that how you helped Calia after she fell, when she tried to fly like a bird?"

Guvnor smiled at the memory, "Yes, but she was still very young then, and it took her rather a bit longer to heal than it took you, today.

Your Neteruian skills are very strong, I only needed to show you how to use them.

Gollosnor believes that you have complete, or almost complete Neteruian DNA, with only a few human segments to code for your physical body. He advised me, that your human anatomy is your weak spot."

Caila laughed, "That is something I am going to have to hang on to for another 107 years, while I'm here on Mesu." Then she added concerned. "Would you mind if I moved to Etherun, after the burn-in period?"

"Why would I mind? I know we had a bad start, and I apologise for that, it was entirely my fault, but I hope we can be friends from now on. Besides, I don't believe Mateos and Devyn would allow you not to move."

He noticed how her face dropped when he mentioned his son and his friend, "They will come around. They love you too much to stay angry with you, especially when they have really nothing to blame you for."

"I don't know about that, but at least they have more than a century to come around. Thank you for opening up to them, it can't have been easy," Caila smiled again. "And thank you for bringing the reactivation of the telumparticula forward."

"That was the least I could do for you, and afterwards you'll find that I left you a small surprise," he anticipated her next plea. "No, I won't tell you what it is, and I won't allow you to scan my memory. You will just have to wait and see."

"Well, if I must," Caila pursed her lips, "but I don't do patience very well."

"No, and you don't do, being a patient, very well either," Guvnor teased her. "Your partner is back, and I still need to talk to Peter and Rebecca before I return to Etherun. Try to get some sleep and stay in bed for the rest of the day.
And, Caila, contact me when you need me. I'll see you again, soon."

107 years

Rebecca knocked, and stuck her head around the Library door, "Juliet told me that you wanted to talk to me?"

"Yes, that's right," Peter and Guvnor stood next to the fireplace, "do come in, please."

While Rebecca walked into the room, Guvnor met her halfway and rested his hands on her shoulders, "Thank you, Rebecca," he said nothing more, but at that moment, the girl felt all his emotions and they brought tears to her eyes.

Peter joined them, and while he gave his star student one of his rare hugs, he whispered, "Thank you, for saving my little sister. …

Come, sweetheart. We got you something to eat."

Rebecca sniffed, as she sat down onto the sofa and accepted sandwiches and a cup of tea. The last time she'd been here was after Jeff attacked her, then she'd cried tears of pain and fear; today it was happiness and relief which brought on her emotions.

"Rebecca," Peter sat next to her on the pink sofa, "Guvnor is the leader of the Neteru and he would like to talk to us."

"I asked Caila's permission to tell you this. Her husband Chris, and two other members of your group already know most of what I am about to tell you. However, after this morning, I believe you ought to be told as well."

Guvnor looked down on the two humans, to whom he owed so much.

"When Earth was seeded, all key species received a string of dormant DNA, which was only to be activated, if Khered were needed for an intervention. The scientist, who led the project, was at that moment grieving the loss of his sister. His twin sister, Calia, and he secretly added her DNA to Caila's ancestor.

It is this extra bit of DNA that makes Caila different from other Khered. Over countless generations, this small string restored to full Neteruian DNA, and when Caila was activated, four weeks ago, she started to develop her Neteru side. You witnessed some of her Neteruian skills this morning, when she attempted to heal herself and, if the damage had been less extensive, she would not have needed my help to recover."

Guvnor moved across the room, to look out of the window. "The girl, the woman, who's DNA was inserted in Caila's ancestor was my daughter. Her twin brother, and the scientist who inserted it, is my son, Mateos. I was not aware of any of this until last week, and four days ago, I met Caila for the first time. I won't go into details, but last Tuesday, Caila took an enormous risk to keep you all safe."

He moved back to the sofa, "Caila's spheream is identical to Calia's, and when I arrived here this morning and found her laying on the floor, I feared that I was about to lose another daughter. If the two of you hadn't been there to help Caila, I would have lost her. There are no words to express my gratitude for what you did for us."

"We could not have done it without your assistance," Peter grasped that the genetic connection between Caila and Guvnor had been crucial to his sister's healing process.

But Rebecca was distracted and twisted her teaspoon between her fingers as she tried to work out Caila's family tree. Two adoptive and two biological human parents, a human twin brother, and two biological Neteruian twin siblings and parents.

She startled when Peter laid a hand on her shoulder, "Rebecca, there is something else that Guvnor would like to discuss with you."

"What you did this morning, was extraordinary; you are a very special and talented young lady," Peter had told him about the girl's exceptional academic progress. "I understand that you are not one of Caila's seven original companions?"

Rebecca shook her head.

"Do you understand the consequences of being activated as a Khered?"

"Activated Khered, can use lectanimo to communicate. And they can be healed by Neteru," Rebecca tried to ignore the glimmer of hope she felt. She'd yearned to be like Peter and Juliet, but she also realised that Caila was only allowed seven companions, that was a strict rule, "They need to stay on Earth for 107 years and that is why they don't really get any older than they are now."

"That is right, but we made an adjustment for younger Khered. They will age normally until they reach the human age of 25, only then will they start to age in Neteruian time. Rebecca, I discussed this with Gollosnor, and we believe that after what you did this morning, we should bend the rules a bit. I also talked it over with Peter and Caila, earlier this afternoon, and they wholeheartedly agree with me. Will you consent to have your Khered DNA activated?"

The lauded teenage surgeon's mouth fell open in astonishment, but a discrete nudge from her human mentor revived her vocal abilities, "Yes, of course I do! Oh, thank you so much."

"It is my pleasure, Rebecca," Guvnor was delighted by the girl's guileless euphoria as he walked around the sofa to initiate the change, "you will notice the effects within 24 hours. Regrettably, I must leave you now. After what happened this morning, I called a number of meetings on my home planet, which I will need to attend personally. But I will visit you again, soon."

"There is more good news, Becca," Peter poured his beaming apprentice another cup of tea, after Guvnor had left. "The repeat Event has been brought forward. It will be triggered tomorrow evening."

"Pffff. It's about time they wiped our beastly benevolent Prime Minister Baldwin of the surface of the Earth,"

Rebecca showed no compassion. "That's not a moment too soon."

West of Hever

Friday afternoon 11 October

Baldwin walked back to his car, a whingeing Eleonor on his tail.

That stupid idiot! To let himself be shot, before he threw that bloody grenade. He'd killed himself, and the only other fool who'd managed to dodge those wretched arrows.

They'd cost tens, no hundreds of thousands of pounds in tax payers' money to be trained, and they had guns and grenades. And still, they were sent packing by a bunch of ruddy amateurs with bows and arrows. Incompetent nincompoop losers!

But he'd be back, that woman hadn't seen the last of him. He'd find other survivors and other weapons. More weapons, and better weapons. He would find them, and then his comrades would follow him, he would lead them into the final battle. Into victory. This country was his.

Baldwin grumbled on, trying to lock out the whining woman who shuffled behind him, when he was startled by a young man running out of a doorway.

"Mr Thurogood, Baldwin! Your Honourable. Wait, please wait, I voted for you. I need to warn you."

Baldwin stopped and whinged, there was a loser if ever he'd seen one. Limping, bruised and grovelling, this man could give Eleonor a run for her money in the cringing department, "Dear me. Please, let me help you, young man. Who did that to you?"

Jeff felt like he'd hit the jackpot, if anyone could help him teach those lowlifes a lesson, it would be Baldwin Thurogood, "It's those rebels at Hever Castle, Sir. They threw me out when I suggested a more formal form of authority, a democratically elected government. Look what they did to me! They beat me up, and then they threw me out, and left me out here to die."

"I know exactly who you mean, Mr ... uhm, what is your name?" Baldwin considered that someone with insider knowledge of the castle might be useful.

"Jeff, Mr Thurogood, Jeff Phatterson, with 'Ph'."

"Please, call me Baldwin, Jeff. We are all equal now, allow me to be your guide, your mentor, in this new reality. Eleonor, my Deputy and Minister of New Order, and I are on our way to muster reinforcements. That is our vehicle, over there."

"Mr Thurogood, Baldwin, there is something else you should be aware of. I overheard it when I was at that castle, it's about the weapon they used on us."

When Jeff had finished his explanation, Baldwin reassuringly held Jeff's hands between his own, "Then we have no time to lose, Jeff. Please, join Eleonor and me; and accept your appointment as my Minister of Strategy and Information."

Mementos

"This is simply heavenly," Caila sighed, as she took the last bite of her carrot cake, they'd made all her favourites.

"Richard baked it fresh, this afternoon. Juliet baked the bread and Steve made the mocktail; he would have made it a cocktail, but Dr Overwood vetoed it," Chris hadn't left Caila's side since Guvnor left that afternoon, she'd been less restless after his visit and had even slept for an hour. "Peter will be here soon, for your check-up. I'll get an overnight bag while he is here with you."

"You can leave me alone for a moment, you know. I feel fine," Caila tried to steal her husband's leftover cake. "Oi, where are you going with that plate?"

"Leaving you alone for a moment," Chris walked over to the window and waved at OOVII. The corvid had visited earlier, to tell them that they had left blackberries on the table in the courtyard for Caila and Gemma, "as requested."

"I meant you, not your plate," Caila muttered, while she fed Jock her last bit of salmon. The cat had jumped onto her bed when she was wheeled out of the operating theatre and had hissed at everyone who tried to remove him.

"Is your wife playing up, Chris?" Peter stuck his head around the door. "I can keep her in here for a couple of days, if you need some peace and quiet."

"Hi, Caila, how are you?" Juliet followed closely behind Peter and Rebecca. "You look a lot better than you did this morning. Would you mind if we stole your husband for a bit? We are having a meeting downstairs about Rory, Gary and Emily. We need our head of security."

"No worries, I'll be fine. Could you let Turgon know what you decide? The repeat Event is tomorrow night."

"Caila, I thought you might like to have these," Rebecca offered her patient a small glass jar; in it, rattled two small pieces of metal.

Caila studied the offending objects intently, "They are larger than I imagined them to be. However did you get those things out of me, with that grabber thing of yours?" She had been told about the hurdled operation, "You know, Becca, I think we should have one each. One for me, to remind me to be more careful, and one for you, to remind you of your first solo surgery."

"Thanks," Rebecca fished one of the bullets out of the jar, before she said with a cheeky grin, "I'm just glad I didn't kill my first real patient. You wouldn't have been able to write me a reference."

"Rebecca, really!" Peter laughingly shook his head at his protégée's unprofessional bedside manner. "And could I request all of you to leave now, please? I need some time alone with my patient."

"How's your hand?" Chris had told Caila, how her brother had crushed his hand between the heavy wooden door and its frame.

"It's fine now, completely back to normal," Peter balled his right hand into a fist and stretched it out again, "for a moment I thought I was done being a surgeon.
Sit still, please," he sat down on the edge of the bed and seized his sister's hand to take her pulse, before he measured her blood pressure. "That is absolutely perfect. But how are you really?"

"I'm fine," Caila quipped, "probably because I finally got a good dose of that sleep you prescribed last night."

"No, seriously," Peter didn't laugh, "Mateos hasn't been around for almost five days now. And I, accidently, overheard your conversation with Devyn, last night." He didn't have the heart to tell her, that Turgon asked Mateos to come over that morning, before she called Guvnor for help.

"Mateos and Devyn believe that I let them down, rather badly. Maybe I did, maybe I didn't. I don't know. I trusted someone, they believe I should not have trusted, and I don't regret doing it. But I wish I could have avoided hurting Mateos and Devyn in the process," she looked hopeful when she asked. "He didn't contact you, did he?"

"No, he didn't," Peter wasn't sure if he preferred the Neteru to stay away, or stop by for him to give him a piece of his mind. "Would you like me to try and contact him for you?"

"No, I promised to leave Mateos alone," Caila bit the inside of her lip, "it's up to him now."

"But you could do something else for me," Caila implored her brother.

"Anything," Peter promised, while he absentmindedly stroked the purring marmelade cat.

"Could you please discharge me? I don't like all this fuss."

"Anything but that, my darling sister," Peter smiled and shook his head, he should have known. "Tomorrow morning. If you behave nicely."

Canada Ultimate East
Saturday 12 October

"Leave it, Mats. I should never have given it to you," Devyn watched Mateos, who studied the wooden cat again, "this is not from Calia. It is from Caila, she is using Calia's memories to get to you."

"Why the hell did she trust my father on this?" Mateos didn't look up, "He lied to me, ever since Tia's death."

"I'm sorry. I told Caila that Guvnor was planning to remove her, or possibly all humans," Devyn grimaced. "She probably put two and two together, after she'd scanned our memories earlier, and decided to take a chance to save her skin. Maybe she even wanted to save everyone in her group, I really don't know. Just like I don't know how she did it. But she got what she wanted, the reactivation of the telumparticula has been brought forward, and removal of all humans is of the table.

She is good at manipulating. She manipulated your father. And she manipulated us from the start, using Calia's memories; calling you 'Sets', flying into that tree, even remembering to fall down afterwards.

And now that wooden cat. Just throw it away, there is a big ocean out there. Forget about her."

"Turgon sounded urgent," Mateos carefully placed the cat on the heavy wooden table in the centre of the room, "we should at least have checked. I heard that there were problems at her location, yesterday morning. Another attack."

"Let it go, Mats," Devyn advised his friend as he stared out of the window. "We would have heard if something serious had happened.
What do you think of my bunch, out here?" he attempted to distract his best friend while he waved at Lucas and Charlotte and their six teens. "Who else than Lucas, would choose six kids as his chosen ones?"

Mateos laughed, "True. You'd expect chaos, but they managed to become the best organised group on Mesu. I love their defence systems. We could have used something like that at ..." He trailed off and picked the little waving cat up again. "Maybe you are right. Maybe I should get rid of it," he paused when he noticed that someone contacted Devyn. "Is that Lucas, calling for you?"

"Morning briefing and hot coffee," Devyn was already on his way. "Would you like to join us? You're invited."

"No, you go alone," he studied the cat, "I need to sort this out first."

Mateos stood in front of the fire, and while he raised the wretched cat to throw it into the flames, he had one last look at it.

He touched its little waiving right paw; that had been Tia's idea. Their own little secret. Even Devyn hadn't known about it, until long after she'd died.

He weighted the cat in his hands and turned it around. Why did it feel like he lost her all over again? He reached for the catch. Surely, it could not have been an act, not all of it.

One tiny raised paw. Those two cats had been frantic, when he moved them to the castle. As he stroked the cat's wooden head, he thought about the day she'd stood quietly beside him, after he'd told her about the day Tia left.

He touched the little raised paw again, she'd left him a message, she'd sent him a note.

Then he pulled the catch.

Dearest Sets,

The other note in this message box is sealed, because I would like you to read this one first. The second note tells you about the circumstances of Calia's partnering, and if your father has already spoken to you about this, as I am convinced he has, then you don't need to read it at all.

But I would like you to know why I did not tell you myself. I can call out to Etherun, that is how I called your father to Earth. So, I could have reached you to tell you. And I could have told Devyn, when I returned to Hever, this afternoon.

It was a great gift you gave me, Calia's DNA. This has, for a very big part, made me into the person I am today. The good, the less so good, and the even lesser so good. And you had the pleasure and displeasure of meeting all of those parts of me.

But Calia's DNA not only gave me her memories, it gave me her feelings as well. Her feelings for you and for Devyn, but also her feelings for her father, her Gunf.

She loved you all very much. She would have been furious about what your father did to you, allowing you to believe that you were somehow responsible for her death, by failing to prevent her conversion to a different species. But she would still have trusted him to tell you the truth, in the end. I had to do the same, I owed her that. But I also owe it to the both of you, to make absolutely certain that you find out what happened. Your father told me how much he loves you, and I know he will have talked to you by now. My second note is only there in the unlikely case he has not.

If I made a mistake in trusting Guvnor when I gave him the opportunity to tell you first, then I apologise, I take full responsibility.

Dearest Sets, if I don't see you again, then I want you to know that I don't blame you for anything. You gave me the gift of who I am, and you have shown me things that no one else on this Earth has ever seen. But most of all you

have given me your friendship and your love.
I thank you for all those gifts.

Thank you, Sets, with all my love, your honorary (little)
sister, Caila.

"Mats," Devyn rushed back in, "something happened that you need to know about." Then he noticed the note in his friend's hand, "You opened it?"

Silently, Mateos handed him Caila's message.

Devyn read the letter in silence, occasionally glancing up at his best friend.

"We made a mistake. Caila wrote this letter just after she returned, on Tuesday. I need to go and see her."

"Wait, there is something you need to know first," Devyn looked over his shoulder, Turgon was still out there, "you may not receive a very warm welcome when you arrive back in England.

There was trouble at Hever, yesterday, serious trouble. Turgon just stopped by to give me an earful. They had a traitor inside the castle. Turgon contacted us to tell that Caila was badly hurt. She had been shot and Peter could not heal her alone, there is too much Neteru in Caila. Turgon was desperate."

"I should have known," Mateos was furious with himself for ignoring the engineer's call for help. "There is no one over there who can help her, she needs someone who can get through to her and show her how to heal herself.

I'm the only one who can do that, I am her brother. I need to go back to her, right now."

"No, wait, you're too late," when Devyn sensed the panic in his friend, he rushed to explain. "She is fine, Mats. Caila is fine, you were not the only one who could help her. We were lucky to assign Turgon to her, she is probably the only one who would have had the guts to contact your father directly. It was Guvnor who helped her, together with Peter and Rebecca, and Gollosnor.

Caila pulled through. Turgon told me that it was touch and go, but she is fine now.

But Peter is livid. He overheard me talk to Caila the evening before, and he caught the gist of your reply to Turgon, yesterday morning."

"Mateos?" both men looked up when Guvnor appeared in the cabin.

"I am aware that you don't want to see me, however, there is something you need to know about, urgently. You shouldn't hear this from anyone else." He halted and looked at the two friends, "Was it Turgon? … You don't have to say anything, but I would like you both to listen to me. I made mistakes which I came to regret bitterly, and I don't want the same thing to happen to you.

I saw Turgon leave, so I assume that she told you what happened yesterday.

Mateos, if anything ever happened to Caila, you would forever regret not having made up with her. She did not tell you what she found out, because she was convinced, I would tell you myself. However, I would be surprised if she didn't have a backup plan, in case I hadn't followed through.

You can push me out of your life, I deserve it, after what I did to you, but please don't do the same thing to Caila. Everything she did, she did to help you."

"How bad was it?" Mateos had to know. "How close was it, yesterday?"

"That's not important. She is better now."

"I need to know," his son insisted, "they called me, and I let her down."

"It was very close," was all Guvnor said about it, "but we got her through."

"She had a backup plan," Mateos showed his father the little wooden cat and the letter. "Would you like to read it?"

Guvnor accepted the letter and read it, "You have to go back, Mateos."

Clearing the air

"Owh, I am never going to get this before tonight," Jenny sat next to Luke on the piano bench. "My fingers are too short and too stumpy."

Luke took Jenny's hands in his own, and studied them, "Your fingers are not short. You have beautiful, long slender hands, you can easily stretch an octave," he carefully rested her fingers back on the keys. "One more time, before Caila comes back."

"Oh, to be young and in love!" while she put the final touches to the floral decorations Juliet watched how Luke and Jenny left the room, hand in hand.

"Is that as opposed to 'old' and in love?" Peter gave Juliet a quick hug and a kiss, before he handed her another rose. "I wish Caila didn't go out alone, just yet. We could have lost her yesterday."

"Don't tell her that, you know how much she hates it when people make a fuss," Juliet nodded towards the window. "She is making up for the peanuts and the chat, she and OOVII missed out on, yesterday; it was really sweet of him to bring her and Gemma those blackberries. Besides, my darling, with you watching her every move from up here, your sister should be safe for a couple of minutes, nothing is going to happen to her.

Where is Rebecca? I haven't seen her for a couple of hours."

Peter had another quick look out of the window before he explained, "She is in her room, sulking. Gollosnor offered her a training place, on Etherun, and she is upset with me because I told her to wait until she has a bit more experience."

"When you see her working and studying, it's easy to forget how young she still is. She told me she hated school because her teachers were slow and boring," Juliet blocked Peter's view on Caila and OOVII, with an enormous floral arrangement, "I'm going to check on the dining room and the kitchen now, and then I'll see if Rebecca is ready to change her stroppy worst for her Sunday best.

Come on, Peter, it's time to change into your finery. Tonight, we celebrate life, and a new beginning."

"Lead the way, my dear," Peter had one last look at his twin sister, before he followed Juliet into the hall.

"What the Dickens!" Peter swore under his breath. "That those two have the audacity to show their faces here, and today of all days!"

Turgon was engaged in an animated discussion with Devyn and Mateos, in the Inner Hall.

"Turgon, may I have a minute with these two gentlemen, please?" Peter interrupted them.

"By all means," Turgon demonstratively turned her back on the other two Neteru and stepped aside, "and don't hold back."

"In there," Peter nudged towards the Drawing Room. "Juliet, would you mind if I had a moment alone with Mateos and Devyn?"

He didn't wait for an answer and in a rare display of temper, Peter slammed the heavy wooden door behind them, "How the hell do you justify coming back here? You almost killed my sister. If Turgon hadn't had the good sense to call your father, Caila would have died.

Nothing that Caila said or did, could ever justify you letting her down like that. How do you think she would feel if she heard that the man, she considered her brother, told Turgon to call a contact centre while she lay there dying?

Don't worry, Mateos, I didn't tell Caila about that. I would never, in a million years do that to her." Peter turned his attention to Devyn, "And you, Devyn. I overheard your conversation with Caila, on Thursday night. She was already tired and depressed, and you found it necessary to knock her down even further.

I want you both out of here, now, before Caila comes back in."

Mateos stood rooted to the spot, Peter's fury was ice-cold and restrained, and justified; leaving him unable to defend himself.

"Peter," Devyn tried, "I admit that what we did was wrong, horribly wrong even.

But most of it was my fault, I held Mats back. He felt hurt and I believed I was protecting him. His first instinct was to come right over when Turgon mentioned Caila.

He will never forgive himself for letting your sister down. And I will never forgive myself for letting you all down.

Please, allow Mateos to talk to Caila. Give them, at the very least, a chance to say goodbye. Don't do it for Mateos or for me, do it for Caila. Please."

Mateos looked out of the window. Caila was outside talking to Turgon, saying goodbye, he guessed; then he quickly moved back into the festively decorated room when she looked up, "I will tell her the truth, I don't want this to stand between the two of you, you are twins. Please, Peter, let me talk to her. She will be hurt, but she will still have you. There shouldn't be any secrets between you and your sister."

Concerned, Peter glanced outside. It was obvious that Caila was restless, she probably sensed that her Neteruian brother was nearby, "Go, Mateos. But I will be here, watching you."

"Thank you again, we will enjoy them tonight. It's the first time I will be roasting chestnuts over a real open fire." Caila looked at the enormous pile of sweet chestnuts deposited in a large wicker basket, "and we'll try to keep the noise down for you."

"It is just a small token of our appreciation," OOVII took another peanut from the well-stocked bird table, which had become a permanent feature in the gardens since Caila and her friends had moved in, "we all chipped in.

Good afternoon, Turgon." OOVII greeted the Neteru, "How are you today? That is a truly delightful cat you have there; a cat made out of wood, is a cat made to be good."

"Good afternoon, Khrhhsh. I am very well, thank you," even the normally frank Turgon was courteous to the stately bird. "They arranged for a permanent replacement. So, I am afraid this is goodbye, for now."

"It has been a pleasure, Turgon. I will give you some privacy now, to say your goodbyes," OOVII turned to address his fellow Khered. "Until tomorrow, Caila."

"See you tomorrow," Caila watched the bird fly away over the maze, before she looked up to the Drawing Room window. She could have sworn …

"I will miss you, you're good company," Caila faced her temporary liaison whilst trying to avoid looking at the wooden cat in her hand, "but I bet, Signe will be pleased to see you again. Who is your replacement?"

"I will be glad to be back in Sweden, with Signe. Nothing against you, Caila, but I need some rest after all the things you put me through," she glanced at the wooden cat. "I believe they have two replacements lined up for you; if you reject the first one, then you can have the second one." She looked at Jock, who lay contently at Caila's feet, "Devyn asked me to give you this carving," she held the figurine with its little raised paw up, and saw Caila's face drop. "If it helps, I told him where he could stick it."

"Oh, Turgon, you are one of a kind," laughingly, Caila accepted the figurine. "Thank you, ever so much. For everything."

Caila felt the cat's tiny waiving paw, he had been too angry to even open it, he'd sent it straight back. She twirled the elegant wooden feline around in her hands. It had been too personal, this was his and Calia's.

"It's not your fault little cat," she whispered as she stroked its tiny wooden head.

Caila touched its little raised paw again; its left paw. She looked again, it couldn't be.

Then, she pulled the catch.

Dearest little sister,

You have nothing to apologise for. I behaved atrociously.

I love the person you are, even if I only met the good parts of you.

You gave me your friendship and your love, and you gave me joy and laughter. You gave me back my life.

I repaid you by betraying your trust. I let you down. Please, forgive me.

I will always love you, Caila, your big brother, Sets.

"Oh, Sets, come back, please," she whispered to the wooden cat, "I miss you."

"Tia?" Mateos stood behind her. "No, don't turn around, please. I need to tell you something that will make you hate me. Please, just listen.

Yesterday, when you were hurt, Turgon called me for help, and I told her to contact the coordination centre on Etherun. I'm so sorry, I could have killed you with my stubbornness and stupidity.

I will leave you now. You will like your new liaison, he is kind and reliable. And my father knows where to find me, if you would ever want to contact me again.

I'm so sorry, Tia."

"I already knew, Sets," Caila spoke softly to the little wooden cat, before she turned around to face her brother, "I overheard you and Turgon, when she contacted you. …

Where are you going? When Turgon mentioned that I had two choices, I hoped that one of them would be you."

"You knew what I did, and you still wanted me back here?" Mateos didn't understand.

"Yes, of course, I still want you back here," Caila walked up to her brother. "We both made mistakes. I foolishly caught a couple of bullets, and you goofed up on a badly timed lectanimo."

"Tia," Mateos didn't know whether to laugh or cry, "this isn't a joke, you could have died."

"Could've, would've, should've," Caila shrugged, "it happened, and it's over now. You are my big brother, and I don't want to lose you. Will you please stay?"

"You'll have to convince Peter," Mateos pulled her close, "your other big brother knows what I did, and he is not as forgiving as you are."

"Mmm, easy-peasy," relaxed, Caila leaned against her brother while they watched the beautiful October sunset together. "If you are both my big brothers, then you both want what's best for me. And since I know best, what's best for me, I am the best person to tell you, what you both want for me."

A new beginning

Saturday evening 12 October

It was a cold evening, but in the Drawing Room it was warm and bright. Juliet's bouquets emanated a light floral fragrance, which blended effortlessly with the aroma of roast chestnuts. The group listened quietly to Luke and Jenny's soft and melodic voices as they accompanied themselves on the piano.

"Do you fall down, you millions?
Do you sense the creator, world?
Seek him above the starry canopy,
Above the stars he must live."

Silently listening to Beethoven's '*Ode to Joy*', Caila moved closer to her husband, as she observed her friends, old and new.

Steve and Richard sat close together. If she could draw, that's how she would sketch them, hand in hand on that frilly sofa, true love personified.

Peter, her twin brother, they were so different, yet so alike. With his arm around Juliet he smiled back at her. Caila was sure that Rebecca, book on knees and Bluebell and Banjo at her side, was already planning the partnering ceremony for this new couple.

Maybe the teen should make it a double ceremony, Luke and Jenny had become inseparable, forming a new family with baby Aurora, who slept quietly in her cot next to the piano.

George and Gemma, Barnaby, Mike, Rory, Gary and Emily. Their community was growing at an unexpected pace.

Then she thought of the billions, who had been removed from this planet, less than four weeks ago.

In her mind, she knew it had been the only option, but she felt responsible and still had the occasional twinge of doubt. Humans had achieved amazing and wonderful things, they could have been great. With such brilliant minds amongst them, how could they have messed up so badly?

She watched Mateos, despite her occasional doubts about the Event, she was glad he was here, and not somewhere high above the starry canopy. It had been less than a month since Sets had woken her up in the middle of the night, but she could no longer imagine life without her Neteruian brother.

The curtains fluttered, and Caila felt a cool breeze as she smelled the familiar fresh scent of spring. Together with her friends she smiled, this was the scent of a new beginning, of a new chance for Earth.

C. Attleya lives in the garden of England, where she writes her science fiction and fantasy novels. Her love for this beautiful county shines through in *The Cool Breeze of Spring* novels.

C. Attleya is notoriously unsociable, however if you would like to contact her, then she invites you to do so at cattleya@haszit.com.

Rumours that C. Attleya has moved to Newfoundland, to write and find inspiration for the parallel novel, *A flying start*, cannot be confirmed or denied at this moment.

Find out more at www.haszit.com

or

Follow C. Attleya on Twitter: @CailaAttleya

38769462R00270

Printed in Poland
by Amazon Fulfillment
Poland Sp. z o.o., Wrocław